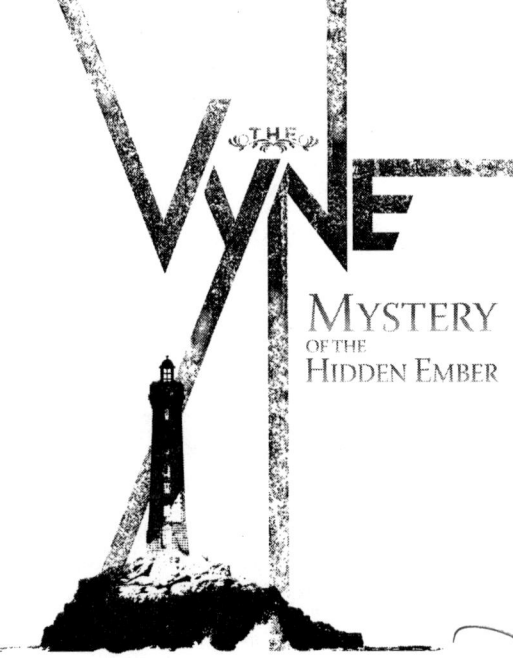

Two Harbors Press
Minneapolis, MN

Copyright © 2011 by Daniel Walls.

Two Harbors Press
212 3rd Avenue North, Suite 290
Minneapolis, MN 55401
612.455.2293
www.TwoHarborsPress.com

All rights reserved. No part of this publication may be reproduced, stored in a retrieval system, or transmitted, in any form or by any means, electronic, mechanical, photocopying, recording, or otherwise, without the prior written permission of the author.

ISBN - 978-1-936198-96-2
ISBN - 1-936198-96-7
LCCN - 2010936036

Typeset by Sophie Chi

Printed in the United States of America

For Maeve & Taye

1 Fear

One
The Dark Creature

If death was a place, this was it. And it wasn't the first time Ash had found himself here, trembling under his patchwork quilt and a layer of beading sweat. With each heavy creak of the wooden steps came the cold certainty that he wasn't dreaming. Blinded by darkness, he assumed that the intruder was his father, bent on taking out his drunken aggression on him once again. But this was far worse.

As his bedroom door slowly shrieked open, long, hair-covered claws curled around it, digging into the chipped paint. The dark creature's shadow poured over the boy's bed like a swelling storm front. Ash remained frozen in fear, his heart pounding through his body like a bell tower. He didn't know how long he could keep his panicked wheezing contained. Any effort to be still was a futile one anyway. For it wasn't a matter of whether the creature could find him. It already had. Ash knew full well that it was now or never. Throwing his blanket aside and leaping toward the small attic window, Ash jumped—but not before the creature lashed out, sinking its claws into his shoulder.

It was difficult to tell what hurt worse: the razor-sharp claws, or busting through the glass pane. After tumbling off the roof and into the frigid mud, Ash quickly picked himself up and began running aimlessly through the night. Writhing with pain, it was all he could do to keep his legs from collapsing beneath his own dead weight. But he had to maintain his pace. The creature would not be far behind. It never was.

For as long as Ash could remember, this vicious creature had been hunting him, lurking in the shadows, ever on the prowl. And its motive seemed indiscriminate, as if the creature might merely be scouring for food. But its persistence proved that this was far more than an instinctive hunt. Ash had a death mark on his head. It was this cruel understanding that kept him up at night, making sleep less and less commonplace.

The forest closed in on Ash as he was beginning to find it harder to keep up the pace. Darkness was everywhere, like a heavy veil, unable, unwilling to be lifted. The lingering rotten stench assured him that the creature was closing in. Suddenly Ash tripped, his face slamming into the mud with a force that briefly stole his breath. He struggled to pick himself up again. But before he was upright, a powerful force thrust him back to the ground.

The creature loomed above him like a swaying tree. Its yellowed eyes narrowed as they locked with the boy's. With its heavy boot crushing Ash's chest, it was certain, there was no escaping this time. Then the creature did something it never had before. It spoke.

"Where is she?" a deep snarl sifted through its lips.

Ash had no idea what or who the creature was talking about. There was no *she* in his life. His mother had been gone for as long as he could remember. And girlfriends were entirely nonexistent. But there would be no response as Ash's voice was locked in a helpless state of trepidation.

The creature repeated the question, its boot growing heavier, to the point of cracking the bones beneath it. A final breath escaped Ash's lungs and soon total blackness bled into everything.

Struggling to untangle himself from his quilt, Ash gasped desperately for air the moment he was free. His eyes darted around his bedroom frantically, vainly searching for a creature he knew full well was never actually there in the first place. But as often as the nightmares were, they were becoming more real with every episode. Yet there was one specific dream that seemed to be recurring more often now—one where he found himself flying above the clouds and into the star-filled sky. Then suddenly the clouds below would grow black and the dark creature would emerge. This was the point where Ash would freeze, breathless and speechless, rendered completely paralyzed by fear, falling, falling …

Looking down, Ash saw two bloodstains soaked into his off-white sheets—damp with fresh blood from scars which mysteriously refused to heal. It was a puzzling sight he had grown to expect after every nightmare. No one knew of this strange anomaly other than his father, Logan. And it would stay that way no matter what. It was bad enough that Ash was a rebellious teen that had earned a tarnished reputation in the village. This was plenty humiliating for Logan. He didn't need further complications brought on by his son's mutant traits.

Myths of people possessing such mysteries were rarely associated with good. According to Logan, Ash was a boy possessed by dark forces from beyond the grave. (It would certainly explain the nightmares.) Logan was inexorable when it came to keeping these unexplainable supernatural abilities hidden from the other villagers. If anyone were to know of these freakish powers he referred to as his *curse*, Logan would certainly be accused of harboring witchcraft. So at sixteen years old, Ash was still completely convinced that his supernatural abilities were every bit as forbidden as his father believed. And he hated it.

Staring into the window's warped reflection, Ash saw the two strange scars on his back, oozing out thin streams of blood. No matter how many times he saw it, it was a gruesome sight—a crude reminder of his curse. He looked through the windowpane at the darkened harbor beyond. It too was a view that never seemed to change. Even the hands of the old, broken-down clock tower hadn't moved in years—a sober reminder of Garbbit Harbor's monotonous, time-locked state. Beat-up steam trawlers littered the bay like a herd of rusted livestock.

Above, the diffused moons appeared as nothing more than ghostly orbs through the cloud cover.

Ash had never actually seen the sky beyond the clouds—aside from a fleeting glimpse of a few stars or the slice of a moon. Nestled into the swampy hills of Willow Lake, Garbbit Harbor was trapped in a spell of perpetual overcast and precipitation. Yet few villagers ever traveled beyond the colorless swamps of Murk. Escape from this lonely place came only in the form of dreams. Or nightmares.

Though the dark creature was merely a figment of Ash's slumbering imagination, the secret of his own curse was a cold reality that tortured him even more.

Two
The Golden Medallion

W*icked. Vile.* That's what people called it. Isla Ruba was a torrid outpost, scorched by volcanic assault. Natives of these southern waters believed that unless their gods were routinely honored by means of bloody sacrifice, the spirits would unleash their vengeance upon them—fury in the form of the island's looming volcanoes. Over centuries, this morbid religion had reduced the local tribes to nothing more than a violent lawless perdition. It was a doomed world in which few dared to step foot; making it the perfect haven for the underworld of piracy.

The luster of twilight moons passed in and out of low-hanging clouds above the silhouetted palm trees. Breaking the tree line, stood Grande Coliseum, the sprawling gladiator arena, built into the basin of one of the island's dormant volcanoes. Orange firelight spilled from the thousands of small portholes drilled through the volcano's skin, like an enormous black lantern.

A single ray of blue moonlight touched down on the arena floor, where two partially armored gladiators stood. The men were the unfortunate random picks, snatched from the bowels of their cells and thrust into this bizarre situation. Though treatment as a slave was beyond horrific, being selected as a gladiator was the epitome of horror. After all, it was nothing less than a torturous death sentence.

The gladiators' eyes remained fixed on the vents of the giant iron gate at the arena's edge. Steam filtered out through the holes from what was awaiting them on the other side. In this case the only thing worse than not knowing was actually *knowing*. And with a shrilling squeal of un-oiled gears and pulleys, the gate began to slowly rise. Two huge eyes peered from beyond the shadows. Then it came forward.

As the sabertooth lion entered the arena with loud thunderous strides, the crowd erupted into a chorus of screams and yells. Four times their size, the giant beast towered over the gladiators. Just its long curved fangs were over half the length of the men's height.

Sabertooth lions were the feared kings of the jungle. Indigenous to the southern peninsula of the Western Territories and this trailing string of tropical islands, the monstrous beast had once teetered on the line of extinction. Oddly enough, if it weren't for the powerful Pirate Brethren of Isla Ruba, the natives' poaching would have most likely wiped them out. But gladiator sports had become such a popular spectacle on the island that the Brethren began breeding these beasts for their own pleasure. Now bigger and fiercer than ever, sabertooth lions were feared nearly as much as the very gods that haunted their jungles.

Before the gladiators even had a chance to formulate a plan, the lion lunged forward with a deafening roar that shook the arena. Its matted, orange fur stood on end at its shoulders, signaling its maniacal state of rage. With the gladiators already scrambling for their lives, the show was on ...

Smoke slithered into the air as Lord Yen relit the bowl of his hookah pipe, observing the gruesome scene unfolding on the arena floor below. Holding the flame in one of his thick, slimy black tendrils, a breath from behind blew out the match. Yen didn't bother to turn around. He knew who it was: Sire Gahm, the old monk scribe.

Gahm's frail physique was wrapped in a brown, loosely woven frock. An oversized hood shadowed his withered face. Though scribes were a dying breed, Gahm was one of the few alive who was still fluent in many ancient dialects. This was exactly why Yen had invited him to his private balcony.

Gahm sat down. He felt insignificant compared to Yen's sprawling mass next to him. After all, Yen was a serpentine—a large, scaly, limbless being, with a tentacle mane that engulfed his heads. His slippery red mass was in a constant hypnotic sway. His beady eye was rich amber and could not be trusted. A black leather patch lay where his other eye used to be. And he coiled his body into the basin of a large, floating brass saucer, which most serpentine Slave Lords preferred as opposed to clambering their way across the dirty soil. This was hardly a luxury, given that Slave Lords were among the richest in the world.

"I trust you brought it with you?" Gahm whispered, purposely avoiding the distraction of the brutal spectacle playing out between the gladiators and the menacing beast.

Lifting his eye patch, Yen pulled out the round, flat, tawny medallion. It dangled from his tendril on a thin chain drawn through the medallion's center. A strange aura of energy seemed to sweep the balcony—perhaps the cool midnight breeze drifting over them. The air smelled with the hint of a coming lightening storm.

It was smooth with thin etching gracing its surface. Yen eased it into Gahm's palm. But when Gahm tried to take it, Yen's tendril tightened on the chain, refusing to let go. Finally, Yen released. It was clear that Yen already held this relic in high regard.

"It's Imcot," Gahm said quietly, after only studying the medallion for a moment.

"I assumed as much," Yen replied unimpressed. "What do the engravings say?"

Gahm squinted his eyes, obviously struggling to decipher the engravings. The Imcot did not standardize many of their symbols or terms, requiring great familiarity with their lore to unravel such enigmatical engravings as found on this medallion.

"This is a very ancient dialect, difficult to discern," Gahm confessed. Yen clenched his tendril around the hide moneybag, compensation for Gahm's services. The old scribe scrambled to accommodate, but the etched symbols eluded his skills. He slowly rotated the medallion in his hand in a laborious attempt to translate the text, which was written in a spiral formation from the edge to its center. "Upon the end of time will come the face of great deception. And the shadow of tribulation shall fall. But from the most unlikely of places will rise the one who will awaken the hidden truth."

"What does it mean?" Yen said as he drew a large hit off the hookah pipe's hose.

"It's a riddle," Gahm said, pulling the medallion out of the light of the pipe's glowing embers. His eyes quickly darted around—making sure no one around could see what he was holding.

"What does it mean?" Yen repeated slowly with growing frustration.

"I … I'm not sure," Gahm stuttered. "Most likely some obscure prophecy. But as I'm sure you know, Imcot engravings were often encrypted with a secondary message. In many cases, the engravings were merely the beginning. The encryption is the real message. Unfortunately, it can take some time to decode an encryption like this. Though I am technically not a code-breaker, if you can part with it temporarily, I could—" Yen shot Gahm a skeptical look, cutting him off mid-sentence. There was no way he was parting with the medallion. "According to Imcot legend," Gahm resumed, "there was a sacred golden medallion entrusted to the order of the Vyne."

"The Vyne?" Yen asked.

"Guardians," Gahm explained. "A sect sworn to protect the secret."

"What secret?" Yen asked again.

Gahm continued incessantly. "Although I cannot be certain yet, you just may have come across the world's most sought-after relic. This may be the Enigma," he said staring at the medallion with trance-like eyes. He began to breathe heavily, as though somewhat overtaken by his own revelation. It was quiet for a moment while Yen digested the explanation.

"And the map," Yen asked, "leads to what exactly?"

"To what?" Gahm repeated, surprised that Yen didn't know. "It leads to their secret: the Chrysalis. The greatest treasure of all time. It possesses the magical formula for turning worthless metal into gold and more importantly, death into life."

Yen quickly relieved Gahm of the medallion—a titillating rush of greed stirring his tendril mane to life, like a nest of hungry snakes. He recalled many run-ins with alchemists over the years. And never did they strike him as anything more than madmen. Still, their mystical obsessions were quite intriguing. *Perhaps this golden medallion was truly the passage to their Magnum Opus: the key to endless life and wealth.* "Your work is done," he said, gazing hypnotically at the medallion. If this relic really was what the old scribe was claiming, then there was no time to waste. "Time to find a code-breaker."

"So how did you come into possession of this relic anyway?" Gahm asked, attempting to shift Yen's focus.

Yen remained silent, taking a long heavy hit off his pipe. He wasn't about to give up any more information to the scribe whose aggressive interest in the medallion was beginning to make him uncomfortable.

"Don't spend it too quickly," Yen said dropping the small pouch of coins into Gahm's lap and motioning for him to leave. "I may be coming to reclaim the money if this turns out to be nothing more than a rock."

"Worry not, my Lord," Gahm said smiling, excusing himself from the balcony. "It's real, all right. The question is: does it actually lead to treasure? Besides, the greatest code-breakers in the world rarely have any luck breaking Imcot encryptions. The codes were not meant to be broken by just anyone." Gahm then made a quick exit before Yen had a change of heart. It wasn't often scribes came into money, especially money in this amount. But on Isla Ruba, blowing it all on mere debauchery would not be difficult.

Refocusing on the bloody gladiator sport below, Yen clenched the medallion even tighter, his head twitching back and forth in frantic paranoia that someone, anyone, might be plotting to steal his prized possession. Tales of incredible treasures littered conversations throughout pirate-infested ports such as this—but no tale as great as that of the Chrysalis. Of all the misguided theories of what this mysterious treasure actually was, Lord Yen's was yet just another shallow interpretation.

He had no idea what kind of power this strange golden medallion actually led to. He had no idea that the world itself was about to change forever.

Three
Garbbit Harbor

Rain fell, turning the streets of Garbbit Harbor into slimy streams of mud. It was hardly daylight when already the village was a bustle with the fowl smells and sounds of fishing crews desperately scrambling down to the wharf. Deathly tired, Ash squeezed through the crowd at a breakneck speed. He knew he was late again.

As much as he loathed working aboard Logan's fishing trawler, he couldn't get to the docks fast enough. If he didn't make it there before the boat left, he would be dealing with the inevitability of his father's wrath. Nothing was worse than that. Had Ash come home before twilight, perhaps he would have woken to Logan's drill-sergeant commands, ordering him out of bed and down to the docks. But Ash and his urchin friend Paulo had been out late, engaging in an array of mischief and senseless pranks. The evening inevitably grew less ambitious after discovering Paulo's uncle's stash of homemade ale in the old shed where they spent much of their time. In fact, Ash had sampled enough to inhibit his ability to recall exactly when the night had ended. As the morning light stung his eyes and his stomach turned over, Ash couldn't help but be baffled by adult's attraction to such fermented concoctions.

Glares of grimace pursued Ash as his gangly physique splashed through the muddy streets. Physically, he was still at the crossroads of puberty; when the body's anatomy is in constant disproportion with itself. Though he was taller than most of his peers, he strode with such a slouch that it made him appear less than average in every way. No doubt, his height he got from his father. But that was the extent of commonness he shared with the man. The rest he got from his mother—someone he had never even met. If fact, the only thing he truly knew of his mother was that she must have come from the Orient, giving Ash his smooth olive skin and sharp features. (But he would never know for sure, as his father refused to as much as mention her name.)

Ash stood out among the other villagers. After all, Garbbit Harbor was an old Viking port, founded by Norse warriors. Hundreds of years later, blonde hair, blue eyes and sturdy physiques still mysteriously dominated the gene pool. By comparison Ash simply looked like someone who didn't belong. Atop his dark slender frame, his unkempt hair looked like oil-covered straw, flopped over his black-bean eyes—eyes that dodged contact. His shoulders seemed to pull away, constantly resisting to the world around him. But there was something about Ash, something that gave him away. If people only knew the real Asher Meadows, they would have understood that his persona was nothing more than an alter ego. But no one in this closed-minded village seemed to go that deep. They couldn't see beyond the stains of his deep-green, hooded coat or his ripped-up, baggy brown trousers, or his muddy boots that were worn to a point near dismemberment. They only saw an immature teen that refused to smile. He was known in Garbbit Harbor for making trouble—even when he tried to stay out of it. But in a village as small as this, once you were typecast, it was nearly impossible to shake the reputation.

The crowds were fierce, as people fought their way down to the docks to get a jump on the rest. Possibly being the season's last official expedition, before winter's chill transformed Willow Lake into a frozen plain, it was each one for themselves. And because most simply gambled and drank their fishing earnings away in the off-season, this was their last chance to bloat their wallets. Right in front of Ash, a fight broke out between two men, arguing over dock space. But while they were wasting time fighting, someone else was already leaving the harbor.

Through the jostle of traffic, Ash could see Logan's fishing trawler pulling away. Black smoke billowed out of its tarnished exhaust chimneys. For a second he pondered just letting his father go. But Ash knew that missing the trip and having to deal with him later would only be much, much worse.

Ash pushed aggressively through the mangled crowd and sprinted clumsily onto the dock. By the time he reached the last plank, the trawler was a good distance away. The large boat was old, beat up, and chugged along slowly through its own coughing of thick smoke. But it was still moving faster than Ash was. Unsure of what to do, his legs made the decision for him.

Eyes closed, Ash's body leaped from the dock toward the boat. But just as his feet left the deck they caught the base of a mooring post. And with a painful cracking thud his body hit the edge of the trawler and flipped over the railing. The moist deck was like ice as Ash slid across its surface on his stomach and came to a crashing halt at Logan's feet.

"You're late," Logan growled in his usual ornery slur. His thick peppery beard and mustache hoarded most of his face, and his long sun-bleached hair was pulled back into a messy braid that looked as though it hadn't been retied or washed in years. He was a brute of a man with broad shoulders that, in spite of his large belly, made him look fitter than he veritably was.

"I know I am," Ash shot back, as he stood to his feet. But he wilted with instant regret, awaiting the repercussions of his cynical reply.

"Keep running your mouth like that and I won't think twice about throwing you overboard," Logan threatened vainly with his sausage-like finger in Ash's face. The dreadful smell of soured booze poured from his words. "You're a waste of skin. Now get to work!" And then faster than Ash could react, Logan slapped him across the face like a stinging snake bite.

Ash's cheek flared red with humiliation. Though, he was lucky this time. He knew that his increasingly cocky remarks were beginning to wear thin on Logan's patience. One of these days Logan would lose his cool and once again Ash would find himself victim to his father's uncontrollable rage. It was a vicious cycle. The more physically aggressive Logan was, the more resistant Ash became.

Looking down, Ash rubbed the long scar on his forearm, which served as a permanent reminder of the night Logan came home violently intoxicated and pushed Ash through a window. Hatred burned his eyes every time he looked at it. But what was he to actually do about it? After all, unlike his half-brother, Ash did not inherit the brooding characteristics of Logan.

Like many fishermen of Willow Lake, Logan fought in the Great War. He was a highly decorated soldier. But years of torture in a prison camp left him wounded and unable to return to battle. Reluctantly, Logan returned to Garbbit Harbor, only to find that his wife had written him off as dead and was now with another man. And Logan's only son was already identifying with a new father.

Logan fell into reclusion, nearly drinking himself to death. Then he met a young refugee woman. They eventually married and bore a son, Ash. But a black cloud soon swept in and changed everything.

While Ash was yet a toddler, his mother was growing increasingly erratic and paranoid, avowing that an elusive dangerous force was pursuing her. Damned by her own dementia she soon ran away, void of explanation. She was never heard from again.

Logan quickly down-spiraled, returning to grief and bitterness—often taking his aggressions out on Ash. They relocated to a small withering farmhouse in the hills of outlying Garbbit Harbor, where Ash was forced to turn a dirty cramped attic into his bedroom. As bad as it was though, Ash knew he was lucky, considering he was nothing more than an unwanted pet in Logan's eyes. It was impossible to look past the boy's *curse*—a secret which till now Logan had managed to keep hidden from the rest of the village. And Ash grew to hate him for the shame he was made to feel. More than anything in the world, Ash yearned for validation—for someone who understood his abnormalities and accepted him for who and what he was. But he knew full well: Garbbit Harbor was the last place in the world he would find it.

Four
The Heist

Her thoughts seemed to blur. Some were distant, not her own, or at least no longer. Then, like emerging from a dream, she heard a voice calling her number.

"Ninety-Seven?" Sixty-One said batting the telescope away from her face. "Are you with me?"

Suddenly her subconscious was steady, where it ought to be. She could see his thoughts again and regained focus. The images and echoes of a forgotten past had all but faded into oblivion. Mental roaming was not only forbidden, it was a *flaw*. Recollection of her mortal past was not an option. But the inevitability of human imperfection always prevails.

Ninety-Seven's pale complexion looked tired and lifeless. Her hazel-green eyes seemed to glow against the darkened rings that encircled them, making her look much older than eighteen. She couldn't remember the last time she had slept. She couldn't remember much of anything. But every now and again there would be something she heard or saw, or perhaps a familiar scent that would transport her to a place in time like an incredible deja vu. It was during these unlawful episodes that she felt most alone and afraid, as if she had just committed a crime.

Isla Ruba looked mysteriously familiar to Ninety-Seven as she refocused the telescope on the rocky shoreline ahead. Early morning fog drifted low across the water's surface like a ghost keeping the island hidden from unwelcome visitors. The port was a nexus for entertainment, trade, gambling, and anything else a pirate might fancy themselves with between voyages. But for Ninety-Seven and Sixty-One, it was the stage where they would soon be carrying out a mission of such guarded secrecy, that if anything were to happen to them, no one would come looking. No one *official*, that is.

Ninety-Seven and Sixty-One climbed down from the crow's nest of the schooner, each cramming into small, brass sub-spheres, hanging where the yawl boat typically hung. A large automated chain lowered them into the sea. Quickly they descended into the crystal clear, moonlit waters.

The vessel they left behind was a drone-spy ship, contracted to the mighty kingdom, aptly called Kingland. It was disguised as a classic cargo-carrying schooner, commonly seen passing through the shipping lanes of the Great Sea. But just like the drone-spies, what lie beneath the outer skin was far more advanced and powerful than what met the eye.

The product of experimental science, and part of a privately owned espionage league, Ninety-Seven and Sixty-One had both been medically enhanced by a synthetic substance so transcendent, so perfect, that the laws of physics no longer fully applied to them. Strength, endurance, even reaction had been elevated to a degree once considered unachievable in humans. Then again, they were more than human. They were drones.

They maneuvered their rivet-covered subs into a narrow cave that tunneled through the island's bedrock, far below the water's surface. They powered down their subs in the filthy waters of a sewer canal beneath the port, emerging through a rusted drainage grate in an empty alleyway. Quietly they made their way into the heart of the old port city.

Their charcoal bodysuits blended into the dead, colorless contour of the surrounding architecture. Clay stone buildings towered above the port's central district, disappearing in the passing fog. Far above the swaying palm trees, in the starry sky, silhouettes of nosferu centurions were policing the city's perimeter like swirling vultures. Mercenary island security, nosferus were as reliant on the Slave Lord's money purses as the pirates who littered the island's ports. Large, winged, rodent-like creatures, they glided through the twilight in constant random patterns.

As two nosferu centurions waddled by, the spies remained perfectly motionless in the shadows. Nosferus walked bat-like, on all fours, their heads tucked into their lumpy shoulders. A thin coat of matted hair covered their dark leathery skin. They wore big black capes and carried long spears. Only the bloodshot red of their beady eyes could be seen through the eye-socket holes of their helmets, which were nothing more than wisent skulls. The narrow skulls were beaked, with tall curving horns, which the nosferus dipped in oil and lit afire. This would be the perfect disguise for the drones.

Ninety-Seven followed Sixty-One's lead, slashing the wrist cuffs of her suit together, igniting its energy—strength enhancement. A matrix of green light illuminated the suits' surfaces. Designed as lightweight body armor, power-suits proved to be a breakthrough invention for combat soldiers of the Allied Kingdoms, augmenting the host's physical strength, endurance, and speed to a point of near perfection. In a flash of green light, Ninety-Seven and Sixty-One rendered the nosferu centurions unconscious.

Recognizing the streets and buildings from the map, which had been downloaded to him prior to the mission, Sixty-One proceeded toward Grande Coliseum with Ninety-Seven close behind. They now dawned the full attire of the nosferu centurions. The other centurions perched atop the circumference of the coliseum paid no mind as the spies entered.

Ninety-Seven and Sixty-One briskly made their way to Lord Yen's private balcony, hunched over and limping along as real nosferus would. They were pulling off their disguise perfectly. But passing by Yen's henchmen guarding his balcony wouldn't be as easy.

The henchmen were towering green creatures, ripped with bulking, greasy muscles. They were lizardens, indigenous to the southern tropical rain forests. Their heads were flat and wide—so wide their eyes extended out beyond the width of their shoulders. But perhaps their most prominent feature was their hatred for nosferus.

As the spies approached, the two henchmen stiffened in defense. The spies didn't slow their stride, but instead raised their spears, razor tips aimed directly at the henchmens' necks.

"We're inspecting this section," Sixty-One said with a voice that was not his own. The synthetic substance flowing through his veins also enabled him to manipulate his vocal cords and mimic the sound of others.

"No one notified us," one of the henchmen growled back.

"We just did," Sixty-One replied in his nosferu-like voice. The two henchmen moved aside reluctantly, unable to even warn Lord Yen of the impromptu inspection. As much as they disliked nosferus, they knew that here, on Isla Ruba, they would have to play by the rules.

Yen didn't as much as turn his head when the spies entered the rear of the balcony, trusting the commotion behind him was merely his henchmen. Unfortunately he trusted their protection a little too much. He didn't know what hit him when Sixty-One shot him in the back with a poisoned micro dart. The dart head dissolved upon penetration to avoid being detected. But the poison worked much faster, knocking Yen out immediately. Ninety-Seven caught the him before his huge limp body slithered off the floating saucer and onto the floor. The serpentine's tendrils were still coiled tightly around the medallion as Ninety-Seven eased it out of his grip. Her master hadn't informed her of what it was. All she knew was that it was priceless.

It didn't look like much as Ninety-Seven held the Enigma in the palm of her hand. She rubbed the engravings on its surface. It was strange. They seemed almost too perfect to be something forged by hand. It was like a relic from another world. One side was etched with strange symbols, while the other looked more like the lines in the palm of a person's hand. Sixty-One grabbed it from her, placing it into a small pouch hanging off his belt. But his attention seemed anywhere but here—strangely preoccupied by the plight of the gladiators on the arena floor below.

The wounded gladiator had sustained further wounds that had now rendered him immobile. The second gladiator was focusing his intentions on merely keeping his counterpart alive. But the sabertooth lion had now shifted into a wild rabid state, foaming at the mouth. The beast shook its crowning mane, roaring to the crowd, its manic state intensified by the first scent of blood.

Knowing that neither would survive if they stayed together, the second gladiator left his counterpart and drew the only weapon he had, his switch-sword. With the flick of a tiny switch upon the sword's ornate hilt, the long, narrow, double-edged blade instantly ejected. But the lion quickly proved that it would take much more than this to bring it down.

The gladiator managed to stab the lion's paw, only to be swiped aside by the other. The impact of the lion's massive claws was more than the gladiator's failing armor could handle. As he clambered on the ground towards his dying counterpart, a trail of red blood was left in the sand behind. The lion thundered an explosive roar to its crowd before devouring its prey. And that was the sight that changed Sixty-One.

Ninety-Seven motioned to Sixty-One to leave. But Sixty-One's mind was still elsewhere. What was playing out in the arena had completely captivated him. As blood oozed from the gladiator's armor, Sixty-

One saw only blood, a different blood, not like the blood that flowed through his own veins. He recognized it, yet it was foreign. Images of a distant past flashed through his mind like a recollection he couldn't understand. He felt naked. He felt violated, as if someone had stolen his identity and replaced it with another—something foreign and synthetic. This wasn't some random delusion he was experiencing. He wasn't hallucinating. This was reality.

"Sixty-One," Ninety-Seven said, leaning into his face. "What is it?" she asked. "Are you with me?" She knew something was wrong. Through his wisent skull mask, Sixty-One's eyes were like glass. She could no longer see his thoughts. But there was no time to figure it out. They had a promise to keep to their master. And their master didn't accept failure.

Sixty-One didn't answer. His eyes remained fixed on the blood. It was beginning to seem clear to him. He wasn't who he thought he was. The foreign substance that now ran through his veins had definitely changed him. Regardless of whoever he once was, he had now been transformed into a mere asset. Looking at Ninety-Seven, he realized just how true this was. They both were nothing more than puppets—they and the many others. In fact, they were all part of the same collective—slaves to the one who owned their motives and orchestrated their actions: Machine.

"Come," Ninety-Seven said, grabbing Sixty-One's arm. "We're leaving." Tossing their nosferu attire aside, they left the balcony.

The henchmen were paralyzed in shock when they saw the two spies slip passed them. *These were no nosferus!* While one of the henchmen peeked around the corner, only to find their boss coiled up, unconscious on the floor, the other henchman proceeded to catch up with the spies. But it was no use; the drone spies were moving at blurring speeds.

Sixty-One stopped the moment they reached the coliseum's entrance lobby, pulling away from Ninety-Seven.

"Leave me," he said to her. "I can't go on."

"What do you mean?" Ninety-Seven asked.

"I know what we are," he said solemnly, as he drew a small blade from his belt and pierced the palm of his hand. Black, synthetic blood oozed through the skin—nothing like the bright red blood he had just seen spilled across the arena floor. As he carved, a small implanted capsule emerged from the scar. He held it up for Ninety-Seven to see and then dug a second one out of his other palm. But Ninety-Seven wasn't as shocked as she thought she should be.

She recognized the capsules as something mysteriously related to the source of her strength, her existence. And she felt that in some strange way she knew exactly what he was talking about. Somehow she knew that her own identity was only skin-deep. The memories that drifted in and out of her subconscious were too perfect and too lifeless to be real. Sixty-One's stare was hypnotic, as black blood continued to pool on the floor. Again, he reached into his utility belt, pulling out a fist-sized, black sphere—an object Ninety-Seven recognized with panic-stricken eyes.

That puzzling emotion, fear, began to swell within her again. She knew what the black sphere was: an atomic-grenade. It was the deadliest hand-held military weapon in existence.

Sixty-One closed his eyes and activated the grenade's detonator. As wrong as he knew this was, he felt powerless against his own actions. Rationale was quickly fading. He couldn't bear it any longer. It had to end now.

Ninety-Seven couldn't allow the mission to be completely lost. Yet something else inside her almost didn't care—or didn't want to care. With every pulse that came from Sixty-One, she knew there was less she could do. She lunged and snatched the medallion from his belt, giving up on trying to intercept the grenade. But even as fast as she was, she didn't cross the stucco entrance trellis before the explosion lifted her into the air and threw her across the street, slamming her into the face of a stone building.

Screams of wounded people spilled out into the street through the settling dust of the fiery cloud of the explosion. Ninety-Seven was slowly coming to. She struggled to determine whether or not the preceding episode was merely another dream. But the smell of smoke and the sound of chaos quickly confirmed where she was.

On the ground next to her a nosferu centurion helmet lie, it's flame extinguished. Ninety-Seven found herself locked in a mesmerizing gaze as she glared into the lifeless eyes of the nosferu's head, still inside the smoldering helmet. She didn't know how to formulate a solid thought or feeling about the sight. She felt numb to the concept of death. Then she smelled something—the powerful scent of a wild animal.

The ground began to rumble. Ninety-Seven was dazed and the dust was thick. But the heavy growl was obvious. It was the sabertooth lion! The beast had escaped the arena through the gaping hole caused by the explosion. It was as disoriented as everyone else, but it was clear that its two victims in the arena had merely whet its appetite. And now Ninety-Seven was in its sights.

The notion to get up and run was almost completely diluted by that strange haunting feeling: *fear*. In a single bound, Ninety-Seven was sprinting down the narrow streets. The thunderous pounding of the lion's pursuit grew louder and louder, closer and closer. Ninety-Seven accelerated. She was exceptionally fast, even for a drone. However, it wasn't fast enough to outrun the giant strides of the lion. So she ignited her power-suit, also activating the suit's wings—two rectangular appendages horizontally erecting from her suit's back capsule.

She leaped into the air, and for a brief moment continued to rise above the buildings, in a green streak of light. Suddenly something struck her and she began dipping into an uncontrollable tailspin, smashing into the corner of a building and falling back to the street. The lion had stood to its hind feet, catching Ninety-Seven's wings with its long claws. Through the flurry of ash, she scrambled to her feet and found her way back to the alley.

As she reached the sewer grate she and Sixty-One had entered the city through, Ninety-Seven threw back the covering and leaped down to where their subs were still waiting, afloat in the filthy stream. The lion came to an abrupt halt over the void, clawing, slamming its paw down inside. Its giant claws thrashed around wildly till it found the sub. The lion instantly gripped it; squeezing it so tight it began to crush. Ripping it out of the sewer it brought the sub above ground, proceeding to retrieve its fleshy prize. But the sub was empty!

Below, Ninety-Seven darted away in the other sub. She felt sick, physically sick. All that had just happened was beginning to bleed together like some ghastly lucid dream. She felt in a strange way that she could vaguely understand why Sixty-One did what he did.

I know what we are. Sixty-One's final words haunted her as she maneuvered back through the underwater cave. She fought vainly to impede it from her mind. There was no time for this. It was now up to her alone to complete the mission. She couldn't leave the island fast enough. Then she saw light at the mouth of the cave. And in the distance she saw the underside of her drone-schooner passing slowly overhead, still safe. But not for long.

A fleet of smaller pirate warships soon joined a flagship, topside. All ships were flying their trademark, black flags, splattered with a huge, white, painted *X*. Great Sea pirates proudly displayed this flag as a symbol of their tyranny.

The ships quickly surrounded the drone-schooner. And as the warship came alongside the drone-schooner, the flagship instantly unleashed her numerous cannons, blasting the schooner's side. But the schooner's hull was surprisingly resistant. The flagship's cannon fire merely splintered the schooner's wooden skin. It was the first sign that it was more than just a small freighter.

On the outside the schooner looked no different than any other freighter. But on the inside was a matrix of state-of-the-art, spy equipment. Like something out of the future, the schooner was unmanned, entirely run by automated machines. But it had a mind of its own—a mind to defend itself.

Ninety-Seven hung back as the entire fleet of pirate ships closed in on the drone-schooner, their barnacle-encrusted bellies sliding through the water like fish. Orange cannon fire lit up the air above the water's surface. But the impregnable drone-schooner remained virtually unscathed.

The perplexed pirates finally ordered a crew to manually board the schooner. Wasting no time, dozens of ravenous renegades leapt and swung by ropes from their ships onto the deck of the drone-schooner. They quickly dispersed to explore the schooner. But once again, this vessel was full of surprises.

Beneath the wooden decking was simply a riveted metal floor. It was like nothing they had ever witnessed. *How was it navigating on its own? Perhaps it was a ghost ship!* Suddenly a loud clang jolted the entire ship, freezing everyone in position. Then a blinding blast exploded from the drone-schooner's side, slamming into the pirate flagship.

From a safe distance below, Ninety-Seven watched as the flagship exploded into a rising ball of fire, settling in a vast dusting of tiny wooden splinters upon the water's surface above. Ninety-Seven knew the capabilities of her drone-schooner. It wouldn't be long before the rest of the pirates were all in full retreat. But then something completely unexpected entered the scene—catching everyone off guard.

Through the underwater clouds of plankton, Ninety-Seven saw something beginning to take form in the distance. It was difficult to make out, other than its magnificent size. The shapeless enormity of whatever it was looked like a giant sea monster. Then its heavy shadow fell over Ninety-Seven. She couldn't tell what it was. It was a submarine of some kind. But it was far larger than any vessel she had ever seen.

She noticed no markings, as it seemed to go on and on as it passed over her, closing in on the drone-schooner.

Topside, the surrounding pirates instantly recognized the approaching submarine as a long row of large, metal, red fins emerged from its upper bulkhead, breaching the water's surface like the fins of a giant whale. It was the *Venom*: the legendary pirate submarine of Sayto Bontey. The largest submarine ever built, the *Venom* was also the deadliest vessel ever put to sea.

Bontey was the most notorious and feared pirate in the world. Refusing to establish an alliance with anyone, he was gravely feared by even his pirate peers. Though he had been imprisoned for the past twelve years, it was said that his first mate, Droku Mox had now assumed the helm. And he was said to be every bit as ruthless as Bontey.

Like a knife piercing the belly of an animal, the huge, sharp, red fins of the *Venom* sliced through the underside of the drone-schooner and ran the entire length of the hull. From below the surface, Ninety-Seven watched in horror as the schooner split in two and began its long slow decent to the bottom of the sea. She barely escaped the descending wreck as it grazed her sub on its way down.

"Agent Ninety-Seven to Master," she said frantically into the sub's transmitter microphone. "Do you copy?"

"What is it, Agent?" a familiar, synthetic-sounding voice replied over the transmitter speaker horn.

"I have to abort the mission," she informed. "Sixty-One malfunctioned. He's gone."

"Do you have the medallion?" the static-filled voice interrupted.

"Yes, it is intact," she assured, holding it up and giving it a once-over.

"Good, then all is not lost," the voice said in an obvious recovery from hopelessness. "Do not abort the mission. I will send a squadron to rendezvous with you at—" Suddenly the transmission cut out as sparks flew throughout the sub's interior. What Ninety-Seven didn't see, was the fatal damage her sub had sustained when the wreckage of the sinking drone-schooner had collided with it. Now, merely a powerless iron sphere, the sub hurdled aimlessly into the blackening abyss.

Watching the dark underwater world spin about through the sub's window, Ninety-Seven felt the instinctive allegiance to her master fading into the darkness along with the horror she was leaving behind. She had felt strangely connected to Sixty-One, not through the puppetry of Machine, but through the mysterious hidden truth Sixty-One had uncovered. Just as Isla Ruba had seemed so oddly familiar to her upon first spotting it, she had felt some sort of connection between these feelings and Sixty-One's revelation.

Rolling the Enigma over in her finger, Ninety-Seven needed no more convincing that somehow she had been lied to about her past. But the more she tried to conjure up a memory, the faster it escaped her mind. It was so strange, almost like there were no memories to remember, just the darkness of the here and now. Little did she know that the fate of the world hung in the very balance of this small golden medallion.

As the darkness of the sea's abyss closed in around the sub, her future seemed no more certain than her past. Fate, however, was only beginning to plot its course.

Five
The Curse

The wind had picked up throughout the day, stirring up rolling white caps across Willow Lake's gray surface. Rain had since turned to sleet, pelting Ash's face like thousands of stinging insects. But he was too tired to care. As of late, sleep had become a rare commodity for him. The unexplainable nightmares were making him reluctant to even close his eyes at night.

His frustrated hands became increasingly uncoordinated as Ash struggled to untie a knot under the dimming evening sky. After a long cold day in constant drizzle, his fingers were beginning to stiffen, as was the rope. But it was more than the cold and the stubborn knot that was irritating him. It was that undercurrent of hopelessness he always felt in the presence of Logan. And the more he thought of his father, the more alienated he felt and the more frustrated he became. But someone who was never far had been watching the whole time.

"Let me give you a hand, Ash," Wick said quietly as his little, pudgy, webbed fingers interrupted Ash's futile efforts. "That rope just doesn't want to cooperate with your hands right now."

Wick McCrow was a wharfling. So his tiny hands were quite good at this sort of thing. In fact, wharflings were the most common choice as deckhands aboard the commercial fishing vessels of Willow Lake, partially because of their stunted size. Indigenous to the bogs of Murk, wharflings were amphibian dwarfs who lived in earthen huts on the marshland plains.

Most people didn't understand the wharflings' way of life, their social or religious rituals. Historically, children were taught to fear wharflings as untamed animals. Regardless, wharflings remained the greatest natural resource for fishing crews navigating the sprawling expanse of Willow Lake.

"So you were out late with Paulo again," Wick interrogated, masked by his irresistibly warm Gaelic dialect.

His pale-green skin was slimy and speckled with sunspots. His eyes were crystal-hazel and his prominent upper lip sagged down over his mouth like a huge tentacle-like mustache that bunched into wrinkles of fat when he spoke. His woven poncho was charcoal, with the exception of a few mismatched patches he had sewn on over the years. Beneath he wore typical wharfling attire: a cable-knit robe made of krugenram's wool. And his chubby webbed feet spilled out of his open-toed shoes.

"We were working," Ash replied sluggishly. He hated Wick's sly guilt trips.

"I smell it on you, Ash," Wick whispered, calling Ash's bluff in reference to the stale alcohol on the boy's breath. Besides, Wick could see it in his eyes. "That Paulo is nothing but trouble. You're better than this."

Ash wasn't in the mood for another one of Wick's lectures. Although Wick was the closest thing he had to a father figure, there were times when he wished he were simply left alone. But before he could step away from Wick's reprimand, he heard a splash.

"Get Wick!" a familiar hoarse voice yelled up to Ash from the water's surface over the edge of the boat. It was Migg, Wick's wharfling apprentice. Migg was holding up a broken piece of pottery, draped in soggy seaweed. Quickly Migg clambered aboard and they huddled in a dripping mess over the find.

They were careful to stay out of Logan's line of sight. He had no tolerance for Migg's little scavenging expeditions, when he was supposed to be tending to the nets below. But Migg couldn't resist. And Wick was a complete sucker for the many underwater treasures often dredged up from the bottom of Willow Lake. Every now and again, a rare find would drift in from Rainy River, which fed the lake from the Great Sea.

"What is it?" Migg asked Wick, as Ash strained over their shoulders for a look.

"It's an urn. But the markings appear to be Atezian," Wick said, squinting his eyes and slowly rotated it in his hands. "Atezians buried their dead. Cremation was an abomination in their culture. So much so that urns were seen as a symbol of evil."

"So what do you think it is then?" Ash asked, as his curiosity piqued. Although he was too embarrassed to admit it to his peers, things like this actually intrigued Ash.

"Judging by the condition of the clay," Wick began with a furrowed brow, "I would infer this artifact to be approximately from the beginning of the late ages, which was after the great insurrection that ultimately crumbled the Atezian society." Aside from his study of magic, and even theories of alchemy, Wick was a bit of a historian, obsessed with ancient societies. "So chances are this urn was forged by an insurrectionist in recognition of their new-found autonomy from Atezian rule."

Ash pondered this for a moment. He knew very little about the Atezians other than the popular legends of their bohemian lifestyle. But he often imagined himself as one of these insurrectionists fighting for their freedom from the powerful dictatorship. It was a situation he felt he could relate to and understand. He liked this fantastical notion. It gave him hope.

"We've got time on our hands I see," Logan growled as his shadow fell over Ash and the wharflings like a swelling plume of smoke. His voice startled Ash, causing him to jerk back in shock. "What have we here?" Logan asked, seizing the urn from Wick's little hands. Holding it up and studying it, he uncorked a bottle of rum, which he carried around faithfully in his other hand. "Did I not make myself clear when I said there will be *no* extracurricular activities taking place aboard my boat?" And with that he smashed the urn down on the deck, shattering it into a scattered mess of pottery shards. "Clean this up and get back to work!" he barked as he lumbered away with his bottle of rum tipped on end in a desperate attempt to retrieve one last drop. But instead of rum spilling out, four black beetles came crawling out and onto Logan's face! He quickly swatted them away and spun around, glaring at Ash with narrowed eyes.

"You—you little freak!" Logan roared as he grabbed Ash by the collar, lifting him off the deck and marching him to the edge of the boat.

Ash knew exactly what he was talking about. He didn't mean to use his curse. It just happened. One moment he was wishing ill on Logan, and the next the beetles appeared. It was almost as though his thought had manifested into physical reality. That's usually how it happened. Then, in a surprising display of restraint, Logan pulled Ash back away from the water. His fist opened and he dropped Ash back to the deck like a stringer of fish.

It was easy to see that Logan was almost afraid of what Ash might be capable of if dropped into the water. The hard part was trying not to laugh as Logan mumbled curses and vain threats under his breath as he stumbled away. Sooner or later, Ash would certainly pay the price for this one.

That night, while Logan's slumbering mass swayed heavily in his hammock, Wick sat across the boat's cabin, quietly studying the only sizable shard he was able to salvage from the urn. With every rock of the boat, Logan's snoring would swell up into a gurgling growl and then dissipate into a series of clamorous lip smacks and inaudible mumbles. The cloud-diffused glow of the moons poured through the cabin's window, painting the small room pale blue. Migg sat patiently waiting for a reaction from Wick.

"Can you tell what tribe the urn came from?" Migg asked Wick about the urn.

"Well, sort of," Wick said in a tone of disappointment. But Migg didn't catch it. He was too excited to hear Wick's final conclusion.

"So?" Migg insisted after a long agonizing silence.

"It's a replica," Wick said plainly as he tossed the shard onto the table.

A laugh spilled in as Ash entered the room. "All of that trouble only to find that it's a worthless phony?" Ash said shaking his head as he pumped the fuel of the dimming lantern hanging above Wick's head. "Sometimes I wonder what your obsession is with this stuff."

Wick turned his head away from the brightening light as Ash continued to pump the lamp. He wasn't shaken by Ash's cockiness. "It's the process of finding that I enjoy, not just the find."

"So you're not let down now, knowing that it's a fake?" Ash asked.

"Honestly?" Wick said as a smile grew across his chubby face, "I am quite relieved. My heart nearly stopped beating when I saw it smashed on the deck."

Ash looked over at Logan who continued to slumber heavily in his drunken state. "Well, it doesn't mean you have to stop hating him," he said, gesturing to Logan.

"Ash," Wick said, suppressing a chuckle as he recalled the beetle incident earlier that day, "I don't hate the man. I feel bad for him. He's a miserable soul."

"He's a monster," Ash shot back instinctively. He could feel his cheek still burning from Logan's slap earlier that day. How badly he wanted to make the hammock untie itself from the wall, letting Logan fall to the floor.

"Yes," Wick said, remaining calm, "he can be. But you are your own person. It's time you stopped evaluating your life based on what others think of you. You are replete with potential just waiting to come out—your Mystery, Ash." Wick's eyes sparkled with something that proved he meant much more than his words said.

This wasn't the first time Ash had heard this. Wick had often spoken of *one's Mystery* as their free will. In fact, outside of religious groups who often hijacked and twisted this notion into commandments of their own, the Mystery was widely accepted as the true full potential everyone possesses. Though most agreed that if everyone were to realize their own Mystery, the world would become nothing less than a utopia, few saw it as completely attainable.

For Ash, Logan was such a powerful and often frightening presence that he had never given the notion of his own Mystery the slightest consideration. And it made it even more difficult to accept when Logan was always reinforcing the notion that Ash had little hope of ever making it in the world, anywhere outside of Garbbit Harbor.

Ash possessed fears of leaving the only place he had ever known—fears that were far greater than he had ever let on. Besides, who was to say he actually could venture off on his own and find his way? He had no direction. All of his dreams and fantasies of changing the world were just that: fantasies. He knew he had the ability to be something more. But how was he to change the world if he couldn't even change his own life?

"Yeah, I know," Ash finally replied. "I just don't want to talk about it right now."

"All right, Ash," Wick said respectfully, as he packed his pipe with a leafy dried weed. "But I don't want you to stop thinking about it for good," Wick continued. "You're at an age now where you must make the right decisions before the wrong ones make themselves for you. We all have a purpose in this world, Ash. But like anything, chances can be missed. You've got to keep your chin up and your eyes open."

"If I could leave this stupid village, I would," Ash shot back in a defensive burst. "But I can't. And there are no *chances* in Garbbit Harbor."

On that note, Wick knew to change the subject.

"Here," he said to Ash. "Hold out your hands, palms up."

Ash rolled his eyes. When he was a young boy he used to squeal with excitement at the thought of Wick's magic tricks. But at sixteen he had outgrown them. He had especially grown tired of how Wick always seemed to pull them out in a vain effort to cheer him up. But he held his hands out anyway. There was still a shred of curiosity in him.

"I'm going to put it in this hand and this hand only," Wick said tapping a bit of his pipe's black ash resin into Ash's open palm. "Now close both hands."

Ash followed along reluctantly, making two fists. Wick then waved his hand over Ash's in a phony magical wave. But when Ash opened his hands he found himself feeling the way he did when he was a boy. His eyes grew wide as his mind raced to figure out how Wick had gotten the resin to transfer perfectly from one hand to the other while Ash's hands were closed.

"How'd you do that?" Migg exclaimed, scrambling over the table, nearly knocking the lantern to the floor. "That's amazing!"

"Shhh!" Wick motioned to Migg as Logan began to stir. "Ask Ash. He seems to be a believer." His pursed grin tried to follow Ash, whose eyes refused to acknowledge. Perhaps out of embarrassment or perhaps out of belief. Regardless, Ash wasn't letting on.

"How did you do it?" Ash finally asked. "And don't say magic."

"You should know, Ash," Wick said with a stare that went right through Ash. "You were watching the entire time. But you saw only what you wanted to see. It's a simple trick of sleight of hand. But because you were waiting for something else to happen, you didn't even see me swipe the resin from one hand and wipe it into the other. It was there before you knew it was there.

"You must be observing with your conscience as well as your eyes if you are to recognize your own potential. Remember, discovery isn't so much about *where* you seek. It's about *how* you seek.

"Take the Imcot, for example," Wick said, sitting back down. His fascination with this particular ancient sect was something Ash never understood. He soon enough would, however. "They were the most respected warriors of their time—defenders of real magic," Wick continued. "But never did they engage in battle. Instead they focused their energy on the search for pure truth, from which, they believed, everything else flowed."

"So what's the moral of the story?" Ash recoiled sarcastically.

Wick's face suddenly grew stone cold, falling into the shadows like a fading ghost. "Stop assuming that you've missed the boat in life just because your father or your peers have claimed it. There's still time. Your true potential finds you, whether you want it to or not. But you must know what it looks like. Quiet your mind and focus on that burning pang within—the one that feels like regret and guilt. For *that* is actually the feeling of undiscovered destiny."

Thrusting his fist to the cabin wall, Ash abruptly left the room and went above deck to be alone. He was now at the age where Wick's fatherly persistence was beginning to simply smother and annoy him. By now, as the realities of adulthood loomed nearer, Wick's ridiculous belief in a greater life only served as a bleak reminder of his own dismal situation—a past unlived and a future uncharted. There was no magical hope for him. There was no *someday*. Garbbit Harbor could never know of his secret. His *curse*—which ironically was the very thing that kept him from ever passing beyond the borders of this small village.

Six
The Count of Cape Sparrow

Off the southern coast of the Western Territories, the Witherland Straits funneled into a long narrow inlet known as Cape Sparrow. Her cobalt blue waters were strewn with thousands of rocky shards, erecting above the crashing waves like giant, crude arrowheads. It was an unforgiving maze, guarding Bald Rock from unwanted visitors. The cape was notorious for snaring unfortunate seafarers, blinded by the area's common fog. Often, the only visible point for those at sea was the lantern of the Bald Rock lighthouse.

Through the years, this towering spire had been refuge to many stranded sailors abandoning their sinking ships, which had fallen prey to the treacheries of Cape Sparrow. But over time trade routes changed leaving fewer and fewer ships passing through the cape. Eventually the old lighthouse turned out its lamp for the last time. Yet in its darkness something continued to stir.

The ghost of the lighthouse keeper of Bald Rock was said to still roam its expanse. In fact, tales of sailors claiming to have seen this elusive ghost were quite common in seaside ports. It was because of these chilling claims that people stayed away from Cape Sparrow. Everyone but one, that is.

He seemed to come out of nowhere. The Count of Cape Sparrow, otherwise known as Count Velkan LePrey, was one day a perfect stranger, the next a household name. Yet he wasn't a name that people talked about lightly. A mysterious recluse, LePrey had become synonymous with the term *madman*. But what drove him to his madness was a dark secret that remained locked away in the shadows of the haunted lighthouse.

Known for his array of fascinating inventions, LePrey was equally known for his incredible wealth. So when he began buying up islands throughout Cape Sparrow, people took notice. Most saw this string of southern islands as a worthless investment, passing off the Count's transaction as nothing more than bad business. LePrey obviously measured wealth in a very different way.

The lighthouse tower and the sprawling bungalow from which it was erected looked as though they might topple off of the cliff's edge and into the crashing waters far below at any moment. Ironically, the lighthouse was once the pinnacle historical site of Cape Sparrow, rich with stories. It was even rumored that it had been visited by members of the Kingland Royal Family at one point in its three hundred year history. But over time, relentless winds funneling down the cape's narrows had made irreversible impressions on its stone brick structure, twisting the tower like a withering tree. The lighthouse of Bald Rock was now nothing more than an abandoned, decaying tower on a treeless rock. But for LePrey it was a means of shutting the world completely out while harboring his secrets safely within.

After the tragic loss of a loved one, LePrey had become obsessed with the concept of mortality. Determined to find a way to cheat death, he turned to the study of alchemy, the ancient scientific practice of trying to achieve an elixir known as the Philosopher's Stone. Success in achieving this alchemical substance was believed to subsequently produce the capability of turning simple metals into gold, but even more importantly, death into life. Eternal life. LePrey was convinced that through this bizarre chemistry he would find the cure. But it never came.

Though rumors swirled about that his obscene wealth was the product of discovering the Philosopher's Stone, thus accumulating gold at his own will, a cure for death still remained out of his reach. In fact, his quest for eternal life ironically resulted in the failing of his own health. Over-exposure to the toxic ingredients required for developing the elixir slowly began to poison his body and mind. That was the moment when everything changed.

With his health deteriorating, LePrey was desperate for a successful remedy. By applying some of his alchemical practices to modern science of the day, he finally had a breakthrough: the development of synth. This extraordinary substance was unlike anything the world had seen. A blackened, mercury-like liquid, synth possessed the ability to regenerate blood cells, enhancing a person's physical state to that of near immortality. Not only did it save LePrey's life, but also it was the core element of the one invention history would remember him for.

Frozen air screamed in like a symphony of tiny voices through the windowpane's imperfections. The chilling sound only blended with the other formless voices encroaching LePrey's mind—ravaging him with their usual prattle. Even the shrieking sound of the six huge windmills on the cliff below seemed to find its way up to LePrey's head. It was a torment he had come to know all too well. The whites of his eyes, leering from the shadow of his hood, were bloodshot with fatigue as he stared motionlessly out the giant bay window.

He was tall and thin, yet housed a daunting physique. His shifty eyes seemed hollow, lifeless. They were sunken into his head along with his cheeks, as if his skin was merely draped over his skull like a thin blanket. His black, well-groomed mustache and goatee hardly looked real against his colorless skin. Beneath his long, charcoal cloak, he wore a crimson velvet vest, which was embroidered in fine vintage texture. Rarely was he seen in anything else. Then again, rarely was he seen at all. His elegant guise certainly preceded his reputation. But his reputation was merely a glimpse of who and what he truly was.

The cape's waters tossed and turned under the high winds. LePrey's eyes remained fixed on something beyond the water—something beyond himself. Alone in the bungalow's foyer he pondered the horrors of the mission's possible failure. Sixty-One was dead, Ninety-Seven was as good as gone and the Enigma along with.

As the invisible voices became deafening, LePrey made his way to the lighthouse's elevator-lift, up to the lantern room, at the top of the tower. Behind the intricately carved elevator door, the shrilling sound of the squealing pulleys came as sweet music, drowning out the chatter in his head—the cruel curse distancing him from his perfect creation …

Countless glass beakers and test tubes littered the darkened room, making it look more like an abandoned laboratory. These days the lighthouse lantern room was void of any lights. Ironically, in place of the giant lantern was a massive black sphere suspended a short distance above the floor. Thousands of tiny rivets peppered its iron patchwork surface like boils on a leper's body. This monstrous orb was LePrey's crowning achievement—his greatest invention of all: Machine.

While LePrey's obsession with death grew, so did his curiosity surrounding his own. As impressive as synth was, it wasn't perfect. LePrey had certainly increased the longevity of his life. But he was still a mortal man. Through lengthy skrying sessions he began looking into the future to discover his own fate. But this ancient practice of staring into a vessel of liquid and entering a trance-like state yielded only the bitter truth of his own mortality. He needed a way out—a methodical diversion from the inevitability of death. So he created Machine, a testament to scientific perfection. Through mathematical precision, Machine was able to predict future events and determine scenarios of probability that could ultimately change the course of history. Immortality had finally almost come to fruition.

Count LePrey slowly placed his gloved hands on the black metal surface of Machine, as an electrical current rushed through his body. On Machine's axis, a round shutter dialed open revealing its optic lens. LePrey stared deep into the darkened glass of the lens. A faint green glow began to swell, refracted by the kaleidoscopic glass. It was as if Machine was staring back into his soul. Large electrical conductors hung around the perimeter of the ceiling like stalactites in a cave. They too rippled with greater surges of green lightening as LePrey and Machine entered into what they referred to as *communion*. Closing his eyes, LePrey whispered a desperate question to his machine. "Where is she?"

Nervous anticipation had rendered LePrey manic after the Isla Ruba incident. News of the mission's failure was one thing. But now, it appeared that Ninety-Seven was deliberately resisting communication with them, leaving LePrey in complete despondency.

It wasn't supposed to happen like this. Sixty-One was the leader of the mission. He was the one who should have been delivering the Enigma to LePrey. But with Sixty-One gone, the most important relic in existence was now in the hands of a drone-apprentice barely able to think for herself. Sure, she was a phenomenon of science, but as Sixty-One had just proven, drones were not as perfect as had been hoped. Finding Ninety-Seven meant everything.

Three floating figures drifted up the stairs, passed the two bald-headed drone-guards with glowing green eyes, and into the lantern room. Their untamed eagerness had betrayed their usual etiquette as they lurked hastily, in search of their master.

"Excuse us, my Lord," One said in his slithery tone. He knew that his master didn't condone Machine being approached without warning. LePrey was adamant that the lantern room be respected no differently than a religious sanctuary. In fact, that's exactly what he referred to it as. But One also knew that LePrey was beyond desperate for any new leads or progress on the recovery of Ninety-Seven.

"I told you never to enter the Sanctuary unannounced," LePrey scolded as he turned away from Machine and drew his hood back, revealing his shaved head sunken into the high, black-fur collar of his cape. His skin looked deathly pale as he whisked the three visitors back down a short spiral staircase and to his private quarters one story below. Their haste was an obvious indication that they had come to deliver only more bad news. It was imperative that their disclosures not take place before Machine. Upsetting it was never a good idea.

One reeled back cautiously as the other two figures cowered behind him in the darkened room. Together the three floating figures were known as the Troika, LePrey's closest advisors. Though powerless and incapable of making an independent decision, the Troika was LePrey's only true loyal asset, far superior to the golems he had briefly brought to life in his early years of alchemical practice.

They were prototypes—first generation drones, explaining their repugnant obscure visage. Victims of a failed experiment, all three were elderly men and little more than skin and bones. Although enhanced by artificial body parts, none had any legs—simply hovering above the floor via their mechanical torsos. But their long, black, hooded frocks concealed most of this, giving them the semblance of black ghosts as they wandered the shadowy corridors of the lighthouse.

"Excuse us, my Lord," One repeated trembling. "We believe we have discovered the whereabouts of our spy." LePrey's impassive silence made One stumble over his words. "First of all," One continued, "the drones most likely suffered a synthetic-meltdown, causing a memory scramble. As you remember, Count, this malfunction was a scenario we had warned against with drones." LePrey's brow lowered into a mean wrinkle. "Anyway, a meltdown would certainly account for Sixty-One's sudden, self-termination. And it would explain Ninety-Seven's resistance to communion with Machine."

"Absurd!" LePrey said, growing angry. He couldn't accept the possibility that his perfect creation might be malfunctioning to such a degree.

"Perhaps, my Lord," One said pleading his case, "but not out of the question."

"And as for where Ninety-Seven may be," Two, the smallest of the three chimed in, "we've tracked her sub-sphere to the Northern Territory of Murk."

"We must find her immediately," LePrey said with wild panic in his eyes. "I hear rumors that Lord Yen survived Sixty-One's suicide attack on Isla Ruba. If this is true, then he will be fixated on retrieving the Enigma back from the girl."

LePrey's motives were complicated. Not only was the Enigma a treasure map, it had become a symbol of hope for those who believed in a world of peace. But LePrey couldn't afford to have delusional zealots dashing the integrity of his life's work. In the wrong hands the Enigma would be his undoing.

"Sir," Three, the third of the Troika chimed in, "that is not all." The Count froze and listened intently. "The situation has already leaked to King Basileus of Kingland. He seeks council with you immediately. Naturally he is quite unsettled about all of this."

LePrey stroked his pointed, black goatee and then curled the tip of his mustache as he drew a long thoughtful breath—a habitual trait that signaled his nervous tension. It was a delicate situation he hadn't anticipated. The same pirates who had destroyed the drone-schooner had since recovered the ship's log; proof of Kingland's illegal espionage on Isla Ruba. If they threatened to use it for blackmail against King Basileus and his secret alliance with LePrey, the outcome would be cataclysmic. He could lose the people's trust immediately. Needless to say, in order to prevent further collateral damage, LePrey would have to be clever in dealing with Kingland, especially King Basileus. Basileus would be looking for any excuse to distance himself from LePrey and this spy program. And lately, no one was more suspicious of his intentions than the King.

Suddenly a crackled voice came through the bulbous transmitter on the head of LePrey's walking staff. "Sir, the Countess is awaiting you."

"Send her up," LePrey ordered, waving the Troika out of the room.

Countess Arona Ivy-LePrey was a most unlikely candidate for the Count's bride. She was considerably younger than the Count—beautiful and simple. A soft-spoken woman with brown eyes that radiated sincerity but also admitted her sadness. She was a captivating sight. But she hadn't always been sad. There was a happier time.

Arona wasn't born into poverty. However, she resisted the lifestyle that attached itself to this kind of wealth and fame. So she abandoned her royal estate and set out for some of the world's most remote places as an escape from the pressures of her prestigious heritage. On her journeys, she met a man who instantly swept her off her feet: Velkan LePrey. On the heels of a whirlwind affair, they fell in love and married. But soon after their marriage, things became strange.

Her new husband fell ill and began to withdraw from her, rarely emerging from the shadows of his secret laboratories. He became obsessed with trying to find a cure for his own tragic ailment. Soon his behavior turned dark and oppressive. And before long Arona found herself a slave-like victim to his many obscure demands—demands as menial as the way she wore her hair, to as ludicrous as forcing her devotion to a monster of his own science, Machine. Though still married, in recent years the two lived apart. Arona remained in another cottage on the grassy bluffs up the coast, while the Count rarely even left the shadows of the lighthouse tower.

Her long, brown curls fell down over her shoulders onto her burgundy gown that flowed sinuously as she entered the room. She carried herself with dignity, in spite of how she felt. LePrey took her hand as she gave a slight bow in an uncomfortable formal gesture. Arona struggled to avoid thinking about what was being harbored just above her in the lantern room. She despised what Machine was—what it had become. To LePrey, this self-aware machine was God.

"Are you ready for the Royal Masquerade?" LePrey asked his wife.

"I am on my way to secure the deal right now," Arona replied quietly, disguising her nervousness as a cold shiver. She avoided eye contact, focusing her stare out the narrow windows that lined the circumference of the room.

"Perfect. Whatever it takes," LePrey said with a hint of respite. "We must succeed."

In spite of her abhorrence, Arona couldn't resists one more attempt to get him to call it off or at least stall it.

"Perhaps the Masquerade Gala is too risky of a place for such a plot?" she suggested hopefully.

For a brief moment Count LePrey wondered if she possibly knew something he didn't. But then he did what he always did. He coiled back in stiffened, defensive skepticism. He knew her too well to fall for this. Her secrets were not her own anymore. "Don't fret. And I have arranged an exit strategy that will ensure complete secrecy."

Arona didn't know what to make of the Count's cryptic reply, so she simply gave a quick bow and hurried away. As she made her way to her private escort carriage, awaiting her at the cottage, she pondered the notion of just escaping for good. But she knew her efforts would be futile. There was only one option: to bring down the number-one enemy of Count LePrey—to kill the man she *truly* loved.

The moment Arona had exited the room, LePrey draped his hood back over his head and proceeded back up to the lantern room. Looking up at Machine, LePrey asked, "Can she be trusted?"

Machine was silent for a moment, as LePrey's reflection stared back at him on its optic lens. Then it spoke.

"No, she cannot," Machine's deep, droned voice said. The voice rang with a familiar tone to LePrey's. Yet it sounded like legions of copies of the same voice, layered over one another. "However, she has no choice but to comply," Machine concluded. A grin threatened to curl up beneath LePrey's hood as a mysterious cool gust hushed through the lantern room like a ghost. Perhaps the ghost of the lighthouse keeper was now present. Perhaps he had never left.

Seven
Wanted

The crumbling buildings lining the narrow streets blurred by as Ninety-Seven streaked through the cold wet shadows of Garbbit Harbor. She had no idea where she was after waking on the muddy shores of a strange lake. But her biggest dilemma wasn't finding her way. It was finding the will she once had to complete the mission. Something wasn't right. Even her short term memory now seemed scrambled and blurry.

Like a yell reaching from a great distance, Ninety-Seven swore she could hear the echo of a familiar voice calling her name. Chills ran over her as it continued to call her number, as though in a desperate search for her. Suddenly she came to a large plaza, surrounded by small cafés.

Everyone seated outside of the cafés dropped what they were doing and observed the strange girl standing in the middle of the plaza, panting as if she was running from some wild beast.

"Can I help you, miss?" one of the locals said as she got up from her chair. Ninety-Seven couldn't understand what she meant.

"Are you okay?" said another, gesturing from his table.

But to Ninety-Seven, these people were nothing more than threats. No one could be trusted. In her bewildered state, she saw it no other way. She struck an instinctive combat pose, causing everyone on the plaza to reel back in their chairs. She wasn't even sure what it was she was defending. But then the most bizarre and unexpected thing happened, something that no one in Garbbit Harbor had ever seen before, as she slashed her wrists together, igniting her power-suit. The hum of the suit's electrical current felt good. It was a feeling of security. She felt invincible. She nearly was.

A large man stood and approached, his fists clenched. He wasn't about to let this girl make threats to his fellow townspeople. But before he could even draw his fist back, Ninety-Seven kicked him square in the chest. His blubbery body lifted off the ground, over tables and chairs, across the plaza and through a large storefront window. It was mind-boggling how that much strength could by harnessed by one skinny girl. No one could comprehend what they had just witnessed.

Ninety-Seven appeared as only a glowing green streak of light as she raced away from the plaza. The crowd in the plaza froze in amazement. Her suit was a technology they didn't understand. Again, she had no sense of direction. All she knew was that she had crossed a serious line. In a few short moments she was about to learn what it was she was actually running from.

Starboard Saloon stood on tall, wooden stilts, lifting it off the muddy runoff at the base of the Garbbit Gorges. Beneath the cracked, wooden floor of the saloon Ninety-Seven curled into the shadows, not to stay dry, but to hide. In the cold shadows beneath the saloon she found it to be quite safe, for now.

Above, debates over trade and tales about fishing filled the smoky air as a drunken, off-key tune competed for attention from an acoustical quartet in the corner. Crumbs of food and spilled ale fell through the wide cracks in the floor, trickling onto her head. She didn't bother to move. She just kept her eyes fixed on the activity of the people above. But then she heard the sound of large feet.

Looking over, she saw the giant, black-clawed hooves of two thunder-stallions splashing through the rain as they drew to a sudden halt at the entrance to the saloon. Thick steam pressed down to the street from the stallions' giant nostrils.

Two huge figures in big black boots and leather, black trench coats stepped down from the carriage's stern, splashing to the ground. Ninety-Seven sank deeper into the shadows beneath the saloon. Something didn't look right. The stallions were pulling a carriage. But from her vantage point it was impossible to see whom the carriage was carrying. All she could see were the three, huge, mud-covered wheels and tobacco smoke curling out from the carriage's windows.

Through the cracks in the floor, she observed the two figures entering the saloon. Once inside, Ninety-Seven could see them more clearly through the cracks in the floor. Together they peeled back their hoods, revealing their green, T-shaped heads. Something about them looked familiar to her. But her mind couldn't quite recognize that they were Lord Yen's lizarden henchmen—the same henchmen she and Sixty-One had out-maneuvered in the Isla Ruba coliseum. The crowd inside the saloon instantly grew silent as the men's boots slowly hammered across the floor. In a deep gravel voice, one of the henchmen finally spoke.

"A girl is thought to have crossed these parts. We need to know if anyone has seen her. She is armed and very dangerous," he said, attempting to make eye contact with every patron in the saloon.

No one uttered a response, nor seemed to know what the henchman was talking about as he held up a yellowed piece of parchment with an illustration of someone's face. But Ninety-Seven knew instantly who it was, without even looking. *It was her!* She knew that it was more than paranoia. She was beginning to understand what was taking place.

"Did he not speak loud enough for you?" the other henchman growled, tantamount to his partner's boiling impatience. They had worked too hard to not even get a reply. Piecing together the girl's likeness from the surviving locals of Isla Ruba was not easy. And it had been a difficult trail to follow to this point. So any lack of cooperation would simply not be tolerated. They had to find the girl.

"We haven't seen any wanderers come through," the bartender replied in a scared voice. "But we'll be sure to let you know if any of us sees anything at all. Right folks?"

"Yes. I'm sure you will," the first henchman said, nodding his large, green head.

For a moment, it was silent as the henchmen surveyed the room. Then, just when it seemed that the worst had passed, one of them whirled around, unsheathing his long rapier and beheaded the bartender. Ninety-Seven scampered away as the head came rolling across the floor, spraying blood down onto her through the cracks and onto her face.

"That was just a warning," the second henchman said as he wiped the blood from his rapier's blade. The two henchmen turned to exit the saloon.

As blood continued to drain down onto Ninety-Seven, she remained frozen, unable to calculate a reaction. Then, above, someone bravely spoke up. "I saw her," an elderly man's voice quivered. Through the cracks, she recognized the man as one of the glaring faces she had seen on the plaza, only moments ago.

"When?" the first henchman asked, towering over the old man.

"On my way here," the old man said.

"Where?" the henchman asked, raising his voice as well as his rapier.

"The main plaza, just down the street," the old man said, sinking into his chair. "She's a ghost or something," he said, convinced that the glow of her power-suit was actually a supernatural aura. "She lit up and then vanished. No one saw where she went."

The two henchmen shot each other victorious grins. They both knew by the description of the suit, they had found the girl. Now all they had to do was retrieve the Enigma she had stolen from their master.

Out of the corner of her eye, Ninety-Seven watched as the two henchmen mounted the carriage. She still couldn't remember exactly who these creatures were. But she knew that things were about to take a turn for the worse. They unleashed their long razor-whips, piercing the thunder-stallions' black-scaled skin. The row of spiking horns that ran from the stallions' nostrils to their lizard-like tails rose high into the foggy air. They were monstrous creatures, filling the narrow streets with their muscular bodies. As they charged away towing the tall carriage, the long red tendrils of a serpentine slithered out from the carriage's window, catching the cold raindrops in the pipe it held.

The wanted poster the henchmen had tacked to a large, wooden pillar in the saloon stared down at Ninety-Seven. People slowly gathered around her likeness as if afraid it might jump out at them. The spectacle tranquilized her. But before she knew what she was doing, she felt cold rain on her face. And returning from what seemed like a deep sleep, she realized that once again she was running. And again, she didn't know where she was headed as the looming evergreens of the Lonesome Pine closed in around her.

Eight
Fallen Angel

"What's eating you?" Paulo asked, his eyes slightly magnified through his goggles and his face smeared in black grease and oil, as he tinkered with his pet project, a homemade jet pack rocket. But Ash didn't hear. His mind was worlds away, as his eyes remained fixed on the overcast that seemed to be suffocating him more and more with each passing day. On the railing of Paulo's balcony, Ash slouched in a deflated manner. "Is it your father?" Paulo asked. He was all too familiar with Logan's abusive episodes with Ash.

"I don't want to talk about it," Ash mumbled back. He was in no mood to elaborate, especially to Paulo.

Paulo was a few years younger than Ash and by all means acted his childish age. Scrawny, with dark brown skin and striking hazel eyes, his kinky black hair was typically home to an array of leaf bits and other tiny oddities he might have picked up throughout his adventurous day. Though there were other boys in Garbbit Harbor that were Ash's age, he wasn't as keen about hanging out with them as they thought he was. There rambunctious competitive nature was something Ash couldn't fully relate to. He had tried out many erroneous versions of himself, in vain attempts to appease them. But in the end he was never quite good enough to be an official member of their cliques.

Ash had a very simple and juvenile side to his personality that he cleverly kept hidden from the other boys. But with Paulo, he could be himself. He could release the real *him* and dare to tap into his colorful imagination. So whenever the topic of Logan came up with Paulo, the reality of his dominance simply diluted the magic of the moment.

"Ouch!" Paulo yelled, sticking his finger in his mouth to sooth the pain after slamming it while tightening the rocket's compressor. Ash looked over, fighting back a laugh. Though he had very little hope in it ever flying, Ash had been loyally involved in the rocket's progress ever since Paulo drew his first schematics. Still, this flying machine was far more Paulo's obsession than Ash's. He possessed an oversized optimism that the rocket would one day be their ticket out of Garbbit Harbor. Perhaps it was that small glimpse of hope that kept Ash working on it at all.

"So you think it will fly this time?" Ash said, pretending to care.

"Positive," Paulo replied bluntly. And with that, Paulo heaved the giant jetpack onto his back. "Now can you give me a hand?" he asked, struggling to buckle the straps while balancing the rocket's massive, heavy wingspan.

Ash jumped up to help. But the moment he touched the rocket, its thrusters fired. "What did you do?" asked Paulo in a panic.

"I didn't do anything," Ash defended, drawing his hands away from the rocket.

"Well shut it down!" Paulo yelled. But just then the thrusters seemed to boost.

Ash looked the rocket over frantically, trying to figure out how to shut the thrusters off. But the fact was he had never paid attention to Paulo whenever he had gone over the details of the rocket's specs. He had no idea where to look. "I think it's malfunctioning," he quibbled as a vain last-ditch effort to avoid responsibility for this mishap.

"Forget it," Paulo said, climbing up onto the railing. "I'm going for it!"

"What?" Ash gasped. "But you haven't even—" Before Ash could finish his sentence the thrusters blasted to their peak and the rocket shot straight up into the night sky. The only problem was that Paulo was no longer attached. Thankfully, Ash was within arm's reach and was able to snag Paulo's shirt before he slipped completely off the balcony.

The boys stood with their jaws dropped open as the rocket swirled out of control, up through the series of clotheslines that webbed from apartment to apartment across the narrow street. And as it crossed each one, the clotheslines ignited like a fuse, burning back to each side of the street. Within a single moment the entire void between buildings was a flaming blaze. And up over the rooftops the rocket continued its swirling journey into the night sky.

Ash wondered just how much trouble he would be in if they didn't fix this little disaster they had just caused. Logan would be infuriated.

"We've got to go find the rocket right now!" Ash said, grabbing Paulo's arm in panic.

They wasted no time, fleeing into the Lonesome Pine to recover their rocket before anyone else did. Luckily, the fires burned out quickly, limited to only the clothes and the lines from which they hung. Still, if anyone found out these two boys were responsible, it would be the final straw, sealing their fate as the blacklisted juveniles of Garbbit Harbor. And Ash didn't want to think of how hard Logan would come down on him this time.

"I smell smoke over here," Paulo said, dashing deeper into the forest. He was more eager than he was wise. It made him seem fearless.

Not only was Paulo much younger than Ash and his peers, he was also far more adventurous, which is what attracted Ash to him. The pointless withdrawn attitude Ash's other friends portrayed was wearing thin on him. And he was tired of always burying his emotions beneath a skin of abhorrence—certainly not his disposition. But if his gang of peers ever found out that he were hanging out with Paulo, he'd never hear the end of it. So finding the rocket and sweeping the entire mishap under the rug was especially important to him.

"Hold on," Ash said, losing sight of Paulo in the darkness. "Wait for me." But suddenly something caught his eye.

Through the trees Ash could see something glowing. It was a faint green light that seemed to be flickering like a failing lamp. As he approached, he began to make out the shape of a person. The person seemed to just be lying on the ground. It was unlike anything he had ever seen. He was afraid. And though he didn't know it at the time, the scars on Ash's back were beginning to bleed again, just like during his nightmares.

An electrical jolt zapped his hand as he touched the person. And the sparks appeared to leap right off of the person. Then the glow dissipated, as if Ash had somehow zapped it out of the person. But when he rolled the body over, he saw the face of a girl who would change his life forever.

"Are you all right?" Ash whispered into the girl's ear as he picked clumps of slimy seaweed off of what appeared to be wings protruding from her black suit. But her suit seemed to react to his touch. The moment he touched it, it reignited, glowing green.

"She's an angel," Paulo gasped, coming up behind Ash. "Look at her wings."

"Shut up, Paulo," Ash said, elbowing his young friend out of the way.

Suddenly her suit went black again and her wings retracted. Though her eyes were open, she said nothing. Her pulse was faint as Ash pressed his fingers to her wrist. And he wondered if she might be in some sort of a coma. Ash drew his hand across her pale forehead, pulling her short, crimson hair back into a more uniform part. Her skin was ice-cold. But she was beautiful—innocent and fragile. The truth was, he had no idea what she was.

"Hey," he said, shaking her shoulders. She seemed to be coming to. "Are you okay? What are you doing out here? How'd you end up out here?" he asked.

"Where?" the girl replied. "Where am I?" Her eyes suddenly locked onto Ash's, as though she recognized him from somewhere.

"You're in the Lonesome Pine," Paulo answered. "Do you know how you got here?"

"I was running," the girl answered as she concentrated hard on her foggy memories. Her expression looked as though she was just beginning to understand an unraveling sequence of ironies. Indeed, she was.

"From what? From who?" Ash asked. Suddenly they heard voices. The girl grabbed Ash's arm and gripped tightly. Her aggressiveness startled Ash. For a girl to cling to him for safety wasn't something he was used to. In fact, it had never happened before. The voices were followed by footsteps breaking through the brush. Ash noticed a light haze growing slightly brighter over the knoll, through the trees. At first he feared that it might be the smoldering remains of Paulo's downed rocket. But it was far worse.

Over the knoll, like an army massing for war, countless villagers holding big torches, lanterns, and light-sticks began to emerge. There must have been at least a hundred of them. Ash assumed that it might have been some sort of search and rescue mission to find this mysterious girl. But as they came closer, Ash could see that some were wielding clubs and pitchforks and even sickles. This was no search and rescue mission. It was an all-out hunt—a lynch mob. *But for whom?* Ash wondered. Then it was obvious.

"We know you're out here, girl," one of the people yelled. "Show yourself! We know who you are. You can't hide forever!" These were people from Garbbit Harbor. It made no sense.

"I told you they would be coming for me," the girl whispered.

As the mass of villagers marched by, the girl clung to Ash in the blackness of the forest. Her grip was tight. And she wasn't letting go. But it wasn't mere physical attraction. It was passion born out of grave disparity. For the first time in his life, Ash felt veritably needed. His own words felt unnaturally bold. But as they fell from his lips, he could feel the girl's spirit collapse in relief. Her cold skin touching his sent a rush through him like an electrical surge absorbing her energy. While his tearful eyes watched the glowing parade of lanterns and glow-sticks disappear into the trees, Ash held the strange girl close.

"What is your name?" Ash whispered into her ear. Expressionless, the girl said nothing.

"Sc-Scar," she stuttered after a long precarious pause. The name seemed to come to her from nowhere. Yet it seemed right. Never had *Ninety-Seven* seemed *right*.

"Scar," Ash repeated softly. Her name seemed peculiar. *Perhaps it was a nickname.* "I'm Asher. But everyone calls me Ash." Suddenly Scar's face turned from exhausted to what appeared to be horribly frightened. "What is it?" Ash asked, noticing her sudden emotional shift.

"Nothing," Scar lied in a whispered. "Nothing at all."

Ash's mind raced as he pondered just who this fallen angel was and how she got there. But the question he should have been asking himself was not *how*, but *why*?

After a short-lived argument, Ash and Paulo decided that the best place to bring Scar was to Logan's fishing trawler. The trawler was unoccupied, pulled out of the water for the season and hoisted into a boat cradle to keep from becoming trapped in the forming ice of late autumn. Suspended by two large leather bands, the trawler floated a dry distance above the water's surface.

When the boys arrived, Wick and Migg were just leaving. They had been secretly retrieving some of their drudged-up treasures, which had been stashed about the trawler throughout the season.

"What have you boys done now?" Wick gasped as Ash wrapped a dry blanket around the girl.

"We found her in the Lonesome Pine," Paulo said, all too eager to give up the goods. And the villagers are looking for—"

"She's lost," Ash cut in before Paulo could go any further. He didn't need Wick getting any more concerned than he already was. "I thought she could stay here tonight to keep warm and dry."

Wick said nothing, studying Scar like a stray animal—a species he had never seen before.

Ash had no idea what was actually going through his mind. "C'mon Wick. It's not like we can just leave her out in the cold."

"It's not my place to say no," Wick said solemnly. "But I'd keep it quiet. And make sure she's gone in the morning."

Ash agreed without knowing just how impossible that would be.

Nine
Premonition

With the changing winds came the dawn of a new season. Silver steam rose from Willow Lake's glassy surface as the first true chills of winter drifted into Garbbit Harbor. Diffused moonlight settled over the harbor in a gentle haze.

While Logan sat amid a hoarding crowd in the warmth of the Harbor Pub, reliving old war stories, Ash quietly padded down to the docks. Logan had insisted that he join him at the pub. But Ash had fallen for that ploy one too many times. He felt like a fool every time he reacted to the flattery of simply being asked to join, only to become the victim of his father's drunken venom. Ash wouldn't set himself up for another round of public humiliation—standing there in front of a mob of hysterical men and women as Logan belittled him to nothing. Not to mention the episodes when things became physically aggressive. Besides, Ash had far more critical things to do.

Moonlight crept into the small dark cellar as Ash lifted the wooden door above Scar's head. She smiled at the sight of him as she had come to expect these visits by now. Ash had come to the trawler with food and water every few hours for the past couple of days.

Climbing down inside the galley's cellar, Ash was careful to step lightly, as the trawler was suspended freely in the air. The slightest movement would cause the boat to sway in its cradle. Ash knew that Logan could see his boat from the windows of the pub. And if he caught Ash aboard it, let alone Scar, there would be a terrible price to pay.

"Paulo thought you were an angel when he first saw your wings," Ash said with an awkward smirk as he pointed at Scar's suit, draped over a small stool. "What kind of suit is that anyway?" he asked. Scar had apologized up and down for changing into an oversized, gray, cable-knit sweater and slim black trousers of Ash's, which she had found stored in a random closet aboard teh boat.

Yet she didn't respond. Instead she wore a consistent sad expression across her pale-white face. Her haggard, hollow eyes seemed to constantly be on the verge of tears. But Ash was amazed how beautiful she still looked, even through the layers of dirt she wore from head to toe. Perhaps intrigue and infatuation was getting the best of him. Either way, he was already finding it difficult to leave her side.

"Here," he continued, handing her a small loaf of bread and a carafe of water. "It's not much. But I see you haven't even eaten what we gave you earlier. Are you okay?"

Scar seemed perplexed by that question. She just stared back with emptiness. "No," she said softly with her shivering knees curled up to her chest.

"What harbor are you from?" he asked as he studied her face. He was struggling to figure out whether or not her scowl was sadness, or if it was simply his presence that annoyed her. He assumed the latter. And void of an answer to his question, Ash stood to leave. He knew there was no use in peppering her with questions she obviously had no answers for. But before he could speak, she perked up with a question—the one question he wished she wouldn't ask.

"Have you lived here long?" she asked. Her sudden change of expression surprised Ash, who froze in his step on the ladder.

"Oh, approximately, umm let's see ..." Ash stumbled over his words, deciding whether or not to disclose that he had never even actually left Garbbit Harbor. "Oh yeah, my whole life," he admitted reluctantly. "But I don't plan on staying," he quickly amended.

"Really?" Scar asked with a sense of true interest. "Where are you headed?"

This was the second worst question Scar could have asked. Now Ash would have to disclose how he really didn't know where he would ever go or why. It was like a balloon of energy deflated inside of him as he slouched down off of the ladder. He was as much of a victim to Garbbit Harbor as he was to Logan. Unable to answer the question without lying, he decided to change the subject.

"The Harvest Festival is in a few days," he blurted out like a little boy. "We should go." Aside from a lack of context to his comment, he had no idea how bad of an idea that actually was. He had no idea how important it was that she remain hidden in the shadows of the boat's galley.

"I don't know how safe it is for me to be seen," Scar said, drawing back into the shadow. Her tone had shifted back into a cold, paranoid state. Much like when Ash first found her.

"What do you mean?" Ash asked with a puzzled expression. He could hardly follow her mood shifts.

"They'll be coming for me," she explained as she peeked out of one of the frosted portholes.

Scar reached for the Enigma only to discover an even worse scenario. It was gone! *She must have left the mysterious medallion in the sub when she ditched it at the bottom of the lake.* But as terrible as this could become, there was something inside, stopping her from going back and searching for it. No good had come because of it so far anyway. Images of Sixty-One's last moments flashed through her mind.

"Who will be coming?" Ash asked quizzically.

Suddenly Scar realized what she was saying. She realized that she was simply speaking her mind and that her mind wasn't even registering clear thoughts. Looking over at Ash, she knew she didn't want to scare him off. After all, he was the only source of hope she had right then. "I don't know," she admitted, shaking her head. "Maybe it was just a dream. It's just so hard not knowing. Not remembering."

"You don't remember anything before coming to the harbor?" Ash asked, wishing he had the nerve to take her hand. Instead, he cracked his knuckles and bit his nails.

"Not really," Scar replied. It was like her entire body was reacting to the thing she had just done: lie.

Over the next few days, Ash found himself spending nearly every waking moment in the dark, musty galley of Logan's fishing trawler. But where he was mattered little, compared to who he was with.

Since being found, Scar had come alive with conversation. And secrets they began daring to share were no longer stammered by clumsy shyness. It was ironic that they found anything to talk about at all, with Ash so unwilling to give up details of his eventless past, and Scar forbidden to speak of whom she really was. But they shared a common ground, a sad and lonely state, in which they could confide in one another without the eyes of others making baseless judgments.

Liberated by a mutual sense of trust, they soon found themselves laughing together—just being young. Ash couldn't remember ever feeling such an overwhelming sense of acceptance by a peer, especially a beautiful girl. Unfortunately, he remained consumed by what he considered a premonition of dark fate. This was too good to be true—too good to last.

Ten
The Clock Tower

"So what would you be?" Ash asked Scar as they sat across from each other in the shadows of the galley's cellar. They had been playing a made-up game in which they each had to choose something or someone they wanted to be reincarnated as. It was one of the many games they had made up over the week she had been hiding in Logan's trawler.

Scar pondered for a while, staring at the sunset through the small galley window. "A tree," she then answered softly.

"A tree?" he asked. Her answer caught Ash off guard. "Why a tree?"

"Because they live so long," she answered quietly, almost in a transfixed state. "They're survivors. They see so much take place around them—and all from the exact same perspective. And as massive and complex as they become, they never lose the ability to bend in the wind."

Ash had never thought of a simple tree so intricately before. It was as if Scar had revealed a hidden secret about trees he never would have discovered on his own. In spite of their awkward situation, hiding in his father's boat, Ash had never been so happy or validated in all of his life.

"How about you?" Scar asked. "It's your turn."

Ash thought for a moment, tying and untying knots on a small section of rope—a nonsensical routine he often engaged in when he was nervous. But he already knew his answer. "A dragon," he said quietly, hoping Scar wouldn't laugh at his boyish reply.

"Really?" Scar asked, surprised. "Why an imaginary monster?"

"Imaginary? Ash asked, obviously put out. "Dragons are misunderstood. People think they were nothing more than that: *monsters*—if they believe in them at all." Ironically, he wasn't thoroughly convinced in their existence either. "But dragons were intelligent. They were magic," he continued. Scar smirked, as though Ash was joking. "You don't believe in dragons, do you?" he asked earnestly.

"I don't know," Scar mumbled. "Sure, I guess. But it's not like I've ever seen one."

"I've never really seen the sky, but I know it's there," Ash challenged, peering up through one of the porthole windows. A subtle drizzle was gently falling from the clouds as he pondered the many dreams he had of flying above the clouds.

"Why do you like dragons so much?" Scar asked after a long silence. It was a fair question. But Ash had no reply. All he could do was ask himself the very same. *Why?* Perhaps it was the countless legends Wick had spun throughout Ash's childhood. Or maybe simply the awesome power dragons wielded? Suddenly Ash saw something that made him freeze.

His shadow, cast by the hanging lantern, was morphing into an entirely different shape. As the shadow grew larger on the wall, the head began to elongate and the shape of giant wings blossomed on either side of him. It was the shadow of a dragon!

Quickly Ash grabbed Scar's arm and turned her back away from the wall.

"Hey, want to get out of here?" he asked with obvious nervous tension quivering his voice. The shadow was normal again. Was his curse now acting out on its own? *No!* It couldn't have been anything more than his overblown imagination.

Ash sighed in relief, grateful Scar hadn't witnessed the odd display. The last thing he needed was for her to discover his curse. Certainly, that would be the end of their newfound friendship, if she even considered him a friend in the first place.

"Outside?" Scar asked with worried eyes.

"Yeah," Ash said. "I know the perfect place." He knew that it would be up to him to choose a destination and route that wouldn't compromise Scar's safety, or his own, now, for that matter: Willow Lake Clock Tower.

Scar agreed as she placed her hand on his—a touch that sent a vibe through Ash's entire body. She knew better. But just sitting there in the bowels of that dingy old boat wasn't doing her any good either. Besides, there was something about Ash, something that made her feel alive.

Behind his geeky mannerisms was a bit of a rebel, and she liked it. Not that he was a bad person. But something about his ability to put his head down and ignore the world around him gave her hope that she might be able to do the same and press on with a new life. And perhaps that life might include Ash.

The evening sky had just grown dark as they sauntered through the shadows of the wharf. In spite of Scar's boldness, Ash was still cautious not to expose her in public for fear that Logan might be around the next corner. So he remained in front of her as they made their way into the heart of the harbor. But suddenly he heard his name.

"Ash!" the voice yelled. "Ash! Up here!" It was Paulo calling from his mother's apartment balcony, five stories above. He sat at the railing's edge, feet kicking in the air and holding a small, metal gadget. "I think I figured out our problem with the rocket! A faulty compressor. See?" he said holding a small metal canister with a hole in it. Hiding Scar behind him, Ash acknowledged with a nod, though he had no idea what the compressor actually did. And right now it was the last thing he wanted to think about. He didn't need Scar knowing about his silly pet-projects, especially with someone who was so much younger than himself. He damned the bad luck he was having trying to impress her.

"Who's with you?" Paulo asked. Ash hardly slowed his stride, wishing he had been smart enough to avoid the street Paulo lived on.

"Nobody, Paulo," Ash answered abruptly. He quickly realized just how rude that sounded in respect to Scar. "Just a friend," he recovered.

"Is it that girl? The angel?" Paulo yelled as Ash and Scar continued into the shadows. Ash rolled his eyes and smiled uncomfortably at Scar. "Is she your girlfriend now? Is that why you haven't come over? I'll see you tomorrow night, right Ash?" Paulo persisted with a note of childish despair in his tone.

"We'll see," Ash trailed off regretfully. Although he had promised Paulo that he'd help him re-launch the rocket, he didn't want to broadcast to Scar the truth of their childish dreams of using it to escape Garbbit Harbor.

On the outskirts of the harbor, Ash took Scar to the clock tower, a common place for teens to hang out at night.

That night, being as cold as it was, Ash and Scar would find they had the tower all to themselves. Though Ash had stumbled through trying to have a girlfriend once, he was as awkward and wide-eyed as a small child when it came to girls. So needless to say, he had no alternant intentions when it came to bringing Scar up to the lookout at the top of the tower.

As they stood at the edge of the lookout railing, gazing out over the sprawl of the harbor skirting the bay below, the usual hum of foot traffic, street vendors, and musicians drifted up into the night air. The new ice of Willow Lake glistened like a scarred mirror. Smoke poured out of a sea of chimneys throughout the harbor, changing the smell of the air for the season.

"It's just a dirty old harbor," Ash said, fishing for a reaction from Scar.

"It's beautiful," Scar replied with a passionate whisper.

"You think?" Ash asked. It wasn't the response he anticipated. He wondered if she was talking about something else. But he could tell by her eyes that she wasn't. Looking down, Ash tried to see what she was looking at. And in a strange way he did.

Simply by blocking out the sound, Ash saw a very different Garbbit Harbor than the one he was used to seeing. In fact, for the first time he saw that the very place he lived in was actually quite interesting and, yes, *beautiful* in many ways. But it didn't erase how he still felt. "Well," he said a little more deflated, "it's pretty dull around here though. Nothing like the stories I hear about other lands."

"What stories?" Scar asked as Ash gazed up at the ghosts of moons passing through the layers of overcast. Indeed, Garbbit Harbor was a sheltered world unto itself—spellbound by a relentless ceiling of clouds.

"Those stories I hear from the traders," Ash answered, the wonderment of a young boy coming through in his voice. "Sometimes I go down to the cafés and saloons just to eavesdrop on the stories they tell when they're passing through. They're fascinating. They talk of great adventures in other lands, battles with pirates, and encounters with giant sea monsters. Did you know that goliath-eels can out-swim most motorized boats?" By the look Scar wore on her face, Ash assumed that she was completely captivated by what he was saying, so he kept going with it.

"Can you even imagine what it would be like to see what's really out there in the rest of the world?" As he spoke, he leaned far over the edge of the balcony's railing, spread his arms and closed his eyes. The chilly wind whipped his face. It felt like he was flying through the air among the clouds, just like his dreams. The fearless freedom of flying …

Scar gazed up at the sky. Her mind began to race with images of places that seemed so real that she swore she could even smell them. But as soon as she saw them, they were gone—gone, like the memories themselves.

"What is it like," Ash asked, calming his delivery, "not remembering?"

Scar paused for a moment. She was troubled. "Empty. It feels empty. Lonely."

"Do you remember anything from the past, from before I found you?" Ash asked, trying to imagine where she might have actually come from.

"Not really," Scar responded. Flashes of cryptic engravings on the medallion's surface began racing through her mind again. She knew that the mysterious medallion was of much importance. *But what significance?* "Some images have feelings attached to them, I think. But nothing makes sense."

"What kind of feelings?" Ash asked, his eyes luring Scar in like a wonderful scent.

Conflict rent Scar like a blade. She knew she had failed her master. But Ash had given her a glimpse of what life could be like if she could escape the prison of her master's rule. With the Enigma missing, perhaps she could slip out of her master's conscience. Though she knew better, she wondered if by distancing herself from the medallion she might simply draw attention away from herself. After all, she didn't even understand what this medallion was.

After a long pause, Scar replied to Ash's question with a shiver in her tone. "Fear."

Looking at Scar, Ash couldn't help but try to figure out where she had really come from. *Was she from the mighty kingdoms? Or perhaps a castaway who had traveled up river from the Great Sea?* The longer he went on not knowing, the more he wanted to simply ignore the details and move on. Though he couldn't help but wonder about his own past as well.

His was also marred by a strange elusiveness. The only distinctions he could make out where the feelings left behind. Those feelings were primarily fear—a deep, dark undercurrent that tormented Ash every day of his life. Somewhere, lost in the recesses of his memory, the dark shadowy figure mysteriously lurked about. Real or not, the image was burned into Ash's mind like an ugly scar. Suddenly it began to rain again.

"Are you cold?" Ash asked Scar, approaching her softly. But her expression was one of confusion—like she didn't know the answer to such a simple question. It was like she was slipping back into the same catatonic state she was in when he first found her. She looked afraid. Suddenly a man's voice echoed up through the tower, startling both of them.

"Hey kids, get down from there!" the man ordered. Ash recognized the voice. It was Ol' Man Morton, the clock tower attendant. He was an ornery old man who had little patience for youth, especially the defiant teens who had made a sport out of breaking into the tower. "This is private property and you're trespassing!"

Scar interpreted the threat as an obvious signal that she had been discovered. *She had to run!*

"Scar?" Ash asked as her figure disappeared into the swallowing darkness of the tower's spiral staircase. "Scar! Where are you going?" Ash's voice echoed down the shaft. But there was no response. She was gone.

It was a familiar emotion Ash had confronted more than once in his life—the feeling of abandonment. Though he remembered little of his mother, he knew that she had deserted him when he was yet a small child. And those feelings had never left. In fact, Ash hated her for it. He hated his mother's cowardliness, her selfishness. *How could someone just up and abandon their own son? How could anyone just run out without an explanation?* Sadness morphed into bitterness as Ash saw Scar's silhouette exit the ground level of the tower and race into the night.

Eleven
Trust

Tears of morning dew ran down her white marble cheeks as King Merrick Basileus knelt at her feet, his head in his hands. The carved statue marking Viana Basileus's grave was so true to her likeness, so hauntingly real, that he could hardly even look at it. Viana had chosen this small, unlikely plot of land on the mountain's snowy summit as the place she wanted to be buried. But she never imagined coming to a final rest here at the age of only thirty-five.

From here the view was spectacular, looking over the majestic Grande Mountain range and pristine expanse of Crown City, the magnificent floating capitol city of the domain of which she and King Basileus ruled, Kingland. At the land's end, where the mountains meet the great Colossiae Ocean, Crown City glistened in the sky like a heavenly kingdom, forged by the hands of angels. It was ironic, since this was the very place she had exchanged vows with King Basileus, all those years ago. Returning here was no easier than the last time he had visited her grave, on the ninth anniversary of her death.

It was ten years ago to the day that Viana's life had been stolen by the hands of dastardly pirates. On a return flight back to Crown City, pirates attacked her private escort, taking Viana's life in the wake of their terror. They were avenging their radical ideals, fueled by the fall of their empire.

The pirate's execution was terrifyingly precise and fatal. It was a moment in time that relived itself in King Basileus's mind every waking day—the horror, the humiliation, and the paralysis of being caught off guard. And in the years since, it ultimately drove Basileus to take desperate and sometimes highly clandestine measures to hunt down the pirates who had murdered his wife. But it was also becoming his undoing. Kingland was slowly slipping away from the graceful kingdom it once was.

Parting his long, wiry hair away from his face, King Basileus wiped a tear from his own cheek. He could feel the lines in his face had already deepened since he had last visited her grave, not so long ago. Indeed, his age was now catching up with him. Even his hair had begun prematurely graying since that fateful night.

"Viana," Basileus whispered feebly as he reached out and touched her statue. "I am so sorry. I have failed you, failed my people. I thought that the only way to justify your legacy was through vengeance. But I have learned since that this only breeds more war, more bloodshed. I have trusted the wrong people and put my credence in the wrong ideals. And it has made me weaker in every way. I kneel before you now and give you my word. I will make it right. I will end this dark and dangerous era Kingland has fallen into. But I will do it with dignity and integrity. I only hope it is not too late."

Suddenly a cold shadow cast itself over King Basileus. Count LePrey had arrived.

Basileus rose, straightened the golden shoulder tassels of his blood-red uniform and began walking without even acknowledging his visitor. Frustration tensed his muscles as he caught a glimpse of LePrey out of the corner of his eye. He would have chosen a less sacred spot to meet, but considering the secrecy of this meeting, Basileus had few options.

"I know what it's like to lose someone close," LePrey said, glancing over at Viana's grave as they walked through the melting mountain snow. "It's like losing a part of yourself."

"I trusted you," Basileus said sharply, ignoring LePrey's shoal condolences. "I trusted you and you betrayed me."

"Never," LePrey responded swiftly.

"Don't play games," Basileus retorted, chopping the air with a frustrated hand gesture. "I know about Lord Yen." Color drained from LePrey's face. He obviously couldn't understand how Basileus knew this. "You told me the Isla Ruba mission was merely to intercept another virus being trafficked through the black market. But according to a certain scribe who had met with Yen only moments before the bombing, Yen had come into contact with some sort of mystical ancient relic. There was absolutely no mention of a rogue virus."

Engineered viruses were often trafficked through the pirate underworld on a regular basis by the Pirate Rogue. In an effort to build a credible insurgence against Kingland's unwelcome occupation of their desert territories, the Rogue was crudely developing lethal viruses in mass. They were used as biological attacks against Allied Kingdom occupation troops.

"What was your hidden agenda on Isla Ruba?" Basileus demanded, stopping with tightly folded arms, his red cape fluttering in the cool mountain breeze.

LePrey regained his composure and begun to spin a cunning response to Basileus's questions. "First of all, I wouldn't trust the word of an old washed-up scribe. I could never lie about something as dangerous as a rogue virus and risk pervasive panic." His eyes dodged contact. "Secondly, I'm afraid, until you agree to institute the drone-vaccine-implants I've developed for your people's protection, the only way to successfully thwart these threats is by intercepting the actual virus itself." His lies sounded so true and convincing, he didn't skip a beat. "Trust me when I say that if the Pirate Rogue were to strike us with one of their viruses right now, we would be completely vulnerable. There would be no way to inoculate that many people in ample time. But if everyone already possessed an implant, we could simply download inoculations to the people instantly."

LePrey's pitch about the implants was a compelling one, once again. Tiny capsules implanted into the palms of people's hands could carry vital, life-saving medical attributes. And with the ability to download specific inoculations, entire societies would be able to receive updated medical necessities at a moment's notice. Indeed, this invention of LePrey's had nearly won the King's endorsement. But Basileus just couldn't get himself to sign on. He knew that the Count couldn't be trusted with that much power. Besides, Basileus was already living with the grave regret for his secret deal with LePrey.

Part of a larger contract deal Basileus had made with LePrey was that if anything were to happen to the King at the hands of the Pirate Rogue, an official countermeasure would be activated: LePrey's contract drone-armada would immediately be deployed in full volume. This would usher in a state of emergency rule until absolute safety was restored. For LePrey, a scenario like this was more powerful than being crowned the next king.

"So now we're in the worst possible situation," Basileus said shaking his head in disdain. "The mission failed, so we intercepted no virus. If there even was one to start with. One of our spies is missing and the other dead after a devastating explosion—an explosion Isla Ruba local's claim we are responsible for. This has gotten way out of hand," Basileus said, throwing his arms open in obvious frustration. "And in case you haven't heard, pirates working for Lord Yen avow that they have solid evidence of this illegal mission—probably the remains of our destroyed drone-schooner. They're threatening to turn this evidence over to the Allied Commission and blow the whistle on this entire espionage program you pressured me into endorsing. Blackmail! This would be the end of me. Do you understand that?" Basileus felt like a child, pleading with a sibling. He knew he was vulnerable.

"And what are Yen's demands?" LePrey asked solicitously.

It was apparent how difficult it was for Basileus to even utter the words. "The release of General Sayto Bontey."

"Bontey," LePrey whispered with aroused interest. It was quite alarming that Yen would be interested in the release of General Bontey. No doubt, Yen was planning to hire Bontey to apprehend Scar for himself. Though Yen had a grand force of henchmen guarding his compound in the jungles of Copi Bienna, they were merely strong-armed thugs—no match for the unbeatable instincts Bontey possessed. This would be vital in tracking the drone-girl. If Yen were to hire Bontey, it would only be a matter of time before he had his hands on Scar and the Enigma back in his possession.

"How do you plan to deal with this?" LePrey asked Basileus, fully aware of what his answer would be.

"I do not negotiate with pirates," Basileus made clear. "But I'm also not going to engage in one of your open fire military solutions either."

After a long, uncomfortable silence, LePrey finally spoke up. "I say we give Lord Yen what he wants." Basileus stopped walking, caught off guard by whatever it was LePrey was about to serve up. "I say we release the General," LePrey said like an epiphany. Indeed it was. He was gravely desperate to find a way to get his hands on Bontey before Yen could.

"Are you crazy?" Basileus shot back. "You can't be serious."

"Why not?" LePrey asked plainly. "Lord Yen has no reason not to turn our data over to the rest of the Allied Commission—anything to weaken the throne of Kingland. And if aggressive force is not something you're willing to consider, then I'm afraid you leave yourself with little other choice." Basileus considered his options with a concerned expression. "You've put yourself in a rather difficult situation here your majesty," LePrey concluded.

"*You* put me in this situation!" Basileus snapped back with a finger in LePrey's face. "Let's be clear."

"Then allow me to take care of it," LePrey offered advantageously. "Perhaps we merely relocate Bontey to a secret facility. And in the meantime, I'll dispatch a battalion of drones to find our missing spy." It wasn't easy for LePrey to conceal his obsessive passion on this topic—

the fact that finding the girl meant more to him than anything else in the world. "As for the pirates who have hijacked our drone-schooner, I have plenty of experience dealing with their type. I can propose a deal that would minimize losses on both sides."

Basileus cut in before LePrey could finish outlining his plot. "No thanks," he said sourly. "You've betrayed me one too many times."

"You're hardly one to speak of betrayal," LePrey whispered coldly.

Basileus froze. The words shivered through him with sharp unease. He knew that LePrey was hiding the truth behind his motives with the Isla Ruba operation. But if LePrey knew of the incredible secret Basileus was keeping from him, nothing would ever be the same again. "What is that supposed to mean?" Basileus asked, pretending that he didn't know what LePrey was getting at.

"I think you know," LePrey said, maintaining his composure in a haunting manner.

Basileus made a quick decision to change the subject. "This situation has raised too many questions about you and your drone-armada to allow any further involvement at this time. The fact that you think you can devise some new course of action for this military and not inform me or the Allied Commission is troubling. You're a loose cannon, Count. That's why I'm freezing all contracts with you until this crisis is resolved and I have a real explanation about what actually went down on Isla Ruba."

"You can't do that," LePrey shot back, raising his hand in panicked protest.

Basileus leaned into LePrey's face and rumbled, "I just did." He then spun around and marched away, his red cape snapping rhythmically behind him.

Alone, on the summit's peak, LePrey knew that although his prevarication had not been fully bought, he still had not given up his secret. "I'm already a step ahead of you," he whispered to himself.

Twelve
The Secret

As if it wasn't enough that she was being forced to contract the assassination of her own lover, Countess Arona Ivy had found herself squabbling over price. Kuta Jedo, the assassin, claimed that she needed more money to ensure a perfectly smooth operation. And it worked. To Arona the money mattered not. All that mattered now was finding a way to spare what little hope she could.

Arona exited the café the moment the deal was secured. She didn't want Jedo to see her tears. As her sky-coach pulled away from the small café, perched on the snowy cliff, the ashen skies were growing dark. Arona could only make out the silhouette of the giant mountain-hawk, whose massive wingspan captured the faint, silver light of the moons as it pulled her coach through the frigid air. Its huge brown feathers were coated in a white frost from the frigid air. Even the coach itself was beginning to accumulate frost inside its inner chamber. But Arona felt very little, as her mind seemed to be drifting off over another horizon. She picked up a small metal box, punched with holes about its surface. A faint white light glowed from within. She then began to speak to whatever was inside:

"My love, if you are hearing this, then our worst fear has been realized. And I, against the fabric of my own being have crossed the point of no return. But I did what I had to, as it was the only way to intervene and save your life. If you do not already, you will soon understand. We must now do the inevitable. I cannot express the heartbreak this has brought me—the torment it has caused me. But these are dark times. And I know you sense as I do, the weight of the shadow that looms over us.

"The Count has perfected his game and is playing his cards close to his chest. But beyond the web of manipulation and lies he has entangled you in, there are secrets so dark and so bizarre that I needed you to hear it from me. After all, there are few who know as much as I do on this matter. And those who do will not speak of it.

"Though the Drone Project is replete with skepticism from the Allied Commission, if you were to know the truth behind it, not only would you put behind you the notion to endorse it, you would put an end to the Count's entire operation. That is, if you are not considering this already. He claims that the Drone Project is merely an army of robots, designed to take the place of human bloodshed in battle. But the truth is that this project is an experimentation that defies science and jeopardizes moral boundaries.

"The Count has developed a substance known as synth, made up of microscopic drones called sythians. This is his secret behind the undying loyalty of his impressive spy agents and the mighty generals who lead his armada. Synth is far more than an enhancement drug. It is poison, like a virus that completely consumes its hosts, turning them into nothing more than android zombies—slaves to his ideals. The drone-implants, which he is so insistent on dispersing across the globe, are the very vehicles he uses to administer this synth. As insane as it sounds, his plan is to poison the population of the world with this stuff, transforming them into what he calls a *superhuman race of immortals*. And this is just the beginning.

"His entire drone-network is controlled by a central beacon called Machine, residing in his remote lighthouse. And this machine seems to be growing in intelligence and independent consciousness. Since the Count has now achieved the power to control the masses through a single source, he plans to unite the entire world into the same collective by means of these drone-implants. It's all part of his ideological vision of social purging and political unity. He's using the Pirate Rogue bio-attacks to force the mandatory distribution of these implanted inoculations for all citizens of Kingland and from there, across the globe. But I beg of you not to let this happen. Though the drone-implants may have some technological merit, the Count plans to use it as a means for controlling the masses. Once you've been implanted, you are owned by the Count and controlled by his machine, slowly transforming you from human to drone. But there's something even larger than this fueling the Count's motives—something he would kill for.

"The legend of the Chrysalis has completely consumed the Count for as long as I've known him. For reasons unknown, he considers it to be his greatest threat. He will stop at nothing to keep it dormant. In fact, the creation of his superhuman race is just one way he plans to suppress it—sheltering the world from whatever secrets it holds. I feel that whatever this secret is, it just might be our only hope against his madness. I don't even know if I believe in the legend, but perhaps unearthing it could be our greatest defense against the Count and his armada.

"Regardless of what transpires between us, I urge you to seek out the mystery of the Chrysalis, even if you don't believe. The Count is on the brink of ushering in a dark new era for the world. He must be stopped. Which is why I must do what I know you won't understand.

"In order to salvage what we can, I have decided to proceed with a plan that most would see as unethical; including yourself. I only hope you will find a way to forgive me."

Opening a small door on the face of the box, Arona whispered inside. "You know what to do."

Suddenly a small pixie, not much larger than Arona's hand, stepped out from the box. The tiny fairy was dainty and albino-white, her black-pearl eyes and pursed mouth merely specks on her large, bald head. An aura of mysterious sparkle glistened above her faintly glowing skin and moth-like wings. Arona handed the pixie a small vile, nearly half the pixie's size. And with a nod of agreement to deliver this message, she simply flew away, out the coach window and off into the evening sky.

Thirteen
The Implants

In the darkness of the galley, Scar sat alone shivering. But it wasn't the cold that made her tremble. It was the conflict within her. She knew that there was no way to escape the wrath of her master if she didn't find the medallion and salvage her failed mission. But what Sixty-One had revealed to her, and the simple sense of hope that Ash gave her made her terrified of ever returning to her life of numbed slavery.

Ash was a friend. At least, that's what he had become. His naive outlook on life brought Scar back to a place in time she couldn't fully remember—a childhood she couldn't see. She was dying to live and Ash made her feel alive. But the dark reality was that she was anything but.

She picked up a small switchblade knife that was sitting on a wooden ledge. Ejecting the small rusty blade, she pressed it to her palm and began to pierce the skin. As the blade dug deep, a tiny, thin object emerged through the oozing, black blood, just as had happened with Sixty-One. A drone-implant fell to the floor. She then dug the second one out of her other hand.

Scar knew little of the implants' real functions. All she knew was that they were something that had been administered to her against her will. She didn't know that besides being a medical and identification instrument, it was also the source for regenerating her synth. All she wanted to do was sever her link to her master. But what she didn't know was that without the drone-implants her synth would eventually die, as would she. Not that this brutal fact would have made any difference. Quickly, she smashed the drone-implants with the butt of the knife and swept their dusty remains into the shadows.

Though she had severed communications with Machine, Scar knew that it would eventually find her. Sooner or later she would have to embrace who she was. Hiding and running could not be sustained. But the secret Sixty-One had divulged just prior to taking his own life continued to replay itself in her mind like a desperate plea for justice.

She wiped the black blood from the scars on her hands and wondered: *Unlike Sixty-One's self-induced dead-end, perhaps I could outrun my past.* All she would have to do is convince Ash to run away with her. Suddenly images began to appear in her mind's eye—images that seemed almost as real as memories. But they couldn't have been. They were of a little red-haired girl. A happy girl. She looked familiar. But it couldn't have been her. Scar had no recollection of ever being so young or so happy.

Fourteen
Betrayal

Like a prodigious wreath of sparkling shards outstretched at varied lengths, Crown City floated among the clouds above the snow-covered Grande Mountains. The capital city of Kingland sprawled across a breathtaking expanse and glistened in the evening sky like a field of crystals. Magnificent chrome spires rose up from each shard. And at the center ring, where each shard met, stood Ares, warrior god. The immense statue was erected in commemoration of Kingland's monumental victory of the Great War. As if wading in waist-deep, the golden statue stood like a towering island in the middle of a grand pool the size of a small lake. With one hand drawing a massive sword, the other pointed west. It was a sight to behold—like none other the world knew. Streams of wind-gliders, zeppelins, and biplanes filled the evening sky, making their way to the event of the year: the Annual Royal Masquerade Gala.

The ballroom was located on the top floor of the Royal Palace, just above the throne room, situated within the hollows of Ares. In fact, the giant windows lining the circular room were literally the detail of Ares's huge crown. From a distance, the windows looked merely like glowing golden gems, inset into the crown. It was a landmark known worldwide, yet few ever actually witnessed it.

The air was fragrant with the blended scent of rich perfumes and the melodic ambiance of stringed instruments. Exotic foods, expensive wines, and lavish decor set the stage for the most glamorous event Crown City would see all year. The Ball marked the close of the Great War, twenty years ago. This historic landmark, which brought about the end of the war, not only dissolved a reign of tyranny, but also skyrocketed Kingland to a superpower status unmatched by any other kingdom of the world. But the price to pay for such an overturn was proving to be far higher and far bloodier than anyone had ever imagined it would be twenty years earlier.

As masked dignitaries from numerous kingdoms mingled throughout the crystalline expanse of the ballroom, King Basileus remained close to the exits, his red royal garments camouflaged by his circle of surrounding aides. He was thankful for the golden mask he held close to his face. Though the masquerade made it difficult to tell exactly who might be approaching, it did make it somewhat convenient when trying to remain anonymous among the crowd. But it was hardly realistic for the King of Kingland to attempt hiding.

The Gala wasn't what it used to be. As Kingland's occupation of enemy territories continued to spiral into a downward trend of civil uprising and deadly guerilla warfare, more and more kingdoms were losing their faith in Kingland and opting not to take part in this annual ritual. And those who did attend were either there to suck up to the most powerful leader in the world, or to pepper him with questions regarding his stand on the failing occupation. In short, this event had become more of a nuisance than anything for Basileus. And just when he thought it couldn't get any worse, someone approached.

"Your majesty," a familiar voice said. It was one of his young, ambitious handmaidens, working the event. "Your majesty, I have someone who would like to speak with you." Stepping out from behind her was the short, round, bald-headed figure of Ambassador Privo, Kingland's Ambassador to the territories of the Zahartan Desert. Basileus reeled back, hiding his face behind his gold mask.

Ambassador Privo had become popular among the people of Kingland after being the first to dare to expose the crude realities behind Kingland's occupation in the desert territories. Even though it wasn't good news, the people highly respected an honest assessment of the situation by someone who had actually witnessed it. However, this created an instant rift between the Ambassador and King Basileus.

Staring through the group of people surrounding the King, Ambassador Privo achieved eye contact with Basileus as the handmaiden ushered him forward. It was too late now. Basileus was cornered. "Ambassador," he managed to say in an almost convincingly enthused voice. "What a pleasant surprise."

"The pleasure's mine," Privo lied before removing his mask. And then he simply budged his way through the crowd, right to Basileus's side. "I need to speak with you," he whispered to Basileus as he grabbed his arm. "In private."

Basileus knew he had no choice but to grant Privo his wish. He waved his aides away and stepped behind a giant pillar with Privo. "What is it?" he asked.

"My Lord," Privo began, appearing almost out of breath, "I have sought an audience with you for some time now. You are a very difficult man to reach. Anyway, I hate to use this event for a topic such as this, but given the subject matter, it might be appropriate," he said looking around at all of the decor honoring Kingland's spectacular triumph in the Great War. Basileus knew exactly what Privo was about to say. "To admit that our occupation in the Zahartan Desert territories is failing is an embarrassing understatement."

"There are platforms in place for such conversations," Basileus reminded Privo.

"Yes, well I'm afraid that by the time the Allied Commission gets around to this topic thousands more will have died," Privo blurted out, unable to mask his provocation. "The bloodshed is beginning to rival the very brutality we claim to have extinguished at the close of the Great War."

"Look," Basileus interrupted, pulling Privo by the shoulder into the shadows, "I know, it's bad. Everyone knows it. Pirate blockades are manipulating trade routes and rogue bio attacks on our soldiers are on the rise. But even though I've rescinded our contracts with Count LePrey's drone-security-armada, I can at any time access this resource as a viable proxy to our physically drained soldiers. Don't underestimate my global perspective, Ambassador."

Privo had been shaking his head since the moment Basileus opened his mouth. "No offense, my Lord, but I'm not talking about the welfare of our troops. With all due respect to them, I'm talking about the state of the desert tribes. I'm talking about the innocent families caught in the middle of this bloody civil conflict. I think it's time we stopped and asked ourselves if we're truly serving the people's best interest by our occupation in the desert."

"Ambassador," Basileus cut in with agitation in his tone, "you have no idea what's at stake here. There's more to this than just policing a civil war. This is about the economy of the world. Zahartan territories are pivotal. These rogue tribes are sitting on top of valuable resources they've chosen to hold as ransom as an attempt to help rebuild their militant empire. If we let the Zahartan tribes fall to the Pirate Rogue, we will end up with yet another ruthless empire, worse than our original enemies."

Privo knew that Basileus was right. The tribes of the Zahartan Desert were the rightful possessors of black crystal, a precious element found only in the depths of the sands of their own deserts. A highly sought-after resource in the world economy, the crystal was also becoming a scarce commodity. Needless to say, the kingdom that controlled the crystal wielded the political power of the world.

"I assume that freezing contracts with LePrey doesn't necessarily mean abandoning your espionage program?" Privo asked. It was his way of letting the King know that he was fully aware of the King's illegal secret deal with Count LePrey.

"Like it or not, the way I deal with our enemies is perhaps the only thing keeping the world from exploding into a full-out civil war and tearing itself apart," Basileus said with confliction and regret in his eyes. He knew he was already eating the promise he had uttered upon his wife's grave. But his rage was far more powerful. "Passiveness accomplishes nothing. But fear demands respect," he preached, growing flushed with fury. "Someone needs to be the dominant voice of reason in the world. That job isn't usually a popular one. But it is necessary for the sake of stabilization."

Privo had plenty to say to that. But, like so often, his words would go unheard. Just as he engaged in what was sure to be a long-winded speech about how military was not the answer, someone entered the ballroom, which completely stole Basileus's attention.

Her brown hair was pulled back and would have revealed her beautiful face had it not been shielded by a large, crimson, feathery mask. But Basileus knew that it was Arona the moment she crossed the threshold, entering the room. He was instantly captivated. Arona wore a long, slim red gown that trailed behind her like a winding, silky river. Her arm was uncomfortably looped through her husband's, Count LePrey. He entered the room with confidence in his stride and an air that seemed to magically control the drifting attire in which he was draped. Only his elongated goatee protruded from beneath the white porcelain mask he hid behind. But his eyes were unmistakable as they caught Basileus's attention from across the room. With a nod, LePrey pulled Arona closer to his side and turned his attention to another group of delegates.

As Privo's words drifted into a distant undecipherable echo, Basileus slipped away from the crowd, dropping his golden mask to the floor. It wasn't until he found himself alone, outside on the balcony that encircled the ballroom, that he realized just how dangerous this affair had become. Gazing out at the appearing moons and stars, Basileus reminisced about how it all began ...

Arguably, it was innocent. Arona was a victim, a prisoner to her own husband. And Merrick Basileus just happened to be in the right place at the right time. Aside from their obvious physical attraction to one another, Basileus and Arona shared a mutual idealism about the world—one that went against the grain of everything LePrey obsessed over. But when they crossed the line and allowed their attraction to turn physical, Basileus knew that his throne would soon be in jeopardy. Not only had moral judgment been dissolved, now the very reputation of Kingland's leader was hanging in the balance.

The mountainous air was cool as Basileus looked out over his floating city. While the soft evening breeze curled around Basileus, he began to shiver. He was nervous and anxious, trembling with guilt. He still mourned his wife's death—still fresh in his mind's eye. But Arona was irresistible. Perhaps she was merely a means to softening the brutal memory of his loss. Or perhaps he truly *was* moving on. Either way, this feeling of guilt was a pending presence, constantly clawing at his conscience. He tried to ignore and deal with it at another time. After all, he had been at this crossroads before.

Rational thinking and what had brought him to this balcony were two forces that couldn't coexist. This was impulse. As much as he had tried to justify it to himself, when all was said and done, he was simply flesh and blood, driven by his own lust. And this was simply infidelity, even if her husband was his greatest enemy. Suddenly he could smell her perfume.

Arona held two goblets of wine in her hands and a soothing smile on her perfectly smooth face as she stepped onto the balcony. The sheer sight of her was tantalizing. Basileus felt his heart pounding so hard he wondered if it was possibly visible as he accepted the goblet. They had briefly discussed meeting here and slipping away, alone for a while during the Ball. But Basileus half-expected it not to happen. He stepped down to the grass of the giant garden plate and took Arona's hand. Together they drifted away from the golden mass of Ares and into the night.

Originally conceived as massive, floating crop fields with the ability to migrate with weather patterns, avoiding drought and flood, garden-plates were later adopted architecturally as the perfect way to integrate green spaces into the floating urban expanses of Crown City. They ranged from simple, small flower gardens to vast acres-wide fields that were sometimes used for sporting events. But tonight, this floating garden would become a romantic escape for their secret rendezvous.

"When can this be real?" the Countess said stepping closer, her bosom gracing his chest. The grief was heavy in her tone.

Basileus looked away, as if trying to see the future. Ares's giant golden arm stretched forth in front of him, proudly pointing west to the darkened ocean, swallowing the last slice of the setting sun. Garden plates drifted like clouds on the outskirts of the city, some of them docking transport-blimps, some of them hosting small party gatherings.

Gazing over the edge of the garden plate, through the passing clouds, to the valley far below, the scattered mining communities that skirted the base of the mountain range looked so small, so insignificant. These communities, though part of Kingland, had all but been forgotten. It was astounding how much of an oversight the rural communities of Kingland had become as the mighty superpower kingdom continued to inflate in size and power. Basileus became overwhelmed by the sad reality that his own lack of focus had wrought. And now he was the only one who could fix it.

"These are delicate times," Basileus finally said. His words seemed cold and unpromising. But Arona knew exactly what he meant as she leaned in and kissed his cheek.

"There is still reason to celebrate," Arona said raising her goblet. Her positive persistence seemed out of character. In fact it was.

"Celebrate what?" Basileus asked with a muddled expression.

"The moment—the here and now. The fact that we are together," Arona said pressing even closer. "Hold me." She then kissed his neck. "Soon everything will be set right and we won't have to hide."

Basileus wanted so badly to believe her. But this is where rationality prevailed. He knew that this affair was doomed from the start. It had no true basis other than the rush of the dare. Besides, Arona was the wife of the very man he had just accused of betraying him. "What do you mean?" he asked, hoping for an answer he hadn't thought of yet.

Arona touched her goblet to Basileus's. "A toast to freedom," she said looking beyond him, out across the city lights.

Just as Basileus took a reluctant sip, a strange hissing sound pierced the air, followed by a sharp sting in his neck. Out of the corner of his eye he could see a small object protruding out of his skin. It looked like a miniature arrow. Suddenly the stars began to spin and blur into streaks. He knew instantly that this was a poisoned dart. Arona's face faded into a kaleidoscope of meaningless shapes. How had this happened? *Who*—? But before another thought was able to even formulate in his mind, he fell to the grass. Arona's crimson gown looked like nothing more than a bloodstain on the sky above him. Then it all went black.

With tears in her eyes, Arona knelt at Basileus's side. She touched his face and then discreetly opened up the pouch she wore. Searching the cityscape behind her, she could barely make out the silhouetted figure of Kuta Jedo—the leather-wrapped, tattoo-covered assassin. Jedo leaped from the rooftops, fleeing the perch from where she had fired the poisoned dart. Little did she know, this would be her last kill.

High above, Count LePrey wore a satisfied smile as he observed from the ballroom's balcony, skirting Ares's crown. Machine was right. Indeed his wife had no choice but to comply with his scheme. Indeed, his scheme was beginning to take form as Basileus slipped away from consciousness.

The lethal poison was meant to work fast. Within only moments all internal organs would dissolve, leaving its victim bleeding to death internally. The job was done. Jedo had proven her incredible skills flawlessly, following her cue of the toast and making her shot in one perfect attempt. Everything had gone exactly according to plan; or so it seemed.

Arona wept.

Fifteen
The Enigma

Migg couldn't swim fast enough as he slithered through the murky waters of the bay. He knew that what he held in the palm of his chubby little hand would most certainly take Wick's breath away. Coming through an outcropping of thick seaweed he could see the bottom side of the wharfling dwellings on the underside of the great bog. Fellow wharflings he passed waved *hello*. But he couldn't even acknowledge. He just kept swimming.

Upon reaching Wick's dwelling, Migg quickly swam up into the entrance hole and breached the water's surface within.

"Wick! Wick!" he exclaimed. But his mentor was nowhere to be found.

Migg poked around the catacomb network of Wick's home, searching desperately. The walls were made of tightly-woven twigs, bound together by mud and coated with a pottery-like substance. Each level that wound upward toward the surface was a little larger than the last. Wharfling dwellings were intricately laid out, designed to economize space and maximize privacy. Suddenly Migg heard something.

"Shh!" Wick's voice came from another room.

Tromping around the corner, dripping water everywhere, Migg could see Wick facing away and standing perfectly still. He appeared to be mumbling something quietly under his breath. Then, before Migg could take another step, a bright flash blinded him and an explosion of blue smoke filled the room.

When the smoke cleared and Migg picked himself back up, Wick emerged from the room wearing a frown and a perfectly dispersed coating of blue soot. Migg did all he could not to laugh. But Wick beat him to the punch and the two roared hysterically for a moment.

"Enough magic attempts for today," Wick admitted as he tossed his little wooden wand aside and brushed off his hands. He had much more practice ahead of him, in preparation for his annual Harvest Festival magic show. "Now what brings you here so urgently my young friend?"

You're going to want to sit down for this one," Migg said, growing anxious.

Wick led him up into his study where he lit a large candle for more light.

"Okay," Migg began with heavy breathing. "So I was exploring off of Dryweed Island when I came across something large, half sunken into the mud. It was a small, single-person submarine." Wick's expression grew from curious to concerned that very instant. "But by the looks of its condition it appeared to have been there no more than a couple of days. There were no identifying markings on it. But it's clearly not from around here. It looks like something from the future inside. You should see this thing."

"You went inside?" Wick asked, surprised by Migg's bravery.

"Yes," Migg admitted proudly. "And I'm glad I did. Because what I found inside is going to blow your mind." At that, Migg held up a small, flat, round, golden medallion with a hole through its center: the Enigma.

Wick was speechless as he fumbled for his monocle to get a better look. He took it into his own hand and held it closer to the candlelight, barely able to swallow, barely able to breathe. The fire atop the candle flickered into a larger blinding fire, the closer the Enigma came. In fact, the entire room seemed to come alive with a ghostly current. Wick had seen many perplexing Imcot relics in his day. But never had he been so mesmerized. The etchings were so perfect and ornate. Even the physical structure of the medallion itself was like nothing he had ever seen. Then, turning the medallion over he saw what, in a small way, he hoped he wouldn't.

The lines etched into the reverse side of the medallion were identical to those of a human hand. But not just any hand. One he knew very well.

"Is it what I think it is?" Migg whispered, looking around, as though someone might be watching.

Wick couldn't answer. As amazing as the discovery was, Wick was overwhelmed with concern. He had a bad feeling that the mysterious sunken sub could somehow be traced back to Scar. And if so, then so could the Enigma. *No wonder she was on the run.*

"There's only one way to find out," Wick finally replied.

Sixteen
The Con

The corridors of the Royal Palace were hushed with whispers. Gossip of the preceding night's tragedy muffled throughout the halls in a ghostly echo. It was eerie, as if death itself had cast a spell across the floating vastness of the city. Even the skies had turned to muted grays with the threat of heavy snow looming on the distant horizon. Traffic was all but nonexistent. And the only figures roaming about were those suited up in midnight-blue body armor with their silver, reflective, featureless masks—Kingland's Royal Police. Until an actual conviction was made, everyone was a suspect. So the best thing to do was to stay in doors and out of the way of the police.

"Is he dead?" a Royal Guard whispered to another, as they stood guard outside of the Allied Commission briefing room of the Royal Palace. Their attire was similar to that of the Royal Police, with exception of their deep-crimson uniforms and golden masks.

"No. I hear he's in a coma," the other guard replied. "A failed assassination attempt."

"By whom?"

"I hear it might be an inside job. Ambassador Privo is a prime suspect."

"A suspect?" the guard asked out of disbelief.

The rumor was that the Ambassador had been meeting with opposition leaders of the King and they had been plotting this for some time. But it was amazing how that small bit of fabricated information, which he had heard for the first time only moments earlier, had already translated into fact. Count LePrey had planned it that way.

LePrey made sure that his propaganda was strategically timed and placed to ensure that the people of Kingland didn't question the accusations he was bringing against the Ambassador. Not only was it the perfect diversion, it was also eliminating yet another opponent of LePrey's.

As the sound of heavy boots began to echo down the corridor, the two masked guards outside the briefing room stiffened in alertness. A cloaked figure approached. Even from a great distance it was clear that the hooded figure was none other than Count LePrey. The guards quickly stepped aside as the tall doors slowly opened.

Ambassador Privo exited the room in a hurry, but not before shooting LePrey a look of sheer contempt. He knew full well that it was LePrey who had fabricated the rumors about his involvement in the King's assassination attempt. Not only could this end his career as a royal delegate, it could end his life as a free man.

LePrey entered eagerly, but pulled himself together quickly once he saw General Athen in full military uniform, surrounded by the small assembly of top Allied Commission delegates. This was the moment LePrey had been waiting for, for what seemed a lifetime—the moment of validation after years of exhaustive work. Finally, the helm of Kingland was within his reach.

Though they operated in secrecy, the twelve representatives of the Allied Commission held the Pinnacle power to start wars, end famines, and ultimately manipulate the course of history. The air was cold and still with gloom. Serious eyes followed LePrey as he made his way to the center of the room.

The council chamber was dark, save for the top surface of the commissioners' large desk, which the representatives sat behind. A single light reached down to LePrey like an operatic spotlight. Indeed, his conning performance would be every bit as theatrical. Finally, General Athen, the Chairman of the commission, leaned forward to address the Count.

"Count LePrey: we the Allied Commission have decided that we must launch a full-scale investigation of your drone-armada and your private compound on Bald Rock." LePrey fought the sour expression trying to twist his face as he foreboded the scheme of betrayal the Commission must have been plotting before he entered the room.

"Pardon?" LePrey asked, prying for a more direct explanation.

Athen's eyes peered intently as a scowl crossed his face. "Until the mystery of this assassination attempt is abated, everyone is a suspect."

"Have we not already caught the criminal?" LePrey asked innocently, motioning to the door Privo had just exited. He was struggling to restrain the anger-filled veins bulging through the skin of his shaved head. He had no time for delays.

"Ambassador Privo is a suspect, yes," Athen assured. "But there will be many suspects in this case." His eyes narrowed in on LePrey's. LePrey knew exactly what he meant. *He* was the prime suspect.

"King Basileus has entrusted me with the largest branch of the military," LePrey defended his reputation. Athen couldn't argue that one. Indeed, when it came to the security of Kingland, Count LePrey was the name that came to mind. His drone-armada was considered invincible.

"That doesn't make you immune to suspicion, Count. You are not inscrutable," Athen warned, growing red-faced. "King Basileus's freezing of your contracts makes way for a very believable motive."

"Motive?" LePrey repeated with a confused expression.

"You must have come to suspect that the timing of all of this is quite curious," Athen prodded. "One day your contracts are frozen, the next an assassination attempt is made on the King. Curious."

LePrey said nothing. He only smiled, which made the Commission uneasy. LePrey knew he had covered his tracks far too well for his secrets to be overturned. Regardless of Basileus's recent outbursts, the secret deal they had sealed behind closed doors was all he needed to impel his agenda. Besides, the trail of evidence leading to Privo's connection to the attempt was far too damning to be ignored. In the end, it would come down to the easiest and fastest solution for producing a responsible party to the masses. The public was anxious to see someone pay for this travesty.

"In your official statement to authorities, you made mention of other sources networking with Ambassador Privo," Athen said after a long silence. "Who are they?"

"Pirate mercenaries," LePrey answered. Gasps swept the room. "As you know, a professional assassin by the name of Kuta Jedo was apprehended late last night trying to flee the city. She is being held by Royal Police as we speak. The very opposition leaders the Ambassador has ties to have already been traced back to Jedo and the Pirate Rogue on numerous occasions."

LePrey had masterminded this scheme wisely. Indeed, Jedo had been apprehended, as he knew she would, since he anonymously tipped off the Royal Police about her presence in the city only moments after she had fired the dart. So far, LePrey's scheme was playing out perfectly.

"A rather aggressive move, even for pirates, don't you think?" Athen asked. "After all, the capture of your drone-schooner is the most aggressive assault they've pulled since the assassination of the King's wife. This impudent move is virtually a declaration of war." His admission of knowledge of the Isla Ruba mission gave LePrey the ease to carry out his scheme as planned.

"Yes. Given Lord Yen's demand for the release of General Bontey, that's exactly what it is: aggressive," LePrey declared boldly. The Commission appeared to be taken aback by his lack of alarm that they were aware of the Isla Ruba incident in the first place. "Investment in the Pirate Rogue is big business on the black market. And Slave Lords like Yen know how to do business."

LePrey knew perfectly well that this was not the case. But if he could convince the Allied Commission to retaliate against the Pirate Rogue with aggressive force and not meddle in his affairs, it would give him the freedom he needed to utilize his armies in ways never seen before.

"So how do you propose we react?" Athen asked, after conferring quietly with his colleagues seated around him.

"We give the Pirate Rogue what they seek," LePrey professed.

"Which is?" one of the other Commissioners asked.

"War."

"Absolutely not," Athen belted out, slamming his palm on the table before him. "We will not fight fire with fire. King Basileus is still alive. And I will not engage this kingdom in war while he sleeps."

But as the final words fell off of Athen's lips, LePrey produced two documents that changed everything: the official secret deal between he and King Basileus.

"Understood," LePrey said stepping forward. He handed Athen two cylinders and then stepped back, avoiding the illumination of the spotlight he had been standing under.

"That is why King Basileus and I sealed a foolproof deal prior to any of this," LePrey spoke softly. "He knows as I do that there is little method to the Pirate Rogue's madness. They want war. They want blood. It's as simple as that. We can't afford for an incident like this to cripple us."

Athen pulled the first cylinder open, unrolling the glowing text on the electric scroll. The letter was an official declaration of Emergency State, stating that all territories of Kingland and their allied kingdoms be placed under immediate marshal law until it can be assured that all threats stemming from the Pirate Rogue are completely nullified. The drone-armada was to lead this charge in a systematic hunt for pirate networks, eradicating piracy from the face of the world.

"This is insane," Athen said after reading it. "You're talking about mass invasion of the entire world! And the notion of relocating General

Bontey—since when do we transfer our highest risk inmates to unsecured facilities?"

In addition to the declaration of Emergency State, General Bontey was being ordered to transfer to a secret facility for his own protection. Never before had something like this been done with such a high profile criminal.

"Look, you and I both know that Yen will not simply take *no* for an answer. If we don't hand over Bontey, he will simply apprehend him himself. He needs this pirate for his dirty work." (If only the Commission knew that LePrey was actually speaking of himself.) "And although the Dungeons of Perg are claimed to be unbreakable, I wouldn't be willing to gamble that against the vigilance of Lord Yen."

The lack of reaction from the Allied Commission came as great relief for LePrey. Of course, no one in the room could have anticipated what LePrey was ultimately plotting.

"You're mad," Athen said with a stern finger shot out at LePrey. The Commission hissed in disgust. "This cannot be real. King Basileus would never go for any of this."

LePrey spoke not a word as Athen unrolled the scroll the rest of the way, revealing King Basileus's official signature of endorsement glowing at the bottom of the letter. Athen's expression was louder than any word spoken thus far. These were not documents that could be fabricated. At least, that's what people thought.

"How can this be?" Athen asked, almost speaking to himself. "The King has frozen your contracts. He has no trust in you. Besides, he can't be planning on an assault of this size with our military stretched as thin as it is already."

"He's not," LePrey said confidently. "Every soldier used to carry out this operation will be a product of my drone-armada. No human lives will be sacrificed. And whatever you heard of King Basileus's plans to freeze contracts, is simply overblown hearsay." Regardless, these documents nullified everything else. "As the document states, the King has named me First Lord of the Admiralty, giving me supreme control over all Kingland armed forces." Horror crumpled General Athen's expression as he read. "I assure you, the King's primary objective remains steadfast: *extinguishing the infestation of piracy once and for all.* Don't forget, he's got more of a motive than we do," LePrey said, referring to Basileus's deceased wife. Hums of whispers swept the room. "Surely, if the King were to wake, only to learn that the attempt on his life was by that of a renegade ex-pirate, he would be even more apt to use military force now."

After a long, breathless moment, General Athen responded quietly. Reluctance dominated his delivery. "This will seal our doom as the most despised kingdom in the world." He hid his sweating face in his hands.

"Misconceptions of war are inevitable," LePrey smoothly reconciled. "But in the end, the people will understand. You have an obligation to maintain a firm stance against the Pirate Rogue—an obligation to the people, a responsibility to the King."

As LePrey spoke, Athen opened the second cylinder, revealing a second scroll—which Basileus never saw. But this time he didn't respond. It was now clear just how LePrey's scheme was going to play out. And with King Basileus's "official" endorsement, there was nothing he could do to stop it.

"The vaccine chip is the only way to ensure certain safety for the people of the world as we enter this trying time," LePrey exemplified, defending the mandate outlined on the second scroll: the ordered dispersing of vaccine chips, otherwise known as drone-implants. "The rogue tribes will be desperate to unleash their viruses on the civilians of Kingland since inflicting disease on my drone-armada will be a futile effort. If you want to salvage any trust the people still have in the allied kingdoms, grant them the security they deserve."

Real or not, General Athen knew that there was no way out. He knew that it would eventually come to this. But he never imagined that the decision would ever be so easy, so simple, and so simple to defend.

Given all of the "facts" on the table, the Allied Commission was backed into a corner

Pirates had murdered King Basileus's wife and he was now lying on his deathbed. The short trail of clues led directly to pirates. So the only question he now had was if he had perhaps waited too long. He was simply left with no other choice.

"Do what you must," Athen said dropping the scrolls onto the table before him.

LePrey wasted no time. With a quick vain bow he whisked out of the chamber to his awaiting escort. A small zeppelin was tied down to the ground on a well-groomed, grass-covered garden plate. As the Troika stepped out of the zeppelin's underside passenger compartment, LePrey's grin could be seen from the far end of the lawn.

"We have our war," LePrey whispered, as he approached the three floating, cloaked drones. "Make sure my proposal makes its way into the hands of General Bontey before Lord Yen has a chance to approach him," LePrey ordered as he handed One a small, metal chest. "We won't have much time to persuade him."

LePrey knew just how intricate his timing would need to be in order for this to go right. He had orchestrated the transfer of Bontey as bait to attract Yen. Even prior to the meeting with the Allied Commission, he made sure that news of the transfer had anonymously circulated to Lord Yen. And sure enough, Yen had fallen for it, plotting to seize the inevitable security loophole of the transfer and break Bontey free. But if played out just right, this would instead work to LePrey's advantage.

"Yes, master," One said loyally. "And what should we do about Basileus? He is still alive. Do you want us to devise a scheme to finish him off?"

"No," said LePrey. "We had our chance. We must be cautious with every move now. The Allied Commission is watching me closely. But I have them right where I want them," he said with a grin. "And Basileus is in a deep coma and won't be waking anytime soon, if he does at all. He will soon be forgotten by the people."

"Yes. However, his chances of survival may be better than you anticipate," Two interjected. LePrey's brow drooped, casting an eerie shadow over his eyes. "We were able to obtain a blood sample from the poisoned dart, which showed traces of seratine in his system."

"Seratine?" asked LePrey in shock. "The antidote to the poison used on the assassin's dart. Are you saying King Basileus was tipped off about his own assassination?" He was growing red with fury.

"Perhaps," replied Two. "But it's more likely he was aided by someone else."

"Helped?" asked LePrey, raising his voice. "By whom? No one else had any knowledge of this assassination besides myself and the Countess."

"Exactly," said Two soberly. "It is my evaluation that it was the Countess herself who aided the King." LePrey's expression turned fowl as a flood of humiliation rushed over him. "Think about it," Two continued. "You have had strong suspicions about her relationship with Basileus now for some time."

LePrey didn't want to admit that his perfect plan had been sabotaged by the very one entrusted to carry it out: his own wife. His entire body shook with anger. He burned with jealousy. He knew that Basileus had crossed a line with his attraction for Arona. But he had no idea that she felt every bit as strongly for him. He had no idea just how deep her feelings had grown for Basileus, or just how much passion she had put into this secret scheme.

Although the toast she and Basileus shared was Jedo's signal to fire the dart, Arona used it as an opportunity to slip him the antidote she had mixed into the wine.

"Damn her!" LePrey shouted, slamming his gloved fist into the other as the epiphany manifested itself in his mind's eye. "I knew she would eventually betray me! Detain her immediately."

"We can't," Three admitted reluctantly.

"What do you mean? Why?" LePrey asked.

"Because she has gone missing," Three answered.

LePrey tensed with rage, like he was about to explode. But he knew that he must remain focused on the objective at hand. The Countess had gone into hiding. But at least now she couldn't get in the way of his plot.

Before long, his drone-armada would be spreading itself across the expanse of the world like a contagious disease. No one was exempt to what was coming: the massive distribution of drone-implants. Soon all of the world would be under the control of Machine.

Everything up to this point had been calculated so precisely, so meticulously that it was unfathomable to conceive anything could possibly stop him from prevailing. But there was one calculation he simply couldn't have accounted for—something about to arise *from the most unlikely of places.*

Seventeen
The Awakening

The chill was cruel, spitting icy rain from the briskly shifting evening clouds. Winter was on the doorstep of Willow Lake as Ash huddled on the roof outside of his bedroom dormer. His only reaction to the cold was to pull his hood forward, blocking the wind, hiding his bloodshot eyes.

From here, he could barely see his father's fishing trawler, cradled at the edge of the bay. And the dim light flickering through the galley's porthole window told him that Scar was still awake. It was all he could do not to go down to the docks to be with her, just as he had done every night since her arrival. But he knew it would be best to stay away. He needed to sort his thoughts—to sort his feelings.

He tried to recall what it was he said that might have set Scar off and sent her fleeing the night before. Perhaps she had suspected the nature of his curse. It wasn't the first time a girl had simply run off without a single explanation. However, it was the first time it had ever hurt quite like this. It was a struggle to keep his thoughts from entering a very dark and self-destructive place.

Ash had never had luck impressing girls. And whenever he had been given a chance he would find a way to blow it, either by trying too hard to impress, or by defaulting to his bad-boy facade. He was now convinced that Scar had become nothing more than another one of his failed attempts. If only he knew how she really felt about him.

Pulling out the crumpled wanted poster, one of the many he had ripped down from around the harbor, Ash studied the rendering of Scar's likeness. He tried to imagine what in the world she could have done to put herself in this situation. It was no mystery that Scar had a troubled past. In fact, this was much of what drew Ash to her. But with the wanted posters of her on every corner of Garbbit Harbor and the townspeople's uprising, Ash was beginning to wonder just how steep of a price he would ultimately pay for his loyalty to her.

He wasn't the type to play against the odds or throw caution to the wind. So the deeper his feelings became for her, the more he felt as though he was falling off the edge of a cliff. The question was: would her past troubles be waiting for him at the bottom of that cliff? Ash balled-up the poster and threw it into the night air. Suddenly he heard something that broke his concentration.

He couldn't see Logan stumbling down the road, but he could hear his big clumsy feet dragging each other through the puddles as he yelled. "Hey boy! You'd better be home! I know about the girl!" Ash swallowed the lump in his throat as he listened intently, trying not to breathe. *Had he found her?* "You thought you could keep it a secret from me, eh?" Logan slurred. "You must think I'm pretty stupid."

Peering over the roof's edge, Ash could see how close Logan was. His drunken slouching posture cast a skewed shadow across the street as he opened the front door to the house. As soon as Ash saw this, he knew he had no time. His heart pounded so loud and hard he could feel it in his throat as he slipped back into his bedroom through the window.

And with every sloppy thud of Logan's boots climbing the stairs, Ash felt his knees threaten to give out, just as they used to when he was a little boy, just as they did in his nightmares. The sound of the raindrops dripping into a tin pail atop his dresser sounded like crashes of thunder in the moment. His eyes dashed about his darkened room, looking for the ridiculous: an escape. But he knew better. There was none. And this was brewing to be a violent episode. Logan was especially enraged and especially drunk. Then the bedroom door creaked open.

Logan used the doorframe to augment his swaying mass. His silhouette was monster-like, with his head hung low and his big fists clenched tight. "Where are you boy?" he struggled to say, through his heavy wheezing. "I know you're in here."

For a brief moment, Ash felt safe, knowing that Logan couldn't see well in the dark. But then his eyes found the boy, and he moved into the room. "You lied," he growled, shoving a thick finger into Ash's face. "And now the whole village is in an uproar. But I'm gonna bring her in." Ash gasped instinctually. "That's right, I'm gonna find her and turn her over to that Slave Lord and collect the reward. Now tell me where she is!"

Ash couldn't believe that Logan still hadn't figured out that she was actually hiding in his very own fishing trawler. Then again, he was never sober long enough to pay that close of attention.

"Never," Ash whispered. He wasn't sure where his confidence was coming from. Suddenly Logan's anger turned to rage. He raised his huge fist over his head and Ash knew that there was no stopping him. But what happened next would all but stop time itself.

Just as Logan began to swing his fist toward Ash, his hand became engulfed in a swirling ball of flame. He belted out a holler that shook the stillness of the room, causing the tiny rodents hiding in the shadows of the attic to scurry away. Quickly he ran over to Ash's dresser and splashed his hand into the pail filled with runoff from the leaking roof. But Ash remained focused. He couldn't believe his eyes; yet he felt as though he understood just what was happening.

As Logan tucked his burnt hand under his armpit, writhing in agonizing pain, Ash looked at his own hands. They shook with anxiety. But then it all faded into an all-encompassing euphoria. A numbing sensation ran through his entire body. He felt powerful—in total control. It felt amazing.

Ash didn't know it at the time; this was but a nexus—an awakening of a childhood secret. It was like he had the ability to absorb energy, be it from someone or something, and manifest it into anything he willed. *This had to be a dream.*

"You cursed witch!" Logan yelled. "Your powers are from hell!"

Ash sank into the shadows, trying to hide. This was too strange to be real. But before he could even focus, he felt his body lifting into the air, almost uncontrollably. Feeling lighter than air, he leaped out of his bedroom window. He ran in a panic up to the peak of his dormer and took one springing step off the shingles. But this was no act of self-destruction.

Though his eyes were closed, Ash could tell that nothing was the same as his body lifted into the sleeting night air. The sensation was thrilling, yet frightening. He felt as though he might not ever come down again. His stomach rolled as he squeezed his eyes shut, afraid of what might come next. This wasn't natural. Gravity seemed to have little effect. It was like his actions were amplified and fueled by his raging emotions. Suddenly, like the slamming of a door, Ash heard a loud crash, and then felt it.

He couldn't help open his eyes as he blasted through the pile of firewood he had just split and stacked earlier that day, clear on the other side of their property. The moment Ash's body rolled to a fumbling halt, he felt the numbing sensation of this strange experience begin to fade. It was like whatever his body had absorbed was now being released. He couldn't describe it, even to himself. It was incredible. But the biting, cold rain quickly began to freeze him to the bone. He crawled out of the mess of split wood and found himself over a frozen puddle. The icy reflection staring back at him was different.

Through tears of mud, it was as if his eyes were glowing. They were. Even his complexion looked different. His skin was pale and tight. Veins he never knew he had were threatening to breach the surface of his greasy skin, like a gray spiderweb splattered across his entire body. *What's happening? What have I become?* he wondered. The scars on his back seemed to burn as warm blood soaked through his shirt.

Fear set in like the cold as Ash curled up next to the wood shed, his body slowly returning to its normal physical state. What scared him more than the preceding episode was that it might be real. Wick was always hinting that Ash would one day awaken to a new sense of being. He had witnessed Ash's curse from time to time and had never acted alarmed. It was like Wick knew exactly what Ash's curse was.

Ash was enough of a social outcast without the aid of this curse. He wasn't about to let this thing destroy whatever chance he had left with Scar. There had to be a remedy for the curse. And if anyone knew what it might be, it would be Wick.

Eighteen
Letting Go

The world smelled different that night. It looked different. It was as if Ash's senses were now on high-alert, amplifying everything around him. So he closed his eyes and just ran.

By now, the watery marshlands of Garbbit Harbor had turned to fields of frost-covered grass, trapped in layers of thin ice. There was a trail cutting through it from the village to the wharfling reservation. Delirious and afraid, Ash took a shortcut that night. He was in a hurry. Every few steps or so his foot would break through the ice, cutting his ankles as they plunged into the frigid, muddy waters. He didn't care. He didn't even notice. He had to see Wick.

The wharfling reservation was located on the outskirts of Garbbit Harbor. Contrary to old tales about wharflings, claiming that they were menacing little trolls hiding underneath the wharf of the harbor, they were simply bog dwellers.

Built on massive, floating bog islands, wharfling cottages were usually cone-shaped clay huts, wrapped in dried grasses on the exterior. This was merely what their topside world looked like. The bottom portion of their homes was much larger, submerged beneath the water level of the bogs, giving them equal access to the bay beyond.

Because wharflings were so small, so were their cottages. But most were at least equipped with a large awning, outstretched from their entrance, in which larger, non-wharfling visitors might be able to fit somewhat comfortably.

Ash ducked in under Wick's awning to dodge the rain. He plopped down on the same stump he always did and picked up a small, broken statue Wick had sitting on the ground. He was always curious to see what new finds Wick might have lying around from recent scavenging expeditions. Wick came to greet him with a small cup of tea and an expression of concern. He awoke and sensed something disturbing the moment he heard the boy running across the marsh at such an hour. It wasn't usual for Ash to visit Wick this late. But recently the visits hadn't been happening at all—with Scar in the picture.

"What is it?" Wick asked calmly. "I know you didn't run that fast just to drink my tea." Wick's humor was wasted on Ash. "Is it that girl?" Wick asked. "They can be trouble you know." Speaking so carefree about Scar didn't come easy for him. She was more than trouble as far as he was concerned.

Ash nestled his steaming tea. The scent of the soaking tea leaves almost hurt it was so pungent. Strangely enough, he had smelled it coming across the marchland. It was like his sense of smell had suddenly become wildly heightened. "Wick," he interjected after a careful sip. "The magic you do in your magic shows is nothing more than sleight of hand and smoke and mirrors."

"Well now," Wick piped up defensively, "I wouldn't say that." Some blue soot still resided under his fingernails from his little disaster earlier that day.

"C'mon," Ash shot back, clearly vexed. "I'm serious. You're channeling no more magic to make a card disappear or an ash to leap hands than any other trickster illusionist." Wick frowned in agreement. "But are there magicians who actually do possess some sort of—something supernatural?"

"If your questions is, are there real magicians in this world, then I say yes," Wick replied. "And wizards and witches and all sorts of people who specialize in tapping into the other side."

"What is the other side?" Ash asked like a little boy.

"The side of this world we cannot see with our eyes," Wick explained. "A world comprised of pure energy. Your Mystery."

"My Mystery," Ash repeated, almost in a trance. He stared at his hands and flashed back to only moments before—his eyes glowing, flying through the air, the incredible energy he felt at that moment. *Was this really what his Mystery looked like?*

Suddenly Wick began to understand why Ash had come. Though it was unclear as to what degree Ash had tapped into this energy, Wick knew that it had to have been significant for Ash to be so devastated.

"Something happened, didn't it?" Wick asked quietly. This was not something he wanted his nosey wharfling neighbors hearing. "You had an experience you can't explain, didn't you?" Ash stared ahead blankly. He couldn't respond. "Did you use it for good?" Wick asked.

"No," Ash whispered, with a frightened expression. He noticed Wick studying his eyes, perhaps trying to detect a lie. "I don't know," he tried to correct, unsure of his motives.

Ash didn't go into detail. He wasn't even convinced he wanted Wick to know what had happened. And Wick wasn't ready for this either. He thought he would be. But now that the time had come, he realized that he just wasn't ready to let go and let Ash become what he was destined to be.

"Ash," he said, lifting Ash's tea bag from his cup, "don't be afraid of what happened. There are two primary forces of nature in this universe: love and fear. Fear is what distances you from your spirit-self, from the other side."

"And what about love?" Ash asked, as Wick was afraid he would.

"If you're asking about the girl, I feel that your infatuation with her stems more out of fear of losing her than anything else."

Ash began to breathe heavily, wearing his anger like a suit of armor. But Wick remained calm. He only wanted to help the boy. After all, Ash was like a son to him—his only son. He couldn't help but feel that this escalated emergence from boyhood was being brought on by Scar's presence. It was all the more reason for Wick not to like her.

"I must warn you, Ash," Wick said. "Scar is proving to be every bit as dangerous as I had suspected she would be." Ash's brow dropped. He didn't like what he was hearing, although he couldn't argue with it. "I've seen the wanted posters around the harbor. She's a criminal, Ash. A thief. And I don't buy the fact that she simply doesn't remember who she is or what she's done. That's an awful convenient alibi for someone who is guilty. There's far more to her than meets the eye, I'm afraid."

"Just because you don't like her, doesn't mean she's a criminal," Ash interceded. "Whatever this Slave Lord wants with her is obviously a lie. The people around here don't like anyone new who comes through the village." That much was true.

"This is more than bad hospitality," Wick argued. "That girl is from another world and has a past that is quickly catching up with her. If she doesn't leave Garbbit Harbor, her problems will soon become ours."

"You're no more open-minded than Logan," Ash criticized, knocking over the small, somewhat valuable statue as he shot up to his feet. "You just want to control me and my life. Well, you know what? I can manage on my own just fine without your help." Ash's words stung Wick. It crippled him with sadness to hear Ash so bitter. He knew that regardless of how tight he tried to hang on to the little boy he wished Ash still was, a young, strong man was emerging.

As Ash stomped away, back across the frozen marsh, Wick struggled to refrain from chasing after him. The secret of Ash's true identity couldn't remain a secret much longer. It was time he knew. Digging the Enigma from his coat pocket, Wick gazed at it and knew right then and there, it was time to let Ash go.

Nineteen
The Dungeons of Perg

It was said there are two types of people in Kingland law enforcement: the over-zealous mavericks and the hopeless burnouts. Marshal Xavier Kane was the latter. After nearly thirty years in service, Xavier had seen his share of criminals, blood, and foul play. Though he still clung to the worn-out belief that Kingland was a kingdom of justice, he was slowly nearing the end of his rope. The growing kingdom he called home was beginning to lose touch with reality and in turn, with him.

Xavier was a legend, an icon of law enforcement. Some hated him, but most aspired to be like him. He had an air about him that made people nervous, even before a word was uttered. He showed little emotion, including fear. A man of few words, Xavier had managed to keep his past a mystery to nearly everyone.

As his huge, albino polar-mammoth trudged through the thick snow of the ice dunes, the lights of the facility slowly became visible up ahead. It was the most relieving sight he had seen in days. His journey across the frozen Arctic Plains had been perhaps the most deplorable experience of his long career, thus far. Bone-chilling temperatures, stinging winds, and the constant, spine-crushing thrusting of riding on the back of a giant snow beast were enough to make him consider an early retirement. Then again, he didn't have much of a life to retire to.

Xavier and the four arctic Eskimos he had rented the mammoths from dismounted, tying the beasts up from their long blackened tusks to rusted shards of metal jetting out of the ice. A layer of ice encased the entirety of the long, bull-skin, Eskimo coat he had traded one of his old pistols for. Though it had kept him from freezing to death, he could hardly move in the frozen hides. The last thing he needed now was to feel trapped.

Finally at his destination, Xavier couldn't help but anticipate how things might play out. Inmate transfers were notorious for prison break attempts. If things didn't go smoothly, in spite of the bloodshed that would be endured, the world's most savage pirate would be back on the loose. That wasn't the kind of mark a Marshal wants on their record.

Once the highest-ranking general in the Krellian Imperial Army, Sayto Bontey went into hiding after the fall of his empire. But the expired regime didn't go down without a fight. While in exile, Bontey found himself in a position to profit greatly as a pirate militant for loyalists to the fallen empire's ideals—the Pirate Rogue. Though many retired Krellian generals have since resorted to piracy, Bontey was the one who made an art of it. His allegiance to the Pirate Rogue went only as far as their money would allow, giving him a leverage he didn't even have when he once bore the medals of a general.

Bontey ruled his crews with a single attribute: absolute fear. He trusted no one and never granted second chances. It was even said that after suspecting a fellow pirate crewmember of going too easy on prisoners he had recently acquired, Bontey forced him to kill his own brother, then eat his eyes and drink his blood. Stories like this drifted about the pirate communities all of the time. True or not, Bontey was by far the most feared pirate history had ever known. But his reign as a vicious captain was short-lived. Kingland was relentless in their quest to take Bontey down once and for all—or until now, twelve years later.

The Dungeons of Perg were massive cylinder-like sinkholes, carved into the depths of the glacial ice that made up Perg's wasteland. A spire rose up through the center of each sinkhole, housing hundreds of cramped prison cells like a hive of insects. It was considered an inescapable prison—an inescapable world.

Xavier left his Eskimo companions on the ice and descended slowly into the depths of the facility in a large, rickety freight elevator within the sinkhole's outer perimeter. Beneath his borrowed fur parka, Xavier wore a fitted body-armor suit, snug to his somewhat-still muscular physique—the suit similar to Kingland's Royal Police, deep blue and white. But his suit, helmet, and face shield were far more beat-up than the shiny, reflective ones worn by inner-city police. Xavier took pride in the fact that his helmet served as a bit of a living testament to his career. Today he wore it for another reason: real defense.

"He's ready," said the gangly prison guard as he limped briskly toward Xavier from the guard shack.

Xavier could see fear and anxiety in the guard's eyes. It was obviously a bittersweet moment for the guard, knowing that the world's most lethal pirate was leaving must have been a relief. But just imagining him on the other side of the bars was a frightful image.

"Bring him out," Xavier said with an uncertainty in his voice he hadn't displayed in many years.

Slowly, the huge door at the end of an iron drawbridge, spanning from the outer perimeter to the prison cells, began to slide up. Heat billowed out from behind the door in the form of thick, white steam. And through its fog stood the towering, shackled and chained figure of Sayto Bontey.

Bontey was a Panthril, the largest and strongest breed of Zahartan Desert natives. Though he walked with a slight limp and his left arm was severed at the elbow, his presence remained ominous, dwarfing the six guards escorting him. His feline-like face and spiking ears erected high above the orange prison robe like a horned beast. Long, thick, black dread locks hung down over his face and onto his furry barreled chest. His long serpent-like tail twitched behind him like the hand of a clock.

As they approached Xavier, Bontey's eyes, one like glowing amber and the scarred other, a milky off-white, shot up at Xavier. Thankfully, Xavier's reaction went undetected behind his masked face.

The last time Xavier had seen Bontey was in this very place, twelve years earlier, when he was delivering Bontey as a prisoner who was to never see the light of day again. The guards quickly ushered Bontey into the elevator and slammed the door shut. They couldn't move fast enough to send Xavier on his way with his cargo. It was like a sigh of relief swept over the entire facility as the freight elevator squealed its way back up to the frozen surface.

Bontey was surprisingly cooperative as Xavier led him up the wooden ramp and into the small cage he would be transported in on their long journey back across the arctic glacier and to the secret hideout he was being transferred to. The cage was affixed to the back of one of the polar-mammoth's backs. It was imperative that this caravan transporting Bontey be small and discrete, as to not draw any attention to itself.

Xavier hung back at the end of the line as they set out, back across the ice dunes. Even through the freezing temperatures, he could still smell Bontey's gagging odor, permeating from the cage up ahead. The creature's dark silhouette was massive against the smear of northern lights in the midnight-blue sky.

After the first day's journey, the Eskimos were about to pull into one of the many ice caves and set up camp for the day. (It was Xavier's order that they only travel at night, as to avoid being detected.) But before they reached the caves, the Eskimos stopped in the middle of an ice plain and dismounted. Xavier was confused as he watched them wandering about up ahead, pointing around and shouting back and forth.

Creaking of thick shifting ice sheets below moaned through the air, chilling the already freezing and unsettling mood. Xavier would have gotten down to join the Eskimos, but it wouldn't have helped since he couldn't understand a word they said. It was an old Galacian dialect only spoken by the arctic natives themselves. Then one of the Eskimos came running up to Xavier, rambling on about something that only confused him more. So Xavier decided to check it out for himself.

As Xavier walked by Bontey, cramped in the cage, the pirate's eyes seemed to be letting on that he knew something Xavier didn't. But Xavier couldn't allow himself to get paranoid all the way out here. He had to stay focused.

When he reached the other Eskimos, he noticed that they were looking at a series of perfectly round holes cut out of the ice. At first he just thought, *so what?* This was how Galacian Eskimos fished—by cutting holes through the ice and spearing their fish through the holes. But then he noticed that no ice had formed over the holes yet, which meant that they had to have been drilled very recently. But if that were the case, then *where were the people who drilled them?* Suddenly there was a jolting blast and one of the Eskimos fell to the ground. Blood oozed out from his skull, soaking into the snow like an inkblot on parchment.

Looking around frantically, Xavier saw smoke curling up from one of the holes. *Gunfire!* Then another blast and a splash from another hole and another Eskimo fell into the snow in a bleeding heap.

Xavier quickly took cover behind one of the polar-mammoths. But the mammoths were now startled too and bucking wildly. With the moons still low on the arctic horizon, Xavier couldn't make out details very well. But after two more shots it was clear that he was now the only survivor—he and his prisoner. Then the ice began to quake beneath his feet.

Turning around, Xavier saw an immense narrow shape piercing through the ice, busting through effortlessly. Whatever it was, it was moving fast—right towards him! Frozen for a moment, Xavier quickly leaped up onto the polar-mammoth. It was the very one Bontey was caged upon. He may have lost the rest of his team, but he wasn't about to lose his prisoner. Suddenly the ice split and the only thing in front of him was open water.

Xavier yanked the reins back, halting the giant mammoth. But when he tried to redirect its course, he quickly realized that he was trapped as they were now floating free from the rest of the mammoths on a large chunk of broken ice. Xavier struggled to repress his panic as he watched the other mammoths struggling to maintain sure footing and slipping into the icy drowning waters.

The mysterious icebreaker came closer and slowed and as it did, Xavier finally recognized the massive red fins: the *Venom*—Bontey's pirate vessel. His old comrades had come to rescue him.

Xavier couldn't help but think about the number of times he had warned his superiors that transferring Bontey would be much riskier than just leaving him imprisoned. The Dungeons of Perg were more highly guarded than any other prison facility in the world. But it was said that these orders had come down from the King himself. So there was no arguing for Xavier. Now Bontey was about to walk away free. Little did he know that Count LePrey had orchestrated this entire setup and was the one waiting in the wings to greet Bontey upon his release.

The deep blue icy waters parted as the massive, black metal hull of the *Venom* surfaced. Its red fins slowly retracted as its huge billowing flag was raised and a small hatch opened atop its surface. Then out stepped the one and only, Droku Mox.

Mox was a Kracnod: a tall, red, insect-like creature. His large-scaled skin appeared perpetually wet and his large, translucent wings seemed to be cursed by a constant twitch that caused them to sporadically flutter in a snapping blur. And his narrow, elongated torso was offset by his huge head and enormous eyes, which rested upon the upper lip of his ever-smiling grin—showing the many rows of his long, spiking teeth.

During Bontey's exile after the Great War, Mox had been his first mate. It was Mox who was right along Bontey's side at every turn during his successful reign of piracy. Together they had become extremely wealthy and powerful through the Pirate Rogue. But when Kingland finally apprehended Bontey, Mox, and the rest of the crew simply disappeared. This was their first legitimate job since then—a lucky turn of events for them after randomly discovering the drone-schooner off the shores of Isla Ruba.

"I think you've reached the end of your trail," Mox mocked, yelling down from a small porthole atop the submarine.

"It all depends on how you look at it," Xavier replied, unshaken. As dire as his situation was, he had an innate knack for maintaining his cool, finding a way to hide his fear from his opponents.

"Well, from up here it doesn't look so good," Mox said. "Unless you're General Bontey, that is. Free him," he demanded, sighting a large pistol on Xavier's head.

Xavier knew he had no choice. Stranded on a single shard of ice in the middle of the Arctic Sea, he literally didn't have any ground to stand on. Almost as a sign of surrender, he lifted his helmet from his head, revealing his untanned, yet windburned skin. Permanent creases and old scars crossed his face like a map. And his graying thinning hair was trimmed close to his skull. His colorless hazel eyes twinkled like lost diamonds through his squinting eyelids as he gazed up at his enemy with regret.

Unlocking Bontey's shackles was the hardest thing Xavier had ever done. He had always won in the end. This was a first, which was why he couldn't help wonder if it might be the end for him.

"Had your King Basileus adhered to Lord Yen's demands, we could have avoided this unfortunate confrontation," Mox said to Xavier as he tossed down a rope to Bontey.

"Kingland doesn't negotiate with pirate scum," Xavier said, watching Bontey leap the incredible distance over the cold waters and climb up the *Venom's* conning tower. It hardly made Xavier feel good to say that. He knew that there had been numerous occasions where King Basileus had secretly contracted pirates to do his dirty work, which couldn't be handled legitimately.

"Obviously," Mox said, glancing down at Bontey. "But now that we have what we want, we have even less of a reason to play by the rules.

I'm afraid the Allied Commission is rather disheartened to learn that Kingland has been conducting illegal reconnaissance missions without their support," he said, referring to the Isla Ruba operation.

"You have what you came for," Xavier said. "Leave it at that."

"That's too docile," Mox replied. "It's high time Kingland started paying for its crimes. Besides, it's too late. We already anonymously delivered the damning evidence to the Commission. If your King ever awakes, he'll wish he hadn't."

Xavier knew just how fatal this was to the stability of Kingland. Already on shaky ground with the rest of the Allied Commission, Kingland was now losing all credibility, which would ultimately thrust the kingdom into political and economic chaos.

Mox and Bontey disappeared into the *Venom*. But just before Mox closed the hatch, he reemerged and said something that Xavier would find himself pondering more than anything he had ever heard spill from the lips of a pirate.

"You know, Xavier," Mox said in almost a thoughtful tone, "you may want to reconsider your allegiances. It's curious as to why you place so much faith and trust in a kingdom that has let you down so many times. Look at where they've left you now." And then the pirate sank away along with the entire *Venom*, beneath the ice.

Xavier couldn't deny the reality of what was said. Kingland had left him high and dry more than once. And if they only would have listened to him, Bontey would still be locked up. And Xavier certainly wouldn't be floating alone on a splinter of ice in the middle of the Arctic Sea.

Twenty
The Chest and the Mutiny

For the crew of the *Venom*, it was surreal watching Sayto Bontey board the submarine again. Still a hulking, massive figure, he was thinner than he was back when he captained the vessel. His oily black hair had since become threatened with hints of silver. He wore the same beat-up leather vest over his bare, hairy chest. And the sound of his huge boots as they thundered across the floor were as distinct as his rancid odor. For some it was just like old times. For others it was quite unsettling.

Though Captain Mox had a wild temper and loved to test his strength against fellow crewmembers, his aggressiveness didn't come close to the violent gruesomeness Bontey often displayed. From strange religious sacrificial rituals to an alleged cannibalistic appetite, no one on the *Venom* felt safe anymore.

Bontey spent little time above deck, as tensions were already growing high between he and Mox. Mox had led Bontey to the main bridge. And in a formal display of honor, he outstretched his hand to the main navigation wheel, as if to say *Welcome home*. But before Bontey could make a move, Mox stepped up to the navigation wheel and took it in his hands. No words were exchanged. Only glares. It was obvious that Mox wasn't about to give up his post as captain of the *Venom*. After all, Bontey had commanded it for a mere five years in comparison to Mox's twelve. And the majority of the current crew had joined within those twelve years and had never even seen Bontey before, let alone sailed under his command. To them, Bontey was a thing of legend. So Bontey made his way down to what used to be his private quarters.

The dark chamber hadn't changed as much as he'd imagined, other than the stench of Kracnod. Seating himself behind the huge desk, Bontey spotted a small metal chest sitting on top of some old crates. It appeared to be a new addition as it was the only thing not dust-covered or scratched in the entire room. Curious, Bontey took the chest and tried to open it. Though its ornately etched surface didn't look familiar to him, the combination lock on the face of it did.

It was a puzzle-lock, with seven rings of characters which, when perfectly aligned, would release the hasp. Mox hadn't mentioned a word about it, but Bontey had a sneaking feeling that this chest just may have been intended for someone else other than Mox. He was about to discover how right he was.

Dialing the seven rings, he spelled out a secret codeword only he and one other person in the world knew. And to his delight, the chest opened. Pulling back the lid, he saw a strange mechanical prosthetic. He lifted the artificial forearm out of the chest, already knowing whom this gift was for, and more importantly, whom it was from.

The arm was made of brass metal and was quite heavy. Just his size. And as he fastened it onto his left arm, a familiar voice flickered through a series of tiny holes on its wrist.

"Greetings, General," Count LePrey's recorded voice said. "This chest contains one hundred thousand in coins. It's yours upon your acceptance of these terms." Bontey noticed that there was a hidden compartment within the chest—another layer beneath where the arm had rested. But this one required a key.

"There is a fugitive on the run," LePrey continued. "A girl, hiding in the swamps of Murk. I need you to find her and bring her to me safely. Upon delivery, I will grant you the key that unlocks this chest.

It's as simple as that. My drone-armada has just been contracted by Kingland to conduct a full-scale invasion of all territories outside of the Allied Kingdoms. It is a hunt and peck mission to root out Pirate Rogue networks. But I want you to imbed yourself in my battalion in Murk and keep your focus on finding the girl. You will lead them. They are waiting for you with more details about this girl.

"Now, as you are surely aware, Captain Mox is under contract with Lord Yen, who has also assigned you and the rest of your crew to find the girl. Play along. Let Yen think that you are working for him. That will keep him out of our way. But in the end, deliver the girl to me. I guarantee you, my reward is far larger than whatever Yen could hope to scrounge up.

"Watch your back with Mox. Don't let him get in your way either. That was the mistake you made the last time I requested your services. Consider your new prosthetic a good-faith gift." And with that, the room fell silent.

Bontey didn't move a muscle. He struggled to believe LePrey, who had a history of twisting the truth to achieve his point. And since LePrey was leading a worldwide campaign to eradicate piracy from the face of the map, it was more than ironic that he would be hiring a pirate to carry out his work. But Bontey knew whom he was dealing with as he recalled how it all began …

Nearly twenty years ago, LePrey had contracted Bontey for a similar mission. Then, like now, there was a young woman on the run. And like now, Bontey ended up tracking her down in the swamps of Murk. But due to an avoidable mistake, she slipped away from him—but not before she severed his arm in a fateful duel. It would be the last time he contracted Bontey. In fact, it wouldn't be long before he turned his back on the entire network of piracy and began lobbying with Kingland to engage in an official showdown with pirates. Bontey knew though, that LePrey would always have a need for his kind. LePrey did too much underground work to remain legitimate across the board.

Bontey clenched his metal fist, familiarizing himself with his new arm. Suddenly the fingers locked into a ball and receded back into the forearm, looking as though the hand had been severed. Then, something protruded from within. It was a knife. But as he adjusted the arm to get a better look, the knife retracted and became replaced by three long, curved claws. As he repeated this, numerous other appendages, such as a saw, a hook, a whip, even a small spear shot from the end of this metal prosthetic. Then, as he turned his locked fist in one last position, a long, double-edged saber ejected, capturing the room's candlelight in its brilliant sheen. He caught his own reflection in the saber's blade and grinned. This was a deal he couldn't refuse. Bontey knew better than anyone that LePrey had access to gold unlike anyone in the world. So money would be no object here.

"There you are." Mox's voice startled Bontey. "I didn't expect to find you down here," he said, emerging from the shadows. He appeared to be less than comfortable with the idea of Bontey sitting in what was now *his* chair. In fact, the entire captain's quarters were technically Mox's private quarters now. After all, he was the captain now.

"I haven't interrupted anything I hope," Mox said approaching the desk, agitated yet nervous. Bontey shook his head slowly and placed his real hand on the chest, carefully hiding his new prosthetic limb. "I see you've found the chest," Mox said. "It's a bit of a mystery I'm afraid. It just showed up out of nowhere, only days ago. We don't know what's inside, and we have no key to open it. I'm apprehensive to pick the lock, as it could be a trap—a bomb. Who knows?"

"Perhaps it's time you retire for the evening," Mox said, gesturing for Bontey to leave the quarters. But Bontey only pulled the chest closer to himself. "You know what's inside," Mox said with worry in his huge eyes. "Don't you?"

Suddenly Bontey sprang from the chair, leaped over the desk and grabbed Mox by the throat. Mox felt consciousness fading as Bontey squeezed tighter. But it wasn't just his breath Bontey was obstructing. It was his mind.

Bontey was known to possess a mysterious, supernatural ability to absorb people's thoughts by means of touch—a supernatural ability he had mastered through the practice of his mysterious dark religion.

"I warned Lord Yen this would happen!" Mox gasped wearily as he stumbled backward. He could feel Bontey's presence in his mind. It was as unstoppable of a force as Bontey himself. "He wanted you to lead the search for the girl," he struggled to utter from his throat. "But I am still captain of this ship!"

"Not any more," Bontey growled in his deep gravelly whisper. He could see Mox's ultimate plan. It was simple: kill Bontey if anything goes awry.

"This is mutiny!" Mox tried to exclaim.

"No," Bontey whispered as the long blade of his new saber shot out. "It's murder," he concluded. And with a single slice, Mox's head rolled off his shoulders and onto the floor.

Above in the control room, the crew was going about its usual maintenance routine. The thud of Bontey's footsteps coming up to the room from below caused everyone on deck to freeze. Mox may have been their captain, but Bontey was the one to fear. And what they saw next only solidified that more.

As Bontey emerged from the staircase he stopped and grinned. Under one arm he held the metal chest close to his body, like it was his offspring. With the other hand he held up the blood-dripping head of Captain Droku Mox. Everyone's eyes widened as the air was perfectly still. Then Bontey spoke.

"The *Venom* has a new captain."

He then walked over to the helm, pulled down a large crank and began the *Venom*'s descent, deeper into the dark cold waters of the Great Sea.

Twenty One
The Harvest Festival

Like the snow's lilting on an aimless current, colorful confetti drifted about the cold evening breeze. Bright streamers fluttered above the streets of the harbor like flags. Small, musical ensembles were on nearly every corner, filling the air with an eclectic assortment of native folk music. The sights and sounds were merry and magical, unlike any other time on the calendar—the opening ceremonies of Garbbit Harbor's Harvest Festival.

At the edge of a small plaza, Wick had set up his magic show. A small, two-wheel cart and rickety wooden table with a ripped-up cloth thrown over it were the extent of his theatrics. As usual, he wasn't attracting much of a crowd. In fact, most of the spectators kept their distance—staying only close enough to heckle. But Wick didn't put these shows on for them. He put them on for the ten or so children with tattered clothes and dirty faces crowding around the table. With excited wide eyes, the children huddled in closer to be amazed by Wick's sorcery.

"And for my next trick," Wick said, fumbling through the jumbled pile of magic trick paraphernalia he had hidden under the blanket on his cart, "I will pull a sparrow from an empty hat." The children gasped. Turning around to face them, Wick held up a black stovepipe hat with a hole in it. He stuck his finger through to prove that the hat was actually empty. Placing the hat top-down on the table, Wick gingerly checked with his other hand to make sure that his sparrow was still in its secret chamber underneath the table. Then, using his sleight of hand maneuver he dropped breadcrumbs into the hat to attract the sparrow. In just a moment the sparrow would fly up from the underside of the table and into the hat. At least, that's what was supposed to happen.

Wick didn't know that the table he had found for his show was also home to a family of giant, bird-eating spiders. And the mother spider was staring right at her supper. But the sparrow was too fast, fleeing from its chamber and into the shadows without anyone even noticing. The out-of-luck spider turned to go back to its nest, but then caught the scent of the breadcrumbs. It was better than nothing.

"So," Wick readied his crowd, "as you are about to see, the hat that was once empty," he said picking the hat up, "is no longer empty, but now possesses a—"

At first he thought his senses were merely deluding him. But when he pulled it out, he screamed with horror as the giant, hairy spider quickly crawled up his arm and down his back, before scampering off. The children screamed and scattered, running to their parents who yelled at Wick in disgust and anger.

Wick felt even smaller than he already was. It was hard enough being a wharfling, a second-rate citizen. Sometimes he felt as though he was nothing more than an outcast. Glancing up at a wanted poster featuring an illustration of Scar, Wick imagined just how bad it would be for him if the villagers found out that he had actually been partially responsible for saving her life and bringing her to Garbbit Harbor. Unfortunately, things were about to get far worse than that.

The music and lights of the festival were merely a faint hum out on the bay. And inside Logan's trawler it was even quieter and darker. Ash swore that he could hear the darkness breathing. Like a ravenous beast awaiting its prey. But his paranoia made no sense. Very little did anymore. Though he didn't understand it, he was changing. So he just tried to ignore it. But in that uncomfortable moment he couldn't find anything to say that didn't sound like cheap small talk. After just showing up unannounced, he wasn't even sure she wanted him there. Scar just sat there, staring ahead blankly.

Ash had hardly harnessed control of the motor skills required to place his clammy hand on Scar's knee; but he was about as stiff as a piece of driftwood. By now, he could feel his breathing turning into wheezing. And he could only imagine how desperate he must have looked, stumbling over words, blinking uncontrollably, weaving back and forth in an effort to evade the impending nausea. He couldn't tell if he was actually causing the entire boat to rock. He clenched his teeth, trying to regain his composure. Then he just blurted it out.

"We could run away, you know." An embarrassing crackle splintered his voice. He wondered if the humility of puberty would ever end.

"You don't want to run away with me. You just want someone to run away with." Scar's words stung. But she was partially right. And even though Ash's feelings for her ran deep already, there was no denying that someone—anyone—to run away with would certainly soften the blow. "I have no reason to stay here," he continued, recoiling his hand out of embarrassment. "I mean, I can't imagine facing my father again after what happened." Logan had already begun spreading vicious rumors about his stepson and his *freakish, evil mutations*.

"What happened?" Scar asked.

Suddenly Ash realized that he had said too much. He had no idea how to explain his strange supernatural experience to Scar. He couldn't even explain it to himself.

"Nothing," Ash resorted to. "We had a fight, that's all."

"Are you okay?" Scar asked, placing her hand on his cheek.

Ash couldn't understand how she could be asking him if he was okay when she was the one who had an entire village hunting her down. But the touch of her hand was about the only thing registering to him in the moment. What he wanted to do was leap over to her and kiss her. What he did, though, was nothing—not even the slightest acknowledgement of her move. For the life of him, Ash couldn't figure out what it was about him that made him clam up the second someone made a move to get close to him.

Over the past week, since meeting Scar, he had felt as though he was on a natural high, floating above the clouds of Garbbit Harbor. The closer they got, the higher he felt. But now that she was beginning to show signs of actually needing him, Ash felt only the cold grip of fear closing in around him—afraid he might lose her—*not so different than Wick had put it.*

Scar withdrew her hand and looked away. Ash couldn't tell if she was put out by his lack of reaction. What he did notice though was the small black stain her hand had left on his coat. *What was it?*

Back in the village, the crowds were inflating into a tight, congested state. The music was getting louder. And so were the conversations, fueled by the flowing kegs of ale. This was the time of night when the dancing began and everyone let their guard down. It was the one moment of the year when the citizens of these small bayside villages felt as though they were the luckiest people in all of the world. Wick, however, loathed the overly jubilant crowds whose drunken stumbles often knocked him around like a piece of rubbish.

The old wharfling was so small that the majority of the foot traffic literally ran him over if he didn't keep a sharp eye. But right now Wick didn't care. All he wanted to do was get home after such an embarrassingly disastrous magic show. As he slowly towed his cart down the narrow, cobblestone-street, a strange green light began to bounce off the puddles in front of him.

Looking up, Wick saw strange circular formations of green lights obscured by the haze of the dense clouds. The lights definitely were not fireworks. They were too faint. And they appeared to be growing brighter—coming closer. Within moments, every eye in the vast sea of people on the plaza behind him was fixed on the lights in the sky. The music, the laughing, everything had stopped. Wick knew it wasn't the light of the moons. These lights were like nothing anyone in the village had ever seen before.

As the crowd began to grow hysterical, Wick felt as though he was alone, standing in the middle of a hurricane of panic swirling around him. He felt as though he was the only one who had a clue as to what the lights may be. And his greatest fear was that he might be right: the arrival of the legendary drone-armada.

There were about twenty green, round lights in each group. And each group formed a circle that seemed to be descending upon the village in an evenly dispersed configuration. As they grew closer they grew larger, brighter, and louder. Wick was now convinced: these were the giant drone-zeppelins of the mighty armada.

Rumors of these massive blimps secretly patrolling the skies had been surfacing over the past couple of years. Traders often spoke of these sightings, avowing that a growing army of drone-zeppelins were now monitoring the world from the heavens. However, the villagers of Garbbit Harbor remained little more than suspicious as their limit of understanding went only as far as the perpetual ceiling of clouds. That is, until now.

Suddenly a giant, black metal sphere, pierced through the clouds, falling from the center of one of the light formations. It was nearly the size of a small building. And when it struck the ground with a thunderous smash, it crushed everything beneath it, shaking everything around it. Its heavy black mass sank nearly a quarter of its height into a crater of mud twice its diameter.

Wick froze as the crowd scattered in a panicked screaming frenzy. He knew now that his premonition had been correct. In the distance, multiple spheres began to drop from the other zeppelins hovering over the village. But what happened next made everything up to that point seem frivolous.

One last giant sphere fell through the clouds, landing directly on top of the Garbbit Clock Tower, causing it to crumble instantly from its roof to its foundation. The sound was like that of an exploding bomb. Through it, the clock's bells could be heard chiming out of tune and out of existence. And as it fell, a massive cloud of dust, as thick and robust as a tidal wave, screamed out from the base of the tower, chasing the fleeing crowds through every singe street and alleyway they could escape to.

If Wick hadn't already made his way out of the center of the congested crowd he would have never had a chance of escaping—especially since no one would have ever stopped for him. So when he saw the crowd of dust-covered villagers emerging from the monstrous cloud, he dropped the handles of his cart and began to run as fast as his little old legs would allow. But it wasn't fast enough. Within only moments he found himself being trampled into the cold, wet, muddy street.

There were six spheres. And since most villagers knew nothing of the drone-armada, many of them assumed this was some sort of alien invasion. For a moment nothing happened. And then, as if a switch was flipped, green sparks began to crackle around the surface of the larger spheres and they began to roll slowly, crushing everything in their path: buildings, statues, vehicles, animals, even people. Though they appeared to be nothing more that giant orbs of steel, the drone-crushers moved in very systematic patterns, obliterating Garbbit Harbor's town square in just moments. As this was happening, dozens of smaller spheres, approximately the size of vehicles, fell from the zeppelins, smashing to the ground.

What appeared to be two long, black, antenna-like tentacles, erected from each smaller sphere until they bent to the ground in a giant arch, falling under their own weight. Suddenly the smaller spheres lifted into the air and the two tentacles began to stride forward. A small green light atop their spherical structure pulsated as it walked. These were the drone-striders—teargas and flame-throwing robots that stood as tall as a two-story building when on foot. They took incredibly long strides as their spherical bodies bobbed in the air at the other end of their arching legs.

From inside the Harbor Pub, Logan watched as these violent events unfolded on the other side of the pub window. A gang of regulars crowded around him like children, as though he was able to do something to stop all of this. Rubbing the bandages on his burnt hand, he couldn't help but wonder if this didn't have something to do with that girl Ash had been hiding. *Could one girl be so important?*

As the giant drones began to spread through the streets, one final wave of spheres descended from the clouds. The sight was quite familiar to Logan as he watched the sky fill with literally hundreds of black, falling objects, drifting down among the blowing flurry of snow. Like a swarm of falling boulders, hundreds upon hundreds of even smaller spheres came down, avoiding fatal impact by the drag of their parachutes.

Once they made landfall, Logan could see that he was right. It was a massive paratrooper legion of soldiers—a drone version of the very type of unit he served in during the Great War. Just before they hit the ground, their parachutes disintegrated into a strange electrical flash, and black silky limbs emerged from the spheres. Without stumbling or missing a beat, the drone-soldiers simply filed into organized squadrons, marching in perfect, short, choppy unison, almost as if they were programmed at high-speed.

They were tall, headless beings with large round torsos and long, thin limbs, which had large, metal armor plates attached to their forearms and shins. Two retractable antennae erected from the tops of their bodies, their tips rapidly blinking green flashes, signaling the state of emergency. The soldiers had a huge single eye in the middle of their chests. When thronged together, the smoky air around them was illuminated in this blinking green light.

The drone-crushers followed the drone-striders, who dispersed and scrambled quickly to the faces of the buildings. With systematic precision, the striders struck first. They shot green tear gas at the buildings with such force that it blew out all of the windows and doors. As the hiding people poured out the other side of the building, they were met by legions of drone-soldiers, who filtered them out in single file. A swarm of small, head-sized floating spheres waited at bay. Once the victims were segregated into specific groups, the floating spheres (drone-inoculators) began injecting mysterious micro-capsules into the palms of every single villager. No one knew what was happening. It was sheer ghastly madness. The only clarity came in the form of a vociferous synthetic voice echoing throughout the streets: "Attention. Kingland has declared a state of emergency rule on all territories of the Allied Kingdoms. Your cooperation is vital for your own protection. Inoculation of everyone is mandatory as a preventative measure against impending plague attacks by the Pirate Rogue. Please, do not resist. Repeat …"

Of course, no one had any idea that they were actually being injected with drone-implants.

Once a building had been evacuated, the crushers would roll in and completely demolish the building, simply by rolling over it. This procedure would be duplicated repeatedly until everyone was accounted for. Through the smoke and swirling snow, the air was lit by the strobe of green, flashing light emitting from the sea of drone-soldiers.

Everyone had fled the Harbor Pub, except for Logan, who remained frozen, standing in front of the window. For the first time in a long time he felt small. But then a familiar figure emerged from the smoke that rendered him completely helpless.

It seemed almost supernatural how General Bontey instantly made eye contact with Logan from outside, across the street. In a few long, hard strides, Bontey crossed the street and smashed through the door and gripped Logan by the throat with his claws, till a thin film of blood began to ooze out from behind his fingernails.

"I know you," Bontey whispered, his rotten breath gagging Logan. He recognized Logan from another time. And as images of that forgotten past flashed into Bontey's mind, he began to see an old farmhouse on a hill. In the attic there was a small room—a boy's bedroom. *It was the same boy he had seen a dozen years earlier.* And then he saw a girl: *Scar! She was with the boy!* More images flashed ... *The boy and girl were on a boat in the harbor.* But there was something about the boy's bedroom that was quite curious indeed.

Bontey looked deep into Logan's eyes. Logan felt consciousness drifting away. He was no longer the hero. Without the security of the people and familiar buildings surrounding him, he was nothing more than a washed-up fisherman. Grief and guilt rushed over him. He knew that he had allowed his own bitterness to destroy an innocent youth. By the time Bontey released his grip, Logan had drawn his last breath. Dropping Logan to the floor like a pile of wet clothing, Bontey turned and left the saloon.

Moments later Bontey entered Ash's attic bedroom alone. The images he siphoned from Logan's mind were not clear. But if what he saw was right, his mission was already about to take a rather interesting turn.

Pulling back the blanket on Ash's bed, the evidence was revealed. Two smears of dried bloodstains were soaked into the off-white sheets. It was the boy! But it was surreal to be standing in the bedroom of the very boy he had haunted so many years earlier. A great epiphany suddenly rushed over Bontey and he grabbed his radio from his utility belt and radioed to his drone-squadrons. "Squadron Three, proceed to the docks. Search all of the boats. She's there. She's with a boy."

Bontey was beginning to suspect the importance of this drone-girl. *Could she possibly have something to do with the Chrysalis?* he wondered.

Meanwhile, Ash and Scar knew nothing of the horrific events unfolding in the village. They were simply too far away. Even the pounding explosions that faintly lit the distant sky over the tree line looked no different than the grand finale fireworks that marked the climax of the annual festival. Besides, Ash's thoughts were infinitely further away.

After his spell of unresponsiveness, Ash had broken the long, uncomfortable silence by trying to be funny. He knew Scar must be desperate, because it worked. He had actually been pretending to be Logan—stumbling about the galley and barking slurred orders into the air. If only he knew what had just transpired.

"Is he really that bad?" Scar asked, trying to calm her own laugh.

It was a good question. And Ash actually pondered it, rather than just blurting out his usual, snappy response. "He's my father. I guess somewhere in there, there's a good man. I feel like I remember him being a kind and even gentle person, back when I was much younger. But he's just so self-consumed now. It's always about him."

"Then why do you stay?" Scar asked.

Ash sat back down and looked down into his lap. *Another good question.* Perhaps this was her way of saying yes to his suggestion of running away. All he could think of was how badly he would have liked to have just kissed her when she made that move.

It felt as though the room was shrinking as he moved closer to her. Looking up, he met her, eye to eye. It was obvious by the look in her eyes that she wavered about what she was doing as much as he did. But something had come over both of them and Ash wasn't about to mess it up this time.

Falling backward, Ash hit his head on a beam as Scar pressed her cold lips to his. She was cold, yet it felt like electricity. Ash had never been kissed before. It was better than flying. But it was short-lived. The loud crunch of a falling tree startled both of them into a frozen state of utter shock.

"What was that?" Scar asked, grabbing Ash's hand as he moved to look out the frosted portal window of the galley.

Ash didn't respond. He couldn't. He was listening. He could hear something stirring in the forest at the edge of the water—something large, something foreign. Then the treetops began to move.

Out from behind a grove of trees at the edge of the wharf, stepped three drone-striders. They were as alien to Ash as they were to the other villagers who had just suffered their wrath, only moments ago. Nothing could have prepared him for this. But to Scar, there was something familiar about them.

Ash shut down, petrified. His mind went blank as he slowly drifted away from the window. *What were these mechanical monsters?* And as they approached, Ash couldn't find the coordination to move any part of his body. It was like one of the many nightmares he suffered from. *This must be what the end of the world looks like,* he thought. For a moment he remembered Scar. But fear's spell had already rendered him helpless. Impressing her was now the furthest thing from his mind as she took his hand.

"Let's go!" Scar said, leading Ash up the stairs. Her combatant instincts had now taken over. But it was too late. She and Ash's commotion had already caught the attention of the striders, who scrambled quickly toward the ice, each marching down a separate dock. One of the striders briefly broke through the old wood of one of the docks, but quickly recovered and continued toward Logan's boat.

On the deck, Ash tried to formulate the best plan he could. But thinking on his feet, especially when he was riddled with fear, was pointless.

"Come on, grab the sword!" Scar yelled, pointing to an old tarnished switch-sword Logan had hanging below the railing. "Cut the straps!" Ash froze for a moment, unsure if this was a good idea. In spite of all of his childhood fantasies of adventure, he hadn't yet imagined actually using a weapon. It was almost like Scar was testing his courage. "Hurry!" Scar ordered in a very stern tone that made him see her in a new light. "Cut the straps and start the boat!"

"But the ice!" Ash yelled back. "We won't—"

"Yes we will," Scar shouted back, with no time to argue. "Just do it."

Ash knew now that Scar wasn't just guessing. She knew exactly what she was talking about. With a loud cough of black smoke, the trawler's motor fired up. And then dashing to the back of the boat, Ash grabbed the switch-sword, ejected its blade and whirled the sword clumsily through the air, slicing the straps. Just as one of the striders hurled a stream of flame at Scar, the rear of the boat fell free of the cradle and crashed through the thin layer of ice, causing the strider's flame to stream just over Scar's head.

Both Ash and Scar stumbled to the floor as the front of the boat slid back out of the cradle. The boat's rear propellers began smashing up the ice behind the boat like an auger, and to Ash's surprise, the old trawler actually began making its way out into the bay. But the striders were now upon them.

As the trawler jerked clumsily in reverse, busting through the ice, the three striders stepped out onto the ice in pursuit. One of them overstepped and rolled right into the wake of open water, cut open by the trawler. But the other two continued, making far better time than the trawler. Their wiry legs slipped around like the unstable feet of a young animal just learning to walk.

"They're gaining on us!" Ash yelled down from the trawler's navigation wheel.

"Open water just ahead!" Scar yelled up, looking further out into the bay. "We'll pick up speed once we hit it."

Suddenly one of the striders shot another stream of flame, catching the trawler's starboard on fire. Ash didn't know what to do as the flames crept further up the boat. Just as the other strider shot its fire, it stepped through the thinning ice, slamming its mass, busting open the ice with the weight of its body. As it sank away into the cold, black waters, the one that remained did something Ash didn't even know it was capable of.

Leaping from the edge of the ice, the strider bounded high into the air, landing gracefully onto the deck of the trawler. Ash and Scar scampered backward, but with the strider towering over them, there was nowhere to go. Ash shook with fear, unable to imagine a way out. But then the feeling returned.

His body tingled with the same numbing sensation he had felt the night he confronted Logan in his bedroom. Specks of light seemed to be glittering about his skin like a swarm of tiny fireflies. Looking up at the strider he then closed his eyes and clenched his teeth.

Scar didn't know what to think when she saw the fire literally leap onto the strider like an attacking animal. The flames engulfed its sphere, swirling around it like a hellish tornado. The strider stammered, trying to shake off the flame. But it was no use as its metal skin began to glow in the infernal heat. And then, like a bomb going off, the strider's body exploded into a ball of sparks and fire. Through the smoke Scar stared at Ash, who had nothing to say.

By the time Ash and Scar hit deeper water, where ice hadn't yet formed, the fire had moved back across nearly half of the trawler, causing it to begin sinking. Staring at her out of the corner of his eye, Ash couldn't imagine what Scar must be thinking after witnessing his freakish abilities. He didn't even know what *he* thought about it yet. All he could think of was what might happen next.

At the back of the boat, Ash and Scar huddled, coughing from the billowing smoke. Behind them, through the flurrying snow, Garbbit Harbor burned like a smoldering forest fire. The reality of it didn't register with Ash yet. He couldn't even get himself to think about who might not have survived. At that moment he was almost wishing that he himself had not made it, so he wouldn't have to endure one more second of this nightmare.

"Is there a life raft aboard?" Scar asked as the trawler continued to sink.

"There was," Ash responded, glancing back at the enclosing fire. "But it's already burned up." Then he turned and saw something. "Look! Reef Point! If we can get close enough we can swim."

It was a stretch, but he was right. If the trawler could hold out just a few moments more, he and Scar could jump overboard and swim the short distance to the peninsula. The real question would be whether they could survive the freezing waters.

Twenty Two
Thieves' Hollow

By now the incredible chill had settled deep into Ash's bones. As the flame-engulfed fishing trawler slowly succumbed to its watery grave, he and Scar sat on the rocky shores of Reef Point, holding each other's shivering, soaked bodies. In spite of the hardship Ash had experienced for so many years aboard his father's boat, it was heartbreaking to see it reduced to a pile of sinking rubble.

Shadows of the giant drone-zeppelins moved slowly across the overcast night as Garbbit Harbor burned in the distance. It was as surreal as it could get. Ash's youth was gone. All he had ever known had been burned away in only a matter of moments.

He knew there was nothing impressive about his uncontrollable tears. But he didn't care. *What was left to prove to Scar anyway? This had to be the end.* It certainly felt like it. He couldn't imagine anything else, even for his future with Scar. All of those dreams of great, dangerous adventures and seeing the other worlds now seemed like stupid childish notions. Ash hated himself for being so naive. All he wanted was his own bed in his own room. He wondered if he would ever have that again.

"C'mon," Ash said, helping Scar to her feet. He couldn't stand to watch any longer. Besides, he was freezing.

"Where are we going?" she asked.

"Thieves' Hollow," he answered, igniting a blue, hand-held light-stick. "Wick told me that in the event of an emergency this would be the best place to hide. It's kind of our secret place." A lump formed in his throat as he thought of what Wick was possibly going through at that very moment, or if Wick was even still alive.

Entering the cave, the air was cold and moist and smelled like dead animal. It was an old mining shaft, which had since become a refuge for giant vulture-bats and countless other nocturnal creatures. The sound of insects scattering about and tiny reptiles slithering away gave it an even creepier feeling. It was as though they had entered the darkened domain of the damned.

Ash kept his eyes fixed on the small area just ahead—the short distance of the light-stick's illumination. Every creak and crack made his heart jump and his skin crawl. The only thing keeping him from turning around and running right back outside was the mental image of his father's burning trawler—that and the fact that Scar was holding his hand. She empowered him to keep going. Suddenly they heard a sound.

"What was that?" asked Scar.

"Wasn't it you?" Ash asked, hiding his expression from Scar—feeling the panic in his own eyes.

"No," whispered Scar.

The sound repeated itself. It sounded like footsteps. Then something moved out of the corner of Ash's eye. He jumped back, raising the light-stick over his head in defense. Drawing his switch-sword hadn't yet become a habit. But it soon enough would.

"It's me!" a familiar voice echoed. "Don't hit me, boy!" Wick yelled, cowering under his own arm.

"Wick?" Ash exclaimed with excitement. He held the light-stick up to Wick, who was covered in smeared soot and peppered in small cuts over his skin and clothing. It was obvious that getting to Thieves' Hollow wasn't an easy task. "What are you doing here?"

"Yes, well nice to see you too," Wick jested. "I fled the harbor the moment everything began."

"The minute what began?" Ash asked. "What's happening? What are those giant machines?"

For a moment Wick said nothing, as he recalled just how he had narrowly escaped.

Had it not been for the fact that Wick was amphibious, able to hold his breath for incredible periods of time, he may not have survived the crushing cloud of dust that swept the village after the fall of the tower. But as he made his way to the wharfling marshlands, he found himself being pursued by a squadron of drone-soldiers. Again, the uniqueness of his species proved to be the difference between life and death.

As the drone-soldiers gained on Wick, he led them right to the edge of the marshlands, where the land is nothing more than a bog. So, just like the striders on the ice, the soldiers simply broke through the ground, sinking into the murky waters. Wick then slipped beneath the ice and swam to Reef Point, completely undetected.

"It's a drone-contract-armada," Wick said.

"Drone? Like robots?" Ash asked fuddled as Scar twitched uncomfortably.

"Precisely," Wick replied, glancing at Scar. "Contracted by Kingland."

"What? But I thought Kingland was a peaceful kingdom," Ash said.

"I thought so too," Wick said regrettably.

"Well I'm sure Kingland will soon come and stop this armada," Ash said naively. "Obviously these robots are acting out on their own."

"One would think," Wick said quietly. "But they do bear the crest of Kingland. I fear they are legitimate." Then he stopped and walked over at Scar, who was staring blankly into the shadows. "It appears something has changed." Wick's expression was grave as he glowered at Scar.

"So what's left of the harbor?" Ash asked, desperate to figure out just how bad things really were. He almost hoped Wick wouldn't respond.

"Not much," Wick said quietly. "Not much at all." Ash's thoughts flashed like a blurry photo-strip of images, racing through his mind. He saw everyone he knew and wondered if they were still alive. *Did his father escape? And what about Paulo?* There were many bittersweet emotions that left Ash sick to his stomach. He wanted answers, yet he didn't.

"My father," Ash stuttered, "did he make it?"

"I don't think so, Ash," Wick said, laying his little hand on Ash's arm. "The drone-soldiers were inoculating everyone with something. They were rounding everyone up like livestock. And those who resisted were eliminated. I know sure as heck your father wouldn't have budged. But I can't be sure," he added, noticing a surprising tinge of sadness in Ash's eyes.

Talking so blatantly about Logan's death felt cold and heartless. But it was such a two-sided coin with this topic. After all, he had spent his entire youth admitting that he actually hated the man. It wasn't until this moment that Ash was able to admit to himself that perhaps somewhere, deep within, he had preserved a bit of compassion for his father. Death was certainly not what he had ever wished upon him—not like this. Not after the pain Ash had inflicted upon him. Guilt washed over Ash like a cold nausea.

"What are they inoculating us against?" Scar asked, clenching her fists to hide her scars.

Wick thought for a moment, noticing the tears in Ash's eyes. "No one seems to know," he said with concern. "I, for one, don't trust any of it. With this new drone-security force, Kingland is beginning to resemble an authoritarian-type regime more and more all of the time. And this is only proof. It's nothing more than a hostile takeover, if you ask me. Little, insignificant harbors like us don't matter. We don't stand a chance."

"So what do we do now?" asked Ash in a tone of innocence that reminded Wick of when the boy was a young child.

"Your father has a friend," he said, pausing in an effort to shake the horrific images from his mind's eye. "He *had* a friend who has access to a secret, secluded cabana in the Glades of Saur. According to Logan, his friend was always more than happy to rent it out for the right price."

"But we don't have any money," Ash said, sinking down.

Wick then pulled out a near-bursting pouch filled with coins. "We'll be fine, boy."

"Where'd you get that?" Ash asked, wide-eyed.

"I may not make a lot of money," Wick admitted. But I spend even less. First we need to go see this friend of Logan's."

"Where?" Scar asked.

"Cobbleton."

"Cobbleton? The big city?" Ash asked, sparking up. He had never been to Cobbleton before. But he had heard many stories of how big and exciting Murk's largest city was.

"Yes," Wick answered much less enthused. "It's about five days' journey to the south. We'll have to use caution though. The swamps between here and there are haunted by things that most don't live to talk about."

Ash tried to pretend he didn't even hear that part. "How long will we stay at the cabana?" he asked.

"Until things blow over," Wick answered, glancing over at Scar.

Ash noticed Wick's shift of attention to Scar. He knew there was something Wick wasn't telling him.

"C'mon kids," Wick said. "Let's set up camp."

On the hills overlooking the smoldering remains of Garbbit Harbor, Sayto Bontey stood assessing the situation. He programmed LePrey's frequency into the radio embedded in his prosthetic arm.

"I am on the girl's trail," Bontey spoke into the radio. "It won't be long before I have her. But she is with a boy."

"A boy?" LePrey asked, obviously confused as to why Bontey would waste time reporting such a minuscule detail.

"Not just any boy," Bontey continued. "He's the one."

The frequency went silent for a long time. LePrey was clearly spellbound with amazement of this news. Bontey knew that this discovery would change everything for LePrey. But he had no idea how much it could change the course of history.

"Do not harm him," LePrey finally ordered with panic. He knew that eliminating Ash would leave the Enigma vulnerable to Bontey. And that was a terrifying scenario no one wanted. Knowing too well Bontey's vulnerability to money, LePrey made him another offer he couldn't refuse. "I will double your fee if you bring him in along with the girl."

Bontey accepted.

Twenty Three
The Vyne

Fire danced, painting a spectacular display of flickering light and shadows on the cave's moist walls. Scar looked as though she was about to pass out. So, using some old blankets he found in the cave, Ash made a modest bed for her. He had watched her fall asleep every night since meeting her. But tonight she appeared especially frail and distant. Seeing her like this broke his heart. His feelings for her had already grown to the point of necessity. And with everything else gone, he needed her now more than ever.

As she curled up in the shadows, Ash and Wick huddled over a pot of simmering soup made from supplies Wick had stashed in the cave—supplies he had always hoped he'd never have the need to use.

Watching Wick busy himself with the cooking, Ash slouched back against the stone wall and pulled out Logan's switch-sword. The weight of the heavy sword wasn't easy for his arm to control. It was much heavier than the sticks he and Paulo often used when playing pirates in the Lonesome Pine. Logan had always made it seem like such an insignificant tool in his giant hands.

"A powerful weapon," Wick mumbled in protest. He still hadn't broken the habit of trying to politely reprove Ash's behavior every time he saw something he didn't agree with. "You must respect its power if you are to use it wisely."

Ash rolled his eyes and quickly retracted the blade, slipping it back through his belt.

"When talking about Kingland and this invasion, you said that something had changed," Ash said. "I don't understand."

"They're after something," Wick whispered, making sure the conversation remained only within Ash's range of hearing.

"After what?" Ash asked, sipping the delectable-tasting soup from the ladle.

Concluding an awkward silence, Wick picked the ladle up and sampled the soup for himself. "Perhaps now isn't the best time," he said, glancing over at Scar.

"What are you afraid she's going to hear?" Ash asked, growing tired of Wick's paranoia regarding Scar.

Suddenly Wick's eyes locked in on Ash's, staring deep into his soul. The expression frightened Ash.

"Okay," he replied while serving up a bowl of soup for each of them. Then, reaching into the pocket of his poncho, Wick pulled out the strange golden medallion. Ash could have sworn that a cold breeze had suddenly drifted into the cave. The look on Wick's face told Ash that this was certainly no arbitrary relic.

"What is it?" Ash asked. Though mysterious, there was something strangely familiar about the medallion.

"The Enigma," Wick whispered, with trembling intensity. Though he hadn't proven this yet to be true, he had a burning feeling he was right.

"Where did you get it?" Ash asked, his eyes steadied on its golden surface.

Wick tried to answer more than once, tripping over his own words. "Migg found it at the bottom of the lake," he finally got out, "in a small, broken-down submarine." He then leaned into Ash's face and whispered, "I believe the sub can be traced back to Scar. If so, then so can this sacred medallion."

"Sacred? What are you talking about?" Ash asked, struggling to swallow a large lump in his throat.

"Let me tell you a story," Wick said, scooting closer to Ash. The orange light of the fire rippled across his face as he began.

"Since you were a boy you've heard me often speak of the Imcot people." *Often* was a gross understatement. Wick was obsessed with Imcot lore. "But what few people know of this mysterious society is that aside from being technologically advanced, the Imcot were keepers of a sacred stellar code—a highly advanced measurement of time. They credit their enlightenment to something quite mysterious they referred to as the Chrysalis. Legend claims that it is the eye to the future, foretelling countless events throughout history—even predicting the end of time."

Ash briefly choked on his soup. "Have any of the predictions come true?" he asked.

"So far, all of them," Wick answered stone-faced. Ash stopped eating. "Let me elaborate," he said, recognizing the awe in Ash's eyes. "According to the Imcot, time expands and retracts in cycles spanning tens of thousands of years. The Alpha and Omega points, where one cycle ends and another begins, have always represented monumental epochs, or distinct periods in the evolution of our world—each one more significant than the last. It has been a hundred thousand years since we last crossed an epoch. That was the dawn of the civilized world. And now we find ourselves at a most unique place."

"Why?" Ash pried cautiously.

With eyes that seemed to tell a story of their own, Wick whispered, "Because we are now upon the next epoch. The apocalyptic prediction. The world is at the threshold of another crossroads of evolution."

"Then this can only be good, right?" Ash fished for a shred of positive news. "We just wait and let it happen?"

"Not necessarily." Wick's disconcerting reply came as no surprise. "The Imcot also referred to the epoch as a Decision Point—presumably a nexus between destruction or our very survival."

Ash recalled the many tales Wick had told him over the years, trying to find a silver lining in this doomsday scenario. "You always said that the Imcot were so advanced because of dragons. You called it their gift of enlightenment." Wick nodded in agreement. He was proud that the boy still remembered his stories. "Where are dragons now? Why don't they come to our rescue like they did the Imcot?"

"Dragons came to this world nearly two thousand years ago, as a form of divine intervention." Wick began to expound, "A way to help our societies progress and avoid self-destruction. That was before the New World settlers. Upon discovering the secluded Imcot society, the settlers didn't understand these fire-breathing monsters living among them. But the prophecy of the Chrysalis was the greatest threat to their industrial sprawl. The settlers declared war, wiping dragons from the face of the map and extinguishing the spread of knowledge of the Chrysalis. What the settlers didn't realize was that in an effort to protect their growing domain, they were threatening the very future of it."

The moment Wick uttered those words he couldn't help but be transported to a similar scene around a campfire, when he was but a youngling himself. His grandfather, a native of the marshlands of Murk, shared with him the true story of what really happened between native wharflings and the first settlers of Murk. It wasn't anything like what most people had grown up being taught.

At first, the settlers of Murk were frightened of wharflings and responded in a violent surge of genocide. The settlers succeeded in killing tens of thousands of wharflings from the northern marshlands and even legitimized the buying and trading of wharfling skin. It took nearly a century before the courts of Murk put a legal end to this travesty.

"And what about the Imcot people?" Ash asked, refocusing Wick's attention. "Were they slaughtered too?"

"Glad you asked," Wick said, warming his pudgy hands over the soup. "They were not like the societies of today. No. The Imcot were a perfectly peaceful society. They lived among the dragons and fed off of their magic." Ash's eyes drew a skeptical expression the moment Wick uttered the word *magic*—skeptical it might become another one of his silly fairy tales. "Tragically ironic, their demise was at the hand of a group of Imcot traitors who broke away and succumbed to the influence of the New World settlers.

"In exchange for money, they joined forces with the settlers and actually became the backbone of this slaughter. The remaining Imcot took it upon themselves to protect the Chrysalis, locking it away until the world is truly ready for the power of its truth. This is where it gets interesting." Ash's eyes grew wider.

"Twelve Imcot were appointed by the Great White Dragon, the queen of dragons, to protect their secret treasure. They referred to themselves as Guardians," Wick continued with more energy. "The White Dragon entrusted them with a powerful gift, one that would save them in their darkest times. She anointed them with supernatural abilities, empowering them for a life indebted to protecting the Chrysalis. Then the rest of the Imcot simply vanished from existence, entrusting their secrets to the Guardians."

"They disappeared?" Ash asked, almost too loudly.

"Gone. Like magic," Wick demonstrated with the same animated hand gesture he used in his magic shows.

"And what about the secret?" Ash asked. "Does anyone know what it is?"

Wick jumped right back into his story, as though he was trying to keep up with himself. "The formula to achieving the elixir of life. It is believed that the Chrysalis is more than a mere eye to the future, bearing the power to manipulate time and create eternal life."

Ash's head was spinning. He didn't know what to believe. "Do the Guardians know where the Chrysalis is?" he finally stuttered out, trying to control the terrible shiver that had since consumed his every mannerism.

"One anonymous Guardian was appointed *the one*. They were given the Enigma," he said, holding the medallion up to the firelight, "encrypted with a map—a set of coordinates leading to the location of the Chrysalis. But legend says that only by means of the Hidden Ember can the Chrysalis be found. This mysterious entity is essential to unlocking the secret of the treasure. Skeptics believe that the Hidden Ember is nothing more than a meaningless fabrication, meant to deter people from going after the treasure. But others, like myself, believe differently. I believe that whatever this mystery is, it is no different than a threshold one must cross in order to achieve the treasure. In fact, the prophecy says that *only the one who is worthy may pass beyond this threshold and be entrusted with the pursuit of the Chrysalis.*" Ash seemed thoroughly confused. "Think of it as a time capsule," Wick simplified. "When the world is ready, the treasure map will be unlocked, the Chrysalis will be found and its secret revealed. You must understand, Ash; this time is now." His actions were now growing slightly manic. "The world is at a Decision Point."

"Are you able to decode the encryption of the Enigma?" Ash asked, studying the medallion in Wick's steady hand.

"No, I'm not that good, boy. But let me explain." Wick continued his story with a slight smile. "The Enigma was genetically coded to reveal the coordinates, only when in the hand of *the one*, the Guardian who was chosen to bear it. With the bearer still anonymous, the twelve Guardians split up, remaining committed to the preservation of the Chrysalis and passing on their supernatural gifts to future generations. They called their underground sect the Vyne.

"Over centuries, legends surrounding the Chrysalis came to consider it as something quite different. In fact, alchemists continue to misinterpret its meaning, considering it synonymous with their sought after Philosopher's Stone. Pirates and scavengers have rivaled in vain to hunt it down, hoping to achieve an endless bounty of gold. Through it all, the Vyne remained true to its oath, keeping their secret perfectly safe. But as happened with the Imcot, it was from within that the Vyne met their most dangerous enemy.

"After centuries of hiding, there came a Guardian leader who simply wanted to know the riddle of the Chrysalis and unlock the power it possessed. He began seeking out and killing off the other leaders of the Vyne in search of the Enigma, which would lead him to it. But there was one Guardian who was able to elude him: the bearer of the Enigma itself.

"For years pirates have obsessed over the Enigma's whereabouts. But they have always come up empty handed."

"So with the fall of the Vyne, is the Chrysalis lost forever?" Ash asked, unsure of where this tale might be headed. "And what does this have to do with anything that's going on around us right now?"

Wick squinted over his soup at Scar's slumbering body. "Hold on," he whispered, setting his bowl on the floor and leaning into Ash's face. "There's much more."

"Ash," he said, staring into the boy's deep brown eyes. "Do you remember when you were young and you asked me if your mother was ever coming back?"

"Yes," Ash said, wishing he couldn't remember that moment in time.

"Well, it's time you knew the truth." Ash shivered at the thought of what he might be about to learn.

"At the close of the Great War, I was running a boarding house for refugees of war-torn territories as well as injured army veterans. That was when I met your father."

"He was a wreck when he first walked through my door. But it wasn't his physical wounds that I was worried about. It was his heart. It was broken. As you know, his first wife and son had written him off while he was struggling to survive in an enemy prison camp."

Ash knew most of this already. Logan seemed to enjoy reminding Ash of how he didn't compare to his first son, Lok, even though Lok wouldn't even acknowledge Logan as his father anymore. It made no sense at all to Ash that Logan couldn't embrace the son who actually tried to love him. But there was nothing he could do about it anymore. He shook his head in a vain effort to purge his mind of these disturbing thoughts.

"One day a mysterious woman came through the camp," Wick continued. "She gave up very little about her past. I think that's what attracted your father to her. They soon fell in love, got a place of their own, and had a child: you. But while you were still very young—"

"Yeah, I know the rest," Ash cut in curtly. His face became flush with anger. He had learned to hate his mother because of her abandonment. "She flipped out and ran away. Look, I already know this stupid story. My mother was a freak!" And he slammed his bowl down, splattering soup onto his pants.

"No, Ash," Wick said, gesturing for Ash to quiet down. He didn't want Scar hearing any of this. "That's what Logan said. But I'm telling you the truth."

Ash picked his bowl up again and slowly stirred what soup was left. He had no reason to believe Wick's version of the truth over what he had believed for sixteen years. But then again, he had no reason not to.

"The bearer of the Enigma was your mother." Ash's eyes shot wide open as he forgot how to swallow. Wick knew this would hit him hard. "She was pursued around the world and ended up in Murk, where she met your father. She thought she had outrun the fallen Guardian. But when you were still quite young, he tracked her down. That is why she had to leave so quickly."

Ash couldn't speak. He felt afraid. He so badly didn't want this to be true.

"Listen," Wick said, attempting to translate the engravings on the surface of the medallion. "*Upon the end of time will come the face of great deception. And the shadow of tribulation shall fall. But from the most unlikely of places will rise the one who will awaken the hidden truth.*" By now, Ash was trembling. "It's a prophetic riddle, Ash," Wick whispered with a smile.

"About what?" Ash asked. He was terrified that he already knew the answer.

"You mean, *about who?*" Wick said poking Ash with the ladle.

There was a very long moment of silence as Ash allowed all of this to sink in. Part of him wondered if this wasn't just another one of Wick's attempts to get Ash's mind off the drama at hand.

"I don't believe you," he said with imperious eyes. "I don't need your stupid stories."

"Look," Wick tried to temper Ash, "before your mother left, she asked me to watch over you. She knew that with her gone, you were now *the one.*"

"*The one?*" Ash asked skeptically.

"Yes," Wick said nodding. "The *one* spoken of in this engraving." Ash felt sick to his stomach. "Look, Ash," Wick continued, "I know what your gift is—the unexplainable strength. The fire." In a strange way, Ash was not at all surprised by Wick's insight.

"You mean *curse*," Ash mumbled with his head hung low. He could feel his scars burning, which meant they were probably bleeding again.

"No!" Wick shot back, a bit louder than he would have liked. "Your mother possessed the same gift. It is a genetic trait every true Guardian of the Vyne is born with—the scars on your back." Ash felt sick with anxiety. His entire life he had wondered what they were. "You were born with wings Ash. All Guardians are—or were. But after your mother left, Logan removed them to conceal your identity."

Ash was speechless, unsure if he should even believe this esoteric tale.

"Conceal it from who?" he asked with a quivering voice.

"From you," Wick answered sympathetically. "He despised what you are because of what it did to your mother. But that was his misconception—a misconception that has stifled you your entire life. But you can free yourself from that now. You were born to fly, Ash."

"Not without wings," Ash mumbled soberly.

Wick had nothing to say to this. It wasn't worth trying to convince Ash of everything all in one sitting. Not now.

"But you are now the last Guardian of the Chrysalis," he informed him, taking Ash by the hand. "And you have the genetic power in your hand to reveal the coordinates to the Chrysalis, to reveal its secrets to the world. You can save the world." Wick smiled with fatherly eyes that twinkled in the firelight.

"From what?" Ash exclaimed. "You don't even know what the end of time means, let alone what the Chrysalis is."

Wick bit his tongue, trying not to get upset with Ash's teenage insolence. "This is not a chart of statistics. It's a prophecy. And it is about you."

It hurt Wick to have to say that. He was no more ready for Ash to graduate into this arena than he was. But he was not in control anymore. He placed the Enigma in Ash's right hand and sat back. An expression of uncontainable anticipation crossed Wick's face.

Ash remembered the time he had tripped over an electric fence on the edge of Paulo's uncle's field. But even that blast of electrical shock was nothing compared to what he was feeling now, holding this mysterious golden medallion. Looking down, Ash could already see white light spilling through the cracks of his fingers. And as his trembling hand slowly opened, he couldn't believe his eyes. A cool breeze swept through the cave, nearly extinguishing the fire. He couldn't find the coordination to draw breath or the strength to even blink. Indeed, this was the real thing. *The Enigma!*

Though the engravings upon the medallion's surface hadn't changed, specific ones were now glowing white. It was like a light within the medallion was glowing through the lines of the etchings.

"What does this mean?" Ash asked with a crackle in his voice. "Is it like a mood ring?" Because the legend of the Imcot had been diluted to mere folklore, similar cheap replicas of medallions like this, and even rings, had been forged and were often sold in the jewelry markets.

When held by a warm hand they would reveal faint glowing markings, no different than a mood ring. But this was no reaction caused by body heat.

Wick leaned closer and read the glowing markings. "The medallion is genetically coded to you Ash. Only in your hand can this secret encryption be revealed. The glowing engravings are the coordinates leading to what appears to be the first cipher on the trail of riddles leading to the Chrysalis."

"Cipher?" Ash asked.

"A cryptic marker on the map's course," Wick replied. Then, gazing into Ash's eyes he uttered quietly, "The Hidden Ember."

Ash trembled. Wick's stare went right through him. And he hated it. This was already a destiny he wanted to ignore. But the more Wick divulged, the less choice Ash seemed to have in the matter.

"It too, is also a riddle," Wick admitted. Studying the glowing markings, he read on. "*That which is hidden must be found. But only by the worthy. Only the one who proceeds in the steps of faith, to the waters' end. Through the gateway to the waters beneath the waters awaits the slumbering beast. Seek not for your own prosperity, but for the deliverance of others. For the hand that fears shall be turned away. And the greedy will be cut off.*"

The cave was frightfully silent as Ash sat frozen, with the glowing medallion in his palm.

Wick then leaned into Ash's face, as if looking right through him. "Are you ready?"

"Ready for what?" Ash asked. He felt as though he couldn't keep up with it all. "Am I supposed to go after the Chrysalis?"

The answer came in the form of silence. In the last few moments, Ash had just gone from a trouble-making juvenile to the prophesied protector of the greatest treasure of all time. Frankly, he couldn't even begin to fathom how any of this was to come to fruition.

"The Chrysalis—it is alive," Wick replied quietly, checking over the boy's shoulder again to make sure Scar was still sleeping. "The prophecy says that when the time comes for *the one* to embrace their destiny, the treasure will reveal itself. It is ready to be found. It must be found. There are forces of evil in this world that will stop at nothing to suppress it. And just as the New World settlers did to the Imcot, or even the first settlers of Murk, a new world order is being instituted across the face of the globe, destroying all that we know, replacing it with utter lifelessness. But I believe the world *is* ready for the hidden truth behind the Chrysalis. It is time."

Ash pondered for a long cold moment. "Then maybe leaving the Chrysalis alone would be best," he suggested sluggishly. "I mean, maybe unearthing it would only put it in jeopardy of being taken by these dark forces."

"We do not fully understand the mystery of the Chrysalis," Wick defended quickly. For Wick, that much was certain. "All we can do is have faith in the prophecies and act accordingly. Remember, the Chrysalis is more than a treasure. The fate of the world balances on this very moment in history—this Decision Point. And you, Ash, are at the absolute nexus of it.

"You've been given a powerful responsibility. One you should not take lightly. The power to save the world from its own destruction lies within your hand. But time is not on our side. If you fail to act now I fear that our course might take on that of the most damning of predictions."

Ash felt as though he might vomit. "I'm scared," he whispered, unaware that his words were even audible. To his dismay, it was all beginning to make sense.

"Fear is natural," Wick said kindly. "How you deal with it is what determines your destiny. This is not a matter of becoming something you're not. It's simply a matter of realizing and facing what you already are. In time you will understand. Embracing the truth is the first step. Everything happens when it does for a reason. You weren't supposed to know about this until this very moment. This is your coming of age,

Ash. It is why your Mystery hasn't been fully realized until now. You *are* ready."

"How do you know?" Ash asked. "I don't feel ready."

Wick's expression grew almost saddened as he pondered what to say. "Because I've waited your entire life for this moment." Wick's eyes glistened with threatening tears. Ash could feel his intensity as he stifled his emotions. "There's so much more to you than you realize. You are ready to be a Guardian—to unearth real truth to the world."

A chill swept across Ash's body like a gust of winter wind as he let it all sink in. "If I'm ready, then why don't you trust me to make my own decisions about Scar?" Ash said.

Wick's agitation at the reemergence of this topic quickly transformed his face. "Scar is a wanted fugitive," he reminded Ash.

"She's no thief," Ash defended again. "She's not hiding anything."

"Perhaps," Wick replied, "but that Slave Lord doesn't know that. And he won't know until they find her. And those hunting her won't stop until she is found. In the meantime, you and I are simply setting ourselves up as victims of her collateral damage. We need to distance ourselves from her, Ash. We need to keep you safe.

"Now, we're heading off to Cobbleton in the morning. Once we secure the cabana, we'll hang low there until this invasion blows over. Scar can come as far as Cobbleton. But—"

"I'm not going to abandon her," Ash said jerking his face into Wick's. "Maybe that's what makes me different than my mother. I don't just leave people."

"You're being naive, Ash," Wick criticized, ignoring the remark about his old friend. "Don't you think it's rather ironic that Scar found you all the way out here in the middle of nowhere?"

"*I* found *her*!" Ash caviled back, even though Wick's string of facts gave him the chills.

Wick boiled with frustration. "The world is crumbling around you and you have the power to stop it. But instead you waste your time wallowing in your own selfish delusions." He was flush in a way Ash had never seen before. But this only made Ash angrier.

"Who says I even believe you?" His condescension burned as Wick couldn't even retain eye contact.

"I can't make you believe," Wick whispered in the darkness. "All I can do is tell you what I know. The rest is up to you." His tone had since shifted to absolute defeat.

As Ash slipped the Enigma into his coat pocket, its glowing etching dimmed. His curse was real. And the devastation of Garbbit Harbor was unfortunately not a dream. But if the end of the world was now staring him in the face, he still felt utterly powerless to stop it. And if it were literally his destiny to do so, would he be able to pursue it without having to turn his back on Scar? If not, then this unproven destiny just might have to wait

2 Courage

Twenty Four
Pursuit of the Dark Creature

Morning concluded a sleepless night without transition. Gleaning his things, Ash felt as though their conversation the night before had been nothing but a dream. He wished. *The greatest treasures in the world are those which are never found*, someone once told Ash. But it never made any sense to him; until now. Sure, the element of intrigue was the most compelling attribute for any hidden or lost treasure. Once it was discovered, no matter how elaborate the loot, the wait was over—the surprise spoiled. And all the ado that inevitably evolved around such a mystery came to a screeching end, replaced by boring facts about who had rights and who got cuts. But not in this case. As Wick had put it, the Chrysalis was far more than a treasure. It could save the world.

As Scar remained asleep, he wondered if Wick hadn't possibly fabricated this entire scheme about her just to make sure Ash didn't ever get too attached to her.

"Are you sure the girl can be trusted?" Wick snuck into Ash's ear as he packed the last of his belongings. "Something's not right about her."

Ash was too tired to argue. He had discovered the smear of black blood she had accidentally wiped on his coat. He tried to hide it from Wick's vantage point, quickly turning away. Indeed, it was strange.

And as strange as it was, Scar's erratic behavior was at times even more of a mystery. But he just didn't want to think about it.

"She's just sick," Ash finally defended quietly, trying not to wake her. "That's all."

"Getting sick doesn't turn your blood black," Wick said, shocking Ash with his keen observance. "You think you were meant to find each other, don't you?" Wick asked. He knew what the boy was thinking. "Clear your mind of this infatuation. Don't let anything get in the way of your fate. Your destiny lies with the Chrysalis, not some girl."

"She's not just some girl," Ash argued back with reprising anger. He had had it with Wick's disapproval of Scar. "You're just jealous because I spend more time with her than I do with you."

Though this truth burned, Wick tried to pull his thoughts and emotions together. He hadn't waited sixteen years to tell Ash about the real meaning of his gift only to have him shrug it off for some strange girl. "Look," Wick said, gesturing for a more peaceful conversation. "I just want to make sure you understand how special and important you are."

"She makes me feel … alive," Ash trailed off, gazing over at Scar, who was now beginning to stir.

At that, the cave fell silent. Wick knew that he wasn't about to change Ash's mind about Scar. Not now. They had a long journey ahead of them.

The deeper they made it into the Ratroot Slough, the more warm and moist the air was, but the quicker it grew dark. Shadows were creeping into the swamps and soon they would have to break for the day and set up camp. Moving through the night and resting during the light hours would have been best for avoiding being seen by the pursuing drone-armada, but the nocturnal creatures that fed by moonlight would be even harder to outrun in these swamps.

Wick was barely still visible through the thick autumn-colored foliage of the swamps as he took another reaching stride in his mechanical stilts. He had been storing the stilts in the cave of Thieves' Hollow, for when he had to voyage out into the swamps. They certainly made a considerable difference in the time it would take for his stubby legs to maneuver through the swamplands. Unfortunately, the little amphibian wasn't able to swim through these root and weed-infested waters. The hydraulic spring action of the stilts gave them a lift that almost made Wick hop.

"Try to keep up," Wick yelled back to Ash and Scar. But after a long, difficult day of winding through the swamps, they had spent all of the energy they had.

The space between awake and asleep was already beginning to narrow, blurring into a constant state of delirium as Ash took Scar by the hand and stumbled forward. He hadn't slept a wink the night before, tossing and turning, trying to understand all that was happening. It was as though he had just been abruptly woken from a simple dream-state, into the midst of a strange new world of unknowns. And there was no time to catch up, no time to let it sink in. They were on the run now. For what was hunting them would not stop until it had won its prize.

As they carefully navigated through the obstacle course of mud, marsh, and uneven ground, Ash pondered a notion: If Guardians were able to willingly control energy, as Wick claimed, then perhaps he could channel some of his energy to Scar and help her regain some of her strength. Perhaps he could save her. Almost inadvertently, he was already doing it.

"I can't go any faster," Scar admitted as she leaned against a leafless tree for support. She tried again, but nothing happened. Her frustration with her own lack of endurance was obvious. A dark sorrow was beginning to permanently transform her expression.

"Don't worry," Ash said, gasping for air, as he un-snagged his coat from the ever-present bramble. "I won't leave without you." And he meant it. It crushed him to see her like this—waning of all strength. He wished so badly that he could find a way to make her feel better.

The deeper they went into the swamps, the more eerie everything got. Nothing was what it seemed. A large thorn bush up ahead suddenly rose slightly as two eyes then opened in the shadows beneath it. Ash stopped in shock, realizing that all of these large, tangled bushes around them were not bushes at all, but the huge mud and grass-covered antlers of giant swamp creatures living beneath the muddy waters. Things were getting eerier by the moment.

"Are you sure you know where we are?" Ash yelled up to Wick, as they entered yet another dark swamp. He had been concerned ever since Wick recommended leaving the trail. Even though the old wharfling was a native to these swamps, Ash knew that he didn't really have a history with navigating them. Wharflings weren't known to venture off too far from home. For most of them, the Ratroot Slough was the other side of the universe.

"Yes, Ash," Wick said. "I could walk this end of the slough with my eyes closed." No sooner did those words come off his lips, than did he run directly into a low-lying tree branch with his face. He was grateful that Ash and Scar didn't see it happen. "But keep a sharp eye for croodies. They come out this time of night," he warned.

"For what?" asked Ash, amazed at Wick's knowledge of the area.

"Croodies," Wick repeated very matter-of-fact. "Little, flying slough-lizards."

"Oh great," Ash said to Scar. After spending a sleepless night in a bat-infested cave, little flying creatures were the last things he needed.

"They're harmless," Wick explained. "But they have a tendency to get tangled in your hair."

Scar laughed. Her hair was too short to be of any worry and Wick had no hair to speak of. But Ash's shaggy mess would probably be a perfect nest for them.

"We'll get through this," Ash reassured Scar. Those words seemed to spill from his mouth, almost out of context.

"The swamp?" asked Scar.

"No. Well, I mean yes," Ash stuttered. "I mean everything. This will all pass," he said, trying to convince himself more than anything.

"I know," Scar said in a much more convincing tone.

As they neared the crest of a muddy hill, the skies were growing black. And the swamps were always the first to fall into darkness. But at the bottom of the hill was something none of them had ever seen before.

Looking around, Ash saw that the trees below were not trees at all, but giant, towering, gray mushrooms, peppered with brown spots. And the underside of their enormous caps were illuminated, like oversized table lamps.

"Well, look at that," Wick said looking around in astonishment. "The famous Mushroom Forest." He had obviously never come this far. "We're making good time, kids."

As they entered the forest, the ground at their feet was lit almost as clearly as day from the mushroom caps above. It was like entering a world of fantasy. For a moment, Ash allowed himself to get caught up, totally lost in the magic of the moment. He had read about this place and seen many paintings depicting its surreal beauty. How this strange forest was believed to be such a dangerous place was beyond him. Suddenly he heard a twig snap.

The snap sounded like it came from the hill adjacent to them. Then, as all three of them turned around to see, rapidly blinking, green light began to glow above the hill's crest. Ash didn't recognize the light. Scar found it familiar. Wick knew exactly what it was.

"They've found us," Wick whispered as he hopped down from his stilts and quietly placed them on the ground. And then, against the blinking green light, a silhouette appeared.

Ash instantly grew cold—surrendering to the entrancing grip of fear. He recognized the dark creature. It was the same menacing creature he had seen so many times in his dreams. *But those were just dreams, weren't they?* It seemed his childhood nightmare had magically come to life—those horn-like ears, the gnarled fangs, and glowing yellow eyes, just like the monster from his nightmares …

It was dark. Ash was barely five years old. Things were already strange around the house. His mother was not there. She hadn't been for days now. His father was frantic—angry and frantic. Ash knew to just stay in his bed and not move a muscle if he heard anything. Those were strict orders from his father. But when the creature entered his bedroom and stood over his bed, he would find that moving was not an option, for he was frozen in fear. Curled up into a ball in the corner of his bed, Ash noticed that the creature was looking for something else …

From the top of the hill, the creature sniffed the air for a possible scent that would give him a clue. But the moisture of the swamps was just too dampening for smells to linger. Peering down into the slough, he couldn't see them like they could see him. And as the drone-soldier squadron reached the crest, they too couldn't see Ash, Wick, or Scar, who remained completely motionless. Ash had been wondering what this drone-armada might look like. But never did he imagine it to be so frightening. He never imagined that the dark creature of his nightmares would lead it. Beneath his shirt, blood dripped down his back in two narrow streaks. Suddenly one of the drone-soldiers shot a large, green spotlight down into the slough.

Ash grabbed Scar and Wick, barely avoiding the light of the mushroom trees. If it hadn't been for the swarm of startled croodies that exploded up from the slough, the dark creature would have spotted Ash immediately. The dark creature struggled to see anything as he batted the swarm of croodies tangling themselves in his long dreadlocks.

"Quickly," Wick said, darting over to a small water hole, speckled in fallen yellow leaves. "Take a deep breath and dive in." With that, Wick dove into the water. Ash and Scar followed.

The dirty water stung Ash's eyes as he struggled to see what was happening above. Green light flashed everywhere. Then the dark creature's silhouette rippled into view again and stood at the pond's small shore. Ash didn't know how much longer he could hold his breath, especially when the sight of the dark creature gave him the compulsory need to gasp. But then a simple bubble escaped his lips and drifted up the water's surface. Ash panicked.

The second the bubble breached the pond's surface the dark creature locked his attention onto it. Ash knew this was it—he had been made. Glancing over at Scar, who looked as though she was about to burst as well, Ash shook his head in a vain apology. But when a tiny rodent slithered out of the pond and scampered away, the dark creature assumed he had just witnessed the culprit. He motioned to his squadron and they marched into the forest of mushroom trees, disappearing into the shadows.

One more second and Ash thought for sure that he would die. As Ash breached the water's surface, Scar flopped onto the shore and began puking. Wick of course was perfectly fine since he was an amphibian. But he was far from fine in every other way as he looked about in paranoia. He saw the green blinking lights of the drone-soldiers fading off into he forest, but he still didn't feel safe.

"Are you kids all right?" Wick asked in a hushed tone.

"Yes," Scar answered. Ash was far too shaken up to speak.

"Ash?" Wick said, laying a hand on Ash's shoulder. He could see that Ash wasn't doing well at all and he knew why. "We'll camp here tonight," Wick said looking around.

"But we should keep moving, don't you think?" Scar said.

"No," said Wick. "They caught up with us, and now have passed on. The longer we sit tight, the more distance we put between them and us. It's best we don't have a fire tonight. The leader of robots has a nose that can pick up scent for great distances. Fire will only lead them right back to us."

Wick knew more about *the leader* than he was letting on. He had instantly recognized the creature as the towering form of Sayto Bontey. He couldn't put enough distance between them and Bontey. Staying put was by far their best option.

Without a fire for light, Wick held the dwindling light of a baby mushroom cap up to an old, yellowed map he had. Ash leaned in, hoping that Wick was merely verifying their position and they were not lost. He didn't dare ask. But then he saw a symbol on the map that made it hard to swallow.

"What's that?" Scar asked, leaning over Ash's shoulder. Ash didn't even know she was standing there, looking at the very same thing. It was an illustration of a skull, right in the middle of a section of the map littered with images of mushrooms.

"P-perhaps it means there's some sort of burial ground around here or something," Wick stuttered, in an unconvincing attempt to cover up his own fearful suspicions of what the skull meant. Ash wasn't buying it. There was something about this forest he didn't trust. But venturing out and possibly running into the creature again didn't seem like much of an alternative either. "Try to get some sleep," Wick said, crushing the mushroom cap in his little chubby fist, extinguishing the light.

As Ash tried to calm his nerves enough to fall asleep, he wondered just where these mushroom trees got their mysterious light. Then he noticed the most peculiar thing on the forest floor.

The cap of one of the baby mushroom trees opened up like a blossoming flower. And from within it a number of long tentacles emerged, winding about like fingers in search of something. Suddenly one of the tentacles jolted toward a passing rodent, slithering by. The tentacle instantly coiled itself around the rodent and reeled it back into the interior of the mushroom as if it was feeding itself. Suddenly the mushroom's light intensified to a bright, white light again. Indeed this forest was like nothing Ash had ever witnessed.

Twenty Five
The Mushroom Forest

The Mushroom Forest was alive with sound. Creatures of all types and sizes scurried in the mud, trotting through the underbrush. And every sound seemed like the sound of danger—even the sound of leaves blowing in the wind, or insects humming. Ash was drenched in a cold sweat. He hadn't even come close to dozing off as he lay, staring at the stillness of the black pond adjacent to him. Besides the impending dangers of the wild animals, there was a creature far more dangerous and far more driven lurking in the very same forests. Suddenly Ash heard footsteps. And they were heavy.

Though the swamp was filled with the sound of nocturnal traffic, this was far louder than any other noise he had heard all night. Ash's heart instantly began pounding so hard that it rocked his body. His eyes shot wide open as they dashed around the dimly lit forest floor. Then, to his horror, he noticed that both Wick's and Scar's blankets were flattened on the ground. They were gone! Fear rattled him once again, as it did when he first saw the dark creature on the hilltop. His instinct was to run, but he had no idea whether or not he was being watched. It was too dark to see. Soon the smell drifted in, filling him with a flood of nightmare images.

Through the mushroom trees, in the shadows, Ash saw two glowing yellow eyes. As the dark creature emerged, Ash tried to get up and run.

But something was wrong. He couldn't move. He was paralyzed! He felt like he had been drugged. The creature's shadow fell over Ash as fresh blood dripped from his fangs onto Ash's face. *Whose blood?* But the blood was black. *What did this mean?* Though Ash didn't yet know the creature by name, Bontey's stench was horrible as he bent down and ripped Ash's shirt open. Inside, Ash felt the quake of uncontrollable trembling as the creature studied his eyes. Then, like a savage beast on top of its prey, he dove for Ash's neck, sinking his fangs deep into his neck. He screamed, but his voice quickly filled with the gargling of blood as Bontey's teeth sank deeper.

"Ash! Ash!" Wick's voice echoed from a distance. "Wake up, boy!" In a state of blurry disillusionment, Ash faded out of the nightmare and back into reality. He couldn't remember falling asleep. He grabbed his throat. It wasn't bitten. It was only a dream. "Quiet down," Wick whispered angrily as he looked around, as if in search of something. "I think you woke them up."

As Ash sat up, Wick noticed two bloodstains on the leaves where Ash had been laying. *It must have been another one of those nightmares.*

"Who?" Ash asked, afraid of what the answer might be. "Woke who up?"

His answer came in the form of a strange rustling and deep moaning at the tops of the mushroom trees.

"You're not dreaming anymore," Wick said with a sober expression of fear on his face.

"What was that?" Scar asked, standing to her feet. Ash's hollering had woken her up as well.

"Remember when I said that these swamps were haunted?" Wick said looking around. Ash and Scar looked at each other and nodded. "I wasn't kidding."

Just then, the tops of the giant caps of the mushroom trees opened like plants blossoming for the suns. And from within, long thick tentacles emerged, drooping down, all the way to the ground. It was just like the small one Ash had seen. But then, like huge serpents, they began to slither in all directions, as if searching for something. *The stories are true! These trees are killers!* Wick thought to himself.

Ash grabbed Wick from a tentacle just as it began to curl its way around Wick's body. Wick quickly climbed onto Ash's back. All Ash felt was panic—no heroism, no supernatural strength. Together, Ash and Scar sprinted through the forest without any sense of direction. Thankfully Scar seemed to have regained ample energy to run. Hopefully it would last.

Tentacles whipped all about like a web of thick jungle vines. One curled around Scar's leg, bringing her to the ground and quickly dragging her backward. Ash dropped Wick off of his back and leaped to Scar, grabbing her wrists. But the tentacle was stronger.

"Don't let go!" Ash yelled, tugging against the strength of the tentacle. The underside of the tentacle was equipped with rows of tiny, razor-sharp scales. It gripped Scar, snagging the loosely knit sweater and digging into her flesh. Ash trembled with rage, but felt helpless against the beast. Suddenly something familiar ran over his entire body like a sizzling fever.

Ash could feel his chest burning and noticed that his hands were beginning to glow again. His entire body was. It felt amazing—a current running through him like an electrical surge. Time seemed to stand still. It was like the world around him froze and only he was moving. Scar's eyes, filled with terror, remained fixed on his. Suddenly something happened that couldn't be rationalized.

The tree's tentacle began to shake and smoke. Still, it held its grip on Scar intensely. Then it began to burn, and before they knew it, Scar was free and the charred tentacle reeled back into a withered, useless coil.

Like returning from flight, Ash felt his body cool and quickly resume its normal state. Pulling Scar to her feet, he felt terribly dizzy. But something inside never felt quite so alive before.

Ash avoided eye contact with Wick, whose eyes were bugged out in utter amazement. The wharfling was like dead weight as Ash flipped him back onto his back and continued through the forest. Wick couldn't believe the miracle he had just witnessed. As the Mushroom Forest thinned, the few last desperate tentacles lashed at them, but Wick didn't even notice. He had waited sixteen years to see this miracle.

Scar didn't understand what had just happened. But there was no denying that the strange feelings she was experiencing were an awful lot like the forbidden ones she had been warned against so many times by her master: affection. Suddenly the forest ended. And so did the ground.

Scar caught Ash's arm, just before he stumbled off the edge of a giant cliff. Looking down, Ash could barely see the river through the mist at the cliff's base. Rainy River merely looked like a winding, thin, black thread so far below. And the other side was just as far away. "What do we do?" Ash's voice echoed across the canyon as a reemergence of tentacles pursued from the forest behind them. They weren't out of range yet. They would have to think fast.

"There," Scar said pointing to an old, rusted cable car that happened to be docked at an old transfer platform on the cliff's edge. "Over there. A way across!"

The car was golden-brown with rust. It looked more like a dwarfed bus with all of its windows blown out. There was no time to surmise whether the car even worked. The three of them dashed over to it, quickly jumped in, and Scar began fumbling around with the car's levers, trying to figure out how it worked. Tentacles lashed out, far over the edge of the cliff as the mushroom trees' moaning echoed horrifically across the canyon.

Scar released the cable car's locks, which had been holding it in place. "Here we go!" she announced as they pulled away from the cliff, leaving the deadly forest behind them in the dark mist.

But the old, rusty pulleys that rode the drooping cables weren't fast enough to pull away before one last, long thick tentacle managed to grab a hold of the car. It began pulling the car back to the cliff's edge!

"Doesn't this thing go any faster?" Ash yelled, terrified of the staggering height they were now at. Heights were one thing, but the tormenting, rock-filled rapids below were certain death.

"There's nothing I can do!" Scar screamed as the pulleys squeaked along.

Suddenly the car jerked violently, causing everyone to stumble to the floor. Looking up, Ash saw the giant claw at the tip of the tentacle, barely hanging onto the car's frame. It curled its fatty mass even tighter around the car's frame, determined more than ever to apprehend its prey. Ash froze. But the strength of the tentacle had halted the car and was now causing the pulleys' sharp, rusty edges to cut through the rope.

"Ash!" Wick yelled, as the frightening sound of unwinding rope whizzed through the air, "your sword! You can beat this thing." His eyes were so sincere and convincing. But Ash was frozen in a state of fear, unaware that the ropes above had just given way. So when he finally mustered up the courage to draw his sword and slice the tentacle free from the car's frame, it was too late. They were falling!

The car rolled end over end, falling into the blackness of the canyon. Icy wind rattled through the open car as the three clenched to its frame. Then with a crushing splash, they stopped.

The impact crunched the rickety remains of the cable car like a tin can. For a brief moment the car was completely submerged in the river. But it quickly resurfaced and was instantly caught in the turbulent current of Rainy River's churning rapids. Dazed from the fall, Ash, Scar, and Wick dared to peek their heads over the edge of the windows to see what was happening. Though the Mushroom Forest was no longer a threat, a new and even more fatal one was awaiting them just ahead: Devil's Falls.

"Oh no," Wick said in a frail voice, anticipating another unimaginable fall. "Not again."

"We have to jump!" Scar yelled.

"No!" screamed Wick. "The rocks will kill us!"

"The fall will kill us!" Scar argued.

But by now, there was no time for any options. They were plowing through the water too fast. Ash closed his eyes as the river before him disappeared. But then, with a sudden jerk, they stopped. Again.

For a brief moment Ash wondered if this wasn't his curse, his Guardian powers at play again. The rolling river splashed into the car from behind, insistent on pushing them forward. No one could figure out what had stopped the car. But as the car continued to surge back away from the waterfall, Ash saw the culprit through the darkness.

A large, harpoon spike was wedged into the corner of the car. Ash's eyes followed the rope it was attached to, all of the way to a strange light coming through the river's mist. As it came closer, all three could see the crude silhouette of a riverboat in the near distance. And it appeared to be bustling with people. Ash's mind raced to imagine who they might be. *Was the riverboat saving their lives? Or were they being captured?*

As the riverboat came through the mist, they could see that a giant, ashen-skinned, bald cyclops, wading through the water up to his chest, was towing it. With one hand he held a rope, towing the raft. With the other he reeled in the cable car. Ash couldn't imagine how strong the giant's legs must be to keep from surrendering to the current. He had never seen a giant before. He didn't even believe they existed. Until now.

Once the giant had reeled the car in, he gently escorted the three of them out of the car and onto the riverboat. Then, like a hobo pulling his simple belongings behind, the giant turned the raft around and began walking back up river, against the current.

Crouched on the wooden beams of the raft, Ash, Scar, and Wick were surrounded by silhouettes, just standing there, staring down. Then the group of people split in two and someone emerged. His soiled skin was coco-brown and weathered. Most likely, his heritage originated somewhere in Hispania. His ears, his lips, his nose, even his eyes were pierced with small silver rings. And under his red bandana, he wore his long, black hair in an array of rugged braids and dread locks, tied up in a colorful assortment of ribbons. The hair on his chin was also tied with a red ribbon and his smile was a sight to behold, strewn with yellowed, gold-capped and missing teeth like a half-eaten abandoned tray of assorted candy. He was thin, with vein-filled muscles that rippled over his dark body. He wore a dirty, blue, loose-fitting peasant shirt—his sleeves rolled up to reveal the extravagant tattoo murals that ran the entire length of his arms. He had a large red sash tied around his waist and his tan leather pants were tucked into his huge leather boots. But the long rapier hanging off his hip was all that Ash really noticed.

"I'd ask where you're heading," the man said in a lazy Hispanic accent. Ash recognized it from some of the traders that came through the harbor from time to time. "But it seems quite apparent." The man smiled intrepidly as he spoke. "You're on the run too?"

"You could say that," Wick replied, standing to his feet and brushing himself off. "Thank you. You saved our lives." Ash and Scar nodded enthusiastically in agreement.

"Sir Lazlo Cornelius Blackwood," the man said, as though he had not heard a word Wick said. Ash swallowed a large lump in his throat. He couldn't believe it. He was looking at one of the most legendary pirates in the world. Or was he? "These are my colleagues: the River Gypsies of the Northern Territories." They all gave a quick bow and then Lazlo turned to walk away. Over his shoulder he muttered, "Come, you must be cold. Let's get acquainted and see if your lives were even worth saving in the first place."

Once again, Ash felt the throbbing heartbreak as he yearned for his own bedroom. He had never traveled this far before. Everything was so strange, so daunting. He was cold, hungry, and tired, and he and Scar hadn't shared a smile since Garbbit Harbor. If this was what life outside of his home village was like, Ash wanted nothing to do with it. If this was what it meant to be a Guardian, he demanded an alternate fate. But turning back was no longer an option. All he could do now was to follow this strange man, who was claiming to be the infamous swashbuckling pirate.

Twenty Six
The River Gypsies

Twilight was barely filtering into the air as the giant waded around the river's bend, towing the riverboat to a fork. The riverboat appeared to be an old trawler that had been junked many years earlier. Typically, fishing vessels that were rendered out of commission, either due to age or an unfortunate encounter with the elements, were simply anchored at the mouth of a river and left to rot. Scavengers would strip them for parts or attempt to restore them to working order.

River gypsies were notorious for confiscating abandoned boats like this and then customizing them in the crudest manner imaginable. The end result was usually an abrasive-looking, unidentifiable vessel that seemed about as seaworthy as a rock. This riverboat was no exception.

It still wasn't clear if they had been rescued or captured, as Ash, Scar, and Wick huddled together on the log floor, at the back of the riverboat. No one seemed to take notice of them now that they were aboard. The crewmembers just bustled about the boat, tending to their individual tasks and joking amongst themselves. Ash wondered how much he might actually be the brunt of these whispered jokes. In spite of his uneasiness, he didn't really care. All he could think of was trying to identify the smell drifting to the back of the boat.

Someone was cooking something. It smelled foreign. Ash realized that the last time he had eaten was the few spoonfuls of soup he had toyed with back in Thieves' Hollow. His mouth salivated like an animal.

"You're welcome to join us for breakfast," Lazlo said, waving them to the cabin of the boat. Ash still wasn't convinced that this man was the actual legendary pirate he was claiming to be.

"We're not hungry, thank you," Wick said quickly.

"What do you mean?" whispered Ash in confusion, grabbing Wick by the arm. "I'm starving."

"You don't want to eat their food," Wick whispered back. "These people are river gypsies. They're filthy. And they can't be trusted."

"You should keep your voice down, wharfling," Lazlo said to Wick, who grew instantly humiliated. He couldn't understand how Lazlo had heard him from where he was seated. "You might offend someone," the pirate added. "Of course, it takes quite a bit to offend this crew. After all, we are all here because of judgments such as yours.

"Take Fynn, for instance," he said pointing to the young, dwarfed knoll-dweller boy, dressed in raggedy mismatched clothes. The shy boy quickly slipped into the cabin to eat. "He's but a boy, but already he's survived odds that most men only see in their nightmares. His parents were murdered right before his very eyes and he spent three of his youthful years in concentration camps before escaping and joining our little crusade of misfits. And all because a certain people's perception of the elfin society changed.

"Or even little Petra," Lazlo said, as a tiny pixie climbed up his arm and onto his shoulder and curled into a ball in the crevasse of Lazlo's neck. Ash couldn't believe his eyes.

The little pixie looked like a person had simply been shrunk down to the size of a bird. Her naked, featureless body was pale, only her backside speckled with faint dots. Her translucent wings twitched like an insect's. And even her movements seemed quicker and more sporadic than that of a human. But the emotion she displayed in her black eyes was every bit as intense as anyone he'd ever met.

"Pixies woke up one day to find that their new neighbors in the area had decided that it would be fun to hunt and kill them for sport. Pet lost her entire family as well. Just for sport." In a strange way, Ash felt as though he and Scar might be in the company of people he could relate to—outcasts. Mutants. "Now pixies are all but extinct. You, little wharfling, ought to know better than anyone, of the prejudice that exists between the converging societies. Wharflings too have a rather dark history," he said referring to the days of wharfling poaching. "So all though I may be on the run, my friends on this raft certainly also know what it is like to not be wanted. Of course, in my case, I'm perhaps worth a bit more money."

"I am truly sorry," Wick apologized. Sitting on Lazlo's shoulder, Petra turned her back and folded her arms in a display of protest—her beady black eyes narrowed and the tiny slit of a mouth frowned. She wasn't convinced of Wick's apology.

"You know," Lazlo began, looking up into nowhere, as if recalling images from another time, "pirates weren't always the black rebels they are promoted as being now. They were once the symbol of true freedom—refusing to align with political or religious agendas. It wasn't until the Zahartan tribal conflict erupted that some pirates chose to exploit their trade by means of terror against Kingland. Now privateers, buccaneers, and pirates have all been lumped into the same pool of convicts. So now, because Kingland finds it easier to round their alleged criminals up en masse, I, a legitimate mercenary, am considered equal with those out thirsting for blood. But on this boat, we *are* all equal. Even Minnow, as daunting as he may appear, is one of us," he said pointing at the cyclops giant, wading down the shallow shoreline, towing the riverboat with his huge rope.

Ash saw the humble innocence in the expressions of the gypsies. It was such an eclectic bunch, but they all shared a common thread:

victimization. For the first time in his life, Ash didn't feel threatened by those around him.

Wick stood and walked over to the cabin as Ash and Scar followed. Lazlo only smiled and held the rickety old door for them. Lazlo's smooth talking and sheer confidence was beginning to persuade Ash to accept his claim to fame.

"So what's your story," Lazlo asked, as Wick dished himself a generous helping of gypsy stew, a medley of meats and vegetables—whatever was available. "Your village got hit too?"

"There's nothing left," Wick admitted quietly.

"These invaders are from Kingland," Lazlo said, blowing the steam from his piping hot bowl of food. "They're contract killers in the name of freedom, false freedom. They've come to thrust Kingland's political agendas upon us and turn us all into slaves to the mighty republic. Ironic, isn't it?"

"You seem to know an awful lot about this," Wick said cautiously. "So what is *your* story?"

"Mine?" Lazlo replied. "Well, you probably wouldn't believe it even if I told you. Especially if you buy everything you hear in the pubs." He shot Ash a sarcastic look that made Ash wonder if he was really making fun of him or simply teasing. "I was once a legitimate privateer, marked by Kingland itself."

"Kingland supports piracy?" Ash asked.

"I'm a privateer!" Lazlo corrected, appearing somewhat put-out. "There's a big difference. Anyway, they do and they don't. There's plenty that goes on unofficially behind the scenes. And I was their number one man. When they needed an enemy freighter taken out or even short-range cargo barges, they would call me and I would do my thing."

"Pillage and plunder," Wick mocked. "The Secret Pirates of Kingland." Petra fluttered by shooting Wick a seething glare.

"You read too much fiction, old one," Lazlo said. "It's no different than the sort of thing a military operation would carry out. The difference is, that while the politicians were in gridlock with the bureaucrats, debating the whole situation, I was out there solving the matter."

"If you're such a hero, then why are you here?" Wick asked, hoping to disarm Lazlo's overgrown sense of certainty.

"Because when they needed someone to blame after a situation went bad, we were the perfect scapegoats," Lazlo explained, deflecting Wick's attempt. "I guess we should've read the fine print before agreeing to enter into business with King Basileus."

"The King of Kingland?" asked Wick, who was struggling to buy a word of Lazlo's story. "Are you trying to tell us that King Basileus works with pirates? Everyone knows what happened to his wife. King Basileus is the greatest opponent of piracy in the world."

"The King doesn't possess the kind of total power you think he does," Lazlo said. "Especially now that he's on his deathbed. There are many subordinate powers within the mega-government of Kingland who have hidden agendas. Count LePrey, the facilitator of the drone-contract armada, is the one who contracted me. He is also the one who turned on me. Never once did I take matters into my own hands or inflict harm upon the innocent. I had a job. I did it well. Kingland turned on me, just like they're doing to Murk and the other territories with this invasion."

"I see," said Wick, resisting the inkling to actually like Lazlo. "So you decided to run?"

"No," Lazlo admitted, confusing Wick. "I had no idea they would turn on me until it was too late. I spent ten years behind bars in the dungeons of Kingland's notorious Isle of Monte."

"And then what?" asked Ash.

"We escaped," Lazlo said with a grin.

The moment Ash heard this, he knew that he was actually looking at the real Sir Lazlo Blackwood. It all made perfect sense. *Why else would such a legendary pirate be so dormant for so many years?* He could have told any other tale of grand heroism. But this was far too humble to not be true.

"And now you run," Wick criticized, finally putting all of the pieces together. "It must be difficult to sleep at night. Always wondering if they might catch up with you."

"You'd know," Lazlo said starring Wick squarely in the eyes. Wick's cynicism quickly faded. "And where exactly are you headed?"

Wick was reluctant to answer, afraid that the gypsies' motives might be nothing more than clever chicanery. But Ash still had much to learn about restraint. "Cobbleton," he answered in unadulterated honesty. "Are you headed in that direction?" Ash pushed further, as Wick shook his head, burying his face in his hands. If there was anything that could keep them out of the forest, Ash was game for it. Securing river passage seemed like the perfect plan.

"Cobbleton," Lazlo repeated with a cynical smile. "We could easily get you within, oh, half a day's walk. Would that help?"

Lazlo's simple reply gave Ash an overwhelming sense of relief and made Wick question whether he should close the book on his jaded conjecture of the gypsies. "Indeed it would," Wick injected almost reluctantly.

"Consider it done," Lazlo claimed, nodding to his gypsy companions.

At just that moment, Ash noticed an old woman sitting at a small table on the other side of a small, fabric partition, adjacent to the dining table. She wore a black robe with a large hood that shadowed her face. With an array of melting candles on the table in front of her, she slowly motioned for Ash to come closer. She was frightening looking. Though not the type of person Ash would typically accept an invitation from, an otherworldly force seemed to be luring him as he took Scar by the hand and approached the old woman.

Twenty Seven
The Hand of Fate

While Wick and Lazlo were entering a debate on the chronology of the greatest pirate raids, Ash and Scar knelt down at the small table across from the old woman.

Multi-colored wax from her candles was melted across the entire table, dripping to the floor. Their light glowed dim amber, underlighting the old woman's face in a way that made her wrinkled, pale complexion look even more frightful. She wore too much make-up, which clumps in the valleys of her wrinkles. And she reeked of cloves. Ash had heard many stories of river gypsies and had even seen a small band of them pass through Garbbit Harbor once. Everything he knew about them was mysterious and dark. Now in their presence he felt less afraid than cautious.

"You wish to know the future," the old woman said in a deep whisper. Ash nodded his head. Her ability to read his mind had already rendered him speechless. "Give me your hand," she said. Ash had a pretty good idea what was going to happen next. Curiosity surrendered to fear as he carefully outstretched his hand. The woman grabbed it quickly, pulling it closer to her bosom. She turned his hand over and ran her fingers over the lines of his palm. Normally this would have tickled. But Ash felt nothing but the creeps.

"You work with rope," the woman said after mumbling what seemed to be some sort of strange incantation. Ash and Scar looked at each other in amazement. But they had no idea how strange this was about to get. "You work hard," the woman said with closed eyes, continuing to run her fingers over Ash's palm. "But your reward evades you, as do your dreams." Ash felt a chill run over his body. "Fret not. Worry not about the things you cannot change. And focus on what lies ahead. You can do nothing for the ones you leave behind." Ash began to sweat and breathe heavily. He wanted to quit already, but now there was almost a strange invisible force keeping his hand there. "The future is yours," the woman said. "Seize it. For in it I see many lands. Many new places," the old woman continued. "Many new faces. But your journey will not be easy. You must be cautious. A dark figure hunts you. And Mystery awaits." Ash felt queasy and began to squirm in his seat. "That which is closest to you is threatened." Ash quickly jerked his hand away from the old woman and told her he didn't want to continue. But she was quicker and stronger than he had anticipated as she grabbed his wrist and pulled his hand back across the table, knocking over a candle, nearly catching his jacket on fire. "You have found love," she said in almost a panicked expression. She seemed obsessed with completing her read. "The question is," she said peeking up at Scar. "Has love found you?"

At that, Ash pulled his hand away once and for all. "No more!" he instructed. "We're done."

But it was as though the old woman didn't even hear him. "Now young lady," she said turning her attention to Scar. "Let's see what lies in store for you."

"No!" Scar said in a panic. But the old woman already had her wrist and was pulling it toward her.

"It's all right," the old woman said softly.

But as the woman uncurled Scar's resistant fingers, the expression on her face changed from one of soothing meditation to one of horror. She didn't say a word. But Ash could tell that whatever she saw wasn't good. Peeking over Scar's shoulder, he couldn't believe it himself.

In the center of Scar's palm was a deep black incision, void of any scabbing. It made no sense. Scars like that would be unbearably painful. He couldn't believe he hadn't ever noticed it before. Scar appeared extremely nervous.

"You're hiding something," the old woman whispered, with a skeptical look in her eyes. "And it's wearing you down, isn't it?"

"What do you mean?" Scar asked the old woman innocently.

After a long silence, the woman threw Scar's hand down and blew out the candles. "We're through," she said rudely as she whisked Ash and Scar away. But just as they were leaving, the old woman grabbed Ash's arm and whispered into his ear, "Don't leave her side or she will die."

As they left the old woman, Lazlo teased them. He said that she was nothing but a harmless old crazy witch. In spite of Lazlo's lightheartedness, Ash felt terribly unsettled about what had just happened, refusing to greet Lazlo's humor with an acknowledgement. Wick, on the other hand, wore an expression of deep concern. Or was it simply hope that Ash had finally been given a glimpse of what Scar really was?

As the riverboat drifted through the early morning fog, Ash and Scar stood at the edge of the port bow, watching Minnow drudge forward. Too humiliated to speak, Scar held her hands close to her chest, refusing to let Ash hold them. Ash wondered what his future looked like. *What did the old woman mean? What were the wounds on Scar's hands? And why had she been hiding them from him?* All of these questions and more were frightening him. He couldn't lose her.

And what if the old woman was right? What if he couldn't leave Scar's side? Did that mean that Scar would be a part of his quest to find the Chrysalis? Then he had a thought …

If the Chrysalis was such a magical powerful entity, then perhaps it could save he and Scar's fate from doom. Perhaps this was meant to be. After all, abandoning Scar couldn't be the right thing to do. As he had just been told, leaving her would kill her.

Twenty Eight
The Hunt

Drawing the bowstring back ever so carefully, Lazlo steadied the sights on the deer feeding in the slough beyond. On his shoulder, Petra sat patiently, trying not to move a muscle. He released the arrow and instantly the deer went down. *Food for the entire crew!* Unfortunately, it didn't stay down.

By the time Lazlo looked up, the deer was already bounding out of the meadow and back into the thicket of the forest. Petra pointed out where she had seen it go down and then crawled into Lazlo's quiver, hiding among the arrows. She knew better than to allow her glow to give her away. That was how she had been discovered and captured the first time.

Lazlo quickly hopped down from the tree and after the deer. The forest seemed oddly quiet that day. He had frequented this area plenty in his travels, and never had it been so still and lifeless. In spite of certain species, which had recently come to extinction at the hand of industrialization, Lazlo could hardly recognize the forest any longer.

He picked up a thick blood trail, left behind by the wounded deer. Now all he had to do was follow it. Dinner was only a few paces ahead. But he was about to learn that this forest was deathly quiet for a reason.

"Here it comes," Ash whispered to Scar, as they crouched beneath the tree. They had volunteered to walk the slashing, adjacent to the meadow, to flush out any deer that might be bedding in the area. This was Lazlo's preferred hunting method when there wasn't time to waste. Ash figured it was better than just sitting around, waiting on the boat. He was reluctant to admit it, but he only wanted to distance himself from the old frightening witch. The only problem now was that every dead stump, every fallen tree, looked like the unmistakable silhouette of the dark creature.

Right or wrong, the witch's premonitions were far too vivid and scary for Ash to digest at that moment. He just wanted to be alone with Scar. Their secluded evenings in the dark, cramped galley of his father's fishing trawler already seemed like so long ago. Suddenly he heard a loud crash.

The deer dashed passed them so fast it sounded like a falling tree. Through the brush Ash could see Lazlo waving as he made his way through the thicket. The three of them met up and followed the blood trail to another small meadow. But before they could enter, they noticed that someone had already discovered the deer.

Three drone-soldiers stood over the dying deer as it lay kicking in the brown grasses of the meadow. The soldiers had detected it running through the forest and followed it to its end, hoping it was the girl. But no such luck. However, the sight of Lazlo's arrow sticking out of the deer's ribcage told them that someone else was near.

Given the type of feathers used on the arrow's tip, cross-referenced with the wood of the arrow, cross-referenced with Machine, they were quickly able to narrow down the probability of the arrow's source to a certain *wanted* pirate: *Sir Lazlo Blackwood*. Though this didn't necessarily lead them any closer to Scar, it did lead them closer to a band of outlaws Kingland had been tracking for years: *the River Gypsies of the Northern Territories.*

Meanwhile Wick coasted through the murky current, beneath the river's surface. Washed-up garbage, which had drifted downstream from larger cities, littered the shallow waters. So Wick dove deeper. With spear in hand, he waited patiently as a school of small, iridescent-colored fish dashed back and forth, feeding off of drifting clouds of algae. The gypsies were grateful for Wick's impressive fishing abilities. It was a refreshing alternative to the constant frustration they endured, snagging their torn fishing nets on submerged trees and hidden reefs. In just a short while Wick had already caught more fish than they typically were able to net after a half day's efforts. But just as Wick was about to unleash his spear, something else pierced the fish, pinning it to the sandy riverbed.

At first Wick had no idea what it was. But looking up through the water, he quickly recognized the terrorizing beast, towering over the river. From below the river's surface, Wick saw the giant drone-strider as it waded through the river along with two others. Out of the corner of his eye he also noticed that the riverboat was already crawling with drone-soldiers. From what he could tell, everyone aboard was being corralled and bound and then led into a large cage sitting on the deck of the boat. Then something fell right next to Wick, almost crushing him.

As the water cleared of unsettled sand, Wick saw that the thing that fell was not a tree, as he had thought. It was Minnow. And he was bound tightly with thick, metal cords. His head was hemorrhaging, staining the water a dark crimson. His heavy eye barely opened, fighting his nearly unconscious state. It was as though he was pleading with Wick to leave him and flee. Suddenly, the giant's massive body was lifted out of the water and up into the sky.

Long cables, stretching into the clouds reeled Minnow's hulking mass into the air. And the large cage aboard the riverboat followed suit, disappearing into the clouds, into the giant drone-zeppelin slowly coasting above. Wick's instinct was to swim downstream as fast as he could. But the only thing he could think of was Ash. *Was he okay?*

Trees blurred by as Ash, Scar, and Lazlo raced through the forest. Scar's feet could hardly keep up with Ash's. Little did she know that merely by holding Ash's hand she was absorbing a surge of energy, which was, if nothing else, keeping her legs from collapsing. Ash tried not to think about the fact that his own physical strength was once again beginning to drain.

Lazlo's legs were longer and faster. He had obviously had much practice running. Indeed, the stories of his heroism were true. Then Lazlo tripped and fell.

"Watch it!" Wick yelled, picking himself up. Lazlo hadn't seen the little wharfling dashing through the underbrush before tripping over him.

"Shh!" Lazlo responded. "They're close."

"More than close" Wick said with a gasp for air. "They're *here*."

"Where are the others?" Scar asked, looking beyond Wick. She was afraid of what the answer might be. She was beginning to remember this drone-armada far too well.

"Taken," Wick said with a sober expression. "The riverboat was attacked. Drones."

"So they're dead?" Ash asked in a panic. He suddenly felt alone—the lurid feeling he had discovered after looking across the bay at the smoldering ruins of Garbbit Harbor. He felt like every step he took, the world behind him was falling away into the hellish abyss of eternal doom. And if he didn't keep moving he would merely suffer the same consequences.

"No," Wick said. "I don't think so. It appeared they were taken prisoner."

"They were," Lazlo chimed in. "The gypsies are worth a lot more alive. Kingland's been looking for them for a long time. They'll most likely be taken to Kingland and detained in one of their top-secret detention facilities. They'll be held indefinitely in an effort to extract as much information out of them about pirate networks and any other paranoia Kingland is fixated on."

"How do you know this?" Ash asked curiously. "How do you know where they'll be taken?"

Lazlo looked at Ash with a stare that went right through him. "Because I've been there."

As the green, hazy lights of the giant drone-zeppelins passed through the gray overcast above, Scar sank into the shadows of a tree. "We have to keep moving," she whispered.

"Yes," Lazlo chimed in. "Let's stay close to the shoreline to maintain reference of our direction."

"Thank you, but we've got it from here," Wick said, grabbing Ash's wrist and marching forward. But Ash pulled away. It wasn't that he trusted Lazlo any more than Wick did. But aimlessly heading off into the dark forest once again wasn't something he felt brave enough to tackle on his own. Wick was no warrior. And Scar was growing more feeble by the moment. He knew they needed Lazlo.

"We don't need him," Wick whispered to Ash. "Remember your gift. Let it guide you."

But Ash ignored him. As amazing as the supernatural episodes he had experienced had been, they scared him. In fact, he couldn't even seem to curb his trembling. All he wanted was for Wick to stop talking as though he was anything but what he knew he was: *a scared, homeless sixteen-year-old boy.*

Lazlo had almost expected a reaction like the one Wick gave him. So, with a stern tone, Lazlo finally unloaded his thoughts. "You seem to forget who it was who rescued you from the waterfall." Wick refused to make eye contact with him as Petra climbed out of Lazlo's quiver and stood on his shoulder, hands on hips. "Look, if you don't want to walk with me, fine. But I'm headed to Cobbleton too. So keep your distance if you need."

"I know what you're trying to do here, Sir Blackwood," Wick said, returning a sharp, pointed gesture with the crooked walking stick he had found in the forest. But at his dwarfed height, Lazlo didn't even notice it. "You're after the reward," he whispered, glancing out of the corner of his eye at Scar.

"I have no idea what you're talking about," Lazlo responded, rolling his eyes. "But I do know what *you're* planning. And yes, I want in." Wick gasped, unaware of how Lazlo could have found out about the cabana. "I heard you mention it to someone aboard the riverboat." Wick suddenly recognized the exact moment this secret had been compromised. "You're trying to secure lodging at a secret cabana owned by the infamous casino owner, Colonel Ormin F. Nootix."

Wick hung his head. Denying Lazlo of access to this refuge would be nearly impossible now.

"Nootix would never allow his cabana to be occupied by a pirate," Wick shot back. "So if you think you can wiggle your way into this deal, then think again."

"On the contrary my little friend," Lazlo said, smiling at Ash and Scar. "Mr. Nootix makes a living at supporting the likes of me. *Privateers*, that is," he said with a wink to Ash. "Besides, have you even ever met him?"

"Not in person," Wick admitted, solemnly.

"Then you have no idea who you're dealing with," Lazlo said, lifting a low-hanging branch for his new friends. "Nootix is crazy. He won't even see you unless you're actually engaged in a poker session at his table. And I don't care who your mutual friend might be, if you don't have money, you might as well be talking to a wall." Wick clenched the moneybag in the pocket of his coat. He had plenty of money for this transaction. His fear, however, was that Lazlo would be after it.

"We can handle ourselves just fine," Wick said, resuming his march into the forest. "C'mon kids," he ordered to Ash and Scar."

Scar grabbed Ash by the hand, but waited for him to take the first step. Leaving Lazlo seemed like suicide. But maybe Wick was right. Maybe Lazlo would only attract the dark creature and his drone-armada even faster. Either option was a gamble. So he followed Wick.

"If you need a hand trying to guess the password the doorman requires before entering Mr. Nootix's casino, just let me know," Lazlo shouted up to the three as they continued into the trees. He couldn't help the smile that drifted across his dirty face. "It's not that it's such a difficult password to guess. But the doorman is not too forgiving. You only get one chance to get it right."

Twenty Nine
Cobbleton

Cobbleton was like something out of a dark fairy-tale. From the summit where he, Scar, and Wick stood, the city sprawled out like a sea of yellow twilight stars at the edge of the estuary. But it wasn't the magnificent metropolis Ash had imagined it to be.

From the sky-scraping chimneys of outlying refineries, black smoke slowly rose to join the gray clouds. Cathedral-like spires towered over the old city's labyrinth of winding cobblestone streets. Snow hadn't consumed the region yet, as it had Garbbit Harbor. But it was clear that something else had: the drone-armada. Smoldering, toppled buildings, piles of rubble and fallen bridges spotted the view, evidence that the armada had already come in and established *peace and order*. Despite the invasion, it didn't appear as though Cobbleton had been hit as severely as Garbbit Harbor. *Perhaps the people of this city simply didn't resist the invasion as intensely as the people of Garbbit Harbor*, Ash wondered. Or perhaps they were just too numbed by the city's stimulation to care.

Cobbleton was an old trading port. As live music, gambling, and prostitution grew in popularity, thus did the small port grow into a massive bustling city. A couple of hundred years earlier it was respected as a competitive hub for trade. But nowadays its reputation had morphed into a bustling nexus of cheap entertainment, the kind that was outlawed in most other lands.

"Ash," Wick whispered, tapping him with his walking stick. "You'll need to be extra careful."

"What do you mean?" Ash asked.

"As you can see, that pirate has no intension of leaving," he said, glancing back at Lazlo who was finally catching up. "He obviously wants something."

"Yeah, he needs a place to stay," Ash said. "He wants traveling companions. Is that so bad?"

"No," Wick shot back. "There's more. And I'm sure it's even more than my moneybag. I think there's a good possibility that he knows something about Scar. The pirate community is a tightly knit culture. He's probably salivating over the thought of her ransom right now."

"Well she's staying with us," Ash proclaimed, pulling Scar to his side. He wasn't about to cave to Wick's drama.

"The city of iniquity," Lazlo's voice proclaimed from behind. It startled Ash and Scar. But Wick chose to ignore it as he began making his way down the slope into the city below.

The chilly breeze carried the scent of burning cigarillos, the incense of Cobbleton. Wick led them carefully through the winding side streets of the city in an attempt to avoid being detected by the patrolling drone-squadrons. Though the mass of saloons and brothels seemed to be closing in like a haunted maze, Ash still found himself oddly relieved to be out of the forest. But the threatening hints of the drone-armada was a whole new level of frightening. It was as if the city had been taken over by the dead. Though the armada had strategically blown many of the major bridges that connected Cobbleton to primary routes, some smaller arching bridges still spanned the many canals that twisted their way through the city's interior. A steady stream of longboats littered the murky gray waters. It was like a mystical, cold drabness had drained the city of all color. Beyond just being foreign to

Ash, Cobbleton was beginning to give him an indescribable sense of uneasiness.

Old stone buildings loomed crookedly over the narrow, poorly-lit streets, which had clearly been built primarily for foot traffic. But with a population that had boomed tenfold and the introduction of steam-powered vehicles, one couldn't navigate without constantly being pulled and shoved in all directions. The dizzying mayhem was beginning to make Ash sick to his stomach.

Ash felt like a little boy again, timid yet fascinated with every sight, sound, and smell. But it all seemed so foreign. A tattered poster was tacked to the side of a building. *Scar's wanted poster!* Shocked and panicked, Ash quickly looked away and kept walking, leading Scar by the arm. Thankfully, she was wearing his jacket and had the hood up, concealing her face from the public. But there was an eerie factor to the entire city that made Ash glad to know that Lazlo was only paces behind. He discreetly turned around just to make sure. Lazlo smiled, showing his discolored, crooked teeth.

Nothing seemed normal, even the people. The faces of bums, lying on street corners and in alleys looked distorted and strange. Beggars slurred and stumbled around in senseless delirium. Even the music that spilled out from the cafés was like no music Ash had ever heard before—out of tune and void of rhythm. Small ensembles of shivering musicians huddled around small open fires on various street corners. The green flicker of passing drone-squadrons quickly marching through the streets didn't seem to faze the locals. Suddenly a loud synthetic voice overwhelmed all other sounds.

The voice seemed to be speaking in unison with many other identical voices. And indeed it was. Though he hadn't actually seen them, Wick recognized the voice from the invasion of Garbbit Harbor. They were drone-heralds.

Strategically dispersed throughout the matrix of the city, the heralds were hovering spheres, about the size of a drone-soldier's torso and with the same large eye on its surface. But within their eyes, images flashed. Fuzzy, colorless images crackled as the heralds floated about through the congestion of Cobbleton's traffic.

"Rescued by Kingland! Rescued by Kingland!" the heralds exclaimed in perfect unison, echoing through the narrow streets. "The mighty kingdom has once again stepped in to save the people from harm! While a deadly epidemic ravages the lands, the medical genius of Kingland has arrived to inoculate the sick and quarantine the uninfected for their own safety!"

"What epidemic are they talking about?" asked Ash.

"There isn't one," said Wick in an angry whisper. "It's propaganda—Kingland's way of covering up the truth. Something these heralds rarely tell."

"You can say that again," Lazlo injected, catching up to them. By now Wick had all but given up on trying to pretend that Lazlo wasn't following them. He would have to find a new way of trying to ignore the annoying pirate.

"To cover up what?" Ash asked, as he tried to circle in front of Wick. He was growing tired of these short elusive answers. He wanted an explanation, an explanation for why his entire world had suddenly been turned upside-down. "Why would they lie about Kingland?"

"Listen, Ash," Wick said, jabbing his walking stick into Ash's stomach, shoving him into the wall of a building. "Be careful of what you believe. You can't afford to be so naive anymore. These drone-heralds are not lying *about* Kingland. They're lying *for* Kingland. The great and mighty kingdom you grew up being taught was so wonderful is not what you think it is. At least it's not anymore."

Ash was perplexed as he watched the heralds' images: android soldiers injecting people with what they said was simply an inoculation for a deadly epidemic. It was exactly what Wick had described, but far more graphic and disturbing. Quickly, he squeezed his eyes shut before he saw anyone he might recognize. He looked over at Scar who seemed less interested in what was on the screen, and more interested and even bothered by three figures in the shadows of an alleyway.

They were gearmen. Originally designed to be nothing more than theatrical entertainers, they looked like walking scarecrows or human-size rag-dolls. In fact, that's exactly what people who disliked their kind referred to them as. After all, beneath the layers of cloth and leather was merely a complicated matrix of gears and hydraulics. Known mostly for their stunning longevity, gearmen literally ran like clocks. They were only meant to resemble people, not replace them. Still, there was something about this artificial life Scar could not stop staring at.

As she slowly began to wander toward the alley, Ash quickly pulled her back, breaking her out of her hypnotic state. But her eyes remained glossed-over, as though looking far beyond Ash's face. *What was she thinking?*

"There it is," Lazlo said, pointing at a brick building up ahead.

The casino was tall and narrow, and had obviously been painted numerous times. A large marquee with flickering, bright-colored lights hung on one side, looking as though it might one day force the old building to tip onto its side. "Lowertown Casino," Lazlo announced. "Let me know if you have any luck with the passwords," he teased Wick.

"Oh shut up," Wick said, whacking his walking stick against Lazlo's leg. "You just get me in and then we'll talk about your stay at the cabana." He knew the topic was a moot point. Besides, the drone-armada wouldn't be wasting their time going after the likes of Lazlo if their true intent was apprehending Scar. He was already in the company of one of the world's most wanted criminal.

Thirty
Colonel Nootix

The air was pungent with stale tobacco smoke and sour liquor. And everyone inside seemed to be covered in a thin layer of soot from the filthy air. Conveniently, it was so dark and smoke-filled that it wouldn't be easy to recognize Scar if anyone were to spot them.

A soft, slow tune wisped through the room from a three-piece ensemble, whose silhouettes slowly stirred the cloudy air. The expressions on the faces of those seated at the bar receded from drunken stupors to stone-faced glares as Lazlo entered with Petra on his shoulder, followed by Wick, Ash, and Scar. Ash couldn't tell if it was Lazlo who they recognized or if it was merely their unwelcoming nature to strangers. Obviously, Lazlo had frequented this place before since he was privy to the casino's secret password, which had served as their rite of passage.

"Excuse me," Wick said staring up at the towering bar, adorned with intricate ornate carvings about its face. "But I am here to see Mr. Colonel Nootix."

The bartender looked around in confusion, unable to see where the voice was coming from. Lazlo nodded with a smirk, motioning for the bartender to look down, over the bar. She craned her neck over the bar and grew an agitated expression as she saw Wick. Cobbleton was notorious for shunning wharflings. "On what business?" she asked in a gravely disgruntled voice. "He's busy."

"I have news to deliver about an old friend of his, Logan Meadows," Wick explained.

One of the casino's waitresses recognized the name and motioned to the bouncer, letting him know that this was indeed a legitimate topic. The bouncer then grabbed Wick by the shoulder and quickly led him to a staircase in the corner.

"I'm coming too," Lazlo said, following Wick.

"No you're not," Wick reprimanded, spinning around and pushing Lazlo back with his walking stick. "Now go make yourselves—umm, unnoticeable," he whispered, addressing Ash and Scar. "And keep your eye on Lazlo." Lazlo grinned and shook his head.

Ash didn't really know what to make of that order. All he knew was that he needed to make sure Scar remained undetected. Though the casino appeared to be void of any drone-soldiers, it didn't mean that there wouldn't be someone who had seen her *wanted* poster. So he took Scar and receded into the darkest corner he could find, huddling into a small booth. Lazlo followed.

The bouncer led Wick down a dimly-lit spiral staircase. In the basement, below the main bar, was the Velvet Lounge, as it was called. It was Mr. Colonel Nootix's private gambling parlor—a place where only the best or the bravest dared to be dealt in—for no one played the game as well as he did.

Red light saturated everything in the lounge, giving the room a surreal vibe. An obese man named Duta sat slouched in a chair on one side of a small round table. His eyes were heavy and bloodshot as he studied his cards carefully. With slow, sloppy coordination he lifted his goblet of liquor to his lips.

"They're playing for Duta's sea clipper," the bouncer whispered to Wick, pointing to the obese man.

Across from Duta sat Colonel Ormin F. Nootix. He was a thin, awkwardly proportioned creature, covered in ratted white, tan, and gray fur. His large ears protruded out of the top of his head and his yellowed, crooked teeth seemed too large for his mouth. He held his cards in one hand and a large cigar butt in the other—both furry hands wrapped in fingerless knit gloves. A bottle of liquor sat aside his pile of chips. Although it hardly fit anymore, he wore his tattered old military uniform with great pride. For him it was a symbol of what once was—a time when his native kingdom was merely one of the many allies seeking justice and peace, and people didn't have to smuggle to survive.

The bouncer whispered into Nootix's ear, letting him know that he had visitors bearing news about his old friend Logan. But Nootix didn't acknowledge that anyone had even entered the room. He just sat there. Eyes fixed firmly on his hand, wearing a crooked smirk.

"He won't speak to you until he's done," the bouncer whispered to Wick.

"With this hand?" Wick asked anxiously.

"No," the bouncer said shaking his head. "With the match."

"What?" Wick gasped a little too loudly. "How long could that take? I don't have much time."

"Well, they've been playing for two days already," the bouncer informed, trying to calculate in his head. "So I can't imagine it going on too many more days."

"Days?" Wick exclaimed. "I don't have days! I need—" Without looking up, Nootix quickly shot a stiff finger into the air, silencing Wick in mid-sentence.

Meanwhile upstairs in the bar, Ash was daydreaming about the cabana. He hoped desperately that it would be a roomy, comfortable place where he and Scar could feel a sense of place and be left alone. He missed those nights aboard the trawler. But Scar and Lazlo were growing solicitous of a certain Kingland Marshal who was seated in the shadows of the corner of the room.

The Marshal's face was obscured by shadow as he poured himself another tall drink from the bottle beside him. But Lazlo had a real bad feeling that the Marshal was watching him. And he had an even worse feeling that he knew who the Marshal was.

"Why is that man staring at us?" Scar asked about the Marshal.

"Who?" Ash asked unaware of the situation.

"That man in the corner," Scar gestured with a nod.

"He's a Kingland Marshal," Lazlo whispered. "He's here for a reason."

"What do you mean?" Ash asked. He had heard so many stories about these heroic icons, but never had he actually seen one. It frustrated him that he couldn't get a clearer view through all of the smoke and low light.

"Kingland Marshals don't just hang out in places like this for no reason," Lazlo said in a serious tone. "He's here for someone."

"How do you know?" asked Scar.

"Trust me," Lazlo said, growing unusually serious. "Let's go."

"But Wick said to stay—" Ash began.

"Don't worry, kid," Lazlo whispered. "We're just stepping outside."

This made Ash feel very uneasy. He still wasn't sure if he could trust Lazlo completely. But if this Marshal happened to recognize Scar, it would all be over.

As the three of them slipped out a side door of the bar, the Marshal stood up, grabbed his helmet and began following them out. But before he even took a step, the casino's entrance half-doors swung open. Standing at the threshold was the towering figure of an all too familiar creature: Emril Fograt.

Fifteen years earlier, this young and energetic Marshal shocked Kingland when he had led a daring operation to apprehend Fograt, one of history's most notorious serial diamond thieves. Since his release, only days ago, Fograt had been relentlessly tracking down the one who put him behind bars.

"Marshal Xavier," Fograt said in a scratchy, tired voice. He struggled to contain the widening grin on his slimy, scaly, ashen face. "You don't have to stand just for me," he joked. "Please, sit."

"Thanks," Xavier replied sarcastically as he watched Lazlo, Scar, and Ash exit the bar.

"Remember me?" Fograt said drawing a pistol from inside his trench coat. The sight of a gun barely stirred the patrons of the casino. Squabbles like this were quite frequent, especially among the gamblers.

"I never forget a face," Xavier said. "Especially one as ugly as yours."

"I see you still have your wit," Fograt said. "You won't be laughing for long. I've come to even the score. You Kingland Marshals think you have absolute power. Well I have news for you, Xavier. You're not invincible."

"Nice speech," Xavier said. "Did you script it all by yourself?"

"Actually I did," said Fograt. "I've had plenty of time to practice, sitting in that dark cell you left me in."

"You deserved every minute of it, Fograt," said Xavier. "And you know it. In fact, if you ask me, they should have thrown away the key."

With that, Fograt cocked his pistol and drew precise aim at Xavier's head. But as he pondered one last statement before exterminating Xavier, the sound of another gun cocked behind Fograt.

"Still cheating to stay ahead," Fograt said to Xavier, leering out the corner of his eye, barely seeing the drone-soldier aiming a rifle at his back.

"Whatever it takes," Xavier said straight-faced.

Then in one last desperate move, Fograt tried to spin around and fire on the drone-soldier. But he wasn't as fast as he was twenty years earlier. The blast from the soldier's rifle blew a hole in Fograt's chest and sent him slamming back into the tables.

As Fograt's bloody corpse lie in a twisted heap on the floor, Xavier dashed for the side door where Lazlo, Scar, and Ash had left. He threw it open and looked around frantically for them. But they were nowhere in sight. Xavier slammed his fist against the wall in utter frustration.

Downstairs, the poker match crawled on. And it was all Wick could do to keep himself from screaming at Colonel Nootix for his stubborn drunken state. Suddenly there was a crash as Duta's sloppy actions sent his goblet of liquor smashing to the floor. Then he began to weave and bob in his chair. And as his eyes rolled back into his head he slouched forward before finally collapsing face-first onto the table. The alcohol had finally caught up with and overwhelmed him as his cards fanned out across the table.

"Ah!" Colonel Nootix said with a mild smile. "He folds." He reached over and lifted Duta's fat hand off his cards. "Too bad," Colonel Nootix continued as he surveyed Duta's hand. "He had a better hand than I. Oh well."

"Can you do that?" Wick asked Colonel Nootix. "He didn't fold. Isn't that cheating?" He wondered just how much money the Colonel was about to swindle from him now.

"Look little fellow," Colonel Nootix said losing his beaming grin. "It's not *how* you win. It's simply *that* you win. And in my casino, the rule is simple. I always win." He then busted into a gurgled laugh, sweeping his arm across the table, consolidating Duta's poker chips with his own. "Now, what news do you have of my friend Logan? Is he dead?"

Wick was shocked at Colonel Nootix's lack of respect. *Perhaps Nootix wasn't the friend Logan thought he was. Perhaps this journey to Cobbleton was all in vain.* Wick was growing dubious of everything.

"Umm, well, yes sir," Wick stuttered. "Yes, actually he has passed away."

"And you've journeyed here from Garbbit Harbor to tell me this?" Colonel Nootix said critically as he counted out his chips.

"Yes," Wick said, as the bouncer seated him at the poker table. He placed his moneybag on the table and picked up the cards the Colonel had already dealt him. "Well, yes, and to ask a favor as well."

"A favor?" Colonel Nootix asked, studying his hand.

"Well actually it was Logan's last wish," Wick said.

"Ah," Colonel Nootix mocked, discarding and drawing a card off of the pile. "The wish of a dead man. Can't argue with that one now, can we?"

"Colonel," Wick began sincerely. "I assure you, I would never speak falsely about a friend. We are in great need of refuge, and I'm told you have a cabana in the Glades of Saur. I was wondering if it might be available for a short stay."

After studying Wick's face for a moment, Colonel Nootix finally answered. "Look, I won't inquire as to why a wee, little old wharfling would be fleeing his home world to seek out a desolate swamp like the Glades of Saur. I needn't know your business. And I don't want to know who or what your cargo is. But I do ask only one thing."

"Yes?" Wick asked eagerly, forgetting to play his hand.

"That you're clever enough to cover your own tracks. Hopefully you're not smuggling fugitives or anything."

It was impossible to tell if the Colonel was totally onto him or not. But at that very moment Wick noticed someone's face peering through the grime-layered egress windows lining the walls around the room. It was Lazlo. He was making an obvious scene, desperately trying to get Wick's attention.

"I may be a smuggler," Nootix continued, while Wick tried to wave Lazlo away without the Colonel noticing. "But I'm no criminal. So if for any reason someone comes around questioning me about you, I won't hesitate to rat you out. And since you will have already paid me, I'm out nothing. Deal?"

Wick didn't know what to say. In a way it all seemed to make perfect sense. But in another way, it seemed as though this entire idea straddled on the whim of a very strange and untrustworthy individual. He didn't have time to waste, as Lazlo was now waving his arms wildly and making ridiculous faces in the narrow window to try to get Wick's attention. "Deal," Wick said in an unsure voice.

"So what's in it for me?" Colonel Nootix asked, changing his tone. "A good name? I hardly care about that anymore. As you see, I'm not half the man I used to be." He then maneuvered himself out from behind the table, revealing that the lower half of his body was completely gone. His torso was affixed into the top of a large glass sphere at his waist. The sphere contained a murky yellow liquid. And a faint plume of yellow exhaust emitted from the underside of it every time he moved. It was an outdated scientific breakthrough that saved his life after a nearly fatal war tragedy.

"My glory days ended after the Great War and Kingland left its allies out to dry," Nootix said taking a large swig off his bottle. "I lost my legs fighting for their ideals, and what did I get in return? A one-way ticket to nowhere with not as much as a pat on the back."

"Well Colonel," Wick said, sliding Logan's military medals across the table. "I think Logan would be grateful if he were here."

"Unfortunately he's not though," Colonel Nootix said coldly as he rolled one of the medals through his hairy fingers.

"So what will it take?" Wick asked candidly, gazing upon the pile of money in the middle of the table.

"How much money do you have?" Colonel Nootix asked with a crooked grin.

"Approximately seven hundred," Wick said laying his cards face down on the table and pulling his moneybag close.

"That will do," Colonel Nootix said without hesitation as he snatched the bag.

"All of it?" Wick asked innocently. He was kicking himself for disclosing the full amount. "But I'll need money for food and—"

"How badly do you want the cabana?" Colonel Nootix interrupted.

"It's all yours," Wick assented with a surrendering hand gesture. "And the key?" Wick demanded. With Lazlo's face in the window, he was finding it nearly impossible to concentrate.

"Oh," Colonel Nootix said while he continued to admire Logan's medals. "The door's unlocked. No one would go out of their way to break into that place. It's far too remote. That's the beauty of it." Maneuvering his chair back around the table, he began to explain.

"The Lowertown Escort service. It's the fastest and safest way to the cabana. Especially if you want to avoid the new checkpoints this invasion has sprung on us.

"Droo," Nootix said to the bouncer. "Show Mister McCrow outside," he ordered, pointing to a sealed, wooden door in the corner of the room. And turning his attention to Wick, he said, "Your driver will meet you shortly and take you down to the sub chambers. Use the code word: *shumai*. They'll know what to do from there."

And with a quick handshake, the deal was sealed.

Droo led Wick out into the back alley, where Lazlo, Ash, and Scar remained hidden behind a pile of garbage. "He will be here soon," Droo said, pointing to a large culvert, trickling with dirty water. He then quickly left.

"Are you crazy?" Wick whispered a yell at Lazlo, as he stepped out from behind the garbage with Ash and Scar. "What were you thinking? You nearly blew our cover."

"Yeah, well I think that's already happened," Lazlo said, dodging Wick's attacking walking stick.

"What do you mean?" Wick asked anxiously.

"There's a Kingland Marshal in the casino," Lazlo began. "And I believe he's on the hunt."

Ash could see the regret in Wick's eyes. Lazlo was proving to be a bad omen to their efforts. It was hard enough to keep Scar hidden. But now traveling with another fugitive, they were only asking for trouble.

"Well we'll soon be far from here," Wick said, stopping to check Ash and Scar out. "You kids all right?" They both nodded.

Suddenly a dirty amber figure emerged from the culvert, looking around curiously. It was a gearman. Covered in what appeared to be a fuzzy knit material, the gearman had extremely long, wiry legs that arched back, connecting to his small, golden, round torso. His long, skinny arms rested gently on his belly as he walked slowly towards them. And his head, which looked like nothing more than a tarnished, rubbery, yellow bag, bobbed in jerky rhythm to his every step. He had cone-shaped metal attachments for eyes, with inner lights that seemed to short in and out, almost mimicking a rapid blinking motion. The rust from the attachments dripped down his face, staining the dark yellow leather with long, brown streaks, like tear stains. And his wide mouth molded over his inner metal skeleton, pinched into awkward arrangements when he spoke. They were crude, but had an uncanny record of remaining fully functional—even long after many of the newer models broke down.

"Um," the gearman said in a masculine, laid-back, Occitan slang. As he moved, his inner workings could barely be heard, ticking and grinding away. "Are you waiting for someone?"

"Uh, waiting?" Wick said nervously. Then he remembered about the code word. "Shu-shumai," he remembered.

"What's that supposed to mean?" the android asked with a head tilt.

"Shumai?" Wick said, afraid that he may have just walked into an elaborate trap, set up by the Colonel himself. "Well uh, it's sort of a password. From Colonel Nootix."

"Oh," the android said, finally recognizing who he was talking to. You're the misfit he mentioned. Well then, in that case, follow me. I'll be your escort to the cabana. I'm Driver Twenty-Eight Twelve."

Thirty One
The Cabana

The sub chamber was cold and dark and smelled of stale rotten fish. But the choking aroma of sea salt seemed to dampen even the worst smells. Green, bubbled cockpit domes were emerged from the grated floor, just above the water's surface. Below the floor the yellow, donut-shaped sub-taxis were docked, remaining submerged in the water.

Driver walked them over to one of the sub-taxis and motioned for them to get in. Everything was happening so fast, Ash didn't even have time to react. Before he knew it, the green, glass dome had sealed shut and they were buckled into the tattered leather seats, submerging deep into the water.

A cloud of bubbles rose around the sub like a swarming school of fish as the cabin of the sub moaned with deafening creaks. The change in air pressure was a pain Ash had never experienced before. And through the murky water Ash could barely make out the reed forest they were about to enter. No one spoke a word for a long time as Driver gently maneuvered the donut-shaped sub through the reeds and into a series of algae-covered rocky narrows.

It was amazing to see what the sea looked like beneath the surface. It was fascinating. There were fish and other strange creatures Ash had never seen before in his life. It was like going to another world. He wondered if any of the other lands Scar had seen were as amazing as this. And then he remembered what the witch on the riverboat had foreseen: *I see many lands. Many new places ...*

"Isn't it beautiful?" he asked Scar. A weak smile crossed her face, as images of fleeing Isla Ruba haunted her mind's eye. "I mean, it's interesting," Ash corrected, unsure if perhaps his phrasing was simply throwing her off.

"Yes, it's beautiful," Scar finally replied, obviously just to ease the moment. Then, out of nowhere she whispered something in Ash's ear. "Don't leave me."

She seemed so desperate. Perhaps she had heard the old witch's warning to Ash on the riverboat.

"Never," Ash whispered back, wishing so badly he could kiss her lips. For a brief moment, he had forgotten about the nightmare he was living in. But reality was quickly creeping back into his consciousness as he could feel Wick's glares.

While Ash lost himself in the sights of the underwater world, one question was still burning with Wick. "So," he said, turning to Lazlo. "What was the password to get past the doorman at the casino?"

Lazlo appeared caught off guard. He thought for a moment, and then turned to Wick. "There isn't one."

"What?" Wick exclaimed. "Then how did we get in? What did you say?"

"I asked him if he'd let us in," Lazlo admitted apologetically, fighting back a laugh. "The doorman isn't there to keep people out. He's there to keep people in—to make sure that Colonel Nootix has successfully taken their money before they leave."

Wick boiled with anger at the lying pirate. He knew that any retaliation would probably not come out very clear at that moment. So he just folded his arms and shut his eyes.

After what had to have been a day's travel, they finally surfaced into a small, swampy lagoon. The moment Driver opened the canopy Ash could feel the difference in the air. It was far warmer and moist. It even smelled different, like something wild. Though winter was coming, it wasn't coming here. But the most eminent feature on the lagoon's shoreline was the enormous goliath-tree, busted half way up its trunk into spiking, jagged shards. Ash had never seen a tree as giant as this. It almost didn't seem real.

"Alas," Driver said, helping his passengers out of the taxi and onto the soupy shore. "The Colonel's cabana."

Ash didn't see anything. But looking closer he noticed that the massive tree trunk had a door affixed to the face of it. And stepping even closer he noticed small, unevenly carved windows.

His heart sank at the thought of taking up residence in a tree. This was even worse than the shack he had grown up in. Scar seemed merely happy to have arrived. And Wick looked right at home. After all, it was a water-logged swamp.

"I'll go check it out," Lazlo offered, as Ash and Scar got sidetracked checking out the large snail shells on the muddy shore.

Scar seemed bothered—almost to the point of coming across as rude. She could hardly get herself to look Ash in the face.

"Is something the matter?" he asked, attempting to peer around her shadowed face and into her green eyes.

"How long are we supposed to keep running?" she answered after a long quiet moment.

"Forever, if we have to," Ash answered with a passion that seemed bigger than him. "Do you know what the Slave Lord is after?" he then asked, hoping he might better understand Scar's state.

"I'm beginning to remember images," Scar finally admitted, as if struggling to conjure them up in her mind's eye. "An engraved golden medallion."

Those words hit Ash like a splash of ice-cold water in the face. No doubt this medallion she spoke of was the Enigma. The very medallion in his pocket! Did this mean that she actually *did* steal it from the Slave Lord? *Perhaps she was a thief,* as Wick had warned. He reached down into his pocket and clenched it in his clammy hand, if for nothing else to simply make sure he still had it.

"This medallion you speak of," he stuttered, testing the situation, "it's yours?"

"No," Scar replied solemnly. "But I have seen it. I've held it."

"And what would you do if you actually had the medallion?" Ash couldn't help but ask with a gulp.

"I'd hand it over," Scar quickly replied. "The Slave Lord is not after me. He's after the medallion."

From the shadows beyond, Wick's eyes found their conversation. Ash knew that vulnerability was more than apparent. He felt Wick trying to read his mind. And he was actually considering handing the Enigma over to Scar!

"Don't you think we'd better get unpacked?" Wick piped up in an attempt to distract Ash from what could have been a most terrible mistake. It worked.

Inside the cabana Lazlo walked slowly through the darkness. The air smelled of mold. Thick spiderwebs draped across every corner and crevasse. It was obvious that the cabana hadn't been used in a long time. But looking down, he noticed something: a watery boot print on the floor. Then it hit him: The front door was clear of any cobwebs. Someone was already there!

"Don't move," an all too familiar voice said behind Lazlo. The barrel of the pistol was pressed deeply into the back of his neck.

"Marshal Xavier," Lazlo said sarcastically. "Sorry I couldn't stick around back there at the casino. It appeared you had an old friend visiting," Lazlo jested about Xavier's confrontation with Emril Fograt.

"I'm afraid your wit isn't going to save you this time, Blackwood," Xavier said shoving his pistol even harder. He had no patience for humor at this point—not after losing Bontey to the pirates. He was bringing Lazlo in, one way or another. He needed to—to help clear his name for what went down in Perg.

"I didn't realize that it had saved me last time," Lazlo said referring to his escape from prison.

"Well, it certainly wasn't your genius," Xavier said. "If you're going to travel with others, you might want to chose people who aren't also wanted by Kingland as well."

"What have you done with my friends on the riverboat?" Lazlo asked defensively.

"I did nothing with them," Xavier answered bluntly. "They were apprehended by the drone-armada. That had nothing to do with me. But it did lead me to you. And in turn, you led me to her. Is she outside?"

Lazlo feared the worst for Scar. If Xavier was after her, then it was over. There was no escape. So he played stupid.

"Who?" he asked. "Scar?"

"Yes," Xavier replied, spinning Lazlo around and digging his pistol under his chin. "You see, there's been a change of plans. As thrilled as I was when I spotted you in the casino, I was quite pleasantly surprised to see that you were in the company of the most wanted fugitive in all of the world. Do you have any idea what that Slave Lord is willing to pay for turning her in?"

Lazlo didn't know. And for as little as he knew her, he was almost kicking himself for befriending her so quickly. Xavier was obviously much more methodical about all of this.

After Bontey's prison break, Xavier took it upon himself to secretly track Bontey's submarine. He followed it to Murk, and kept a safe distance until the drone invasion began. He soon learned of a small band of gypsies reportedly being apprehended and transported from Rainy River to a Kingland detention facility. Xavier quickly traced the gypsies' steps back to Lazlo. And from there, his luck only turned better. But it took purposely losing a high-stakes hand of poker to Colonel Nootix to get tipped off about the secret cabana.

"I guess it's my lucky day then," Lazlo said, assuming Xavier would let him go if he turned over Scar.

"Not quite," Xavier said as he took Lazlo firmly by the arm and led him out of the cabana. "Your road still ends here. It's actually *my* lucky day. I get to arrest the both of you."

"Oh," Wick said with surprise, looking up to see Lazlo emerging from the cabana. "How is it inside?" Then Xavier emerged right behind Lazlo.

"Occupied," Lazlo joked unenthusiastically.

Though he had been hard to see in the dark smoke, Ash and Scar recognized Xavier from the casino as he stared deep into Scar's eyes. Ash had a bad feeling. Suddenly Xavier turned the gun on her and shoved Lazlo away.

Lazlo was already cuffed, unable to help. But Ash discovered that his instincts were far more aggressive than he had thought. Before he knew it, he had Scar tucked behind him and was dodging back and forth to block Xavier's aim.

"Give up, kid," Xavier said, approaching them. "She's a criminal. And now, so are you. But cooperating can certainly help your outcome."

"Let him take her!" Wick pleaded to Ash from the lagoon, where he and Driver had been conversing quietly.

Ash felt the strange sensation rush through his body. As Xavier's pistol pressed into the skin of his forehead, Ash closed his eyes and dared to allow his curse to manifest itself in him. But there was a gun pointed right at his head. Nothing happened.

"Either you give her up and live or I kill you and then take her," Xavier outlined. "Either way, she's coming with me."

Ash clenched his teeth, almost trying to squeeze the power out of himself. But it was doing no good. He felt tired and deflated. Collapsing to his knees in the mud, he felt Scar's grip release from his and then heard her footsteps splashing away as she followed Xavier. He knew that he had failed everyone, including himself.

Xavier was quick and orderly, filing everyone back down to the sub-taxi. With his pistol to Driver's bag-like head, Xavier ordered him to get in and drive. And in a few short moments they were re-submerged.

"You told the boy to be ready for a sudden change of plans," Lazlo said to Wick with a subtle grin. "Well, here we go."

But Wick didn't see the humor. His perfect plan had been perfectly spoiled.

Thirty Two
Making the Deal

Xavier disarmed his prisoners, locking their weapons in one of the sub's interior compartments. So he didn't bother handcuffing them, as they were little threat to him now. But the deeper the sub-taxi submerged into the depths of the sea, the harder it was getting Xavier to look at their faces—especially Scar's. There was nothing criminal about her. She appeared as nothing more than a scared girl. But he quickly extinguished these thoughts. She *was* a criminal. She was *wanted*. And he was soon to collect a healthy ransom for her capture.

"What is it?" Lord Yen's voice crackled over Xavier's large wrist transmitter.

"I have the girl," Xavier said, struggling to contain his excitement.

"Does she still have the—" Yen seemed to catch himself in mid-sentence, before continuing. He wasn't about to disclose his secret to a stranger. "What is her condition?" he asked calmly.

"Weak, but stable," Xavier described, fighting the inclination to turn around and get a quick look at her.

"Good," Yen replied. "Bring her to my compound in Copi Bienna. Come straight here, as quickly as you can. Dock at Port Conga. There you'll be met by two of my agents, who will escort you to me. The full reward will be waiting for you the moment you hand her over. Now hurry."

Xavier switched off the transmitter. His hands shook with guilt. The only way to remain focused was to ignore the inner voices in his head. But that hardly worked either. He wondered if he wasn't just simply losing it after all of these years. If the subsequence of his assignment to the Dungeons of Perg was any indication, then he was.

Leaning over to Driver and pointing out of the green canopy, he whispered, "Head straight south-west."

"You're not heading into the Graveyard are you?" Wick asked, recognizing the coordinates.

"Relax yourself, wharfling," Xavier said with a hand gesture to quiet Wick. "It's a shortcut. Time is of the essence. Sit back and enjoy the view. Because the next one you have will be the inside of a jail cell."

"But those waters are infested with goliath-eels and, worse yet, pirates," Wick said, ignoring Xavier's threat.

"Then you'll be among friends," Xavier said glancing back at Lazlo. Lazlo grinned with pride, his facial piercings glistening in the dim light of the sub.

"I suppose you've forgotten that most people who venture through these waters never make it out alive?" Wick continued like an annoying parent.

"Enough, wharfling," Xavier barked back. "I know the sea a lot better than a little old mud-hole troll like yourself."

"You're not going to get away with this, you know," Wick persisted angrily.

"Well then I'll die trying," Xavier said, finally turning around to face him. But instead his eyes caught Scar's. Her fear had seemed to turn to sadness by now. Xavier looked away.

Thirty Three
The Graveyard

The darkness was so thick now that Ash wondered just how Driver could even tell where they were. As expressionless as a gearman's face was, Ash was certain he recognized Driver's uneasiness while struggling to navigate these haunted waters. Suddenly Ash felt something pressing into him.

Looking down, Ash saw that Scar was now resting her head on his shoulder. An electrifying sensation ran over his entire body. How badly he wanted to kiss her. He felt awkwardly heroic. To feel this wanted, this needed—it was like no other feeling he had felt before. He almost felt like a man. Almost.

"We're entering the Graveyard," Driver announced.

Ash quickly craned his neck to see. But it was so dark that all he could see was more blackness. Suddenly Driver switched on the sub's flood lamps, and what appeared before the sub sent shivers down Ash' spine.

The ghostly silhouette of an immense galleon mainmast towered like a half-fallen tree in the murky water. Carrageen moss-covered ballast stones, spilled from the belly of the sunken ship, littered the sea floor. Thick algae fluttered off of its mast like the hair of an animal. It was ghostly looking. And then looking further, the view grew even eerier as Ash saw what had to be hundreds more ships strewn across the sea floor. It was like some sort of strange, supernatural force brought an entire fleet down all at once. The truth was far scarier.

"Sailors used to believe that it was the gods forbidding voyagers from venturing into foreign waters," Driver explained like a tour guide. "But they soon learned that ships were being attacked not by gods, but by giant sea monsters breeding in the area. And the most feared and deadly is the goliath-eel—one of largest and most deadly of the sea."

"Are you done?" Xavier asked, annoyed. "Plenty of people take shortcuts through here."

"Yeah, but very few live to tell about it," Lazlo responded, staring at the array of sunken ships outside.

"Look," Xavier said with growing agitation, "I wouldn't get all uptight because of what some talking rag-doll says." Driver's head jerked in response to the snide remark about him. Suddenly there was a loud bang and the interior lights of the sub flickered off and on.

"What was that?" asked Ash, grabbing Scar's hand. He wasn't sure if he had grabbed it out of security for her or for himself.

No one answered as everyone's eyes became affixed to the canopy window above. Searching for the culprit. Nothing looked out of the ordinary. But then it happened again.

"Falling asleep at the wheel?" Lazlo teased. "Just let me know when you want me to drive."

"Nice try," Xavier said shaking his head. But it was obvious in his tone that he was preoccupied with something taking place outside of the sub.

"Well, there's good news and bad news," Lazlo said, looking behind the sub. A flash of white light streaked overhead as the interior lights dimmed again.

"What's the good news?" Wick asked picking himself up off the floor.

"We're not sinking," he answered.

"Then I don't think I even need to ask what the bad news is," Wick said as color drained from his face and the corners of his mouth dropped. Ash knew without a doubt, the eels were near.

"You called it, wharfling," Xavier said as he looked about a bit more frantically. "I hope you're strapped in. This is gonna get bumpy."

Outside the monstrous goliath-eel kept in tight formation with the sub, as though it was locked into the sub's draft. But Driver was pulling no punches as he raced the sub wildly around some of the larger coral outcroppings.

The eel was long and flat, moving like a fish. Its translucent skin glowed white as the electrical current pulsated throughout its body. And as it gained on the sub, it began to glow even brighter, preparing for another electrical strike. Opening its large jowls, a bolt of electrical current shot out of its mouth, slamming into the sub like lightening from a storm cloud—capturing the sub in a temporary flux of blackout.

Scar squeezed Ash's hand even tighter. But as much as it flattered him, he had no idea what to do with it. He was every bit as afraid as she was.

At the speed they were going, Ash wondered how long it would be before Driver lost control of the sub. But soon the eel was joined by a school of others. The sub became engulfed in their swarm. The only thing keeping the sub from becoming instantly destroyed was the fact that the eels didn't work together to bring down the sub. On the contrary, they fought and competed with one another over the sub. And with one final electrical strike, the victor was established.

Blackness entombed the crew of the sub. Only the settling dust cloud could be seen as the sub tumbled slowly through the murky waters. Ash swore that his heart was going to leap from his chest as he anticipated the sight of the dreadful monsters. He caught a quick glimpse of them as the sub looped around. The one who deactivated the sub's power was already attached to the sub's underside. Ash could hear it as it tore away at the sub's hull with its large fangs. Eating its way to the prize that waited inside, the crew.

"Doesn't this thing have auxiliary power?" Lazlo asked Driver without the usual sarcasm.

"This isn't some military rig," Driver shot back in a way that made him seem much more human than gearman. "It's a taxi. You can blame

Mister Over-Eager here for getting us into this mess," Driver said, pointing to Xavier.

"Well that eel appears to be in more of a hurry than even we are," Lazlo said as the floor began to distort and bubble from the impact of the attacking monster. Suddenly the sub began to spin into a slow descent.

Ash closed his eyes and let go of Scar's hand. He had to know if he had it in him to do it. He had to know if his curse could be summoned.

Letting go of everything around him, Ash began to see white light in his mind's eye. The sensation returned. But this time it came over him in a wave that nearly made his entire body thrust forward. And then concentrating his thoughts onto that one source, he tried to seize the eels' energy from them.

Only Wick had any idea of what was actually happening as an incredible pulse of white, sparkling light engulfed the entire school of goliath-eels. The light grew into a blinding mass, illuminating the vastness of the Graveyard, exposing hundreds of more shipwrecks. And then, like a bursting geyser it imploded upon itself, dissolving the eels in an explosive flash. Ash slumped into a brief state of unconsciousness, only to quickly wake to the implosion's shockwave slamming into the sub. His ears popped painfully as the powerless sub sank deeper and deeper before crashing to a jolting halt.

"What in the world was that?" Lazlo asked wide-eyed. Catching Ash out of the corner of his eye, he had a sneaking suspicion that he already knew the answer.

Crumpled and powerless in the shadows of a giant, coral crevasse, the sub was wedged into a place the eels couldn't even get at. The only problem was, the crew was now trapped inside.

"Are you all right?" Scar asked Ash. In the darkness, Ash said nothing as his hands feebly searched for hers.

Thirty Four
Left for Dead

It didn't take long for the frigid waters to grip the sub in its spell, as frost began crystallizing on the windows. No one had yet moved. It would be a toss-up as to what would kill them first: the depletion of air or the freezing temperatures.

"Is everyone all right?" Xavier coughed up as he struggled to his feet. The craft had landed lopsided and the crew was strewn everywhere—battered and dazed.

"Great!" Lazlo said sarcastically. "Nice shortcut by the way. Got any more good ideas?" Petra fluttered away shaking her head in disgust as a trail of glowing dust dissipated behind her.

"You're still alive I see?" Xavier said rolling his eyes in disappointment.

"Not for long," Lazlo noted. "How long till our air runs out?" But Xavier ignored him. He was busy doing what appeared to be packing.

Everything was a painful blur as Ash slowly came to. He felt lifeless. Lazlo's voice seemed distant. But it was a relief to hear something familiar.

"Where's Wick?" Ash asked Scar, who appeared to be no more or no less distraught by the preceding events.

A grunt came from the shadows as Wick struggled to move. Ash tried not to worry as he helped his old friend sit up. A large cut on Wick's forehead was bleeding and it appeared that he had injured his arm. But his familiar smile told Ash that he would be just fine. But when Ash turned around, he noticed that Scar was gone.

Looking up he saw that Xavier had her by the arm and was making his way to the rear compartment of the sub.

"What are you doing?" Ash asked Xavier. He was having trouble seeing with all of the dust that had settled in his eyes since the crash.

"I'm going for help," Xavier answered sternly.

"How?" Wick chimed in as Ash helped him to his feet.

Xavier hit a switch that opened a hatchway to a small rear compartment. In the shadows hung a yellow, rusted sub-sphere. It looked almost like a small version of the sub-taxi itself. "In that," he said pointing to the sphere. "And I've only got room to take one of you." He pulled Scar closer.

"Take me. I'm your prisoner," Lazlo offered. Petra climbed down Lazlo's back and into his shirt to hide from the confrontation.

"Not anymore, Lazlo," Xavier said. "She's worth a lot more."

"Let her go!" Ash blurted out as he grabbed Scar by the other arm. "She's innocent!"

"I told you once, kid," Xavier said gripping Ash's arm and twisting it painfully behind his back. "Don't get overzealous. It'll only get you hurt."

"You came for me," Lazlo said straight-faced pulling Ash away from Xavier.

"You were never about the money, Lazlo," Xavier admitted. "I don't make one extra coin by bringing you in. I get a pat on the back and the comfort of knowing that one less pirate now roams the sea. And that much I've already accomplished," he said looking around the interior of the sub. "Welcome to your tomb."

Ash knew now that Xavier wasn't going for help. He was merely leaving them for dead. And with that, Lazlo finally lost it, lunging at

Xavier with a drawn fist. But before he could strike, Xavier's pistol met him directly between his eyes. "Don't try to be a hero now," Xavier warned. "It's a little late for that. You chose to be a pirate. I'm afraid that's simply unredeemable."

"What about me?" Driver asked from the shadows. His arm was in a twisted mess, but otherwise, most of his bolted and stuffed parts remained intact. "I'm an innocent bystander."

"You're a freaky talking rag doll," Xavier said without bothering to break stride in what he was doing. "No one cares about you. Especially me."

Scar's eyes were like that of a scared child as Xavier backed her into the shadows of the rear compartment. Ash was too weak to fight back and his broken heart was literally hurting. They had seen an overwhelming amount of terrible things in a short period of time. But this was the most damning. Xavier was right. There truly *was* no way out. Once Xavier was gone with Scar, Ash and everyone else aboard would be left to die. It was as simple as that. He watched in horror as Scar and Xavier disappeared behind the door. And after a few brief moments they jettisoned in the small yellow sub-sphere, fading into the murky distance.

After a few, long, cold hours, consciousness was becoming a challenge. The fear of death and his worry for Scar was the only thing keeping him awake. But the most disquieting thing since Scar's disappearance was that the medallion was now missing as well. After searching every corner of the sub, Ash still hadn't located the Enigma. Yet in a strange way, he couldn't get himself to care as much as he knew he should. He could feel its absence. And now his painful chill had turned numb. Even thoughts seemed to slow down, taking on the distorted surreal likes of a dream. Thick frost had now corroded the entirety of the sub's interior, slowly transforming it into an icy cell.

"You really care about her, don't you?" Lazlo asked Ash, breaking the ice-cold silence. "We'll save her. Don't worry, kid."

"I think we'd better be concerned with saving ourselves first," Wick said, vexed that Lazlo was sympathizing with Ash's childish infatuation.

Ash was astounded by Lazlo's optimism. "How can you claim we'll save her?" he asked with a shiver in his voice. "Look at us. We're stranded. There's no way out of here."

"Sometimes," Lazlo began, "you've just got to trust that there are larger powers at work, and know that in the end, everything works out."

"But maybe this *is* the end," Wick said in a vanquished tone.

"Nice touch," Lazlo said annoyed with Wick. "Way to keep the spirits alive."

"But maybe it is," Ash said agreeing with Wick. "I mean, after all, Xavier just left us here. And if we don't run out of air first, we'll freeze to death. And if not that, there's still other eels or worse yet, the Graveyard Pirates. I've heard a lot of stories about pirates who trawl the Graveyard. They say that the—"

"They're just stories, kid," Lazlo interrupted. "Just stories."

Suddenly red light began to spill in through the frost-covered glass canopy. It was impossible to see what the light was through the kaleidoscope of icy build-up. But suddenly a loud rumble shook the sub with powerful vibrations.

"What is it?" Wick asked frightened.

"Larger powers," Driver mocked himself.

Ash scraped a tiny hole through the glaze of frost on the glass—just enough to see a huge thick cable descending down to the canopy. At the end of the cable, a giant iron hook was attached. Out of Ash's line of sight, it hooked onto the sub's frame. And with a heavy jerk began raising the sub up from its muddy grave.

The red light soon brightened, consuming the little sub-taxi. Then it came to a stop. Silhouetted figures appeared through the frost-covered canopy above, diffused like an image against a stained glass window. Wherever they were, it was much warmer than the frigid air they had been surviving in. Again, Ash wiped away the frost, which came off much easier now that it was melting. But to his horror, he wished he hadn't touched the glass. They were surrounded. *Pirates!*

Thirty Five
Captured

The darkness smelled of death—souring hygiene, trumped only by the stench of rotting animal flesh. Everything was old, dark, and wet—either rusted or molding. The intense pressure on the submarine's hull moaned and creaked like weeping ghosts. Since he was a small child, Ash had imagined what being aboard a pirate vessel might be like. But this was nothing like he had ever imagined. It was hell in comparison.

The shadowed figures marched their victims down the cold, dark corridors of the submarine, shoving them with the butts of their rifles and randomly smacking the backs of their heads. They stopped on a grated mezzanine, cutting through two enormous, metal-constructed catacombs with barred doors. And with strength that seemed almost unnatural, the figures tossed them in through a darkened doorway, into one of the cells.

"Pirates," Lazlo grumbled to himself in a disgusted tone as he brushed himself off. "Never much on hospitality."

"But they do know how to throw a party," Driver said with a raised finger. He was busy mending a small tear on his arm, yet still listening to the discourse around him. The situation he now found himself in didn't seem to affect him much, or at all. Whatever simulated emotions these gearmen had, they usually didn't align with reality.

Wick grew instantly angry. "I'm afraid we do not share your lighthearted cynicism," he said taking a stand right next to Ash, who was still struggling to make it to his feet.

"Look," Lazlo tried to amend, "I know these thugs. They're cowards. It's all theatrics with them." Petra sat on his shoulder, arms folded and nodding her head in agreement.

"Smoke and mirrors," Driver chimed in.

"What if they're after the treasure?" Ash whispered to Wick, hoping no one else heard. "You said that most pirates are probably well aware of what went down between Scar and that Slave Lord."

"I wouldn't give them too much credit, Ash," Wick said. "Like Lazlo said, they're just thugs." But secretly, Wick was every bit as worried as Ash was.

"I didn't say that they weren't determined though," Lazlo interrupted. He had heard every word Wick had said. "In my line of work, word like this gets around fast. And though he's kept a tight lip about his true motive, Lord Yen hasn't been too shy with his campaign for bringing Scar in. How do you think we got into this mess?" he said, referring to Xavier. "I'm afraid that odds are, these pirates *do* know about the Enigma."

"Enigma?" Wick asked with a confused and almost panicked expression. "Who said anything about the Enigma?"

"Well that's supposedly what was stolen from Lord Yen," Lazlo explained. "Hard to say if the rumors are true, but at least that's what people are saying."

"So Scar *did* steal the Enigma?" Ash whispered with wide eyes. His stomach turned at the thought of her lying to him.

Wick couldn't help but appear smug. "Yes. And she seems to have stolen it back from you."

No one spoke for a while, as Lazlo continued to comb the cell for a weakness he could exploit in an escape attempt. But it wasn't as easy as he had hoped. "Escaping the cell is plausible," he said, studying the cell's structure. "But escaping this vessel is another story. That will take more than charm, I'm afraid."

"We're part of their crew now," Driver said nonchalantly. "But piracy isn't such a bad gig. It pays well, right Blackwood?"

"I wouldn't know, Driver," Lazlo answered annoyed. "I was a privateer." He wondered how many times he would have to defend this title with these new acquaintances.

Suddenly a feeble voice spoke up from across the aisle. "You think you can escape Sir Blackwood?" the prisoner asked. Then he laughed and coughed. "Do you not know who you're dealing with?"

Lazlo knew full well whose vessel he was aboard. But he opted not to say anything, for fear that it might send Ash into a state of panic.

"Oh go back to sleep you bum," Wick scolded the prisoner. He too didn't want Ash to know.

Heavy chuckles of other prisoners came from some of the other cells further down the corridor. Ash wondered just how many prisoners the submarine was detaining. *Who were these pirates?*

But the bum refused to listen. "You're in hell now," he said in a deeper, morbid tone. Interestingly enough, that's exactly how Ash referred to this place. "And you're about to meet the devil himself."

Petra climbed onto Lazlo's shoulders and took a look around. Ash saw that her tiny face didn't appear to possess even the slightest expression of optimism. Though they had survived the goliath-eels, they had now found themselves veritably in a situation where even good luck and insight didn't trump the heartless ambitions of those controlling the situation. They had fallen into a trap few had ever escaped.

"So," Driver piped up, as he tapped out a tune on the wall with his metal-tipped fingers. "I say we just tell these pirates that the girl is with the Marshal. That way they will have no need for us." Ash shot him a glare. "C'mon, kid," Driver urged. "You're telling me that you'd risk your life trying to save some girl whose *wanted* poster is plastered in every major port of Murk?"

"Leave him alone, Driver," Lazlo jumped in. Ash was grateful for the support. At that moment he needed it. He found it strange that Wick didn't even bother to defend him. It was almost as if he agreed with Driver.

"Then let the kid get himself killed and let's get out of here ourselves?" Driver said.

Lazlo said nothing, only raising a stern finger to silence the gearman once and for all. Petra mimicked his every action, perched upon his shoulder. Her tiny facial features were practically nonexistent in context of her crude expression. She had grown quite fond of Ash by now.

Driver took the hint, shaking his head and turning away in disdain.

The night was sleepless, and the next day a quiet terror-filled wait as the five of them sat in morbid silence. There was an occasional yell or scream of other prisoners that would echo throughout the corridors. But otherwise, they were all alone, with not even a drop of water to wet their tongues.

Even the imp-like prisoner across the way had since gone silent. *Perhaps he had died in his sleep?* Ash pondered. Hunger and thirst began to obsess him as he tried to fall asleep the next night. But just as his eyes began to weigh heavily, a figure emerged from the darkness.

The cell door flew open and a long, slimy, scaled arm reached in and snatched Ash. Resisting seemed like it would only do more harm. So Ash simply followed as the creature marched him away. Long claws pierced Ash's peasant shirt as the creature led him down the corridor. Glancing back, Ash saw the horror in Wick's eyes. It was like losing a child.

"Where are you taking me?" Ash yelled.

"You're having dinner with the captain," the creature rumbled back.

"Oh boy," Driver said quietly. He knew how pirate ships worked. Unless you were part of the crew, or an distinguished guest, if the captain wanted to see you, it meant you would most likely be walking the plank very soon.

The exclusive invitation sounded almost flattering to Ash. But if these pirates were as horrible as the prisoner across the way had let on, then, in spite of his raging hunger this was a dinner Ash would rather have skipped.

Thirty Six
Dinner With the Captain

Darkness was like a life form unto itself, ever-present and consuming. Ash felt blind and helpless. Fear he had never thought existed caused his insides to literally hurt. Swallowing, even breathing, was painful. But once they reached the captain's cabin door, all of the random thoughts and emotions he had been feeling seemed to melt into a singular overwhelming presence of hopelessness. The door opened.

The pirate's clawed, slimy hand shoved Ash over the threshold of the rusted door, slamming it behind him. A row of large, oval porthole windows lined the walls of the darkened room, allowing only the dim blue marine light in. Schools of silvery fish dashed back and forth among the passing coral spires. In the center of the room was a fire, rippling out of what appeared to be a goliath-clamshell pan, suspended just over the floor by thick chains hanging from the ceiling. From the firelight, Ash could see that a long, elaborate table was set low to the floor. An array of fish, oysters, and other mysterious shellfish was spread across the table. There had to have been enough food for more than twenty full-grown men. Ash didn't know what he was supposed to do. The sight of water and the smell of food would have made him drool had he any spit left. Then something moved at the opposite end of the table.

"Sit," a deep, thick voice growled. Though merely a whisper, the voice seemed to pierce the air like thunder. And there was something about it that seemed oddly familiar to Ash. Without even knowing it, he found himself sitting on the floor, at the end of the long table.

He tried to adjust his eyes and get a better look at the silhouette against the porthole windows. And then, as the figure leaned forward to skewer a slice of raw meat, its features became defined by the firelight. In one horrific moment Ash finally recognized the captain. *The dark creature!*

The fish was stuck onto a short spear erected from Bontey's prosthetic arm. His long dreads hung into his cat-like face, and fire danced in his yellowed eyes as he looked up at Ash. Ash didn't move. He even tried not to breathe. *Who was this familiar creature he had seen in the Ratroot Slough?* Nothing, not the drone-armada, not the mushroom forest, or even the goliath-eels made Ash tremble like this. It was an entirely different type of fear. His scars burned worse than ever before.

The fire had now dwindled down to a flickering smolder, as Bontey finished the massive fish, which he skewered and ate with etiquette unbecoming of his nightmarish persona. It seemed as though an eternity had passed before Ash even remembered to blink. He even forgot to quench his dying thirst with the water right in front of him. He had no comprehension of time.

Ash assumed him to be nothing more than a savage beast. But somehow knowing that this dark creature also possessed a sense of reserved dignity frightened Ash even more. Though he had regained some of his strength in Scar's absence, unable to channel it to her, Ash felt like *he* was now the one being drained. It was like every passing moment he was less alive.

"Eat," Bontey rumbled as he chewed.

Instantly, Ash reached for the nearest piece of food. He studied the chunk of raw fish and gave it a sniff. It had little to no scent. Still, the texture of this slimy meat nearly made him vomit. But hunger was beginning to consume him. Not to mention, he wasn't about to insult the captain by not eating. So he closed his eyes and dropped the raw meat into his mouth. Surprisingly enough, it didn't taste half bad. But then something strange happened.

He first felt it in his throat. But the numbing sensation quickly spread throughout his entire body until all he could do was let his body fall backward. What he now realized was that in his hungered haste, he had just eaten the legendary poisonous puffer fish.

The poison worked swiftly, rendering him completely paralyzed from head to foot. His mind was perfectly aware, but every muscle in his body was now as useless as the very meat on the table.

Out of the corner of his eye, Ash could see Bontey as he licked the meat juice off of the skewer and disengaged it back into his arm. Then, with heavy eyes he looked up at Ash's limp body and stared intently. The stare was hypnotic. Suddenly dishes flew everywhere, the fire flipped out of the shell-pan and Bontey was on top of Ash.

His claws tightened around Ash's throat, digging into his skin. His switch-sword blade had erected from his prosthetic arm and was pressed up to Ash's throat, threatening to pierce the skin. *Paralyzed. Just like the nightmares!*

It was the most horrific terror Ash had ever known as Bontey's black, hairy face slowly leaned into Ash's. He sniffed the air, as if recognizing the boy merely by his scent. It was the blood soaking through the back of Ash's shirt that Bontey smelled. He was the one.

"Where is she?" Bontey whispered with sour, rotting breath. The very question he asked in what Ash now realized to be a *precognitive* nightmare.

Ash could do nothing. He could feel his thoughts being trespassed. He was right. As Bontey squeezed tighter, more and more images from Ash's mind flashed through his mind's eye. And then it all went black.

Bontey released Ash, leaving his unconscious body on the floor. He was glad he had taken the precaution to paralyze Ash, given the supernatural powers this boy might possess. But he had gotten what he needed. Scar was with a Kingland Marshal. Find the Marshal, and he would finally have his prize. He was now one step closer.

Thirty Seven
Escape Attempt

"Ash," a familiar voice echoed. "Ash, can you hear me?"

Blurry images began to manifest as he slowly opened his eyes. Above him, Wick, Lazlo, and Driver were looming. His head ached.

"What happened?" Wick asked. "Where did they take you?"

Ash couldn't answer. For a moment he couldn't remember. Though he had regained his ability to move, his body still felt numb. Violated. Then the haunting recollection of the dark creature entered his mind's eye. He broke out in a cold sweat just thinking about it.

"Did they torture you?" Lazlo asked, recalling the many times he had found himself in the same situation. He hoped, for Ash's sake, that this wasn't the case. Pirates had no reason to place parameters of principal on how they conducted their torture procedures. They showed no mercy.

"How long was I out? Ash asked.

"They brought you back last night," Wick answered. "It's been an entire day."

"Where did they take you, Ash?" Driver insisted.

"The captain," Ash whispered as he shook. "They brought me to see him."

Wick and Lazlo looked at each other with deep concern. They both knew who this captain was. And if the rumors of his prison break were true, than surely he was back at the helm of the *Venom*. But Wick knew what this especially meant for Ash—something Ash didn't even know.

"He's the same one we saw in the swamp," Ash said to Wick. "Who is he?"

Wick was apprehensive to divulge. "His name is Sayto Bontey," Driver jumped in, making Wick cringe. "He's an ex-general for the Zahartan army. After the Great War he went into exile and became the most deadly pirate ever to sail the seas."

Ash was fully aware of this legendary pirate. And although he believed the bizarre tales, he couldn't believe that this dark creature was actually him.

"The question is," Lazlo interrupted, "what does Bontey want with you?"

"They say that Bontey likes to get to know his prey personally before he kills and eats them," the annoying prisoner interrupted from across the corridor.

"All right," Wick reprimanded the prisoner. "That's it. The boy's gone through enough, don't you think?" Shifting his attention back to Ash, he whispered, "What did Bontey say?"

"I think he's looking for Scar," Ash said. "Even in the swamps, he seemed to be searching for something—someone. But he was leading a platoon of drone-soldiers. He can't be working for Kingland, can he?"

"Not directly," Lazlo said solemnly. "But as I said before, Kingland has a history of contracting pirates to do their dirty work. So technically, somewhere down the chain of command, yes, he probably is." He was speaking from experience.

"We've got to get out of here," Wick whispered, leaning over to Lazlo to hide his words from Ash. "If Bontey's after Scar, then we're nothing more than a means to an end for him—which means, once he has what he wants, we're as good as dead."

"You're right," Lazlo said, looking around the cell. "This won't be easy."

"You did it once before," Wick said, referring to Lazlo's prison break from Isle of Monte.

"Yeah, well that was different," Lazlo admitted, continuing his study of the cell.

"Why?" Ash asked, quickly losing hope.

"Because I was able to dig a tunnel that ended on the other side of a wall," Lazlo explained. "Digging through walls isn't a real good idea on a submarine."

"Trust me," Driver added. "I tried it once. Not a good idea."

Then Ash saw something. "Hey, check this out."

Looking through the barred door, and through the floor grates, they could see two pirate-guards conversing on the mezzanine, two levels down. A large ring of keys jingled from the belt of one of the guards as he slowly stumbled back and forth.

"I think I see what you see," Lazlo said with a grin.

"The trick is, how to get our hands on those keys while still locked inside the cell," Wick said.

"Unless you're small enough to fit between the bars," Lazlo said, his epiphany taking the form of a wide grin.

"I'm not that small," Wick said, rubbing his protruding stomach.

"No, but she is," Lazlo said, as he lifted Petra off his shoulder.

They quickly drew up their plan and then sent Petra on her way.

Petra fluttered down to the pirate-guard's side, careful not to allow her glowing figure to meet his line of sight. Unfortunately, the more excited or anxious a pixie became, the brighter they glowed. There, right in front of her was the huge ring, with dozens of keys—each one as large as her entire body. But the guard was playing with them as he conversed with the other guard. The pixie had to find a way to distract him. As the guards wrapped up their conversation, she had an idea.

While one guard walked away, the other just stood there, still playing with his keys. Then the voice of the other guard echoed from behind him, repeating the last thing he had said: "I'm going to go catch some shut-eye." The guard with the keys was startled, as the voice was too close to be the other guard. It wasn't the other guard. It was Petra.

A trait all pixies possessed, which most people assumed was some form of magic, was the ability to absorb and mimic sounds with perfection. Though pixies were mute creatures with a vast language of gestures, they were able to use their vocal cords for this incredible gift, playing back the sounds as a near-perfect tonal match.

As the guard reached for his pistol, finally lifting his hand off his keys, Petra went for them. With no time to weed through all of the keys, Petra decided that it would be faster to just take the entire ring.

Ever so softly, she unclipped it from his belt. But as soon as it came loose she almost dropped the entire ring to the floor. It weighed far more than she did. With one arm looped around the ring and the other clasped to a rusty metal beam, she didn't realize that she wouldn't be able to fly. She would have to climb.

Below, the guard was finally figuring out that he had actually been tricked. Out of the corner of his eye, Petra's glow caught his attention as he glanced around frantically in search of the source. Petra knew she had to move much faster now.

The moment she reached the grate and began sliding the keys through an opening, she slipped! She quickly caught herself by grabbing onto the ring as one of the keys luckily became lodged in the grate. From above, Ash, Wick, Lazlo, and Driver watched with unblinking eyes.

Dangling from the ring, just below the grate, Petra regained her composure. Not for long, however. Below her, the large gloved hand of the pirate-guard reached and tried to grab her leg. Instantly, Petra curled up into a ball, out of the guard's reach—her glittering dust tickling his fingertips. She quickly climbed up the ring and onto the grate above and pulled the ring of keys through the opening just as the guard's fingers reached through to snatch them. Now that he had detected her, she really had to move. It wouldn't take long before the entire *Venom* was swarming with angry pirates.

"Throw them up," Wick yelled down to Petra as she struggled to climb back up to their level.

"She's a pixie," Lazlo defended. "She can barely carry them, let alone throw them. You're doing good," he yelled down to Petra, cheering her on.

Heavy footsteps rattled the grated floors of the corridor as Petra finally handed the keys over to Lazlo. He quickly unlocked the door and the four of them sprinted into the darkness of the catacombs.

The ship was a maze, but Lazlo seemed to be privy to the logic of its design. But suddenly the ease of their escape narrowed into a snared trap as six silhouettes rounded the corner in front of them.

"Here," Driver said quietly as he reached through a loose seam and into his torso, retrieving Ash and Lazlo's switch-swords. "I grabbed them from my taxi before we got hauled off to our cell," he said, handing them over. "Thought they might come in handy."

"Nice work, gearman," Lazlo said, quickly snatching his sword.

"Thanks," Ash whispered, ducking halfway behind Lazlo as the pirates engaged them.

"I hope you know how to fight, kid," Lazlo said to Ash, who had completely forgotten to eject his blade. "This is going to get ugly."

Then, just as the pirates got within a few steps, Lazlo dashed forward with a yell, whirling his sword high above his head. His blade was met with an equally aggressive one, the hammering of their meeting rattling through the air.

Instantly they were surrounded. "Get back!" Ash yelled to Wick and Driver. And then a rapier caught his arm, gashing his flesh wide open. It stung far worse than he had imagined it would. But there was no time to care. He had to fight back. Still not used to the heavy switch-sword, Ash made a wild attack on the air around him, failing to come even close to the surrounding pirates. One of his attackers closed in with his rapier cocked back over his head. He deflected the pirate's blow with his switch-sword, but not without losing grip of it as it clambered to the floor. Standing over Ash, the pirate taunted with an evil chuckle and his long rusted rapier. But suddenly Ash's hands went numb.

Opening his fingers, Ash saw a small ball of orange light beginning to swell upon his palm. Quickly the ball manifested into a fist-sized sphere of fire. Looking up at the looming pirate, Ash didn't think twice.

The fire slammed into the pirate's face, boiling layers of skin off his skull. The pirate screamed in a high-pitch, sprinting into the darkness. Ash's throw had been hard and precise, spraying flames everywhere. Just as Ash found himself stepping away from two more attackers, their swords began to smoke and then glow from the poignant heat they were magically channeling. *His thoughts were manifesting!* Instantly the pirates dropped their swords, screaming in pain as they held their scorched hands. And just like the pirate before them, they spun around and dashed away in terror. This left only one pirate, who quickly calculated his odds and followed his comrades.

Ash stood staring at his smoking hand. He couldn't help but remember the pain he had inflicted on his father only nights earlier. Lazlo's eyes were wide as he dragged his sword behind him like a broken stick. Ash would certainly have some explaining to do to his new friends. Lazlo disengaged his blade and turned to Ash, his eyes locked on Ash's hands. Ash only looked away.

"Okay, kid," Lazlo said with narrowed eyes, "have you got something you'd like to share with the rest of us?"

But before Ash could say a word, Wick jumped in, attempting to shelter Ash from Lazlo's sight. "He has nothing to say to you, Blackwood. You seem to be a well-traveled man. So no doubt you've seen your share of anomalies. Perhaps a thank you might be in order." Lazlo said nothing, just staring ahead at Ash. "Surely you don't think you could have defeated all six of those pirates on your own."

"Thank you Mr. Meadows," Lazlo said with the hint of a grin as he studied Ash's eyes. Ash knew that Lazlo was fully aware of what he was. But he seemed more impressed by it than anything.

"Follow me," Lazlo whispered, leading them into another narrow passageway and then further into the depths of the *Venom*. Again, the construction of the walls seemed to resemble smaller catacombs. But instead, each opening was filled with what appeared to be an airtight door.

"Hurry," Lazlo ordered, motioning the rest of them through the doors.

The room was dark, except for a small pool in the center of the floor, which was slightly lit from beneath.

"What are we doing?" Ash asked in a panic.

"We're going for a walk," Lazlo said, pointing to the three gold scuba suits hanging along the wall like unconscious, bubble-headed beings.

"What?" Ash exclaimed. He couldn't even imagine putting one of them on. He felt claustrophobia chocking him, just thinking about it. "We can't. There are not enough suits."

"Sure there is," Lazlo said, putting one of the suits on. Petra fluttered into it before Lazlo had a chance to seal it. She could fly. She couldn't swim. "Wick doesn't need one either."

Wick couldn't argue. Still, the thought of just abandoning ship at the bottom of the sea didn't really seem like such a good idea.

"Look, kid," Driver chimed in, "we don't have many options here. Sure, you might die out there. But you'll certainly die if you stay aboard this vessel. Make sense?" Unfortunately, it did.

The water was freezing as the weighted boots of the suits pulled Ash, Lazlo, and Driver down to the sandy bottom of the sea. Wick swam alongside. The boots made it impossible to move fast through the blue waters. Sunrays streamed down, casting long strange shadows across the sandy floor as they passed through a field of giant reeds. Up ahead,

Lazlo pointed out a school of giant jellyfish, rising from the depths. Ash's heart pounded. He knew just how deadly these things were. Lazlo made a gesture that told Ash to *calm down*. But then he froze as the school appeared to be coming closer.

Ash could see the concern in Lazlo's eyes through the small porthole window on his huge, brass helmet. And Wick crouched down behind a large pile of rocks, motioning for Ash to join him. Suddenly a massive swarm of colorful fish jetted around them, circling like a cyclone, stirring up a huge cloud of dust. These fish were reacting to something. Something big.

A massive cloud of sand swirled into a blinding haze, and before Ash knew it, he was being sucked up into the draft of the fishes' random course—they all were. Then a shadow fell over everything and Ash found himself engulfed in strange moist air.

Thirty Eight
Deception

"My Lord," the quivering voice of One whispered. Count LePrey stood on the lantern room catwalk, overlooking the crashing sea, too enthralled in thought to realize that the hovering drone was right next to him. Voices ravaged his mind like a circus of dizzying mayhem. He struggled to even focus his eyes, let alone his mind. So many years of toiling had led him to this point. Looking back it all seemed like another lifetime.

LePrey knew that creating the drone-armada was not something he could do on his own. Even if all resources were at his disposal, the sheer size of the operation would have alarmed those watching him closely—those like King Basileus. So LePrey had devised a scheme to have only precise parts for unique pieces of his armada built at specific public facilities. Each facility was under the impression that they were simply building parts for random pieces of machinery, such as water purification systems or energy generators. LePrey tracked when and where each shipment of parts was going from there. He would then contract pirates to raid these shipments, stealing the parts for him as they kept the rest of the loot for themselves. All that remained was the mere assembly, which he had completed in the caves of his island. And now with their global march underway and the dispersing of drone-implants successfully in progress, the population of the world would soon be transformed into a perfect, superhuman race, loyal to only one: Machine. It was the perfect plan.

If LePrey was startled by One's unprompted appearance, he didn't show it. He merely turned around and glared, as the Troika huddled together nervously.

"We-we have a problem," One stammered, getting right to the point. "The girl has been located."

"Good," LePrey said with uncontained excitement. He couldn't get his hands on the Enigma fast enough. The world could never know its secrets. "That doesn't sound like a problem to me."

"But not by Bontey," One said. LePrey's face grew instantly worried. "It's complicated, sir. A Kingland Marshal apprehended a refugee pirate. The girl was with him."

"Who is the pirate?" LePrey asked.

"Sir Lazlo Blackwood," Three answered.

"Blackwood?" LePrey said, baffled. He had gone to great lengths to erase this pirate's name from existence. Though he had heard rumors of his prison break, he couldn't imagine that Lazlo would have any luck running for long. "I thought he would be dead by now."

"Well he happened to be traveling with a band of renegades," One continued. "Most likely, the Marshal recognized the girl from the wanted postings circulating around Murk by Lord Yen. Yen's reward for the girl is attracting a lot of attention in that area."

"Whatever you do, make sure news of this doesn't find its way back to Bontey," LePrey said.

"It's too late for that, sir," One said. "He's the one who informed us that the girl was apprehended. And he's quite distressed about it. He thinks you've broken the deal. He's back aboard the *Venom* awaiting a response from you."

"We can't have this turning into a battle between the pirates and the Marshal," LePrey said stroking his chin. "It places the girl in jeopardy. Tell Bontey that his information is incorrect. In the meantime, send another drone-squadron out to track down this Marshal. He should be easy to find. The trick will be finding him in time, before he hands the girl over to Lord Yen. Because Yen won't hesitate to kill her if she doesn't cooperate."

"On a separate note," Two added, "the Pirate Rogue is becoming a real concern in the occupied territories. The recent surge in violence is threatening to overshadow any progress made since the invasion of our drone-armada. The Allied Commission has grown weary of the number of human casualties their armies have sustained." LePrey nodded in thoughtful agreement. "Shall we send in more drone-security forces?" asked Two.

After a brief moment, LePrey replied. "No."

This answer didn't compute with Two. "But the conflict might erupt into a full-scale war if we don't act first and wipe the Pirate Rogue completely out," Two warned. "It could easily escalate into a bloodbath, depleting what's left of the occupation forces."

"Exactly," LePrey said with a grin. "We need to seize the opportunity and allow chaos to work its-its magic." He chose his words carefully.

The Troika was now quite muddled. This was completely against the grain of LePrey's initial plan for wiping out the Pirate Rogue.

"Two," LePrey said, laying a hand on his shoulder as they began walking around the circumference of the catwalk. "Who is our greatest enemy?"

"The Pirate Rogue," Two answered.

"Wrong!" LePrey shouted spinning him around face to face. "Kingland and the Allied Commission are. And this is exactly why I say you are not perfect yet." He ran his fingers across Two's cheek. "You *must* realize this, if we are to succeed. People hate you and the very existence of your kind. Kingland has reduced the notion of artificial intelligence to a mere scientific commodity they reserve either for menial tasks or those they wish to wash their hands of. Although we have been successful in establishing a worldwide presence of our drone-armada, until the Ally's army of ancient ideals is eliminated, we have not truly won. The current armies of Kingland and their Allied Kingdoms are flawed. Their flaw?: their own mortality—a sad attribute they proudly flaunt in their sick emotional dementia. Mortality, my friend, is an attribute this world will soon be void of. Soon my entire drone-network will be one singular global mind. Invincible. Anyone who resists will be removed."

"So what is your plan?" One asked, ringing his hands in anticipation for his master's grand scheme.

LePrey looked at his reflection in the lantern room windows, knowing full well that Machine was studying him from the other side. He then revealed their new plan.

"I'm ordering a full withdrawal of our contract drone-armada in the occupied territories," LePrey began. "This will serve as a diversionary tactic of good faith on our behalf, cooling the heat coming from liberal idealists of the Allied Commission. But in turn it will leave their human occupation army vulnerable, which is exactly what we want. The Pirate Rogue will interpret our withdrawal as abandonment. And they will not hesitate to engage in full-blown war with the remaining occupation troops.

"Machine has calculated the probability of this scenario, and in the end, the Allied Occupation Forces and the Pirate Rogue will have all but wiped each other out. Another perfect plan. They both fight to the death while we remain unscathed. Our two greatest threats will simply do the work for us, simultaneously."

"Brilliant," the Troika raved in unison. "Consider it done."

Thirty Nine
Copi Bienna

Dozens of local fishermen sat, perched on rickety stilts made of dead trees, submerged in the crystal blue waters off the shore of Copi Bienna. They didn't move a muscle, waiting intently with their spears in hand—waiting for an unlucky fish to pass by. It was an admirable sport, taking patience and skill most people simply did not have. In fact, the younger generations of Copi Bienna didn't even bother with this style of fishing any longer. They simply boarded large boats and cast even larger nets. But every now and then their nets caught more than they planned.

On the white sands of the shore, a massing of shirtless, dark-skinned men stood, crowded around the spectacle. One of the day's fishing boats had netted a black whale, one of the largest monsters of the Coral Sea. Even lying on its belly in the sand, its dorsal fin rose twice as high as the tallest man.

Though its flesh was poisonous to eat, the whale's skin, fins, and giant black tusks were highly valuable on the local trade market, meaning these villagers would be living well for a while to come. The crowd cheered relentlessly as they hovered around the dead fish. But suddenly it moved.

Backing away in shock, the crowd watched intently as the whale shifted in the sand. Its mouth opened and the crowd took another step back. And then something happened that sent most of the crowd scattering away in all directions. It spoke.

"Help," the whale said. Its voice was muffled and seemed to be emitting from deep within. "Give me a hand here," it spoke again. Suddenly something emerged from its mouth and all but one of the fishermen fled the scene.

Standing to his feet, Ash tried to wipe the slimy clumps of seaweed from his scuba suit. But it was no use. He was just glad to have escaped the wretched bowls of the whale that had swallowed him. Looking up he noticed a shirtless man standing on the beach before him. The man's jaw dropped open, as if broken. Behind Ash, Wick, Lazlo, and Driver finally emerged from the whale's mouth as well. The fisherman said nothing as his eyes rolled to white and he fell backward into the sand.

Discarding his slimy scuba suit on the beach, Ash grew instantly mesmerized. Looking up, he was overwhelmed by the blue vastness. Never had he seen a cloudless sky before. The bright sun stung his eyes, but it was the most beautiful sky he had ever seen. This sultry tropical world was like something out of a dream.

The endless sea was a color he had never seen before—a turquoise that didn't even seem real. White sands stretched in either direction for as far as the eye could see. And blowing against the bright blue sky, a wall of towering palm trees met the sands like a wall concealing the jungles beyond.

Ash left the beach with Wick, Driver, Lazlo, and Petra. He was speechless when he took his first step onto the fern-covered soil of Copi Bienna's jungle floor. The air was thick with humidity and smelled like fresh, tropic rain, not like the muddy, sour rains of Murk. Everything was thicker and bigger, bloated by the lingering moisture. And the colors hurt his eyes with their vivid intensity as he struggled to adjust to his newly heightened senses.

The trees were enormous, looking over him like green mammoths. And every sound was new. Every squawk and howl echoed through the jungle, claiming their territory from these new invaders.

"Where do you think we are?" he asked.

"Copi Bienna," Lazlo answered without reservation. "The tropical peninsula of the Western Territories."

"Where are we headed?" Ash pursued.

"The village of San Gallopi," Lazlo answered. He seemed to not question for a moment where they should be headed. "It shouldn't be far from here," Lazlo said, wiping a drip of blood from the small scar on his forehead. He was trying to find the position of the sun in the bright blue sky, so he could determine their coordinates in the jungle.

"You know these jungles?" Ash asked, as he brushed the huge, hanging palm leaves from his face.

"I've stepped foot on every one of the world's continents at one time or another," Lazlo explained. "Being a fugitive can be a great way to see the world." He winked at Ash and continued through the jungle.

"Why San Gallopi?" Driver asked.

"Because there's a train terminal there. And if we're going to find Scar before Marshal Xavier turns her over to Lord Yen, then we'd better get a move on. The fastest way is by train."

"Ash," Wick whispered with shallow breath, as he struggled to keep up. "I need to talk to you. Before you go wasting your time trying to save a wanted criminal, I need to show you something."

Ash stopped dead in his tracks and spun around to face Wick. "I'm sick and tired of you discrediting my feelings for Scar. She's my friend—the only one who actually accepts me for who I am. I don't care what you think of her or what you think I should be doing. I'm my own person making my own decisions. And my decision is to find Scar before wasting my time on some fantastical treasure hunt."

It was final. They were going after Scar. Regardless of everything Wick had explained to Ash of his true identity, destiny would wait. Ash would soon learn the contrary.

"I think I see something," Driver said, trudging further ahead.

Crouching down at the edge of a fern-covered ledge, the five of them looked down at a large dome surrounded by a spread of smaller buildings in the distant valley. Petra heaved the large telescope out of Lazlo's backpack and onto his shoulder. He thanked her, took it, and looked through it.

"Yep, that's it," Lazlo said. San Gallopi. And unless they've changed the schedule recently, quite soon we should be able to catch a train to the Gedharah Plains, where Lord Yen's compound is.

"Wait a moment," Wick said with concern. "How are we going to pay for our fare? Mister Nootix took all of my money."

The expression on Lazlo's face was all too easy to recognize. He was hiding something.

"You didn't," Wick said, glaring at Lazlo with a furrowed brow. "You did," he answered himself.

"I had to," Lazlo admitted.

"He did what?" Ash asked, perplexed.

"He stole my money," Wick shouted with a shaking fist.

"Only some of it," Lazlo defended. "But I had to, otherwise Nootix would have taken all of it. I knew that we'd eventually need money. And all of my money was on the riverboat. Look, here," he said, handing over a handful of coins to Wick. "Take it. It's yours. I was just holding onto it for you."

Wick snatched the coins from Lazlo's hand. Ash thanked him. Still, *could this pirate really be trusted?*

"Pirates," Wick pouted to himself, gesturing to Lazlo.

"Privateer," Lazlo corrected again.

"Let's go," Ash said, starting down the slopes to get away from another round of pointless bickering. Now that they were this close, he wasn't about to slow down. The lonely whistle of a distant train howled through the trees.

Forty
Derailed

San Gallopi was an old city. In fact, its ritualistic social structure was so closed off from the rest of the world that in most ways things had remained as they had been for nearly two thousand years. With the exception of specific modern technological advances, one would hardly be able to tell the difference between the current city and that of generations gone by. But since being invaded, the city was now crawling with drone-soldiers. Soon this spot on the globe would be transformed into a new-world city, wiped clean of any remnants of its expired history.

In the dead center of the city sat the train terminal, the nexus of technology and the one thing that connected this place to the rest of the world. The terminal was enormous. Its domed tiled exterior had once glistened in the sun of Copi Bienna. But over the centuries, the tropical heat and rains had weathered the building, washing away much of its color and decaying the beautiful artistry and craftsmanship of its tile work.

Huge, double-decker commuter trains lined the floor of the terminal, as hundreds of people boarded and exited. Their silver steel exteriors were rusted and strewn with graffiti across each car. The loud, echoing voice, announcing departures and arrivals, was in a different language—one Ash had never heard before. It was one more reminder that he was in a foreign world.

The moment Ash stepped aboard the train, the moisture grew even thicker. The air was like a wall of thick humidity—a gagging blend of sweat and smoke, trapped inside the rusted confines of each car. Most people wore only thin, colorful robes and cloaks. And many covered their heads in defense against the heat. The quarters were hot and cramped with people around each other moving frantically, as if in an aimless race against time. As hot as it was, Ash never felt colder, never so far from home. Still, there was something about it that reminded Ash of Garbbit Harbor—the blurring bustle of so many strangers.

While Wick and Lazlo situated into their seats, caviling about something relating to the elevation level of San Gallopi, Ash and Driver decided to go down to the lower level and have a look around.

Ash had never been aboard a train before. It was fascinating, especially one of this size. Although this wasn't the fastest model to date, and was certainly showing signs of age, the train was still an impressive piece of machinery. With a sudden jolt, the train lurched forward, causing Ash and Driver to stumble into a pole. They were officially on their way to the Gedharah Plains, the residence Lord Yen.

The churning of the engine's gears filled the train with a moaning hum that vibrated throughout the walls and floor. The power of the train's speed was overwhelming, almost dizzying. But then Ash saw something that seemed to make everything stand still.

Her face was shadowed by the cloak's large hood, yet the Marshal seated next to her looked familiar. Though his helmet's shield concealed his face, Ash was almost positive of who it was. He didn't recognize the two large, green creatures sitting across from them. But then, the hooded person opened her clenched fists, discretely exposing her scars to Ash.

Ash was frozen in shock. He knew he had to make a move. *But what? How?* Unfortunately, it was that moment that Xavier decided to make his move.

"Oh boy," Driver whispered. He knew that there was no way this would end peacefully.

Still handcuffed to Scar, Xavier dashed from his seat, yanking her with him. He dragged her to the stairs, to the upper deck. Yen's two henchmen stood to their feet, but their thick, lumbering legs were not quick enough to catch up to Xavier in time.

"Asher!" Scar cried as Xavier jerked her forward.

The sound of her voice rattled Ash like thunder. It was one thing to hear her voice again. Yet it was another to hear it in such desperation. Before he had time to think, Ash found himself sprinting down the train after them, leaving Driver in the dust.

His legs were moving far faster than he had ever felt before. And he was maneuvering over and around obstacles in ways he had never experienced. It was as though someone or something else was in control. This surge of power was beginning to feel natural. And he liked it. Through the blur he noticed his skin beginning to glow. Suddenly he found himself flat on his face, on the floor of the train.

Looking up from the gritty floor and unaware of what he had tripped over, Ash saw Scar and Xavier entering yet another car. The last car of the train! In spite of the cut he had just received on his forehead, Ash shook it off. He got to his feet and made it to the final door. But this time Xavier had locked it. Scar's eyes were desperate as he pulled her away. She looked so tired and weak. Ash cranked on the handle with everything he had left, but nothing happed. Then he had an idea.

Before Ash had a chance to weigh his options rationally, he closed his eyes and focused his energy on the window. As his rage built within, a crack began to run down the pane and suddenly it smashed to pieces. Everyone around him scattered at the sight of the glowing boy as Ash found himself climbing out and onto the exterior of the train.

This was unlike anything he had ever even dared to do before. As he carefully scaled the train he felt as though all rational thought and logic had left him. There was strength inside of him that he felt had always been there, but until now had never awakened. It was more than adrenalin. He was becoming something new.

The jungle blurred by like green liquid as the train cruised through the depths of the bamboo forest. The metal hull was cold, chilled by the intense speed. The train shook with persistence, like a giant lizard trying to lose Ash. But he held on with everything he had, and more. Hand over hand he slid is body down the car, crossing the threshold to the very end. His eyes filled with tears from the whipping wind. He could barely see what he was doing. As light began to pour through the thinning palm trees, he could see only blue sky up ahead—no more trees. Suddenly he knew why.

The train was skirting the very edge of a cliff that rounded a giant mountain. Just the sight of the incredible cliff made Ash slip, as the turquoise sea stretched eternally far, far below. He quickly regained his grip and dared to move forward. But looking up he caught a glimpse of Scar inside the car, struggling to get away from Xavier, who was making an attempt to enter the roof of the train. He was too weak to use his curse on another window again. So with a single blow of his elbow, Ash smashed the glass, cutting his arm. But he didn't have time to think about a simple cut.

Quickly he climbed in and made it to his feet. Scar looked as though she could collapse to the floor at any moment. All Ash wanted to do was hold her—hold her and smell her hair. But before he could engage Xavier, the door blasted open in a rapidly dissipating fireball. Through the smoke entered Lord Yen's two henchmen. The lizardens drew their guns on Xavier who instinctively whirled Scar around in front of him and shoved the barrel of his pistol against her head. Ash felt his heart flip at the horrific sight. His *Mysterious* glow instantly dimmed. Everyone froze.

"Give her up Marshal!" the first henchman growled. "You had your chance to bring her in, you've got too much heat on you now. Hand her over and we'll spare your life."

"Back away or she's dead!" yelled Xavier as he recoiled into the corner. Ash clenched his teeth at the sound of all of these threats on

Scar's life. "I know how you work. Don't think for a second that I didn't know what you were up to. You'll bump me off the moment I hand her over to Lord Yen. Why pay the reward when you can just kill the delivery boy?"

The henchmen didn't even try to defend themselves. Xavier was right. "You have nowhere to run," the second henchman said. "And there's two of us and only one of you."

Suddenly a whir sliced through the air and the first henchman's head slid off of his shoulders. His limp green body fell onto the floor. And behind him stood Lazlo, with his sword dripping in warm red blood. With pistol in hand, Driver stepped out from behind Lazlo. Wick peeked around from behind Driver's leg with scared eyes.

"I see only one greasy lizard-man standing," Lazlo replied to the second henchmen's remark.

Ash was relieved to see them, but in a strange way felt envious of Lazlo's heroic entrance. It should have been he. Never before had Ash cared about being a hero. But something was changing. He needed to save Scar. He felt that in a way he was responsible for all of this. Had he not rescued her in the Lonesome Pine, her path would have ended up vastly different. But at that very moment, all he felt like was a useless tagalong to the swashbuckling pirate hero.

"I'll split the reward with you," Xavier pleaded with Lazlo, knowing that it would take some serious persuasion to talk himself out of this situation.

"I'm not interested in the money, Xavier," Lazlo replied. "You should know that by now."

"C'mon," Xavier shot back. "You're a bloody pirate! Don't get all ethical on me now. You're not going to get a better break than this!"

"Privateer," Lazlo corrected. The second henchman seemed to be frozen in a state of shock, listening to this ridiculous conversation. "And I'm not looking for a break," he informed, raising his rapier and nudging the first henchman out of the way. "I'm looking for a girl. Now hand her over."

The henchman spun around and pressed his rifle into Lazlo's stomach. But before he could do anything, Xavier tossed a tiny gas grenade down onto the floor. Instantly, everyone was consumed in the choking smoke. And when the smoke cleared, Xavier and Scar were gone. Xavier's boots thundered on the metal roof above. Concurrently, Ash, Lazlo, and the second henchman fought their way to the roof through the same exit Xavier used. Wick stayed behind with Driver, knowing full well this type of confrontation was not for either of them.

With his rapier in one hand and pistol in the other, Lazlo dashed forward on the rooftop, against the pressing wind of the moving train. The henchman followed closely behind firing vain shots as he stumbled in pursuit. Ash steadied himself as he climbed onto the roof as well.

"Careful, Ash," Wick yelled instinctively, pacing the floor below. He couldn't quite let go of his need to look out for the boy. "This train's moving faster than you think." But Ash heard none of what was said. The only thing he could see or hear was Scar, with Xavier's pistol pressed to her head.

"Stop right there!" Xavier yelled, with Scar clenched tightly. But Lazlo didn't listen. Either he was fearless or something inside told him that Xavier didn't have it in him to actually pull the trigger. And perhaps that was true. Because with every step Lazlo took, Xavier simply took another one back. But suddenly a shot fired and Lazlo went down to one knee.

The henchman had finally locked his sights and was able to get a mostly clean shot. Although it wasn't a kill shot, it had disabled Lazlo enough for the henchman to engage Xavier and Scar. Ash raced forward to check on Lazlo just as Xavier and the henchman began to exchange gunfire. But at that instant, the world went completely black.

The tunnel wound through the jungle-covered mountains of Copi Bienna. But because these tunnels were so old, few of them were equipped with any form of lighting. And the tunnel's curved path made it impossible to tell when the end would ever come.

Ash held on to Lazlo's sleeve to steady both of them. The gunfire had ceased. But by the sounds of things, some form of tussle was taking place between the henchman and Xavier. Suddenly Scar screamed and there was the sound of broken glass, a shattering window. And then it was silent.

The sunlight was blinding as the train finally exited the tunnel. Ash struggled to see. But as he focused, he only saw Lazlo and Xavier. He looked around frantically, but Scar was nowhere to be found. His heart sank once again. The momentum of defeat was shifting Ash to a very dark place, a place he had never been emotionally. His fear was slowly melding into a most powerful anger-fueled rage.

"He took her," Xavier said in a waning voice, holding his ribs in pain—his plot derailed. "Thanks to you, she's gone now."

"No!" Lazlo said lifting his head. "Thanks to you!"

Inside the train the henchman escorted Scar through the cars, brushing bits of broken glass off of himself from the broken window he had escaped through with his prisoner. But then, just as they were passing from one car to the next, the henchman stopped and thrust his huge rapier down into the giant lock, linking the two cars together. Twisting it violently, he disengaged the lock, separating the train into two.

The front cars slowly pulled away, crossing onto a giant bridge spanning the immense void of a canyon. Quickly he pulled out a grenade. However, this one wasn't a gas grenade. Pulling the pin, he dropped it onto the tracks and took off running, dragging Scar behind.

"Back inside!" yelled Xavier as he, Lazlo, and Ash scrambled off of the roof. They saw the rest of the train pulling away, but they had no idea what the henchman had just tossed down onto the tracks of the bridge they were about to cross.

As soon as they reentered the train, the rear cars crossed onto the bridge, still coasting at a brisk speed. And just as the front cars, still being pulled by the engine, crossed over to the other side of the canyon, the grenade went off, blasting the bridge into a splintering cloud of wood and twisted metal. The back half of the train launched into the air and off the rails …

Like a gliding aircraft, the train soared in a giant arch toward the other side of the canyon, smashing into the matrix of metal and wooden bracings holding up the far end of the bridge.

The impact was a violence that convinced Ash that he was already dead. He felt the timeless cold grip of darkness nearing. *This is how I will die*, he thought to himself. His lanky body was thrown around, as if caught up in a tremendous funnel cloud. Finally, the train jerked to a stopped.

The only way Ash knew up from down was by the fact that his floppy hair was standing on end. Carefully, he maneuvered himself back to an upright position, hanging on to the headrest of a broken seat by his fingertips. His body hurt, but he didn't have time to figure out exactly what it was. The inside of the train was a mess of torn seats and bent metal. Through the dust he could hear moaning. But he couldn't tell who it was. Then, from above, he heard the blood-curdling, bone-crunching sound of a body slamming into the unforgiving frame of the train—then dropping lifelessly away.

Looking down, Ash saw Xavier falling through a gaping hole in the side of the train into the thick mist below. It wasn't clear where he had fallen to. From what Ash could tell, the train had ended up entangled in busted underbracing of the bridge's remains. All Ash could think about was his fingers. They were already numb from hanging on the outside of the train for so long. His hands shook painfully, struggling to keep their grip on the seat, in which he hung. Who knew how far down the bottom of this gorge actually was, beneath the passing mist? Wick's words echoed in his foggy mind, *You were born to fly.* But Ash wasn't about to test his luck with gravity. Not now. *Probably not ever.* Then, like the last breath on a deathbed, his fingers gave up.

Forty One
The Ginka

The mist smelled of rotting grass and animal feces. And it was much cooler and breezier here, wherever *here* was. Ash opened his eyes to a gray formless world. But when the mist passed, he discovered that he had landed in some sort of a crater composed of mud and straw. Lifting his head even further, he then realized exactly where he was. And that's when his stomach turned.

The vertical rocky gorge of the canyon sank into a sifting fog bank far below, and was littered with what appeared to be giant nests. And Ash was in one of them. Large fowls circled in the skies above, but these were not their homes. Whoever had made these were much bigger. The winding river was so far below, the sound of its waves could not even be heard. But the sounds of the jungle above were loud and uninviting. The crying howl of the wind was like the scream of a rabid animal. Then he heard something.

It sounded like a yell. It sounded familiar. He looked around but saw nothing. Then Ash heard it again. It seemed to be coming from below. Looking over the edge of the nest he couldn't believe his eyes. Lazlo was curled into a ball in the middle of another nest. And in yet another, lie Driver, who appeared to be kicking at something. Then Ash saw something that made the hair stand up on the back of his neck.

Two, gray, hairy hands appeared from a crevice in the gorge, grabbing Driver's legs and dragging him into a cave within the gorge. Only moments later, the same happened to Xavier, who appeared to be unconscious.

Ash was now overcome by a whole new sense of fear—the kind that made him almost feel like he hadn't survived the fall. As he huddled in the nest, he did the only thing he could: wait. There was no way down and no way out. The gorge was far too steep and smooth to climb. Looking into the blackness of a narrow crevice in the rock from where the nest seemed to grow, Ash wondered how long it would be until this mysterious creature might come for him. But there were already eyes waiting in the shadows of the cave.

His head banged off the wet, rocky cave floor, as Ash was drug by his feet. The creature's grip was tight, dragging him through a maze of tunnels before finally reaching the light. The sun was screened by the woven texture of the walls. From what Ash could tell, it appeared he had been taken to some sort of a giant hut. Unlit lanterns hung from the high, domed ceiling and torn linen sheets were draped across the hut as dividers, sectioning the hut into various rooms. But his view soon became eclipsed by the growing multitude of furry creatures surrounding him.

They were Ginkas—natives of the Bamboo Forests. But they were primarily cliff-dwellers. Although they bore webbing, which connected from their wrists to their ankles, they were gliders rather than flyers. They were more primate than fowl, with a thick coat of hair that covered their entire body and a long, bushy striped tail that seemed to have a mind of its own. They looked like bandits, with their beady eyes hidden within the large, black patches of hair that wrapped the upper half of their face. Tuffs of long, gray whiskers curved down from their upper lips, like overgrown mustaches. To Ash, they were alien. And he could only imagine what they were thinking at that very moment.

One of the Ginka lit a large fire in the center of the hut. Though they appeared quite civilized, there was no telling how vicious they just might be. Ash had heard many stories of how dangerous these jungles could be. He tried to escape the image of himself being roasted over the flame.

"Looks like they're having us for dinner," Lazlo's voice came out of nowhere.

Sitting up, Ash noticed that they had all been brought to the same hut. Assuming Petra was still safe and hidden within Lazlo's backpack, they were now only missing Xavier. As grateful as he was to see all of them, he wondered if this might be their last moments together.

"Do you think they'll eat us?" Ash whispered as the Ginkas loomed above with their spears and clubs.

The Ginkas all froze, staring at each other. Then, after a deathly silence, laughter roared through the air. Every Ginka in the hut was doubled over in hysterics. "Get over yourself," one of them said in a high-pitched tone, slurred by a thick, broken dialect. "I'd rather eat mud," another one joked.

"That's the advantage of being a gearman," Driver said, leaning over to Ash. "Cannibals tend to pass on you."

Ash was shocked, partially by the fact that the Ginka could talk and partially by the fact that they were not interested in eating their prisoners like the tales he had been told. *Perhaps they were not prisoners after all.*

One of the Ginka leaned down with a stone crock filled with water. She gently poured it into Ash's mouth. "I'm Boota," she said meekly. The cold water tasted heavenly—so cold on his parched lips. And for a moment it seemed his thirst would never subside. Then another stooped down with a large clay bowl of fresh, bright-colored fruit. Ash grabbed a couple different ones and shoved them into his face like a toddler who still hadn't learned the art of feeding himself. The moment their tart juices touched his tongue, it nearly made his eyes cross, *his newly heightened senses performing brilliantly.*

"Where's Xavier?" Ash asked with a mouthful. Wick, who was sucking the last bit of fruit juice from a core, only shrugged his shoulders.

"Your friend is with the Hoodu," Boota said, pointing to a small, rope-suspended staircase, leading to an exit.

"Who's that?" Ash asked.

"The witch doctor," Boota answered.

"Witch doctor?" Lazlo asked. "Why? What's wrong with him?"

"He's dead."

Forty Two
The Witch Doctor

The sun, bloated and distorted in the cooling evening sky, slowly sank away into the orange horizon. The view, from the small earthen balcony in which the tribe's huts were affixed was stunning—looking out over the winding ravine, out to the vast tropical sea. Ash realized that the nests they had fallen into were simply these balconies. He gazed into the naked sky and became overwhelmed by the sight. Stars he had never seen before glittered like a field of diamonds. It was far bigger than he had ever imagined. It was so much more magical than he ever dreamed. For a moment he felt he understood what the Imcot were so mesmerized and inspired by when they too stared into the center of the sky.

The old witch doctor puffed on a long, curved, wooden pipe, gazing out peacefully over the sunset. His hair was whiter than the other Ginka, his whiskers much longer and his posture was hunched from his age. The giant feathers of his headdress swayed in the evening breeze in steady communion with the treetops around.

Ceremonial drumming filtered through the air from beyond like the rhythm of a distant engine. Incense filled the air with a strange smell that almost gagged Ash. The sight seemed too serene. *Could Xavier really be dead?* he wondered. It was a strange emotion he was feeling, having hated Xavier so deeply. But just like his father, death was not what he wished.

In the middle of the small balcony lie Xavier, swathed in white linen. Neither Lazlo nor Ash knew exactly why they had come or what they thought they would find. After all, *dead* is a pretty conclusive state. But there was something about this witch doctor that gave them hope.

"So, Mister Witch Doctor?" Lazlo said, entering the hut with a limp. Although the lizarden's gunshot had barely grazed his leg, his cut had now become slightly infected. Boota had already treated it with a strange concoction of spring water and crushed leaves. "What now? Are you going to bring him back to life? Is that what you do?"

Ash cringed at Lazlo's cocky lack of respect for the old native. Nonetheless, he had mixed emotions about the entire situation. After all, Xavier had left them for dead at the bottom of the sea. And the last time Ash had seen him alive he had a gun to Scar's head.

Hoodu remained silent, puffing on his pipe. Ash recognized the scent of the weed. Then it hit him: *Ginka Weed. Of course!* It was the same type Wick smoked. Only Wick had to have his imported to Murk and paid a high price for it.

Then the witch doctor answered quietly, in a soothing foreboding whisper. "No. I do not possess the power to raise the dead. That will be up to your friend here," he said pointing to Xavier.

His answer was nonsense to Lazlo. But Ash felt like he actually knew what Hoodu meant. He had heard many stories about people who had been declared *dead*, but then mysteriously came back to life. They often spoke of a turning point where they could either turn back and reenter the world, or continue on into the next life. *Perhaps this was the place where Xavier was currently residing.*

"Come in," Hoodu said to Wick and Driver, who decided to join them. No one really knew if this was about to become a memorial service or some sort of séance.

They all sat next to Hoodu in a long, buffed log. Lazlo was careful not to sit too close. But when Hoodu began passing around his pipe, he knew that there was now nothing to fear. It appeared he didn't assume that Lazlo was a pirate, like everyone else did.

"I know you were once a pirate," Hoodu said. His words made Lazlo choke uncontrollably on the pipe. Smoke went everywhere.

"P-privateer," Lazlo corrected through his cough. "I was a legitimate privateer under the flag of Kingland."

"I know," said Hoodu. "I fail to see the difference. But don't let that scare you. You now know as well as I do that this is a failed strategy. Look where it got you. You're now a fugitive."

"Yes, but I was a victim of corruption," Lazlo defended. "There was an insider who wanted the King dead. My knowledge of this is what put me behind bars."

"Yes, I know, Lazlo," Hoodu said.

The fact that Hoodu knew Lazlo's name sent chills down everyone's spines. "How do you know who I am?" Lazlo asked with a bewildered expression distorting his face.

"I know far more about the world than you think," Hoodu said as Lazlo handed back the pipe.

Hoodu was old enough to have had many brushes with pirates over the years. Someone like Hoodu would have done extensive research on a pirate like Sir Lazlo Blackwood. "While the rest of you are busy jumping from one continent to the next, we Ginka remain quite still, observing."

"But how can you claim to have a worldview from just sitting here?" Ash asked.

"It is not merely seeing which gives one insight," Hoodu said lifting his head to the dawning moons. "It is listening. The wind. It is timeless and transcendent. It has always existed and travels the globe by its own will. It carries the voices of all living things upon its wings. The wind speaks very simply, if one is only willing to listen."

If this was anything like Ash's mysterious, recently heightened senses, he was oddly enough was beginning to understand what the witch doctor was talking about.

"So the wind can see the future?" Lazlo asked skeptically.

"No," replied Hoodu. "It is merely a reflection of what is happening. Or of what has happened. But by understanding the past, one needs to only open their eyes to then see what lies ahead."

"I don't get it," Driver said.

"See those creatures across the way," Hoodu said, pointing to two small animals erratically scuttling around the edges of a clearing at the edge of the jungles on the other side of the gorge. "They are sparring, preparing for a fight—a fight to the death."

"How do you know?" Ash asked, intrigued by Hoodu's impeccable insight.

"Because neither will give up," Hoodu analyzed. "It's their instinct. It's how they claim their territory. But they are too evenly matched. So they'll both wind up dead."

"So no one wins," Wick whispered, deep in thought, as he took a large hit off Hoodu's pipe. He was amazed how much more fresh this weed was than the stuff he had imported to Willow Lake.

"Wrong," Hoodu said. "Look over there," he said pointing to an adjacent, large tree. Through the thick leaves Wick could barely make out the silhouette of another Ginka.

"Yeah, I see him," Lazlo said. "One of your tribal guards."

"Hunters," Hoodu replied. "He's staking out the two animals below. First, he bated them by placing a carcass in the clearing. The two animals you see are the elected warriors for their clans, chosen to claim the carcass for their own clan. But the real winner here will be the hunter in the tree. And most likely, he will not even spare a spear tip to reap the reward of not one, but *both* animals."

"Why do you tell us this?" Lazlo asked even more bewildered now than he was before.

"The shadow of darkness has been cast across the world," Hoodu said, lowering his tone and shifting his focus to Lazlo. "The magical language of the dragon is all but dead. And now there is one who aims to dismantle our freedoms and silence the voices of the past forever.

An insider with relentless persistence. Word has reached the jungles of Kingland's crippled state."

"The wind told you that?" Lazlo asked, about ready to dismiss himself from this outlandish conversation.

"Actually the birds told me that," Hoodu admitted. "They are quite keen observers, you know." This answer was pretty mind-boggling too. But it was just believable enough for Lazlo to remain seated.

"Kingland's supreme powers have fallen victim to a heinous puppet-master," Hoodu continued. "And with meticulous manipulation, the puppet-master has secured his position and weakened even the strongest kingdoms.

"The world's greatest rivals will not stand down until war is had. And like the animals across the gorge, neither will they withdraw till the other has fallen. But also like the animals, they are evenly matched. The puppet-master knows this, which is why he sits, waiting on his perch while his two primary obstacles eliminate themselves. It is the perfect plan.

"With no blood to wash from his hands, the puppet-master absorbs the chaos of a crippled world and claims to be its savior by means of militant rule. Once the greatest kingdom to ever rise upon the face of the world, Kingland is now on the verge of collapsing into nonexistence."

Though Hoodu's parables were vague, everyone in the room was beginning to understand what he was saying. The real question on their minds was, *Why was he telling them this?* It's not like they could do anything about it.

Turning to Ash, Hoodu whispered, "You don't know it yet, but you play a vital role in all of this. I can see it."

Ash swallowed the lump in his throat and nodded, clueless as to what Hoodu was talking about. Wick, however, knew exactly what Hoodu meant.

Then the witch doctor changed the topic. "The one you seek is within your reach," he said to Ash. "But you will need a plan if you have any chance of saving her."

Ash was spooked by Hoodu's telekinetic-like abilities. It was like Hoodu was reading his mind.

"We need to get to the Gedharah Plains," Ash explained. "Scar, the one I seek, is being held there, in the compound of Lord Yen."

"Slave Lords are bad business," Hoodu said, shaking his head. If there was one thing the Ginka feared most, it was the Serpentine Slave Lords that lived in their stone towers above the treetops of the jungles.

For centuries Slave Lords had been kidnapping Ginka younglings and forcing them into slavery to help build their compounds. Sure, there were jungle beasts far more ravenous than Serpentines, but death in the jungle was preferred over life as a slave.

"But their compounds are heavily guarded," Ash said, hoping Hoodu would have an idea. "We have no resources for a mission like this. And we don't have much time."

"What are those?" Wick said, pointing to a massive flock of giant moths, flying in a loosely patterned *V* through the darkening skies. They were flying south.

"Those are megamoths," Hoodu said. "And a good eye you have, wharfling," he complimented, placing his hand on Wick's shoulder. "They will come in quite useful for your journey to the plains tomorrow. Yes, quite useful indeed."

"Wait a moment," Wick said. "I didn't mean that. I was just asking—"

"But in asking the wrong question, you have discovered the right answer—the one you were looking for," Hoodu said.

"I think the old coot needs some sleep. He's not making any sense," Driver whispered to Ash. But Ash just ignored the gearman.

"Get a good night's rest," Hoodu said, addressing them all. "You'll need it. In the morning I will divulge."

"Have you got room for one more on your journey?" someone asked. But the voice made no sense. It wasn't right. *How could it be?*

Slowly turning around to see, everyone gasped as Xavier stood in the center of the room, unwrapping the white linen from himself.

Forty Three
Lord Yen

Dawn came, breathing life back into the jungles. A vast array of chirps and whistles echoed throughout the mangrove as the native birds repeatedly announced the arrival of a new day. Tiny lizards scurried about the forest floor as larger, more mysterious creatures leaped about from tree to tree. Ash had never experienced a world so alive. In fact, though the hammock in which he had been put up was perhaps the most comfortable bed he had ever layed down in, he was up most of the night just listening to creatures he had never before heard. This was truly another world.

Ash wished he had gotten more sleep. But with Xavier coming back around, the entire tribe was abuzz for most of the night. According to Hoodu, Xavier had only partially died, refusing to completely cross over to the other side. Ash didn't fully understand the explanation, but he believed it. When asked why Xavier had decided to come back, Hoodu simply replied, "Perhaps he has unfinished business to tend to." Perhaps Hoodu was right. After all, the Xavier that had awoken seemed nothing like the one who had died.

"Look, you're going to need someone like me. I know these jungles," Xavier argued with Lazlo. Surprisingly enough, not only did he want to join their crusade to rescue Scar from Lord Yen, he was insisting that he *lead* the charge. Indeed, something had radically changed about him.

They say that near-death experiences have a tendency to change one's perspective. Though Xavier wasn't about to expose his emotions to these misfits he now owed his life to, he felt little urge to protect his hardened ego any longer. Life was clearly too short for that. Now, instead of fighting for another bloody dollar, he felt an overwhelming sense of compassion—especially for those he had hurt so badly—especially for Scar. *But was it real?*

"I know these jungles too," Lazlo argued back. "Don't you think you should rest? I mean you've only been alive since last night."

Xavier choked down a laugh. "I'm a little foggy right now, so forgive me. I don't think you understand. I need to be a part of this."

Lazlo paused for a moment and studied Xavier's expression. It was nearly impossible to tell whether Xavier was being honest. This shift in behavior was all just a little too suspicious. But giving him the benefit of the doubt was no different than what Lazlo had been asking of Ash and Wick since meeting them. "Okay, if you insist. But no arresting us again, got it?" Everyone busted out in laughter, even Xavier.

Leaning into Ash's face, Xavier whispered, "Besides, if I have to hang around here listening to that old witch doctor speak in aimless riddles any longer, I think I may die again." Ash chuckled, but then realized that somehow Xavier had obviously heard everything that was being said in the hut the night before. The concept of death had just become a bit more perplexing.

As Ash readied himself for the adventure ahead, Wick approached him with the obvious intention to discuss something.

"If you're here to preach about going after Scar, save it," Ash barked proactively. But Wick held up his hand in defense, clearly disinterested in stirring the pot.

"No, Ash," he began humbly, "I only want to wish you luck and to tell you that I'm proud of you." His words were sincere. "So much has happened recently that I have trouble keeping up myself. I never imagined it would happen like this. That your awakening would be some overnight revelation. And never did I imagine that you would be forced to use your gift like this."

"Like what?" Ash asked, puffing up his chest. "To save Scar—"

Wick didn't even let him finish. "No. To save the world." Ash didn't know what to say. "I always knew you were special, Ash," Wick continued. "But even I didn't fully understand the significance of your gift. And you are growing stronger. You may not see it yourself—caught up in the chaos of the moment—but you are becoming more powerful all of the time. You are becoming a true Guardian. Like Hoodu said, you play a vital role in all of this."

As flattering as it all sounded, Ash wished more than anything that his role was far less impressive.

"They're coming," Boota yelled, as a subtle rumble began to sift through the jungle.

Through the thick foliage of the jungle, Ash could see something moving. And some of the smaller trees, those that didn't pierce the clouds, seemed to be bending and twisting—pushed aside by something giant passing by. Then they emerged and Ash's eyes grew wide.

Megamoths were one of the oldest and largest species known to Copi Bienna. They always traveled in herds, for protection. Although these nocturnal beasts were the largest land animals of the jungle, it was the smaller, faster, pack-hunting predators that were their most deadly threat.

Every evening, massive herds of megamoths, reaching numbers of over a thousand, flew to the Bamboo Forest to feed on the leaves of the trees. Since it was the one time megamoths ate in the course of a day, they would eat obscene amounts of food. Then, when twilight came, they would begin their long journey back home, through the Western Jungles. To conserve on energy they conducted their homeward journey on foot, right through the Gedharah Plains. Now all Ash had to do was build up the courage to follow through with this ridiculous scheme they had devised.

The golden sun was diffused through the megamoths' translucent wings, propped up like a giant, vertical fin, as they slowly herded through the jungle plains. They looked very similar to tiny insect moths—only they were larger than a house. Gray and marked with smoky, swirling patterns, they were not the most beautiful creatures to roam these jungles. Swarms of birds and insects followed the mass of megamoths, like a lifting cloud as the sprawling herd moved across the vastness of the jungle.

Their journey took until late morning. As they neared a vast plain, from which Yen's towering spire erected, dozens of shirtless lizardens slowly parted, making a large path for the megamoths to cross. Though it was a daily occurrence, the passage of the megamoths was a sight to behold—hundreds and hundreds of giant, insect-like creatures moving in unison across the plains. Every morning, at the exact same time, the scene was the same, except for today.

As the herd crowded the plains, everything looked as normal as it always had. But suddenly four of the megamoths leaped up from the rest of the herd and spread their wings. And there, hidden between where the megamoths' wings had been clasped together was a person.

Ash, Lazlo, Xavier, and Driver were saddled onto the backs of four separate megamoths. In one hand they clenched the spine hair of the megamoths like reins. In the other they wielded a weapon. Xavier had his pistol, Ash and Lazlo their swords, and Driver carried a spear he had borrowed from the Ginka. *Whatever works*, as he put it.

The lizarden guards instantly drew their swords, as the megamoths lifted into the air. Though riding a wild megamoth was a far cry from riding a stallion or other tame creatures, Ash found that steering the megamoth was actually much more literal than he had feared. As they approached Lord Yen's sky-scraping spire, he pulled back on the megamoth's hair. But the beast wasn't quite that tame. Ash had to make a quick decision. So he jumped.

The sound of his body slamming into the side of the spire was not good. He was certain that something was broken. But before he could think about that, he had to grab something. His fingertips barely curled around a thin lip on the shallow balcony protruding from the spire.

Ash noticed that Driver didn't have such luck when he jumped. His hand had hooked onto a protruding piece of structure, made of bamboo. But the thrust of his impact had caused his arm to disconnect from the rest of his body. A long, thick band of threads were unraveling from his arm, all the way down to his falling body. Quickly, he climbed his way back up, if nothing else, to save his arm. Lazlo and Xavier, however, remained on task, getting their megamoths to land on a large, open patio at the top level of the spire.

Ash scrambled over the edge of the balcony. He was completely exhausted from hanging off the ledge. His wind was shot. But he now had a spiraling staircase to climb and this was the moment he had come for. Only a few flights of stairs stood between he and Scar.

Ash closed his eyes and focused his energy. But doubt and fear clouded his thoughts, rendering him no more capable than any worn-out boy. Then he heard gunshots in the chamber above. He couldn't climb the spiral staircase fast enough to get to the top.

Lord Yen's chamber was an open-air expanse, consuming the entirety of the top level of the spire. Flowing red curtains, suspended between thick pillars, were all that stood between Yen and the outside air. Upon entering the chamber, Ash saw that Lazlo and Xavier had already taken out Yen's chamber henchmen. And Xavier had a large gash across his arm, oozing blood through his jacket. As they stepped over their bulky, green corpses, Lazlo kept the tip of his sword and Xavier the barrel of his pistol pointed right at Yen, who was slowly backing away, adjusting his eye patch with his slimy tendrils. Ash and Lazlo were thinking the exact same thing: *What if Xavier turns on us?*

Yen's red, slimy body was curled up on his floating saucer as his narrow eye glared at the intruders. Ash looked around frantically for Scar. Then he noticed the thick chain, connected to the saucer.

The chain was long, running down onto the floor, across the chamber and underneath a curtain door, leading to a dark room. Ash followed the chain. And parting the curtains, he then saw her.

Scar was hunched over, looking as though she was about to spill out of her chair. A twitch of her hand came as overwhelming relief that she was still alive.

"Are you okay?" Ash asked, as he discovered that the chain was securely attached to a big metal ring around her neck. But she didn't answer. Her eyes were rolled back into her head and her mouth flopped open, drooling uncontrollably. Only a faint sigh gurgling up from her throat told Ash that she was trying to communicate with him. Then the chain jerked, yanking Scar out of the chair and onto the floor. The voices yelling from the chamber told Ash that things were only getting worse.

"Give her up and I'll let you live!" Xavier shouted at Yen, who was reeling the chain into himself, tendril over tendril. Lazlo remained poised, but allowed Xavier to lead the charge on this one. It was clear that, as Xavier had put it: *he needed it.*

"I was still planning on paying you," Yen equivocated, hoping to entice Xavier with his money.

"It's not about the money anymore," Xavier said engaging Yen steadily.

"It's always about the money," Yen insisted. "I'll even double the amount if you just drop your weapons."

Both Ash and Lazlo became worried that Lord Yen's proposal was beginning to attract Xavier. This was a lot of money Yen was talking about. And even though Xavier had endured some sort of change of heart, there was no telling what his threshold of temptation might be. They were about to find out.

"This is your last chance, Yen," Xavier said, backing Yen to the edge of the chamber floor. "Don't be foolish," Xavier warned.

Yen was not about to back down. Instead he yanked the chain even harder, reeling Scar across the floor by her neck. But Xavier was too fast. He spun around and shot the chain, splitting it in two, freeing

Scar. Ash ran over to Scar and pulled her away. Now the struggle between Xavier and Yen was merely a matter of pride verses vengeance.

"A coward with a gun," Yen hissed. "That's all you are, Marshal. And that's all you'll ever be. Don't be stupid. You're passing on a once in a lifetime opportunity."

Xavier pondered Yen's words. As much as he hated the serpentine, he knew that there was some truth to what he had said. But Xavier was determined to alter this course. He would not die a coward.

"Throw me your sword," he ordered to Ash.

Without hesitation, Ash tossed his switch-sword to Xavier, who in turn dropped his pistol onto the floor. And wasting no time, he whirled around, cleanly slicing Yen's head fin two.

As Lord Yen's blood-soaked corpse uncoiled from the saucer, spilling over the edge of the balcony. Xavier whispered to himself, "I'm no coward," and tossed the bloody sword back to Ash.

Forty Four
Chase Through the Jungle

Sweat stung his eyes as Ash hurdled over a fallen tree. Glancing behind, he noticed Scar barely keeping up—her legs tumbling over one another, about to give way any moment. Ash quickly grabbed her hand and she held on tight. Like a slow leak, physical energy instantly began waning from Ash—flowing into Scar to keep her from completely dropping to the ground.

The jungles of the Bamboo Forest were much thicker and trickier to navigate than the swamps of Murk. It reminded Ash of getting lost in the vast mazes of the grain fields on the outskirts of Garbbit Harbor. But the bamboo trees grew so tightly together that it was virtually impossible to see anything up ahead, other than what was right in front of his eyes. The only way to truly navigate this portion of the jungle was to keep one eye on the giant behemoth trees looming high above.

Ash felt it even hard to breathe in the crowded forest. Suddenly, like an impulse that was as alien as his newfound powers, he stopped, spun around, grabbed Scar by the face and kissed her.

Her lips were cold and stiffer than Ash remembered them being from their one and only kiss in his father's fishing trawler. But a rush of emotion, as her hands gripped his shirt, pulling him closer, made him forget that he was even standing on his feet. He became lost in a world of his own in the crowd of bamboo. Far more than when he had grabbed her hand, Ash could feel energy fleeing his body as his tongue interlaced with hers. Still, his heart raced on.

"I was so afraid," he whispered, his lips pressed against Scar's cheek. He had to catch his breath from the kiss. "I thought I might not ever see you again."

Scar gripped him even tighter. "You shouldn't have come for me."

"What are you saying?" Ash asked, pulling back to get a look at Scar's hopeless, blank stare. The rings around her bloodshot eyes were especially dark. "Nothing could have stopped me," he admitted passionately.

But his words didn't seem to have the effect on Scar he was hoping for. She just remained silent. In fact, it seemed as though she was now beginning to fade, letting go, falling away.

If only Ash knew the weight of guilt Scar was carrying for refusing to come clean—for refusing to admit that she was not only a spy and a thief, not only a drone, but a killer. Ash deserved to know the truth.

"Ash," she said, struggling to catch her breath. "You have to let me go."

"What are you saying?" Ash asked in obvious disbelief.

"I'm not who you think I am." Ash pulled away with a look of horror. "I'm beginning to remember who I was. *What* I was. And some things cannot be changed."

"That's not true," Ash argued. "I don't care about whatever it is you're being accused of. We both have strange pasts. That's okay."

"No it's not, Ash. This isn't a matter of whether or not we are compatible. You are obviously a very special person in this word. I've seen your power and it is beautiful."

"It's a curse!" Ash said slamming his hands together.

"It's who you are!" Scar corrected with more energy than she had displayed in a long time. "You can't throw it away on me. I won't let you. Look, I want things to be different as much as you do. But the fact is, I'm a wanted fugitive—wanted by the most powerful people in the world. Even if I believed in my own innocence, I still wouldn't stand a chance against them."

Ash had no response. His insides hurt. This was a blow he wasn't prepared for—one he didn't have the strength to confront. So he simply tried to pretend that it never took place. Suddenly he could feel a vibration in his feet. It felt like a distant thunder. But as it swelled, he could hear it growing louder. *Footsteps.* Ash feared that the tales he had heard about these jungles *might* actually be true. He couldn't look and didn't want the verification that it might actually be what he thought it was: a sabertooth lion. Ash grabbed Scar's hand again and ran, trying to catch up to the rest of the gang. He couldn't look her in the eye now though.

"Did you hear that?" Lazlo asked as he slashed his sword through the thicket of bamboo. Xavier merely nodded as he raced ahead. "A lion," Lazlo clarified, crippling Ash's hope for a safe passage back to the Ginka tribe. The look of concern in Lazlo's eyes told Ash that this was about to get really bad.

"Sabertooth. And I think it smells your blood," Lazlo said, lifting Xavier's bloody arm. A splattered stream of his blood trailed behind him on the dense underbrush. Suddenly a roar rumbled through the air, filling the jungle like the thunder of a coming storm.

It was difficult to see, given the thick foliage. But from the size of some of the trees it was smashing to the ground as it ran, the lion was every bit as large as the tales had said. It mowed down the bamboo trees like a sickle cutting through grass. All Ash could do was run.

The lion was so much faster than Ash had anticipated as it blurred through the jungle, effortlessly trampling everything in its path. The lion's roars rattled through Ash, almost crippling him as he struggled to keep his legs beneath him. There was something about the beast's feline features that reminded him of the horrific face of Sayto Bontey. Then he tripped.

Scrambling to his feet, Ash quickly realized that the taller he stood, the closer he was coming to the long saber-fangs of the lion. The beast was standing right over him! In the background, Ash could hear Lazlo and Xavier arguing over whether shooting the lion might only attract more lions. Its hot breath poured over Ash like a deadly ghost.

Ash could hardly look as the lion towered over him, growling and dripping thick, slimy saliva onto his face. As the lion opened his mouth, Scar screamed. Then a shot rang out and the lion's monstrous body slumped straight down, pinning Ash's shirt to the ground with its fang.

"Hey, who did that?" Xavier yelled.

"You did," Lazlo said, helping Ash out from beneath the dead lion.

"Finally," Ash added as Scar helped clean him off.

"No I didn't," Xavier admitted, looking around in paranoia. "My gun was jammed."

"Then who did?" Driver asked, his rubbery head jerking around frantically in search. Suddenly a rain of fire-dipped arrows gleamed over their heads, penetrating the jungle ahead, blasting the underbrush into a giant blaze of fire. Then a bullet whizzed through the trees.

"Pirates!" Lazlo whispered loudly, with a look of disappointment aimed at Xavier.

"Again," Ash added, shaking his head.

It didn't take long for the pirates to spill into the slashing, followed by a legion of drone-soldiers. But when Sayto Bontey emerged from the bamboo trees, Ash instantly felt his knees go weak.

With the pirates close behind, Lazlo led Ash, Scar, Xavier, and Driver to the gorge, bridged by a massive old fallen tree. It was far faster than trying to climb through the deep bowels of the gorge. And now the yells and chanting of their pursuers were closer than ever. But before they could even cross, the pirates had completely caught up with them.

"We've got company," Lazlo warned as he began leading them over the gorge on the fallen tree. He unsheathed his switch-sword and instantly began dueling with the pirates as they quickly crowed the fallen tree.

Ash's foot slipped on the moist moss. He jerked and Scar fell. But their grip was stronger. Xavier's arm came swooping down to help. For a brief moment, Scar and Xavier exchanged stares, as if choosing the only moment they could spare to reconcile their fateful differences.

For a brief moment Ash drifted into a lucid dream state, unable to move in any direction. But then Scar let go of his hand, unsheathed his switch-sword and handed it to him. "You can do this," she whispered with tired eyes. Ash ejected the blade and with uncertain feet stepped forward into the heat of battle.

There must have been a dozen or more pirates crammed onto the fallen tree, yelling and screaming and wielding their swords wildly, as though they were nothing more than mere animals. In their possessed ravenous state, this wasn't far from the truth. Even though the tree was immense, its moss-covered surface made it slick and difficult to keep a steady foothold. It was obvious that for Lazlo, who was a master swordsman, this made it a bit easier for him to hold off his surrounding attackers. If his sword didn't get them, they simply slipped off the tree, down into the rushing stream below.

Ash quickly realized that if he didn't start fighting back, he too would end up falling subject to the same fate as these pirates. The moment he raised his sword to fight, he felt the surge.

Again, time seemed to stand still. But this time he seemed to be channeling a power that literally transformed him. Instead of stumbling around with the heavy sword, he was now wielding it with as much strength and control as Lazlo. In fact, as he dueled his way across the fallen tree, his maneuvers were almost impossible to follow. The Guardian within was coming alive! But then something happened that he felt was beyond his control, as his sword burst into flames.

Like something out of a dream, Ash whirled through the entanglement of pirates, blocking every offense with his fire-filled sword, knocking his attackers off the giant log. Lazlo could hardly stay focused, watching this supernatural display. Suddenly the fallen tree began to roll, rocked loose by the wild foot-traffic on it surface.

The first to fall from the tree was Driver, who had almost made it to the other side before losing his balance. Luckily he became entangled in the vines and sagging strands of torn moss hanging down from the underside of the tree. But as pirate after pirate began to fall from the slick rolling tree, they too became entangled in the vines. And with one final roll, everyone had fallen.

Though some simply fell into the stream, Ash and Lazlo found themselves in a relentless duel with the pirates who were now strewn throughout the web of vines beneath the tree. It didn't take long for everyone to figure out that the best way to attack was to simply go for the vines themselves, cutting the enemy loose, causing them to fall. Pirate after pirate continued to fall victim to Ash's unmatched skill as Lazlo caught himself frozen in a trance, bewildered by the sight of Ash.

Lazlo had seen many strange things in his travels, but nothing quite as strange as this. When Bontey emerged over the edge of the gorge, the magic of the moment instantly dwindled. He was followed by the green flashing strobe lights of the drone-soldiers signaling their arrival.

Surrounded by the squadron and more pirates, Bontey paused, assessing the situation. Rage flared his yellowed eyes as he gazed into Ash's. Heavy footsteps shook the vines below as he stepped onto the tree, followed by his squadron. Suddenly he spun around and snatched a giant axe from one of his pirate mates, before shoving him off the log. He then jumped up and grabbed a hold of a thick vine, hanging down from the giant trees above.

Kicking his legs, Bontey began swinging back and forth in a large arch, like a wild primate. And every time he crossed the path of the fallen tree, he took a large swing with the axe, slamming it into the tree.

It didn't take long to gouge a considerable wedge into the tree, causing it to begin breaking in half. And with every impact of the blade, Ash felt the attack of fear dissolving his strength. Suddenly, with a loud crunch, the fallen tree busted into two, falling away at the center, slamming each half into the opposite sides of the gorge.

Blood splatted onto the walls of the gorge as some of the pirates became flattened between the tree and the rocks. As for Ash and his friends, their fate was only slightly better as they fell the rest of the way into the swirling stream.

Emerging from the water, Ash searched desperately to find Scar. Looking closer, he noticed her arm breaching the water's surface in a vain attempt to be rescued. Ash quickly began trudging back up stream, through the shallow waters. But then something fell from above, slamming into the water like an explosion.

Bontey slowly rose, water cascading from his oil-coated fur. As he continued to uncoil, rising like a plume of black smoke above Ash, a growl gurgled in his throat and he stepped back to guard his prize: Scar.

Reaching down, Bontey pulled her limp body out of the water and raised her up like a hunter's trophy. He proudly discharged his new bionic saber, holding its blade to her throat. Ash's heart sank, watching the horror before his eyes. But his trembling feet instinctively repelled backward. He felt like nothing more than a worthless dastard, crippled by his own boyish fears. Once again, Scar was slipping through his fingers because of his failure to overcome his own fears.

"Get down!" Xavier yelled at Ash, causing him to stumble to his knees. But as soon as Ash went down, Xavier began firing his pistol at Bontey in a desperate attempt to hold him at bay.

Hiding behind a series of rocks, marking the crest of a large series of rapids, Xavier continued his assault on Bontey as Ash quickly made his way to the safe side of the rocks. He patted Ash on the back, as if to say, *It'll be okay. I've got it from here.*

Years of chasing criminals around the world had taught Xavier never to panic, never to give up, even in the face of uncertainty. And this was no exception.

After first being recruited into the military academy of Kingland, Xavier's determination was completely unmatched by those around him. At a very young age he acquired a reputation as a force to be reckoned with. But his skyrocketing career soon came crashing down after the assassination of the King's wife.

In the wake of this tragedy, Xavier found himself on a list of sideliners, forced to prove their worth to a leader obsessed with finding a culprit. And as the years passed him by, so did any chance of validation. In fact, Kingland, the very kingdom he had once sworn an oath to defend, had now become a symbol of the very corruption he was trying to exterminate. It took nearly dying for Xavier to realize just how vain his oath had become.

Ironically, he was now willing to put his life back on the line to save the girl he had once considered a mere ransom token. Since awaking back in the Ginka tribe, Xavier felt a strange burning sensation inside of him—a yearning to vindicate himself and prove his loyalty to Scar, after nearly delivering her to her death sentence.

Bullets peppered the water as Bontey fired back with his rifle. Facing this menacing beast was hardly a winnable situation. A multitude of thoughts and memories screamed through his mind as he pondered the countless scenarios of how this might play out. But only one seemed right. Only one was inevitable as he glanced back at Ash's hopeful eyes.

"Go," Xavier ordered Ash in a sincere whisper.

Ash paused. There was no way he was going to just turn and leave Scar behind like that. Still, he knew that there was no time to argue—no alternative. His own strength was all but nonexistent in the shadow of Bontey. And if Xavier, of all people, was telling him to leave, he knew better than to argue.

Downstream, Scar's eyes rolled around like weighted balls in the hollows of her eye sockets. Life was draining from her again like a deflating balloon. Only Bontey's clawed grip was keeping her from stumbling back into the water. And as Ash's vision finally gave way to the obstruction of tears. He took Xavier's advice and continued over the rocky crest and down the rapids to meet the others.

Ash came to a slippery, stumbling halt, just before vaulting off the edge of a narrow but terrifyingly deep waterfall. Wick, Lazlo, and Driver had already managed to make it out of the rushing stream and were there instantly to help Ash out of the rushing water. But before Ash could even get to his feet, the gunfire of the shootout behind him came to a stop.

Within a short moment, Ash found himself in a pool of red blood, filtering into the water from upstream. As Lazlo helped Ash to his feet, he looked up to see Xavier's lifeless body slumped over the rocks from which he had been fighting. And beyond, Bontey stood victoriously with Scar still clenched in his massive grip. The surviving drone-squadron was trudging downstream behind Bontey, guns drawn.

"Come on, let's get out of here," Lazlo whispered. The gravity of the situation had yet to sink in. Xavier was dead—an ironic sacrifice trying to save Scar. But Lazlo knew that if they didn't keep moving, they would be Bontey's next victims.

Lazlo pulled out the ram's horn Hoodu had given him before departing for Lord Yen's compound. In the event they got themselves entangled in a situation requiring backup assistance, he was to blow it. He wished he would've pulled it out much sooner as he began to blow.

The echoes quickly traveled down the winding route of the canyon in which the waterfall spilled. And soon the sight of their gliding Ginka comrades began to appear in the shadows of the canyon.

There was no time to waste as Bontey and his squadron loomed behind. The Ginka swooped down to pick up Ash, Wick, Lazlo, and Driver. As they flew off, a haunting sound filled the jungle air.

With Scar still clenched tight, Bontey stood at the edge of the waterfall howling like a wild canine. The sounds echoed through the canyon like a pursuing force, promising more bloodshed. Indeed there would be, once he discovered that Scar wasn't even in possession of the Enigma.

Forty Five
Destiny

The cliff-hanging huts glowed like lanterns in the evening dusk. Boota stoked the burning logs in the fire pit as sparks floated up through the hut's open top and into the night sky like a swarm of fireflies.

The sound of the fire was ear-piercing next to the uncomfortable silence, which had since consumed the hut. Wrapped in a patched-up blanket, Ash sat on the floor, back against the grass wall, glaring across the room at Wick and Hoodu, who had been whispering about something ever since Ash had returned from the jungle.

Wick had hardly commented on the details of their harrowing adventure, let alone Xavier's death, let alone, Scar's capture. The only thing that really seemed to be on his mind was the discovery that Hoodu was not only an enthusiast of Imcot lore, but also incredibly fluent in the ancient dialect. Ash wanted to hear none of it.

"He deserves a proper burial," Lazlo said, as he rummaged through Xavier's jacket, the only article he had left behind. Petra was nested into his neck, still beaming with excitement about her master's return from the tortures of the jungle. She was glowing more than usual.

"I'm afraid the vultures will have gotten him already," Boota explained. But she quickly realized just how unsettling those words were. Petra's tiny eyes grew bigger and she scampered down into Lazlo's shirt. "I mean, not yet," she stuttered, trying to redeem herself. Ginkan culture didn't share the same level of sensitivity around the concept of death, in comparison to most cultures. "We can retrieve his body in the morning if you'd like."

"No. You must stay out of the jungle," Hoodu interrupted calmly. Everyone seemed perplexed by his comment. Fear tainted his words.

"Why is that?" Lazlo asked with a curious expression.

"Because of what hunts you," Hoodu said, gazing deep into Ash's eyes. Ash shuttered at the thought of what Hoodu meant. "It seeks terror and thirsts for the possession you keep hidden."

"What possession?" Lazlo asked. He was becoming more confused by the moment, as was Ash. Suddenly Wick became fidgety, eyes dashing around the room, paranoia consuming him. But as he clenched his money sack tighter, something slipped through the small tear on its underside.

It hit the floor with a loud thud and rolled across the room on its edge, right over to Ash—as if steering itself toward him. His eyes shot open as it coiled to a spinning stop, right between his legs. The air seemed to fill with a strange electrical charge, as Ash's hair began to stand on end.

"The Enigma," Hoodu whispered with large eyes. He carefully made his way over to Ash. Ash's heart raced.

According to Wick, Scar had snatched the Enigma back from Ash before disappearing with Xavier after the goliath-eel attack. Then again, according to Wick, Scar was the enemy. Either way, the old wharfling had a lot of explaining to do.

"Did you say Enig-Enigma?" Lazlo asked, crouching down to have a better look. "As in the legendary Imcot relic? No way."

"It is," Wick admitted solemnly, unable to look Ash in the face. Hoodu seemed less surprised and more intrigued.

"You stole it!" Ash yelled at Wick. "You stole it from me but told me Scar did it—all just to turn me against her."

"I tried to tell you," Wick cut in with pleading eyes. He had relieved Ash of it just after the sub-taxi crash at the bottom of the sea. But with every intention on handing it over to Ash once they reached the cabana, he knew that the medallion was no safer in the boy's hand as long as the girl was still around. Unfortunately, the deal Wick had originally made with Driver to simply bring Scar back to Cobbleton and turn her in never came to fruition, thanks to Xavier.

"No you didn't," Ash argued back, standing to his feet. "You've been hiding it from me all along."

"I told you that Migg found it at the bottom of Willow Lake," Wick tried to clarify as he trembled. "And that we traced it back to Scar. She has no business with this medallion."

"Scar and Xavier are gone and you're still just sitting there obsessing about this stupid fantastical treasure," Ash shot back.

"The Chrysalis is very real indeed," Hoodu interjected, closing in on Ash. "You curse it, yet you know this to be true," Hoodu said, locking his stare in an almost hypnotic state.

"I'm so tired of being told what my destiny is," Ash shouted, throwing his arms down. "I told you before, I'll decide for myself." And with that he picked the Enigma up from the floor. A numbing vibration surged through his body the moment it touched his skin. But he tried to ignore it, throwing it back at Wick. But to everyone's amazement the medallion went nowhere.

In the exact place it had left Ash's hand, the medallion simply hovered in mid-air, spinning continuously. Even Hoodu appeared to be perplexed by the sight. Then, as if bound by some invisible, magnetic force, the medallion shot back into Ash's palm, snapping his fingers back around it.

"Destiny isn't something you choose," Hoodu said folding his hands calmly. "It chooses you."

"Yes, the Enigma is yours, Ash," Wick added, daring to approach the boy again. "I've been trying to tell you for some time now. But you won't listen. It leads the way to the Hidden Ember—and ultimately the Chrysalis. And you are the key, which unlocks it. There is no other way."

Looking down, he could see the white light spilling through the cracks of his fingers again. He slowly opened his hand. Markings on the medallion were glowing.

"I know," Ash said condescendingly. "It's a treasure map."

"To the greatest treasure of all time," Hoodu said in a mesmerized state.

"I'm just not ready for all of this," Ash admitted, hanging his head. "I never wanted to be important. Why can't I just be a normal person and not have to chase some pre-ordered destiny?" Wick was furious with Ash's insolence.

Then, the last person Ash ever imagined confronting him spoke up. "Because that's what it means to live," Lazlo's voice pierced the air sharply. Ash's expression drained to nothingness as Lazlo spoke. "I hate to break it to you kid, but you don't get to just pick and choose every step of your path. We all have a purpose in this world—one that precedes our very birth.

"Look, I know that your childhood was a mess. And I know that your daddy was less than a hero in your book. But you can't go on blaming every little problem you have on him." Ash burned with humiliation. *How could this pirate be so intuitive?* "You are the luckiest kid I know," Lazlo continued. "I can't imagine being honored with the gift you have. Yet instead of being grateful you reject it. What a waste. Stop seeing your Mystery as a curse and accept it as your destiny."

Ash had had enough. He knew that every word of Lazlo's was true. But embarrassment and guilt were crushing him.

"So what am I supposed to do?" he yelled out with vulnerable eyes. He really didn't know.

"Follow the map," Hoodu said gently. He then stepped closer, pulled Ash's wrist close to get a good look at the glowing markings of the Enigma.

"To where?" Ash asked impatiently.

For a long, quiet moment, Hoodu poured over the Enigma's glowing markings. Then, with a tone of concern that seemed to send a chill into the air, he spoke. "Only a *true* Guardian of the Vyne would dare go to such a dark place."

"What place?" Ash asked, his hands beginning to tremble.

"The place between places," Hoodu demonstrated in an eerie whisper. "A coordinate that exists only in another realm."

"What do you mean? Ash asked. "Why are these coordinates so different?"

"Because they don't exist," Hoodu said, his eyes following the rising sparks of fire through the hut's open roof, into the starry sky. "This place is off the map."

"What place?" Lazlo probed, growing quite curious himself.

"The Abyss," Hoodu whispered.

By the look on Lazlo's face, whatever this legendary place was, it wasn't good. In fact, Ash hadn't seen such a terrified expression cross the pirate's face since meeting him. Ash's entire body was now beginning to tremble. "What is the Hidden Ember?" he whispered to Lazlo, hoping it wasn't nearly as bad as his expression was letting on.

But his hopes were quickly dashed. "There's a legend," Lazlo began thoughtfully, "which tells of a lost abyss, doomed by the curse of gods. In the bowels of this place is said to reside the greatest beast known to mankind. Shrouded in darkness, the beast guards its prized possession: the Hidden Ember."

"The foolhardy who dares cross into the realm of the Abyss will surely meet their end," Hoodu added.

"That sounds like incentive," Driver said, shaking his head. "Count me *out*."

Suddenly Hoodu began to read the actual text upon the surface of the Enigma. "*That which is hidden must be found. But only by the worthy. Only the one who proceeds in the steps of faith. Through the gateway to the waters beneath the waters awaits the slumbering beast. Seek not for your own prosperity, but for the deliverance of others. For the hand that fears shall be turned away. And the greedy will be cut off.*"

"Does anyone even know where this Abyss really is?" Lazlo asked, daring to break the uncomfortable silence. "If I had a coin for every theory I've heard over the years—"

"It is only for the boy to know," Hoodu interrupted, staring at Ash.

"This already doesn't sound like much of a treasure," Driver said. "I thought treasures were made up of precious jewels and golden coins."

"*Seek not for your own prosperity*," Hoodu repeated to Driver sternly. "Whatever it is stirring within the heart of the Abyss, be it beast or be it not of this world, it is surely protecting the Chrysalis from ill motives such as yours." If it was possible for a gearman to get embarrassed, Driver was. Then, turning to Ash and taking both of his hands, Hoodu concluded. "The Hidden Ember is not what you think. Nothing is. As there are forces working feverishly to keep the Chrysalis dormant, you have an obligation, a calling to unveil its truth for all the world to see. Destiny is a gift. Accept it with courage."

Ash's hands shook as he held the Enigma. It was like every tiny detail of his life, every memory he had ever had, was all a progressive build-up to this very moment—a crossroad of inescapable decision. *Why me?* he wondered. That hopeless mantra repeated itself through his mind like an infinite echo.

Since Scar's arrival, he had been fighting for her approval with Wick. And it seemed that with every little twist and turn in their adventure, Wick was always looking for a reason to discredit her. Choosing to not acknowledge her was one thing, but stealing the Enigma from her, while allowing her to be hunted and arrested was unacceptable. It crossed a line Ash could not forgive. Looking over at Wick, Ash couldn't resist the temptation to lash out one last time.

"Now I know why you gave up on Scar so long ago. You wanted the treasure for yourself." Wick tried to interject, but Ash cut him off. "I knew you were a scavenger, Wick, but I never took you for a thief." He then whisked himself out of the hut before Wick could utter a response.

Forty Six
The True Guardian

Standing on the earthen decking, looking up at the night sky, Ash weighed his options. His gift could not be denied. But if destiny meant giving up on Scar, it just didn't seem worth it. *Why was letting go of all that he loved so critical to his destiny?* It was so unfair. As he opened his palm, the light of the glowing etching painted his face in light. He tried to imagine his mother holding this very same medallion and what she must have thought. He then slipped the Enigma into his pocket.

"You okay?" Lazlo's voice drifted out of the hut as he joined Ash on the balcony.

"Yeah, I'm fine," Ash lied. But Lazlo knew better.

"No you're not," he replied, placing a hand on Ash's shoulder. He remembered being Ash's age, in a constant struggle to understand his own turbulent emotions. "Your entire world just came crashing down around you. But sometimes we've got to just stop making excuses and pick ourselves up and move on. Trust me, I know. There have been plenty of times when I've felt I was misdealt in life. All those years in prison weren't what I had in mind when I first set sail. And what about Xavier?

"He was so adamant about going after what *he* thought was right, he never stopped long enough to realize that every move he made only resulted in disaster." Ash thought about it and Lazlo was right. From the goliath-eels to the train-wreck, Xavier's efforts were anything but smooth. "It wasn't until he embraced his moral obligation to Scar that he was finally successful."

"And now he's dead," Ash reminded him.

"Yes, now he's dead. But not prematurely. He consummated his destiny. That's all one can ask for in life."

"What about Scar?" Ash asked. "Is she void of destiny? Does she not have a purpose in this world?"

Lazlo looked concerned as he pondered his words carefully. "I don't have to tell you that there is something about Scar that sets her apart from the rest of us. She knows this too. She's a drone, Ash."

Ash looked away. He couldn't let Lazlo see his bloodshot eyes. "I know she is," he whispered.

"Then you understand that she can't be saved," Lazlo replied.

"No!" Ash shot back with narrowed eyes. "I *will* save her. And I won't let Xavier's death be in vain."

"But what runs through her veins is poison," Lazlo explained. "It has no cure."

"Well I believe differently," Ash argued. "I believe Scar *can* be saved. You said so yourself," he said, referring to promises Lazlo had made earlier on.

"That was before I knew she was an android zombie," Lazlo said, wishing instantly that he had chosen his words more carefully.

Anger filled Ash's eyes as he glared back at Lazlo. But the inclination to retaliate quickly faded. Letting out a huge breath, Ash slouched back against the clay and twig constructed railing as tears streamed down his face. He knew that Lazlo was right. Scar could not be saved.

"Do you believe in this crazy legend?" he asked Lazlo.

"I don't know what I believe anymore," Lazlo answered, shaking his tired head. "But I do believe in one thing."

"What's that?"

"I believe that you are meant to go after and discover the secret of the Chrysalis. I believe that you have a gift, a power few dare to wield. And you wield it like a true Guardian."

"I still don't understand how a treasure, even magic, can change what's happening in the world," Ash admitted, as he pulled the Enigma back out of his pocket.

He just didn't feel special enough for such entitlement. He was just a kid with a bad attitude from Garbbit Harbor, of all places. But deep down Ash knew that there was an incredible chapter yet to unfold in his life. If the prophecies were true, then he was holding the power to save the world right in the palm of his very hand. This was more than destiny. It was fate.

Hoodu stood, nodding in the doorway of the hut, as if to reiterate what Scar had told Ash in the jungle: *You can do this*. Wick remained inside, unable to make eye contact with Ash.

Across the canyon, Sayto Bontey crouched on the large branch of a tree. Only the twitch of his long, thin tail moved as he peered through a large telescope onto the Ginkan village. *The boy has the Enigma*, he thought to himself. Bontey knew what the Enigma was.

Through his vast travels Bontey had been introduced to many bizarre traditions and rituals, but none as intriguing and promising as the study of alchemy. If he could get his claws on this simple relic, he would be within reach of the greatest treasure of all time. No longer would he have to scavenge for gold like some washed-up panhandler. He would possess the power to create it himself. But the Chrysalis's power didn't stop there. Eternal life would also be his to harness. Never had he been so close to such an incredible treasure, an incredible power. No pirate had. Unlimited riches. Eternal life. Both were merely a stone's throw away—across a narrow tropical gorge.

But Bontey also knew who Count LePrey was. He was aware of his mystical lineage back when LePrey had hired him the first time, all those years earlier. In fact, LePrey was the reason Bontey had become so obsessed with the Chrysalis in the first place. If Bontey were to strike prematurely, LePrey would certainly find a way to exploit his rashness. The plan had to continue as planned. For now. With the Enigma glowing brightly through the lens of his telescope, he began to salivate with envy.

Forty Seven
Dark Horizon

Boota glided down to her old rickety sloop, docked at the base of the gorges. Once talk of going after the treasure began to surface, she instantly threw in her bid for escorting her new friends out to sea. And with no other real options, they agreed. Besides, it was a good idea to have a native along when headed toward such an uncertain horizon.

Ash couldn't get himself to look back as the sloop pulled away from the docks. The Ginkan tribe cheerfully waved them on from the shores, but Ash's stone-faced expression remained unshaken. Across the bow, Wick's eyes were heavy with grief. Yet Ash's anger outweighed any compassion for his old, broken-hearted friend.

Ash hadn't uttered a word to Wick since storming out of the hut the night before. There may have been a better way of handling the situation, but Ash couldn't see it. After all, Wick was the one who had crossed the line. Maybe he would have apologized, if given the chance. But it was too late for that now as the sloop drifted into the tropical blue waters.

Boota's sloop was smaller than most and crudely constructed. But she was intensely proud to be commandeering it for such a monumental occasion. The sloop's wooden skin was hewn and in need of much cleaning. Its patched-up mainmast looked like a giant quilt, patched together in a rudimentary manner out of whatever materials were available at the time. The smaller sails were an array of colors and indeed *were* nothing more than sheets and blankets, recovered from the landfills of outlying villages. And its rigging resembled that of a bird's construction—a mixture of stripped bamboo and colorful rope. Ash wondered how the small boat even made it out of the inlet, let alone how it was supposed to sail across the sea. But he felt even less certain of his own fate.

The Tropical Sea was rich, crystal-clear blue. Looking down over the sloop's edge, Ash could see far down to the coral bottom as swarms of colorful, shimmering fish skirted around the reefs. Watery reflections glistened up onto the sloop's hull as Boota cranked the steering wheel to move it into the wind's current.

The open sea stretched out for as far as Ash could see. And the cliffs of the Bamboo Forest soon shrunk into a mere sliver on the horizon. For Ash, leaving these shores was almost more difficult than leaving Garbbit Harbor. At least in these jungles, life still thrived.

It was impossible for Ash to sleep aboard the sloop that night; so he sat up with Driver, who took a shift at the tiller as Lazlo and Wick slept. Even though the waters were calm, his guts were rolling with anticipation as he held the Enigma in his hand. He had no idea what mysteries lie at the end of this quest, as he gazed out across the deep blue sea.

Reflections of the moons and stars danced upon the water's surface, interrupted only by the sloop's path cutting across the water. Cool breeze sifted through Ash's hair like a breath of fresh air as a shooting star glittered across the sky—a sign of *good luck*, as Wick had always avowed. But the faint horizon ahead was filled with secrets that would soon be reveled. Nothing had transpired the way he had plotted in his mind's eye—something Wick had warned him of back in Cobbleton. Everything he had imagined adventure to be was so much more vivid and frightening.

When Ash was a young boy, the mundane routines of learning the ropes aboard his father's fishing trawler seemed more like punishment than it did adventure. Sure, he was young and unappreciative. But with such a distance between he and his father, Ash spent most of his time anxiously waiting to reach the shore at the end of a fishing trek, so he could escape into his own worlds of fantasy. But his peers had since shifted their interests into things like racing boats, daredevil stunts, sneaking into saloons, and worst of all, girls—something Ash knew from the start he wouldn't be a natural at.

Although all of Ash's friends and most of the villagers had become convinced that he was a *bad seed*, no one but Wick knew just how self-conscious and lonely Ash really was. Girls thought he was just another hellion. And Logan thought very little of him at all. It wasn't until Scar came along that Ash felt his first sense of truly *being*. All of this talk about destiny couldn't erase the feeling Scar gave him. He tried to escape into the only memory that made him feel somewhat normal …

As he closed his eyes he imagined Scar's lips. He could still taste it. Be it naive thinking or the triumph of credence, reliving that moment in his mind made Ash feel as though he possessed the power to change his future, maybe even to save the world. Just then, lightening crackled in the distant sky. Ash looked up to see a dark wall of clouds spread across the horizon like a growing mountain range.

Lazlo and Boota were now locked in a heated exchange over how to determine their location. Needless to say, without actual coordinates to refer to, it was debatable as to whether they were even close. But the signs around them quickly answered that question as the wind suddenly began to course correct the sloop, summoning it toward the distant storm.

Forty Eight
The Maelstrom

It took nearly all night for the old sloop to finally reach the strange wall of clouds. And by now, everyone aboard the vessel was huddled together, staring speechlessly at the black mass before them, crackling sporadically with magnificent flashes of thunderous white lightening. The winds blew harder, the sky turned darker, and the clear waters of the sea churned relentlessly, stirring up clouds of sand. Ash was regretting ever stepping aboard the sloop.

A swirling storm cloud threatened them from above while the mountainous swells tossed the sloop back and forth like a toy. As they entered the wall of fog, the air grew painfully cold. Time seemed to stretch and warp, as if caught in some other-dimensional vortex. But shockingly, the moment they cleared the fog bank, the waters instantly became as still as glass and the sky above them brightened. It was like entering another world. No one had ever lived to make it this far. Or so it was believed.

Around them, the wall of fog seemed to go on forever, encircling this mysterious coordinate. In the middle of the still waters was what appeared to be a giant spire of mist. All eyes were fixed on it, wondering if it might be the source of the great beast. Then the sloop stopped.

"We're not moving anymore," Wick acknowledged in a panic, as he looked around.

"Because there's no wind," Lazlo pointed out, licking his finger and raising it to the air.

"No," Boota added, peering over starboard. "Because we're not in the water anymore."

"What?" Driver exclaimed, rushing to the edge.

To everyone's utter amazement, the sloop was mysteriously suspended in mid-air, a short distance above the water's surface. For a moment, no one could speak. But suddenly Wick remembered something.

"Ash," he said, grabbing his arm. "Let me see the Enigma." Ash jerked his arm away and shot Wick an angry stare. "No, I don't mean to *have* it," Wick clarified. "I mean I want to read it again." Ash reluctantly opened his palm to Wick.

Carefully studying the medallion, Wick began to read. *"Only the one who proceeds in the steps of faith, to the waters' end."* Ash looked up at Wick with fear in his eyes. "Ash," Wick whispered. "Look at it." He was pointing to the giant spire of mist emitting from the core of the churning waters.

"The eternal maelstrom."

"Eternal?" Ash asked, confused. *How could this be?*

"Imcot legend tells of a massive maelstrom in the middle of the sea," Wick answered, clearly putting together all of the pieces of this strange riddle. "Of course, the gateway to the Abyss."

"And the steps of faith?" Ash asked as he gazed horrifically out upon the water's surface.

"I think you already know what it means, Ash," Lazlo said, his eyes expressing every bit as much fear. "This is crazy," he whispered to Wick, unfortunately loud enough for Ash to hear.

A cold sweat broke out all over Ash's body. He understood the riddle far better than he wanted to admit. And he knew that there was no turning back. Looking into the eyes of everyone on board, he imagined the consequences of turning his back on his fate. It was now or never.

His sweaty hands nearly slipped from the tattered rope as Lazlo lowered him down from the hovering sloop to the water's glassy surface. The privateer wasn't as masterful with covering up his doubt this time. It was obvious that he had since relinquished any desire to control this strange situation. His eyes said all of that and more.

The moment Ash's foot touched the water he knew something was different. He felt it. Instead of submerging into its wetness, his foot simply flattened, no different than standing on solid ground. Only subtle rings of water rippled away from his feet as he stepped down. Everyone aboard the sloop gasped in unison, eyes threatening to burst from their sockets. Ash was standing on water!

Unsure if it was a testament of his faith or simply the mystical energy of this strange place, Ash's legs shook uneasily as he took his first step. Schools of fish darted about beneath his feet, giving him the sense of dizzying vertigo. *Don't look down! Don't look down!*, he chanted in his mind, desperately struggling not to panic.

Fear was so intense, his knees felt as though the bone had been removed and any wrong movement might cause him to completely fold over himself like a piece of wet parchment. The massive spire of mist seemed so far away. So far away. He considered running, just to get it over with, but he wasn't sure if that might cause him to sink.

The audacity of this entire concept angered him as he stepped carefully. *Why such a ludicrous test of faith? And what mystery lies at the waters' edge?* It made little sense, yet seemed like an inescapable task to complete.

"Why can't things just be simple?" Ash whispered to himself. Utter exhaustion flooded his body as he anticipated what treacheries lie beyond reaching the massive whirlpool. But as he began to near its swirling core, the water's pull began to cause his feet to slip and sink, like he was stumbling in a shallow river, cursed by a massive current.

Water misted in an explosive hiss as Ash squeezed his eyes shut. He had to keep moving forward. He worried that if he didn't, he might completely sink. Then, where the water began to dip in an immense arch, off into nothingness, Ash stood perfectly still, his body being washed by the spray of the mist rising up from the whirlpool's interior.

The maelstrom was massive, like nothing Ash could have imagined—like a giant hole in the middle of the sea. Then, as though being pulled by an invisible force, Ash's body slipped beneath the surface, sinking, sinking …

Forty Nine
The Hidden Ember

Ash's body breached the water's surface with a powerful splash. He was still alive! At least, that's what he thought as he floated in total weightlessness. The water's surface rippled beneath him. Or was it above him? He couldn't tell as he slowly drifted away from it. Suddenly something bumped him. He quickly realized that he had gently come to rest on the surface of a giant boulder. *Land?* But when he lifted his head, he noticed that the boulder, along with a sea of others, was floating in the air as well, just above a dark chasm.

Ash made it to his feet, surprised that he was feeling so well. He was disoriented to say the least. But from what he could tell, he was in some sort of airtight cave. *The Abyss?* An underwater cave was feasible. Floating boulders and an upside-down pool on the cave's ceiling was not. Perhaps this was all a dream. Hoodu's words revisited his mind: *The Hidden Ember is not what you think.*

The shadows of the cave's cavity quickly enveloped Ash like a thick, cold cloak as the boulder on which he stood slowly rotated, turning the cave on end. Ash smelled the air. It was scentless. He tried to steady his own breathing to listen. But fear had a painful grip on him now, causing his breathing to sputter uncontrollably. Through the echoes of his gasps, he swore he heard something.

It seemed to be growing louder, like a bubbling stream. It was a voice. *A woman's voice?* Whatever it was, it was repeating the same thing, over and over. Then a warm whisper filled his ear. "Ashhh."

He felt faint with fear. *How did they know his name? Whose voice was it? A ghost?* Ash began seeing things too—flashes of light. *Was it real?* He wanted to close his eyes but was afraid that it might throw his balance off, causing him to fall from the floating boulder. The flashes began to increase in number and speed, slowly illuminating the entire cave. Gold, shimmering fragments of light danced everywhere. Ash was surrounded. Looking down, he finally saw its source.

A blinding gold light seemed to be emitting from below the surface of the watery chasm, which was now beneath him, causing some sort of mysterious reaction that initiated a slow moving whirlpool. A glowing, glitter-like substance rose from the center of the whirlpool, swirling around the cave like a swarm of dancing fireflies. And as the swarm passed by the cave walls, it lit a streaming path of light, allowing Ash to see that the walls were actually covered in strange, ancient Imcot engravings. Then something moved.

Out of the corner of his eye, Ash saw a white mass slowly rising out of the water. Though shrouded in shadows, it was gigantic, filling the cave with its mass. It emerged only partially. But as it lifted its head, Ash could finally see that this white thing was a monstrous beast! *The beast guarding its lair.*

Its skin appeared to be smooth—white with black-splattered markings. Its narrow head was crowned with what looked like giant white feathers. The beast's orange eyes almost glowed as they peered down at the trembling boy before her. Then, in a language Ash had never heard before, the beast spoke.

"Why have you come?" the beast asked with an authoritative yet benign delivery. But what was even stranger than the question, was the fact that Ash could understand it. After all, it was a dialect he had never even heard before: the ancient language of the dragons.

"Be-because the Enigma led me to you," Ash stuttered with uncertainty.

"The coordinates of this medallion are not coordinates to a place," the beast revealed. "They are coordinates of time."

"What time?" Ash asked, wondering if the medallion might have simply been misinterpreted—wondering if he was about to be eaten alive by this beast.

"Now," she answered.

"But the coordinates led me here, to this abyss," he informed her.

"No," she replied. "Your heart led you here. And the Hidden Ember is not what you think it is," she mysteriously echoed Hoodu.

Ash tried to make sense of what the beast was saying. Then he had an epiphany. He had finally figured it out. "So *you're* the Hidden Ember!"

"No," she repeated. Ash was growing more perplexed with every answer she gave. He was beginning to doubt that he had any business being there at all. "You are," the beast concluded, narrowing her fiery eyes as she studied the boy.

"I don't understand," Ash admitted. No way could this be true. It made no sense.

"Since the inception of the Vyne, the Hidden Ember has always been a chosen one—a child hidden from the rest of the sect," she said, drawing closer. Either she was admiring him or sizing him up for a meal. Ash wasn't sure yet. "If the sect were to crumble, this child would be the only safe one left. And that is precisely what took place. *You* are now the last remnant of the Vyne. The Hidden Ember is simply a metaphor for what you are, Asher. But the time has come."

"For what?"

"Courage," she replied simply. "To challenge the dark forces draining this world of its Mystery." By *Mystery*, Ash wondered if she was speaking of it in the same way Wick always had. "The full potential of this world has been diluted by the self-destructive nature of its own people. That is why we dragons came." Ash almost fell off the rock as he suddenly realized that he was looking at an actual real-life dragon. *The White Dragon herself!*

Since he was a child, Ash he had dreamed of what these beasts might look like. And now seeing it, the dragon was nothing like he had imagined. Nothing like any painting he had ever seen.

"We chose the Imcot people to shine as an example. To show the world that by overcoming their fears of the unknown they could tap into an energy that few have ever experienced. A transformational energy that unites the body and spirit into a symbiotic being, void of the constraints of time and space.

"You see, the entire universe is made up of energy. Positive and negative. Light and darkness. Every living being has the unique gift of channeling these energies, manifesting whatever it is they wish." Ash knew that she was speaking of his powers. His *Mystery*. "This is what we call one's Mystery," she validated. "However, few have ever even glimpsed the existence of their own Mystery.

"Though the Imcot were beginning to understand this gift, they were slaughtered out of fear before they ever had the chance to spread their truth. The secret sect of the Vyne was put in place to carry forth that truth. But there were those who chose power over peace.

"Even the Vyne, as well-intentioned as they were, misunderstood their true purpose. Out of fear they hid the Chrysalis away. But it was never meant to be hoarded like some exclusive secret. Dragons came to free the world, not to segregate. That was what the Vyne was to carry out upon our ascension from your world. To go forth and prepare the world for the next epoch in time, not to hide like an underground cult."

For a moment it was perfectly silent. Ash hated the fact that Wick had been spot-on with everything he had ever told him about the Imcot. Still, he knew the one question he needed to ask. He was just too afraid to ask it. "Does this epoch represent *the end of the world*?" his tongue hardly delivered.

The dragon closed her eyes, as if meditating on the question. "It depends."

"On what?" Ash asked eagerly. The suspense felt like it was killing him.

"The will of the people," the dragon said. "There is a shift in the universe that takes place, igniting a moment of enlightenment for those who are willing to embrace it. This epoch is a Decision Point between the evolutionary advancement of the world or its own self-destruction. Currently the fate of the world is destruction. But it can be changed."

Ash didn't know what to say. He felt he might throw up. Growing up in the closed-minded village of Garbbit Harbor was proof enough for him that the world was not headed in a good direction. But when he saw the even sadder state of Cobbleton, he realized that the world's lust for money and self-stimulation was beginning to spread like a disease. If this was something that could be changed, he couldn't understand why it had to be *him* to initiate it.

"Why is all of this so cryptic?" he asked, shaking his head. Frustration consumed him. "I don't understand why I was led on this wild chase, only to find out that *I* was the very thing I was looking for. It seems like a game. A very unfair game."

"The leg of the journey you've completed thus far has merely been the first part of your awakening," the dragon explained soothingly. "You needed that experience to lead you here. And this very moment is what is preparing you for the journey ahead. In spite of your fears, I deem you estimable for this quest. You must find the Chrysalis. It is the only way to save the world."

"Why can't you simply tell me where it is?"

"It is not my place to meddle in your affairs," she admitted. "Dragons came to enlighten, to guide. Not to puppeteer. Even I do not know of the Chrysalis's resting place." That came as an utter shock to Ash. "Your journey must be your own if you are to overcome the fears and doubts that plague you now. You have the natural gift of free will. Use it to guide your path. But be wary of the darkness that haunts you. Keep the Enigma close to you."

"So, what is the darkness that haunts me?" Ash whispered as a rhetorical question. He knew full well that she was speaking of Bontey.

"You already know the answer to this," she informed him gracefully. "There are those who are greedy, futilely craving a treasure they don't understand. But there are others who do understand the true power of the Chrysalis and strive to suppress it from the world.

"The Enigma remains safe as long as you remain strong. Until now it has been protected under the will of its former bearer: your mother. Now it is yours. But if you willingly choose to turn your back on your destiny and give it up, the power of the Chrysalis returns to neutral energy and can be consumed by anyone. Good or bad. Light or darkness."

"If the Vyne couldn't survive, then what hope do we have?" Ash asked.

"You," she said simply. "We have you, Asher. The greatest adversary ever to surface now threatens the world. The free will of the people is being eliminated as they are forced into submission of fabricated will. Even the most powerful armies are no match for these artificial legions. But by striking at its core, it can be vanquished."

Ash stared the dragon in the face. He felt so small, so vulnerable in the presence of the beast's powerful energy. He closed his eyes and absorbed the moment, allowing the warmth of her energy to rush over him. The cave became full of light and life, pulsing and sparkling like electricity. He had never felt such a sense of power in all of his life. It felt incredible. He then opened his palm to find that an entirely new set of engravings upon the Enigma were now glowing.

Then, leaning down to Ash, the White Dragon concluded. "These are the coordinates to the second cipher: the Koda. The Koda is the key to unlocking the Chrysalis. Only you have the power to truly defeat the darkness." The dragon finally sank away, back into the shadows and asked one last question.

"So I ask you again," she said, stiffening her towering posture. "Why have you come?"

Ash didn't know how to answer the question. He had already gotten it wrong the first time. So he wasn't about to blurt out the first thing that came to mind. But after pondering it for a long while, he finally had to say the only thing that came to mind. "Because this is my destiny."

The dragon instantly submerged into the water—the surrounding light quickly fading to black. Fear was in the cave again and Ash grew cold. Out of breath, he felt alone, naked. He wasn't sure if his answer was what the dragon was looking for, or if he had made her angry, causing her to leave. Then, drips of water began to rain upward from the lagoon, splashing into the pool of water on the cave's ceiling.

The upsidedown rain quickly grew into an upsidedown waterfall. Ash found himself caught in the powerful rush, and before he knew it his body was turning over and over in the cold, dark water.

The sloop slammed back down to the water as the crew stumbled to the floor. A blinding flash of light exploded just beneath the water's surface, causing the water to ripple. Then a sudden gust of strong wind billowed the ragged sail, turning the boat and setting it on a course out through the wall of fog.

"What's happening?" Lazlo asked, trying to help Boota crank the wheel the other way. But it was no use.

"I don't know," Wick answered, fearing for Ash. For a moment, Wick wondered if he hadn't misinterpreted the encryption. He began to panic.

No matter how hard Lazlo and Boota cranked the wheel, the sloop continued on its new course. Above them the clouds grew dark again as lightening crackled thunderously across its underbelly. The waters on the other side of the wall of clouds were far more rough as the sloop sailed on. Suddenly Wick saw something floating in the water.

"Ash!" he yelled, as he noticed the boy's unconscious body bobbing up and down in the stormy waves. "It's Ash!"

"Here," Lazlo ordered to Wick, handing him a rope. "Tie me off."

Lazlo tied the other end around his waste and dove into the water.

Fifty
Asher's Decision Point

That evening, aboard the sloop, Wick tried to get Ash to talk again. He was worried that the boy may never be the same after this bizarre supernatural experience.

"Look," Wick said, approaching Ash, who was curled up into a ball, slouched against the stern. "You don't have to talk, but you really should eat. Lazlo's got soup cooking and he's—"

"How long was I down there?" Ash asked, trembling.

"Down there?" Wick asked, obviously baffled. "I'm not sure what you mean. One moment you were walking on water, and the next, the winds picked up again and we were sailing back out of the fog. That's when Lazlo saved you from downing."

It was obvious that Wick had no idea of what Ash had just experienced. But then again, perhaps it was because it hadn't happened at all. Perhaps it had all been nothing more than a hallucination. After all, he had nearly drown. If Wick hadn't confirmed the fact that he had witnessed the miracle of walking on water, Ash wouldn't have given it another thought.

"I saw her," he admitted in a monotone voice. His eyes were glossed-over like a blind person.

"Saw who?" Wick asked, hoping the answer wasn't *Scar*.

"The White Dragon," Ash answered.

Wick stumbled backward, catching himself on the railing. "The White ... are you sure?" he gasped, not believing his ears.

"What did you think I'd see down there?" Ash asked, finally making eye contact with Wick.

It was clear that whatever happened during that split moment when the sloop fell back to the water, was something quite remarkable—something that took place in another dimension of space and time.

"What did she say?" Wick asked with heavy breathing.

Ash repeated what she had said about him leading the people, his eyes glossing over again. But although Wick recognized the dialect, he understood none of it as Ash was speaking fluently in the language of the dragons.

Wick had to sit, for fear that his legs might give out. Ash was transforming into something more powerful than he could have ever imagined. The boy he remembered was no more.

"Where are we headed?" Ash asked, looking up over the bow. Only open water lay ahead.

"We're headed back to Copi Bienna," Wick answered. "It's perhaps the only safe place for you right now."

"It's not about keeping me safe," Ash said sternly as he stood to his feet. "The dragon told me that I have the power to confront whatever it is controlling this invasion. I need to find out." He then rushed past Wick, down into the galley where Lazlo stood over a pot of boiling soup.

"You seem to know a lot about this invasion," he said to Lazlo. "Who's at the center of it all?"

"Look who decided to start talking again," Lazlo teased. "Welcome back, kid." Petra waved to Ash from the countertop, where she was sitting.

"I'm serious," Ash insisted. He was obviously in no mood for humor.

"At the center of the invasion?" Lazlo reviewed the question to himself. "Well, like I mentioned earlier, at the center of the drone-armada is Count LePrey."

"The Count of Cape Sparrow?" Ash asked.

"Yes," Driver joined in from the adjacent room. "The same guy."

"Why do you ask?" Lazlo inquired as he stopped stirring the soup. Ash looked away and didn't answer. "You want to take him down, don't you?" Lazlo said with a slight grin that revealed his many shades of teeth. It was obvious that this seemed like a good idea to him.

"Maybe," Ash said quietly.

"Ash, wait," Wick exclaimed, out of breath from chasing the boy into the galley. "The White Dragon wasn't necessarily speaking literally when she mentioned you confronting LePrey. You have a job to finish. The Chrysalis remains hidden. Find it and you will surmount everything that plagues this world."

"Enough, wharfling," Lazlo warned Wick with a dripping ladle in his face. "You've helped the boy enough. Now let him be."

It was obvious that Lazlo was on to Wick's fear that Ash was merely choosing LePrey as a physical target as a means for getting to Scar. But even if this was the case, Lazlo still at least trusted in the boy's capabilities.

"Well then, my young prophesied messiah," Lazlo jested, dropping the ladle and wiping his hands on a towel, "we'd best turn this boat around." He winked at Ash with a smile and then banged on the low ceiling. "Captain Boota! Set sail for—"

Suddenly a deafening crunch busted through the air as the sloop rocked violently to one side. Water sprayed up through a massive break in the floor.

"We've got company!" Wick yelled from starboard.

Climbing back up to the deck, Ash saw the giant red fins of the *Venom* slicing through the water like a fish. One had already slammed into the boat and two more were just about to do the same, as the massive submarine sliced through the water.

"Brace yourselves!" Wick cried as he hit the deck.

The *Venom* rent the sloop like a knife through clay. Bailing water wasn't even a consideration. In one swift moment the boat had been completely destroyed, awaiting a slow descent to the depths of the sea.

Two motorized skiffs circled around the sinking sloop. As they neared, three pirates from each skiff leaped aboard the sloop and began searching.

It didn't take them long to locate Ash, who strangely enough didn't put up a fight. Lazlo tried but was quickly overcome by the butt of a rifle, which rendered him unconscious. Wick watched in horror as Ash was whisked away to one of the skiffs. It was as though he knew that this was something that had to happen. Did he know something Wick didn't?

The submarine's massive metal bulk sat like a giant black monster, dead in the sea as the pirates re-boarded with their prize. Then, from the edge of the sinking sloop, Wick watched as the submarine vanished into the blackness of the sea.

Like many pirates of the Coral Sea, Bontey had tried numerous times to enter the elusive waters of the Abyss. And like the others, his attempts failed. In fact, after following Boota's sloop there, he tried one last time. But this time the supernatural forces nearly crushed the *Venom*. Barely escaping, Bontey now knew that the Chrysalis was *only* attainable by means of crippling the boy's mystic powers. Through fear alone, he was certain he could achieve that.

As the *Venom* dove deeper, one of Bontey's crewmembers stepped into his quarters, holding his severely burnt arm.

"Captain," the tattooed man said, trying to hide his pain. "We now have both of them, the girl *and* the boy. We're keeping them separated. The boy has the Enigma, but he's not talking. And when I went to take it from him, this is what happened." He then held up his blistered arm. Layers of skin had already fallen off from the burn. "How shall we proceed?"

Bontey knew this would happen. He knew the legend well enough to know that the bearer protects the Enigma from the hand of the ill-intentioned. A symbiotic relationship. It would take everything Bontey had learned through his practice of the dark arts to breach this mystical barrier and retrieve the Enigma from Ash. But first he had to eliminate his competition.

An evil grin threatened to streak across Bontey's face. "Let's go claim our reward from the Count. Set a course for Bald Rock."

Fifty One
The Messenger

Night fell on Crown City like a shadow carrying a lurid omen. With much of the city's power out, even Ares assumed a frightful presence, his massive silhouette looming over the city against the storming skies. Squadrons of drone-soldiers marched the web of sky-bridges, congregating in massive legions on the city's countless garden-plates like an insect infestation. Hundreds of drone-striders lurked through the confines of the floating city, hunting for anyone who might dare step outside. Crown City was under fastidious lockdown after riots had briefly erupted during Colonel Athen's public declaration of marshal law.

Large wet snowflakes pelted the porcelain face of King Basileus's private quarters. Inside, the room remained as it had since the night of the assassination attempt: perfectly still. The only signs of life were the fuzzy green blips glowing on a small monitor screen. Wires reached from the monitor beside his bed to various parts of his body. Though his vitals were stable, there was no telling if or when he might ever awake from his coma. Suddenly across the darkened room, a tiny pixie awoke. She had been instructed by her master to remain dormant until this very moment. Though it had been many days of hiding in the shadows of the king's quarters, the pixie had been loyal to her word, loyal to her master. After all, she would do anything for Arona.

The pixie slipped out of the shadows and hovered over King Basileus's chest, who lay motionless on the bed. She then pulled the small vial off her back. Though to her it was a large load to carry, to Basileus it was merely as large as his fingernail. Then she pressed it against his neck and the tiny needle pierced the skin.

It only took a moment for King Basileus to stir. After all, until this very moment, the King would have been in too deep of a coma for this small amount of antidote to take effect. Next his eyes sputtered open and soon he found himself awake, yet still in a world of complete darkness.

"Who's there?" his voice cracked, as he felt around with his hand. "I can't see. I'm blind. Who goes there?"

The last thing he remembered was Arona's face. *Was he still alone with her on the garden plate? Wait, there was a sharp pain in his neck.* He was confusing the sharp pain of the antidote the pixie had just administered as the same sensation as the poisoned dart. He knew that something bad had happened. *But what?* Little did he know that it all would have been much worse had Arona not slipped a small portion of antidote into his drink at the Masquerade Ball. Little did he know that she had instructed this pixie to imitate her message, hibernate in his quarters until it was safe, and then administer the remaining portion of the antidote to him. Once the rest of the antidote worked itself through the King's bloodstream, he would awake and the pixie would deliver this message:

"My beloved," the pixie's imitation of Arona began, "if you are hearing this, then our worst fears have been realized ..."

Basileus's panic instantly subsided the moment he heard Arona's voice. He reached forward, only to feel the miniature slender figure of the pixie. His heart sank, realizing that it was not Arona herself delivering the message—his crippled eyes only able to detect the fairy's faint glow. He only hoped that Arona was still alive.

"...Regardless of what transpires between us, I urge you to seek out the mystery of the Chrysalis, even if you don't believe. The Count is on the brink of ushering in a dark new era for the world. He must be stopped. Which is why I must do what I know you won't understand.

"In order to salvage what we can, I have decided to proceed with a plan that most would see as unethical; including yourself. I only hope you will find a way to forgive me."

Fifty Two
The Last Stand

By now the sloop had all but completely sunk. Besides the colorful array of torn fabrics, which had once served as the mainmast, only the bow and the tips of its tallest sails breached the early morning waters. It had been a frightening night as they scrambled to keep Lazlo's unconscious body from slipping into the water. But now, with everyone awake and aware, there was nothing left to do but huddle at the peak of the bow, waiting for either help or fate.

Since last watching the *Venom* slip back beneath the surface of the sea, Wick had hardly spoken a word. He kept only to himself—his expression pruned up like a withering, lifeless fruit. For Wick, watching Ash being whisked away by the pirates was like losing a child. His emotions were a sour blend of abandonment and guilt, knowing that wherever Ash was now, somewhere deep inside he was still raging with anger at Wick for what he thought was a great act of deceit.

There were only so many things an old wharfling like Wick could do now. He could choose to curl up and grow old in a cocoon of self-pity, or he could dare to consider the opposite: doing something.

Wharflings had earned a reputation of falling into the shadows of ambitionless stalemate—hiding behind the immunity of their own tortured past. And although their terrible history could not be denied, the sad reality of how Kingland had simply bought them off in an attempt to quiet them had since turned to an even sadder state.

Nowadays it was common for the younger generations of wharflings to refuse to even earn an honest living. There was even a name reserved for these social outcasts: *bum-dwarfs*. But wharflings like Wick refused to be lumped into that stereotype. At the end of his life, Wick wanted to be known as someone who actually lived it and never turned his back on the prospect of opportunity, if it were indeed a means to help make the world a better place. And the prospect before him now was bigger than any wharfling from the cold swamps of Murk could have ever imagined—that is, if he lived to see it.

Fog had settled upon the waters of the sea, dropping the visibility range considerably, which had everyone a bit jumpy that morning. Even though Wick was amphibious, going into these waters was not a good idea. Boota and Lazlo knew all too well. These waters were infested with black whales. And morning meant only one thing: feeding time.

Through the fog Wick saw something approaching. It was big. And before he even had a chance to think, it was upon them.

Once the galleon cleared the fog, Driver yelled in excitement. Boota sighed in relief as she hugged Lazlo. *Saved!* But their celebration was short-lived as a row of cannons emerged from the ship's side, pointing down at the castaways.

The galleon pulled up along side the wreckage with armed men standing at the rail, pistols and muskets aimed right at Wick, Lazlo, Driver, and Boota. Ropes were lowered, which came as a sign of respite, even though these strangers refused to lower their weapons.

They didn't look like pirates, but they weren't legitimate military either. Wick and the others were given blankets to warm themselves with. Suddenly someone wrapped in a gray hooded robe emerged from belowdecks and approached them. Perhaps this wasn't the rescue they thought it was. Then she peeled her hood back.

"Arona?" Lazlo gasped, like he'd seen a ghost.

"It has been too long, Sir Blackwood," Arona replied with a beautiful smile, as her band of insurrectionists lowered their weapons. Wick was beginning to add the situation up—enough to know he had little to fear anymore.

"Awe, c'mon," Lazlo said, taking Arona by the hand and kissing it. "Please, call me Lazlo. Just like old times."

"Old times," Wick whispered to himself. This was the first piece of solid evidence that Lazlo had been telling the truth about his past. *Indeed, he had been connected to Count LePrey and possibly even the King. Perhaps this pirate really could be trusted.*

"Time is of the essence," Arona said, with an undercurrent of urgency that told Lazlo he was about to get an earful. "I'm not sure what you are all aware of, since being on the run. But the Count's drone-armada is advancing far beyond Murk." Lazlo shook his head, already aware of this much. "The entire world is in danger."

"Wait a minute," Lazlo cut in. "Isn't this drone-armada just a contract army for Kingland?"

"Yes," Arona replied. "But remember, they are run by the Count—or worse yet, by his machine. And with the King out …" she paused for a moment, recovering herself, "out of the picture—"

"So it's true?" Lazlo asked, unsure as to why she was referring to his old friend in any other way than his first name. After all, they were all once good friends.

"Yes, Arona replied with a crack in her voice. "He was targeted for assassination. He's in a coma." Lazlo could see the life drain from her expression as she spoke. "But it's too late. Marshal law has been put into order over all Allied Kingdoms. They are on a crusade in pursuit of those responsible for the assassination attempt."

"I'll bet everything the Count was behind the assassination," Lazlo said. "A pretext to release his army into the world."

"He was," Arona informed him, straight-faced. "Trust me." Her eyes were filled with remorse. "But now the King has been rendered powerless."

Lazlo's thoughts fell on the dire situation Hoodu had warned them of when observing the Ginkan hunters in the jungle. Indeed the Count's scheme was taking shape and taking the world down with it. The efforts of Allied Kingdom occupation troops were becoming more and more futile. If the Count played his cards right, he could quickly spark a devastating conflict between these ground troops and the war-torn territories they were ironically claiming to protect.

"The drone-armada is an unstoppable force as long as the Count's machine still functions," Arona continued. "The vast network of communication is carried out by means of his drone-zeppelins. But their homing beacon is the machine itself. The one hidden in the lighthouse of Bald Rock."

"Look, I appreciate you coming here to tell me this," Lazlo said with defeated tone. "But why are you *really* here?"

"Because I need you," Arona said, laying her hand on Lazlo's shoulder.

"I'm flattered, but confused," Lazlo laughed.

"Like I said, the drone-armada is far too large to take on," Arona explained. "Even for Kingland and its Allied Kingdoms. But Machine *can* be taken out. If Bald Rock's blockade can be breached, Machine is vulnerable. It *can* be destroyed."

"Destroy it with what?" Wick interjected. "Lazlo has nothing more than a sword and a quiver of arrows. And a pixie," he added as Petra fluttered over to him.

"And my charm," Lazlo slipped back. "Look, even if one could get past the blockade, it would take an army of fighters, not to mention weapons and artillery we simply don't have."

"You don't have *yet*," Arona replied.

"Excuse me?" Wick asked, nervous of what he might be getting into now.

"The Pirate Rogue," Arona said straight-faced. Lazlo didn't even bother to respond. *She had to be kidding.* But she wasn't.

"As we speak," Arona continued, "hundreds of pirates are preparing for one of the largest assaults on the Allied Kingdom Occupation Forces of the Zahartan Desert. Rumor has it that they have engineered a new virus more deadly than ever before. And they are not afraid to use it.

"The desert tribes are infuriated by the recent surprise withdrawal of all drone-security forces. Though they're not supportive of our foreign military presence, there are those who see this withdrawal as yet another broken promise—abandonment. With these forces gone, the region has erupted into chaos. In retaliation, the tribal leaders have urged the Pirate Rogue to rise up against this abandonment. This assault could be the deadliest we've seen in the region yet."

"So you plan to talk them out of it?" Lazlo asked with a look of confusion.

"Kind of," Arona said, searching for the right words. "The Pirate Rogue is less motivated by the political struggle and more by the money the tribal leaders are paying them. But if the Pirate Brethren could be persuaded to shift their initiative to where it really counts, they might feel like their fight is much more legitimate."

"You plan on paying these pirates to fight?" Lazlo asked. He wasn't convinced.

"Absolutely not," Arona clarified. But this isn't about money. This is about giving them a chance to redeem themselves by fighting for a real freedom. After all, real freedom is what pirates stand for, right?"

"Have you lost your mind?" Lazlo laughed.

"No," Arona said, straight-faced. "But we are running out of time. And options." Lazlo refocused, giving his old friend the benefit of the doubt.

"I think you underestimate just how vile these pirates are," Lazlo said scratching his head. "They really don't care about a cause unless it's going to affect their wallet. And even if they could be convinced, who's going to go meet with the Brethren."

Arona said nothing as her eyes remained locked into Lazlo's.

"Oh no," Lazlo said shaking his head and backing away. "You're not getting me to do it. These guys hate the likes of me. They think that my friendship with Merrick was a sellout. They —"

"Listen to yourself, Lazlo," Arona interrupted angrily. Lazlo stopped in his tracks. "What happened to the intrepid rebel I once knew? What happened to doing whatever it takes?" She turned her eyes to hide a stubborn tear. "You have no idea what I've gone through just to be here right now. A good friend once told me: *If something is worth fighting for, then risk is inevitable.*"

Lazlo pondered the plot for a moment, imagining the devastation if full-out war were to erupt in the occupied territories. The Allied Kingdoms would eventually disband and the drone-armada would become the most powerful force in existence. Count LePrey was in a position that could grant him the type of power no one was meant to wield. No way in hell was Lazlo about to give him this. He had been in hiding for too many years because of this madman's ideals.

"Okay," he finally said with an outstretched hand. "It's worth the risk." Arona smiled. After all, the friend who had once told her the proverb was Lazlo.

"What?" Wick, Driver, and Boota exclaimed in unison.

"Looks like we're heading to Isla Ruba," Lazlo said, patting Wick on the head.

Fifty Three
Council of the Brethren

Thankfully, the journey to Isla Ruba wasn't a long one from where Arona and her crew of loyalists had rescued Lazlo and the rest. Had it been any longer, the anticipation would have eaten Lazlo up. Still, he wasn't convinced that he was going to leave this island alive.

The Brethren held council in an abandoned temple, built by a long-gone religious order, which tried to convert the island natives from their wayward ways. But their well-organized efforts quickly evaporated in the fervor of the native's devout ritualistic beliefs. Ironically, the entire order wound up being sacrificed to the gods of the jungle.

As he approached the old temple, Lazlo hummed to himself to keep himself focused. He had to, as to not make eye contact with the eyes peering at him from the shadows of the jungle. The island natives were always on the hunt for fresh victims for sacrifice. Lazlo knew this, which is why he kept his hands hovering just above the handles of his pistol and sword.

He had to travel alone, as to not upset the Brethren any more than they already might be. So, anchored offshore, the crew awaited the outcome of Lazlo's efforts. Wick almost tagged along, had it not been for the argument he and Lazlo were still in the heat of. This entire scheme with the Pirate Rogue was just more than Wick could take. He was finally convinced that Lazlo had proven where his true allegiances lie: with the pirates.

After surviving the long hike through the moonlit jungle, Lazlo was greeted by two fiery-masked, nosferu centurions guarding the temple doors. Slave Lords often paid them in either worthless coins from long-gone kingdoms or broken mechanical gadgets from the New World. And by the looks of the electrical wires strewn around them like necklaces, these nosferus had been hired before.

"Nice," Lazlo whispered to himself as the nosferus parted. Thankfully, they had been informed of the pirate's arrival.

Only candlelight flickered from within the vast sanctum of the terracotta-domed building, as the large wooden doors slowly opened. Though the temple wasn't used as a place of worship any longer, it still maintained a certain reverence within its intricately etched walls. The natives stripped Lazlo of his weapons and proceeded.

The six council members of the Pirate Brethren were seated on an elevated platform, where most likely an alter once stood. They were of every race and creed—proudly representing every corner of the world. Lazlo had to remind himself why he had come.

"Sir Blackwood," Captain Barnacus Pelt addressed before Lazlo had even reached the council. The head of the council, Pelt was a large, thick man with long, silver hair. His peppered beard reached down to his chest and his clothes were tattered to the point of depletion. Milky, washed-out tattoos lined his dirt-smeared skin. "We thought you were dead."

"So did I, a few times," Lazlo responded, wishing he had left his sarcasm back on the galleon.

"What brings you before us?" Pelt asked, refusing to acknowledge Lazlo's attempt at humor.

"Well, it's complicated," Lazlo began. He wished he had rehearsed his plea. "You see, I know that the Pirate Rogue is readying for a full-scale attack on the Allied Kingdom Occupation Forces in the Zahartan Desert. And I am aware of your newly engineered rogue virus. But releasing it will only justify the drone-armada's enforcement of their implants. It will be the nail in your coffin." Six stone-cold expressions glared back at Lazlo.

"Though I sympathize with the motive, I am here to inform you of another threat, far more critical, that could use your military might even more." Not one of the six as much as blinked. Lazlo was pretty sure that he was going to die on this island.

"Look," he continued, stepping up his tempo, "As radically fueled the dessert tribal leaders are, the Allied Kingdoms are not responsible for the withdrawal of drone-security forces."

"Then who is?" one of the other six asked.

"One man," Lazlo answered. "The Count of Cape Sparrow. The greatest pirate-hater in the world. He is the proprietor of the entire drone-armada, and in this state of marshal law, the one pulling all of the strings with Kingland's entire military. You may not know this, but his primary initiative with this invasion is to wipe you out."

"So what does that mean to us?" Pelt asked, gesturing for Lazlo to speed his explanation up.

"It means that you're focusing your attention on the wrong enemy." Lazlo could hear his own breathing, as all skeptical eyes remained fastened on him. "Bald Rock is home to the Count and the central nervous system of his grand armada. By striking at the core, you could take out the entire network in one shot."

"Are you suggesting we redirect our fleet from the Zahartan Desert to Bald Rock?" Pelt almost laughed out.

"The remaining forces in the desert are still considerable," Lazlo said, glad he was even being given the time of day. "I fear you may be too evenly matched to achieve the outcome you wish for, even with your rogue virus." The council members grew uncomfortable in their seats at that comment. So Lazlo quickly proceeded.

"But the blockade protecting Bald Rock is minimal in comparison. Given the secrecy the Count surrounds him in, he obviously doesn't want to draw attention to his lair. You have a window of opportunity here to bring down the largest army that has ever walked the face of the globe."

Lazlo's words had definitely not fallen on deaf ears. He watched intently as the Brethren whispered amid themselves. The candles burned nearly all of the way down, and still, the Lords were discussing. Finally, as the room grew silent again, Pelt spoke.

"So how much is your offer?"

Lazlo was now positive that Isla Ruba would be the last stop on his journey through life. He even smelled the air, just to get a good sense of the place where he would obviously be put to rest.

"Well," he stammered out weakly. "I don't really have one."

"We can give you a price then," one of the Panthril Lords offered in almost a benevolent tone.

"Yes, but I'm not offering money." Lazlo squeezed his eyes shut and tucked his head into his shoulders, waiting whatever verbal bombs were about to be dropped. But there was nothing. Only silence. And as he dared to open one eye, he noticed that the expressions on their faces were as somber as when he had last checked.

"No money," Pelt finally reiterated. "Your allegiance to the King of Kingland was reason enough for us to nearly refuse your entry to our council. But exile has clearly diluted your judgment. Coming here with such an insulting offer. You are no longer worthy to call yourself a pirate."

Knowing that his own death was probably only moments away, Lazlo decided to go for broke.

"First of all," he began, approaching the council proudly. "I'm a *privateer*." Looks of confusion crossed their faces. "Secondly, this is not about money. It's about freedom. The core virtue you stand for. It's about validation. As honorable and powerful as you are, the Pirate Rogue as a whole has become synonymous with cannibalistic terror in the world." It was obvious that this offended some in the room. "But if you really want to flex your power, do it against your greatest threat."

No one spoke for the longest time. And then Pelt stood to his feet and approached Lazlo. Lazlo bowed his head, knowing this was it. Then Pelt laid a hand on his shoulder and said, "You forgot one." Lazlo was bewildered. "It's about time."

"Time?"

"It's about time we redirect our fleet," Pelt concluded with a grin. And then addressing the entire council he shouted, "We have a new plan. Cape Sparrow is about to be paid a little visit!"

Lazlo sighed, about to drop to the floor. He would be leaving Isla Ruba alive after all.

Fifty Four
The Lighthouse

A stiff chill permeated every pore on Ash's skin, like a wicked virus creeping into his body. Since torching the arm of the pirate who tried apprehending the Enigma from him, Ash had been tossed into a tiny, rodent-infested cell, void of light, void of hope. Though his capture had reunited him with Scar, it was looking like more of a dead end than anything. Besides, she was still unconscious in the cell across from him.

As the *Venom* slowly surfaced through the waters of Cape Sparrow, the impending doom consumed any ray of hope that had ever existed. At the edge of the grass-capped cliff, the lighthouse loomed tall and daunting, like a massive headstone. In a sad, odd way it reminded Ash of the old clock tower of Garbbit Harbor, so tall and alone and void of function. The submarine entered a cave, carved-out of the island's stone perimeter. Desolate and treeless, Bald Rock certainly lacked the romance and charm that Ash had seen in picture books as a child. On the contrary, this was by far the most disturbing and frightful place Ash's journey had taken him to thus far.

They docked beneath a giant blimp, hanging from above, consuming the entirety of the blackness of the island's cave. It was overwhelming to see one of these drone-zeppelins so close. Then Scar awoke in her cell, appearing more ill than ever. She hardly acknowledged Ash. He wondered if they had already spoken their last words to one another. He had to know.

"Since finding you in the forest, Wick has warned me that you are not to be trusted. Can I trust you Scar?" He dreaded her reply.

"No."

Her answer felt like being stabbed. He had worked so hard to win her approval. He had fought so tirelessly to resist Wick's admonition. *Was it really all for not?* After what he had already lost, he didn't know if he had it in him to lose anything else.

The pirate-guards came to get Scar. She went with ease. But as they pulled her from her cell, she turned to Ash and said, "Leave me. Save yourself. I will only hurt you."

Even though he knew he had to let go, even though she had warned him too, Ash couldn't help but wonder if she might still be able to be saved.

The two were quickly ushered from the *Venom*, across the cave's elevated iron docks and into to a large freight elevator. Ash kept his eyes closed as to not catch a glimpse of Bontey. Scar's ice-cold hand was the only successful distraction. Ash held it tight, whether she wanted him to or not. The elevator rose upward at a stomach-turning speed, and then abruptly stopped after only a short commute. When the door reopened, two drone-soldiers led them into the darkness.

The room smelled old and musty, yet carried an acrid sulfurous scent that reminded Ash of some of the magical potions Wick had often concocted. A layer of dust had evenly settled across the surfaces of the sparse furniture arrangements, de-saturating the interior's colors into a life-drained world of grays. Only the blue sea through the skirting windows drew any color into this place. Ash tried to forget the many stories he had heard about this haunted place. He couldn't help but think that every movement out of the corner of his eye was the ghost of the lighthouse keeper. Little did he know; ghosts were the least of his worries here.

The pirates' boots pounded like thunder, stirring up a cloud of dust as they climbed the spiral staircase, up to what should have been the lighthouse's lantern room. But instead of the room housing a large lamp, in the center was a massive black iron sphere. It floated above the steamy floor and had a strange lens of fractured glass, which seemed to be staring right at Ash, like the eye of a cyclops. *What was it? Was this the machine Scar had spoken of?* As featureless as the deathly black mass was, there was something about it that seemed *alive*. Ash's heart was racing as Bontey stood next to it, eyes narrowed on him, as if he might dive for his neck at any moment. Then, a tall, thin figure emerged through the darkness like a spirit manifesting from the shadows.

He wore all black. His pale shaved head seemed to drown in his tall, black-fur collar as he drew his large hood back. It was a man Ash recognized from books: *the Count of Cape Sparrow himself. The legendary alchemist.* He was pallid and sickly looking, save only for the dapper attire he donned. An apparent sense of tragedy shaped his eyes into narrow slits. He looked as though he might snap into a violent rage at any moment. But by the look of Scar's reaction, he was also someone from her foggy past—someone she feared. Ash couldn't believe it as he began quickly putting it all together. *The Count of Cape Sparrow was also the "master" Scar had spoken of so many times!*

LePrey twisted his mouth into an pruned smile. It was apparent that the sight of Scar came as intense relief to him. Approaching her, he reached out and gently touched her pale cheek.

"My prodigal child," he whispered to Scar. "Do not tremble. You are home now."

His words seemed to meet her with much resistance as her face pursed and her eyes darted away. LePrey's cunning manner terrified Ash.

"You have taken the long way around," LePrey continued. "But it was worth the wait, for you have not only brought me the medallion, but you have also delivered the last remnant of that dead cult," he said, turning to Ash as though he knew him. "This has truly been a mission of fate. Your work here is finished," he said, motioning for Scar to leave. "Guards, take her to debriefing. It looks like she could use some rest." The two drone-guards of the Sanctuary quickly apprehended Scar and escorted her from the room.

Ash vainly reached out for her, knowing full well that by *rest*, LePrey meant termination. The rifle of a drone-soldier held Ash back. But as Scar left, he couldn't help but ponder upon LePrey's words: *the last remnant of that dead cult*. This count knew exactly who Ash was.

LePrey then reached toward Ash's shirt pocket and attempted to retrieve the Enigma. But suddenly a blinding flash of white light shot from the medallion, blasting LePrey back, bursting his hand into a ball of flame. It looked no different than Logan's hand the night Ash had inadvertently unleashed his curse upon him. The difference now was that Ash was discovering the ability to control his manifestations. The flash quickly dissipated. LePrey stood motionless and wide-eyed, holding his raw, smoking, burnt flesh. His black glove had melted into his skin. But he didn't even bother to remove it as he struggled to suppress his surging rage.

"Interesting," LePrey whispered to himself through his teeth. "Very interesting indeed." His green eyes studied Ash's. In a strange way it seemed as if the blast was the boy's instinct to protect the Enigma.

"Well then," LePrey announced, shifting his attention to Bontey. The dark creature stood holding a small chest. "First things first. I too have a little surprise. And as always, I am a man of my word."

With his good hand, LePrey handed Bontey a large silver key. Bontey took the key, and with a snarl quickly inserted it into the keyhole on the chest's inner chamber. His greedy impatience to retrieve his reward was as obvious as a child's behavior as he opened it. But the expression on his hair-covered face instantly morphed to rage as he looked inside. Then, in an instant, something black leaped out of the chest and attached itself to Bontey's neck.

It only took a moment for the spider's poison to render Bontey completely unconscious. And as the dark creature's hulking body slammed to the floor, his drone-soldiers squadron turned their rifles on his pirates.

"Don't think that I am not grateful for your contributions," LePrey addressed Bontey's unconscious corpse. "The retrieval of this boy and girl was imperative to this treasure hunt," LePrey said, cradling his burnt hand with the other. He then turned his attention to the drone-soldiers. "Take Bontey down to the dungeons. When he wakes he'll understand the repercussions of attempting betrayal."

Ash didn't know whether to be afraid or relieved that Bontey had been taken out. The drone-soldiers quickly cleared the room, dragging Bontey by his dreadlocks and marching his pirate comrades out of the lantern room.

LePrey circled the room, gloating in the glory of his magnificent creation: Machine. They were alone now—just Ash, Count LePrey, and his mysterious machine. "And now for you," he addressed Ash. He suddenly stopped, leering into Ash's eyes.

Ash suddenly grew cold with paranoia. *What did he see?* Then it hit Ash. Looking down at the floor, Ash could see drips of blood pooling at his heels. The scars on his back were hemorrhaging like never before! There was no covering up. If LePrey had any idea what this meant (and surely he did), then Ash had just been made.

"You don't know me, do you boy?" LePrey asked, pacing the floor slowly. The iron mass of Machine loomed behind LePrey like a giant, black moon. Ash had no idea what LePrey meant by his question. *Most everyone knew who this legendary Count was.* Ash wanted to react but fear had rendered his tongue useless. And the expression LePrey wore appeared to be a mix of anger and obsessive satisfaction.

"But I see it now. You have your mother's eyes," he said. Strangely, LePrey's green eyes almost seemed to glow. "Then again, you probably don't even know your mother, do you?" LePrey asked. "She ran away when you were but a small boy."

The fact that LePrey knew these details made Ash feel nauseous. "I must admit, meeting you is like going back in time. I had no idea your mother even had a child. But it makes perfect sense, now that I think of it. She hid you from the world. A smart woman. *You're* what they call the *Hidden Ember*. The last smoldering remnant of your kind. And it is even prophesied that you will rise up and save the world from its peril." Ash swallowed painfully. "How's it going so far?" A quiet laugh hissed into the darkness.

LePrey studied Ash's eyes for a moment. "Oh dear," he said wearing a sad expression, realizing that Ash had no idea what he was talking about. "You really have no clue what you are, do you?"

"I'm a Guardian," Ash said, wishing he had come off a bit more brave. But deep down he was convinced that LePrey actually knew more about what a Guardian was than he.

"Awe, so you *do* know a little something," LePrey reacted, pointing his burnt hand at Ash. "You know about your mother's past. But do you even know what it means to be a Guardian?" Ash was now questioning weather he really did. *Had Wick actually told him everything?* After all, Wick hadn't been perfectly truthful about many things.

"Well I'm afraid the Vyne withered away long ago," LePrey continued, suppressing his sinister laugh. "But it doesn't mean you won't still fulfill your destiny. You will." There was something in the way LePrey delivered those last two words that gave Ash a sense that LePrey was far ahead of him in this game.

"You were probably told that in order to protect the secret of the Chrysalis, you must exploit it to the world," LePrey continued. "But that is just an uniformed myth—a crooked twist on the truth." He shot Ash another prying look. "I see your scars." Ash shuttered. "A fatal curse I'm afraid. Trust me. I know."

"It's not a curse," Ash argued back. Still, he wasn't even convinced himself.

As LePrey turned away, he dropped his cape to the floor. Ash saw two wet stains, soaking through the backside of LePrey's vest. The stains looked exactly like Ash's bloody scars. But the blood that had soaked through was black, not red, not human. *Synth*. Ash's mouth dropped open.

Like a chilling epiphany, things were beginning to fall into place. Not only was LePrey a Guardian, he was the traitor who had killed off the rest of the Vyne!

"If anyone knows about curses, I do," LePrey said, his green eyes bloodshot with what looked to be heartbreaking grief.

"You see," LePrey continued as he slowly approached Ash, "I come from the same line of people as you. I too was a Guardian. But this inherited mutant trait is nothing more than literal damnation. Living a life of sworn secrecy under an ancient oath established by dead forefathers is the definition of insanity. The Vyne once understood exactly what it was they were protecting. But over time the truth of it had become mired by exaggeration and diluted by myth. As the world evolved, the Vyne became feeble and meaningless.

"I couldn't live my life as a cursed outcast, protecting something I had no comprehension of. I had more foresight than the other Guardians, shedding my wings and denouncing their dogma. I freed myself of that ancient curse and turned to a new source of magic." Gesturing to Machine, LePrey exclaimed, "This miracle of science is the most powerful force in the world.

"Now, separated from the bias of that sect, I understand that the so-called *truth* the Vyne wanted to spread was never meant to be *harnessed* by the people of this world. Even for the Imcot, this *Mystery* eventually became their downfall, proving just how mortal they really were."

Then, like echoes from another place in time, Ash felt as though he was channeling her thoughts. *But whose thoughts? The White Dragon? His mother?* "You know nothing of the Mystery." These words seemed to rip through LePrey like a blade. Truth burned him. "It's not as simple as that. It's not a thing you can simply hide. Our Mystery is our freedom. Our free will. My mother knew this. But she understood that the Vyne wasn't meant to hide it from the world. That is why she tried to expose it."

"She betrayed the order of the Vyne!" LePrey yelled frantically. His eyes were wild.

"No!" Ash argued back with a confidence that scared him. "You did! Dragons came to this world to free our Mystery—to free us from our own inhibitions and save us from our self-destructive nature. The Vyne was meant to protect and spread this magic, not suppress it."

LePrey seemed to be caught off guard by those words. He then began to speak reverently again. "You've seen the White Dragon, haven't you?" he pried, his eyes locked with Ash's. "She told you this tale." Ash couldn't respond. "Listen to me," LePrey erupted again and jabbed his staff into the air to make his point. "The Chrysalis is dangerous! You've been told that awakening people's Mysteries can save the world from self-destruction. But I ask you this: Do you really think that such a power can be trusted in this world?"

When considering the menace of the Pirate Rogue and the violence they embodied, Ash couldn't deny that an untamed awakening of supernatural power was dangerous. Bontey had obviously tapped into this power, with the ability to read people's minds. There was no one more dangerous than he.

"In the right hands it can be controlled," Ash replied solemnly.

"The right hands?" LePrey asked. "And you believe *yours* are the right hands?" Ash didn't know what to say as he studied the lines of his palms. "Are you so foolish to think that simply unleashing a power like this could ever work? What you call *enlightenment* is nothing more than unfiltered power. Look around. The world is a pirate-infested disaster! We're more divided now than ever before in history. In the end, it is our nature to want more, to trample over the weaker. It's our survival instinct. If people were to one day awake to possession of this raw power, they wouldn't know how to control it. The world would be destroyed faster than you'd be able to react." Then LePrey locked eyes with Ash and uttered words that rendered him speechless. "By releasing this power to the world, you alone will have brought the ancient apocalyptic prophecy into reality. Do you really want that blood on your hands?"

Ash had never had it put quite this way to him before. He thought of his power and how unpredictable it seemed at times. And even if he was able to control it, he had often wondered if it might quickly become an addiction he would soon grow to rely on. *Was this the inevitability of power? It seemed so.*

"Freedom scares you," Ash hurled at LePrey. His hatred for the Count was thickening his skin with every passing moment. "Yet freedom is the true essence of the Chrysalis. Not the alchemical attributes you've mistaken it for. Your plan is to enslave the world to your machine. A silent global society that has no will of its own. But you can't bring peace to the world through science and mandates."

"War is merely a means to an end," LePrey responded cryptically. "The Pirate Rogue has transformed the world into a chaotic landscape of fear and terror. Even the seemingly innocent people of the Allied Kingdoms do not understand that their own apathetic behavior is only fueling this threat. I wish there was another way. But right now there isn't. And now is the time to act. Yes, in the end, the path war leaves behind is silent. But silence is peace."

As harsh and disconcerting as it sounded, Ash found it impossible to respond. Suddenly LePrey's mood shifted again. A softer smile graced his boney white face like a garment that just didn't fit.

"You and the girl have a bit of a connection I see," he said studying Ash, as if reading his mind. Ash found it impossible to respond to such an intimate detail. "I sympathize with your quandary. Your curse is not one that others find …" he paused briefly, carefully choosing his words, "pleasing." Then he stood face-to-face with Ash. He rested his hands on Ash's shoulders, the pains of his torched hand apparently not of concern any longer.

"I need you to trust me," LePrey said in a half-whisper. "I can free you of this curse you've been born into. The one your mother burdened you with before abandoning you. The one that keeps you from the things you yearn for in life." Ash knew he meant Scar. "And as for the girl," he continued with his proposal, "she is currently scheduled to be rejuvenated: her mind wiped clean of anything up till now." Ash imagined Scar being strapped to a table, her head painfully being injected with foreign medical instruments. "However, I could see to it that she remains as is, remembering everything and *everyone* as is. You can have her. You and she can be together. But first you must do something for me."

"Do what?" Ash whispered. He burned inside with guilt. But if the Count was actually offering a way out from this burdened destiny, even the Guardian power in Ash couldn't find the strength to turn it down.

"I need you to give me the Enigma," LePrey requested with an intensity in his eyes Ash hadn't seen yet. "You were told that it is your destiny to protect the Enigma from people like me. But again, that is nothing more than a lie. The truth is, it is poisoning your mind. This medallion is brainwashing you and forcing you unwillingly into its service. You know what I'm talking about, don't you?" Ash was afraid. He couldn't deny that since the Enigma had come into his life, his will had not been his own.

"You think the Chrysalis is the elixir of life," Ash called LePrey's bluff. "Well, you're mistaken. It is far more than some random scientific elixir. It is truth."

"That's the White Dragon talking," LePrey mocked angrily with a stern finger on Ash's face. "The power to create and sustain life is not one that belongs in the hands of the masses. And it certainly isn't intrinsic to a boy who doesn't even know what he believes in." LePrey's words stung with precision. "Few fully understand what the Chrysalis is. Your mother didn't. In fact, I wonder if you even do." This made Ash question the very same thing. "You can have the girl, but give me the Enigma," LePrey pleaded with an outstretched hand. Ash's lack of response caused LePrey to tremble with anger. "You don't understand the dangers of releasing the power of the Chrysalis to the world. Now release the Enigma to me and give up your futile quest," he demanded, slamming his hands together.

This was the moment in time that would ultimately define Ash as a person—the crossroads that could take him down two entirely different paths. The White Dragon herself had laid out his destiny in detail. Ash could change the doomed course of the world. But knowing that Scar's very existence hung in the balance of this decision was just too much for him to overcome. He *had* to save her. Reaching into his pocket, Ash pulled out the Enigma and looked at it. He closed his eyes but couldn't find the strength to lift his hand. It was like an unseen force was holding his arm down. It wasn't going to happen.

LePrey slammed his staff down onto the floor. "You fool!" Then he motioned to his drone-guards, who had since reentered the lantern room. The guards approached Ash with their glowing green eyes fastened on him intently. One of them slashed his cuffs together, igniting his power-suit, and the other quickly repeated. They ejected the double-ended switch-swords, drawing their blades up to Ash's chin as they marched him backward, towards Machine. Ash's eyes grew wide with panic. He was mystified. LePrey glared hostilely, his green eyes almost glowing in their dark sockets.

"What are you doing?" Ash yelled.

"Perhaps you'll be a bit less stubborn after Machine is through with you," LePrey said, pointing to Machine. "After all, I promised that you *would* fulfill your destiny. You *will* save the world—save it from the curse of the Chrysalis."

Ash could hardly think as the guards backed Ash up towards Machine. He tried to summon his Mystery. But fear and overwhelming hopelessness overruled.

"You see," LePrey began describing, "through transmutation, all of your imperfections, your delusions, your inadequacies, even your fears will become obsolete." Ash assumed that by *transmutation*, he no doubt meant: *transforming into a drone*. He was right. "Machine will wash you, white as snow, and you will live again in perfect peace."

Then LePrey looked out the window, as if dreaming of another time. "Fear is what stifles you more than anything," he said in a bone-chilling manner. *How did he know so much?* "Fear of the unknown. Fear of loss. Fear of the dark beast: Bontey." Ash could hardly breathe as he backed away. "When you were still a small child, I hired Bontey to hunt down the Guardian who possessed the Enigma: your mother. Certainly you remember seeing this beast." Ash couldn't believe what he was hearing. Yet, like a perfect puzzle, it all seemed to be fitting together. Bontey had been haunting him since he was a boy. "I'm surprised he spared you," LePrey continued. "Especially since your mother got away. But enough about them. Let's get back to you."

At that moment, Ash looked up and saw that one of the guard's power-suits had disengaged. A swirl of green fire and lightening manifested before Ash. Suddenly Ash grabbed the fiery mass like solid matter and threw it at the guard, knocking him across the room and into a motionless heap on the floor. LePrey only watched as Ash then engaged the other guard. But he was no match for the guard's ignited power-suit, as the guard threw him into the air.

An unseen aura kept Ash's body from slamming into Machine's iron surface. For a brief moment he hovered motionless. He could feel the heavy forces of this dark place doing everything to bring him down. Then, as if an intense magnetic pull had gripped him, Ash abruptly became attached to Machine, like thrown clay splattered on a wall. But this was hardly a sign of good luck.

Suddenly an excruciating, stinging pain flashed over Ash like an electrical surge. What he couldn't see, were the thousands of tiny needles erecting from Machine's iron surface, the likes of emerging hairy stubble—pushing into him, piercing his skin like a bed of nails. Ash screamed as the needles sank deep into his skin, injecting him with something he instantly detected as very foreign, painfully synthetic. Out of the corner of his eye he could see the needles as they moved through his palms. The skin on the topside of his hands rose as the needles threatened to puncture completely through.

"Machine," LePrey finally ordered. "Make him one of ours." That was when Ash felt it.

It was violating—like when Logan used to bust into his bedroom late at night, barking ridiculous and often indiscernible orders. Most nights Ash was just lying there, still awake, imagining what life would be like outside of Garbbit Harbor.

The lantern room was alive with electricity as the transmutation process initiated. The electrical conductors hanging down from the ceiling crackled wildly with green sparks. Machine surged with lightening as Ash's body quivered atop its surface like a half-dead laboratory animal.

The strange sensation of the needles' injections felt as though his very soul was being siphoned out of his body. Emotions he had known so well were beginning to fade. Fear, regret, hatred—they were quickly being replaced by a complacency he didn't understand. But to his own dismay, he mysteriously wasn't resisting the transmutation any longer.

His eyesight slowly began to fade. His thoughts were quickly receding to places of undecipherable context. And as much as he tried to tell himself that there wasn't a certain sense of numbing comfort to it all, deep down, Ash knew that whatever was happening was an irreversible procedure. Though his instinct was to resist, Ash was beginning to almost like its effects.

Fifty Five
Attack on Bald Rock

Arona was right about the Brethren. Lazlo had to give her that. But he still wasn't sure how thirty galleons and a host of only two hundred goliath mountain-hawks were going to penetrate the blockade guarding the heart of the most powerful army in the world. For the first time in a long time, Lazlo was finding it difficult to remain cool.

Towering palm trees blurred by as the giant, brown mountain-hawks soared through the canyons, on their way to Cape Sparrow. Seated upon the back of one of the many massive feathery raptors, Lazlo surveyed the horizon carefully. But as his hawk rounded one last corner of the jungle-covered canyon, the waterbed opened up to the mouth of Cape Sparrow. In the distance, through the fog, Bald Rock sat on the horizon like an unassuming predator, patiently awaiting its prey.

The plan the pirates had devised was simple, but aggressive: Lazlo led the pack of pirates on mountain-hawks, escorting the thirty galleons. Ready for attack, each galleon was commandeered by Pirate Rogue's deadliest captains. It would be Lazlo's job to get the galleons within firing range of the lighthouse. But first they had to make it past the blockade.

As the pirates crossed the cape, Lazlo could see the spire of the lighthouse spiking into the low, fast-moving clouds. Drawing nearer to the island, Lazlo noticed something very strange. There was no blockade. "Where is it?" he whispered to himself. For a moment he wondered if he hadn't lead them to the wrong island. But as the towering lighthouse came more into view, he was reassured that indeed, this was Bald Rock.

Raising his arm, he signaled for the fleet to keep moving forward. He and the Brethren had anticipated that the Count's blockade would be a mass of patrolling war ships. But if he had to deal with being wrong, this was one time he didn't mind it. Taking out the lighthouse just might be easier than he had thought. Suddenly the water below began to ripple.

The mountain-hawks quickly scattered in a randomness of panic, as sixteen strange massive objects slowly crested the water's surface. The rising giants were quickly recognizable as drone-fortresses: massive spheres erected on three, narrow retractable stilts. They stood even taller than the galleons, like towering robots wading in the water. Narrow smokestacks billowed with thick black smoke atop their iron shells. Before they had even completely risen, eight portholes about their axis's dialed open and large cannon barrels protruded from within. They instantly began firing at the swirling host of hawks and the fleet of galleons closing in.

"Somebody's home," Lazlo said sarcastically to himself as his hawk dodged oncoming cannon fire. With one hand on the reigns and the other wielding a sawed-off musket, Lazlo was continually looking back to make sure that the galleons were still advancing.

The midnight-blue air lit up with orange explosions as the galleons fired their cannons at the fortresses. The technologically advanced drone-fortresses were able to spit out gunfire much more rapidly than the galleons' traditional cannons. Then massive shadows began to fall over everything.

Turning around, Lazlo saw four giant drone-zeppelins closing in. They seemed to come out of nowhere as they drifted through the low-hanging fog. Hatches on the zeppelins' under-carriages dialed open as swarms of small, black objects poured out like insects.

As the swarm closed in, Lazlo saw that it was a multitude of flying drone-solders. With their rectangular wings erected like a beam across their backs, the drones flew into the evening sky, their silhouettes like crucifixes. Each held a long slender rifle in its synthetic hands, firing rapid shots at the host of hawks.

"Oh boy," Lazlo said to one of his comrades flying next to him. "This is going to get fun." Then, raising his musket above his head, he commanded his mountain-hawk and dove into action.

The only thing keeping Lazlo and his pirates from instant defeat was their instinct, a trait that the drone-soldiers were void of. All they had was a pre-issued mandate. So although their precision and speed was remarkable, they only operated perfectly in so many variables.

Lazlo and his pirates continued reconfiguring their approach in a timed manner that seemed to continually throw the enemy off. They even managed to lure one of the zeppelins in closer to the battle, where one of the galleons managed to blast the helium-filled blimp, sending it crashing into one of the drone-fortresses and blowing it into a massive cloud of fire. Though this threw the swarm of drone-soldiers off their game for a moment, they quickly regained focus. In fact, it didn't take long for the enemy to adapt as they began coordinating their flight patterns with that of the drone-fortresses, leading their pirate prey directly into the line of cannon fire. They too were now adapting their strategy.

Fifty Six
The Wharfling

Through the telescope, from the galleon's deck, the battle in the sky was difficult to assess. But by a simple calculation of odds, it wasn't hard for Wick to understand that their efforts were on the verge of becoming completely futile. If something weren't done quickly, this mission would be as good as over. He couldn't help but wonder where Ash might be at that moment—*so far away, trapped in the bowels of the Venom.*

"Off the deck now!" Captain Pelt's gravelly voice yelled out from the ship's cabin. Wick and a handful of other shipmates scrambled off the deck and into the cabin.

"What is it Cap'n?" one of the pirates asked.

"Those drones are eating us alive," Pelt answered in a frustrated tone. "We must act quickly."

"What do you propose?" asked another pirate.

"Even though we outnumber them, they outgun us. Our galleons are clearly no match for those drone-fortresses," Pelt admitted.

"We took out one," another pirate reminded from across the cabin.

"A zeppelin crashed into it," Pelt reminded angrily. "But sometimes the only way to bring down a giant is not by trying to reach their head, but by tripping them at the feet."

Wick wasn't sure he was following. "And you have a plan?"

Captain Pelt glared at Wick with a look that was either one of total intrigue, or of complete disgust. Wick couldn't tell.

"Unless *you've* got one, then yes," Pelt assured defensively. "We have a small arsenal of atomic-grenades aboard this ship. If we could manage to plant these at the base of these drone-fortresses, we could bring them down with one hit."

Indeed, it sounded like a good plan. "And how do we plant the grenades?" Wick asked enthusiastically.

"That's where *you* come in my little wharfling friend," Pelt said with a grin.

Pelt then described how Wick, being both quite small as well as amphibious, made him the perfect choice for the job. This is exactly what it would take for relaying the grenades to the five remaining drone-fortresses. And to remain undetected by the island's sonar, Wick had to conduct this operation alone. Needless to say, he was less than enthused about it. In fact, he was quite resistant, until one of the pirates insulted him by calling him a *bum-dwarf*.

Visibility was terrible in the stirred waters as Wick swam up to the base of the first drone-fortress. The sights and sounds of the battle above was muffled by the murky water, making Wick feel as though he was trapped inside of a glass jar.

He pulled the first grenade out of his sack and found a nook at the foot of one of the fortress's legs, sunken deep into the seabed. He pulled the pin, placed it in the nook and quickly swam away. He would have to repeat this fourteen more times in the length of time that it took for the first grenade to go off or he might get caught up in the draft of the explosion. But the operation went faster than he had anticipated—that is, until he reached the fifteenth fortress.

As he rounded the legs of the fifteenth, he saw a familiar silhouette in the watery shadows of what appeared to be a massive cave on the island's perimeter. In the cloudy darkness it was hard to tell what it was, other than enormous. Then he recognized the detail. It was the *Venom*. *Ash is here!* What he couldn't see was what else was patrolling these dark waters. Suddenly an explosion ripped through the water. The first grenade had gone off!

Wick scrambled to lodge the last grenade. And he couldn't swim fast enough before the others began going off, one by one. When he reached the surface of the water he was greeted by a multitude of cheers as Captain Pelt's crew pulled him aboard the ship again.

"Nice work, Wick," Pelt congratulated him with a pat on the head. In the waters beyond, the crippled drone-fortresses slowly sank away, back into the sea like wilting giants. But in the skies above, the battle waged on between the flying drone-soldiers and hawk-riding pirates.

"Who's the hero now?" Lazlo yelled, as he landed his mountain-hawk on the deck of the galleon. Dismounting and running over to Wick he said, "I didn't take you for a risk-taker, wharfling. Looks like I could learn a few things from you." He shot him a wink. "Now it's time for the big one," he said, pointing to the lighthouse. Wick panicked.

"No!" he yelled. "We can't blow the lighthouse."

"Why?" Lazlo asked with a look of complete confusion.

"Because Ash is in there."

Wick had just put all of the pieces together. If Bontey was here, then he was working for LePrey. And if he was working for LePrey, then Ash was now in the hands of the Count himself.

"What?" Lazlo asked. "How do you know?"

"'Cause I saw the *Venom* down there," Wick answered, pointing to the water. "He's here. Bontey is working for LePrey. And LePrey's after the Enigma."

"Look," Pelt cut in, "I don't know what you're talking about. But all I know is that we've got a very small window of opportunity here. It's anyone's guess as to where the rumored drone-submarine fleet is."

"Or if it even exists," another pirate chimed in.

There were many speculations about a massive drone-submarine fleet patrolling a vast range of waters—from Cape Sparrow all the way to the North Sea. But although ships often disappeared without a trace from time to time, no one had ever actually seen this fleet.

"Real or not, I'm taking no chances," Pelt promised sternly. "It's now or never, guys."

"Yes," Lazlo agreed with the captain. "We have to do it, Wick. We have to do it now."

"You can't!" Wick pleaded in what was almost a scream. "Ash is—"

"Listen little guy!" Lazlo cut in, trying to settle his old wharfling friend down. "He'll be okay." Though Lazlo had much more faith in Ash's ability to take care of himself at sixteen, he knew full well that between Bontey and LePrey, the boy's chances of survival were dwindling. He then turned to Captain Pelt.

"Look, if I can get inside the lighthouse, I can rescue the boy."

"*You're* the one who talked us into this!" Pelt roared at Lazlo. His eyes were red with anger. "And now you want to delay us?"

"No," Lazlo warded, waving his hands crazily. "The boy is a friend of ours. I *have* to do it. You must understand. I just need—" he looked up at the cloud-wrapped moons to judge the time.

"Here," Pelt said, tossing Lazlo one of two tiny hourglasses he had. "You have until this runs out. Then we start bombing. Got it?" Thankfully, the code of the pirates included a clause in regard to never leaving a comrade behind unless they were actually dying. Thankfully, this pirate still considered Lazlo one of his own.

Turning back to Wick, Lazlo promised, "I won't leave the lighthouse without Ash. Or I'll die trying."

At that, Lazlo flipped his hourglass and walked away. He remounted his hawk as one of the crewmates threw him his musket. Wick felt sick. As nice as it was to hear a promise such as that, it wasn't going to be as easy as simply walking in and rescuing Ash. Wick had a terrible feeling that the last time he would ever see Ash again had already happened.

Fifty Seven
Revenge

Even the encounter with his greatest fear, Bontey, wasn't enough to shake Ash from the half-alive state he was now in, plastered against Machine's cold surface like a crucified outlaw. It was just like his nightmares—being paralyzed, yet fully aware of what was taking place around him. It was a trepidation he had often pondered. But suddenly he remembered something.

Although Wick's suspicions about Scar had been fueled with much paranoia and prejudice, Ash recalled one thing Wick told him the evening he went to visit him at his hut on the wharfling reservation: *If your questions is, are there real magicians in this world, then I say yes … wizards and witches and all sorts of people who specialize in tapping into the other side … the side of this world we cannot see with our eyes … comprised of pure energy.*

Ash considered that notion far more deeply now than he did that evening on the reservation. His journey since leaving Garbbit Harbor had seen many strange things, but none as alien as this new aura of energy he had inherited. *Was this power really "the other side"? The place we think of as death? If so, could it be channeled to overcome the consuming powers of something as powerful and as un-human as Machine?* It would take every trace of belief in this power to even raise Ash's head from its dropped and trapped state.

Struggling to keep his mind awake and his eyes open, Ash saw what was happening. In his delirious state of mind, he couldn't quite decipher what was real and what was part of this new, dream-like reality, slowly absorbing his being. But the strange sound that began to swell seemed to be all too real as LePrey himself appeared obviously perplexed. Suddenly a large shadow began growing up the wall of the stairwell.

Even Machine seemed to react in surprise as the green lighting flashed across its surface more sporadically. And as the beastly frame emerged from the stairwell, the beastly silhouette of General Sayto Bontey stood towering over Count LePrey. Broken chains dangled from the busted locks, clasped to Bontey's wrists. Barely able to see out of the corner of his eye, Ash couldn't imagine the strength this beast must possess to tear these loose with his bare hands. LePrey's expression was lifeless. He hadn't anticipated Bontey's emergence from the bite of the poisonous spider.

"You'll have to try harder than that," Bontey growled in a creepy rumble to LePrey. His words seemed to literally drop the temperature of the air. "If Kingland couldn't keep me restrained, what makes you think you can?"

"It was my handiwork that freed you from the Dungeons of Perg!" LePrey defended harshly, as he backed away.

"Then you've betrayed me for the last time," Bontey said, marching forward. Suddenly the large saber shot out of Bontey's prosthetic arm, poised for attack. But LePrey would not be a simple victim. Motioning to his drone-guard, the guard reignited his power-suit, ejected the dual blades of his switch-sword, and lunged at Bontey.

The drone was faster and far more agile than Bontey. But when he did make contact with the drone, Bontey's powerful thrusts were mutilating. After being knocked to the wall and stabbed in the shoulder, Bontey's rage quickly boiled over. And with one massive swing, his saber slammed deep into the drone, reducing him to a sparking, smoking heap on the floor.

Bontey stepped over the drone's corpse. His eyes were fixed on LePrey, who was pale with what should have been fear. Instead LePrey seemed more intent on trying to devise a way out of this situation.

"I made you what you are," he said to Bontey, who may as well have been deaf. "You *owe* me."

"Indeed I do," Bontey whispered like a heavy-breathing lion. He then grabbed LePrey by the throat, and pulling him closer ran his saber through his chest. Black blood spilled to the floor. *Revenge.*

LePrey smiled, as though he had somehow convinced himself that he still had the upper hand. His mind had become so diluted by synth that he couldn't even comprehend the reality of his own defeat. *After all these years of meticulous scheming, this couldn't be the end!* But then the chill of mortality finally gripped LePrey like a hand of ice. His head flopped back like a broken doll and his entire body went completely limp.

LePrey dangled by the throat as Bontey drew his arm back and threw his limp corpse. A mysterious trail of black dust appeared to exude from Bontey's hand, propelling LePrey all the way across the lantern room.

With the object of his obsession just across the room, Bontey could hardly contain himself. But when he turned to face Machine, he was horrified. The boy was gone.

3 FREEDOM

Fifty Eight
The Gift

Breaking free from Machine was the most painful thing Ash had ever done. The transmutation needles had embedded themselves deep beneath the skin. But besides the physical horror, the psychological strain of emerging from the place he had just been abducted to—that strange synthetic world—was like waking up from death. He wondered if Xavier's experience might have felt similar.

Ash had snatched the drone-guard's switch-sword, knowing it would probably be useless against the dark creature. And Bontey quickly pursued him with large, thunderous strides. Before Ash reached the elevator, Bontey pulled out his large musketoon and slammed the bullet-filled clip into it.

When he tried to fire, the gun jammed. Re-cocking it, he tried again, but still, nothing. Then, as if all of the bolts and screws holding the gun together had been removed, the musketoon simply fell apart in his hands, spilling onto the floor in a random scattering of metal and wooden objects. Glaring deep into Ash's tired eyes, he knew this was nothing more than a trick of the boy's magic—his Mystery. So he lifted his prosthetic arm, engaged a crude bionic pistol and fired every round of bullets it was armed with. But Ash was too fast, every shot merely blasting into the wall as Ash entered the elevator. Bontey then ejected his bionic saber and engaged the elevator's closing doors.

As the elevator slipped down the shaft in a blur, Ash fell against its wall in exhaustion. He couldn't keep up with all that was happening. If it hadn't been for the speed in which things were progressing, he might have simply fallen over at the sheer sight of Bontey. Then suddenly the elevator stopped with a jolt.

Ash knew exactly what was happening. Bontey had somehow disengaged the elevator's gears. What Ash didn't know was that the dark creature had done it by summoning his own mysterious powers. So he drew the stolen sword, ejecting only one of its blades, and with it, pried open the escape hatch on the elevator's ceiling. He quickly climbed out and onto a ladder that stretched from the top to the bottom of the shaft. Above was a small opening, barely illuminated by light. It would lead to somewhere—anywhere but here. But as he approached, the ladder began to shake. Looking up he saw that someone else was climbing down. *Bontey!*

Ash climbed with everything he had. He couldn't even look up. And the second he reached the opening he jumped in and began to crawl towards the light. As the light grew brighter, Bontey's pursuit grew louder. The beast's huge physique smashed through the crawlspace, sounding as though the entire lighthouse was falling apart. Then Ash reached the threshold.

Kicking the grate free, Ash leaped from the crawlspace into moonlight. Leaping into the night air, he fell a short distance onto the roof of the bungalow. He could hear the crashing sea far below as his body spun off the roof, rolling through the grass to the edge of the cliff. A storm was brewing on the horizon, igniting the sky with lightening, and the air with its delayed thunder. Far below, hundreds of spiking rocks littered the shoreline like the fangs of a starving leviathan. He tried to back away from the edge, but then Bontey's feet landed next to him.

Wasting no time, Bontey lunged forward at Ash with his saber. But he was met with the same, strange blast of energy that had thwarted LePrey when he had tried to retrieve the Enigma. Bontey's powers were not enough to breach this barrier after all. A low growl accentuated

Bontey's peaking rage as he paced the ground. *This boy was every bit as powerful as his mother had been.*

"Give up!" Bontey growled with wild eyes as he whirled his saber over his head.

Ash quickly redrew his sword and backed away. Sparring with Lazlo in the jungles of Copi Bienna had proven to be a priceless experience as Ash realized his inability to effectively use his powers to attack Bontey. He could feel the scars on his back burning and bleeding like never before. He felt only partially in control as he teetered at the cliff's edge, barely keeping up with Bontey's aggressive assault. *Perhaps Machine already had some sort of hold on him. Perhaps he had already been poisoned beyond the point of no return? After all, the transmutation process was well under way before being interrupted.*

Ash had to fight these thoughts of doubt as hard as he had to fight Bontey. But suddenly Bontey managed to strike Ash across the chest, opening his flesh into a deep wound. The burning sting shocked Ash into near paralysis for a moment, spilled blood soaking into his tattered peasant shirt. And with his guard down, Bontey quickly moved in and kicked Ash in the stomach, knocking him over the edge of the cliff.

A strange numbness of this deathly reality seized Ash's consciousness as his body rolled over and over on its fatal descent. So many nights he had dreamed of falling to his death. But the nightmares had always been interrupted before he hit the bottom. Always. And this was no exception as the speed of his fall suddenly slowed to what felt like almost a complete stop.

His spine was suddenly gripped by a terrible stinging sensation, followed by what felt like breaking bones. Then Ash caught a glimpse of something as his body mysteriously swooped away from a rocky spire and out over open water. But he couldn't make sense of it. It appeared as though something was protruding form his back. His skin glowing brighter than ever before, he felt the strangest sensation he had ever experienced—like he was controlling these protrusions. These were wings! His *gift*!

He didn't have time to consider how this was even feasible as his torn shirt fluttered in the wake of his draft. Ash was closing in on another jagged spire, further out from shore. He knew he had to make a move or suffer slamming into it. And it was at that moment that he realized that, *yes*, he was in control of these wings. He *could* fly, just as Wick had told him he could.

Curving back toward the cliffs of the island, Ash made his way down the coast, away from Bontey. A line of six huge churning windmills towered over the crest of the gorge. Maybe he could hide there for a while—at least until he could make some sense out of all of this.

Ash's ribs cracked against the rocks as his unpracticed landing resulted in crashing directly into the side of the cliff. Grabbing onto anything he could, Ash clenched onto a thick vine and pulled himself over the edge. Quickly he scrambled to the giant withered windmill.

Fifty Nine
Ghost of the Lighthouse Keeper

Moonlight poured into the room beneath the lantern room as Lazlo quietly navigated the darkness. Outside, the sky battle had all but ceased, as the mountain-hawks had now become spooked by the coming storm. Lazlo hadn't seen a soul since entering the lighthouse, making the old tower feel even more haunted than he already believed it was. As much as he didn't want to admit it, the lighthouse keeper legend was one that had always made him feel oddly uneasy for some reason.

It was all he could do not to search the lighthouse and hunt down the man who falsely accused him of treason and put him behind bars. But he wasn't there to seek revenge with LePrey. He had a promise to keep. Then a bright light blinded him.

When his eyes adjusted he saw the figure of a man standing before him. Count LePrey. He was wearing a form-fitted power-suit. (If only he had been wearing it when Bontey had attacked him.) Like his drone-guards, the surface of the suit glowed, only his glowed red.

Lazlo couldn't believe whom he was staring at. He studied LePrey's glowing green eyes. The Count looked so different than he had remembered all those years ago. He looked dead. Then Lazlo realized that it wasn't even the man who was speaking anymore. He was nothing more than a half-alive puppet, manipulated by synthetic energy. A black bloodstain was seeping through his power-suit. LePrey had obviously received a considerable chest wound. How he was even standing was a mystery in itself.

"Your kind is a dying breed, pirate," LePrey said as he unsheathed his sword, which had been housed inside of his walking staff.

"We all die," Lazlo said with a faint grin. "You of all people should know that."

"Once I get my hands on that golden medallion your friend is holding, I will all but be in possession of the Chrysalis, the elixir of life. I will be invincible, as will my army."

"Your misinterpretation of the Chrysalis's secret will be your undoing," Lazlo warned.

"Your misinterpretation of my army will be yours," LePrey shot back. "Your assault is quite in vain I'm afraid," he said, pointing out the windows with his sword to the advancing pirate fleet.

"I don't know," Lazlo replied. "It looks like we managed to take out your blockade, no problem."

"The blockade?" LePrey asked. "Oh, that wasn't the blockade." Lazlo couldn't help his eyes from growing wide. "Those were my greeters," LePrey said snidely, speaking of the drone-fortresses. "They will know the blockade when they cross it."

Lazlo grew terrified for his comrades. He wished he had a way to warn them of the danger they were about to face. But as LePrey lifted his sword over his head, he realized that his own immediate danger was about to become fatal. LePrey exploded into a state of wild rage as he leaped forward with superhuman strength. Seeing this older man move like that didn't even seem real. It wasn't.

Though LePrey's artificially advanced strength was dominant, Lazlo was still a master swordsman. He matched the Count's every move as they dueled throughout the expanse of the window-rimmed room. Then, as his sword sliced across LePrey's arm, he noticed the red glow upon the power-suit's sleeve dissipate. If he could manage to sever power to the entire suit, he might have a chance. But as Lazlo began to tire, he knew he wouldn't be able to keep this pace up. So he backed his way up the spiral staircase and into the lantern room.

He realized quickly that this was just as much of a dead end, as LePrey bounded after him. The giant black sphere, consuming the majority of the lantern room, had to have been the machine—the hub controlling the drone-armada. To be this close to it sent chills down Lazlo's spine as LePrey began to accelerate his attack.

"Give up and I'll spare your life," LePrey offered vainly.

"You're getting soft in your old age, Count," Lazlo shot back, the only way he knew how.

"Then I'm afraid your time has come." And with that, he backed Lazlo to the windows, with no place to go.

Lazlo knew that he was cornered. He had to think fast. But even that couldn't save him.

"You, along with the rest of the world, are about to see that I am immortal," LePrey said in a crazed stare. "See, the lighthouse keeper is not a ghost, as so many believe." Lazlo was confused as to why he would bring up this ghost story now. "*I* am the lighthouse keeper. And I do not die." The revelation was like a winter's wind. Lazlo imagined just how many years the Count had been toiling and scheming his demented plot to take over the world. Indeed, he was a madman. "And like I said," LePrey concluded, "you are a dying breed."

As he ran his sword through Lazlo's side, Lazlo's life flashed before his mind's eye. Never did he think it would end like this. Then stumbling forward, his body smashed through one of the giant lantern room widows, slipping into the cruel night.

At the threshold of the broken window far above, LePrey stood, his red glow like a devil. A sinister smile drew across his colorless face as he watched one more enemy become eliminated. Then, turning his gaze out to sea, he watched as the pirate fleet approached their snare.

Sixty
The Blockade

As the last grain of sand passed through the neck of the hourglass, Captain Pelt looked up at the lighthouse. From where he stood he couldn't see that Lazlo had just taken a plunge out of the lantern room window. But regardless of Lazlo's fate, the time had come to attack.

Wick pleaded mercilessly for more time, only to find that these pirates were fixated on completing their mission, with or without his endorsement. As one of the crewmates held Wick back away from the captain, all remaining galleons turned to align their cannons with the lighthouse.

"On my mark we fire!" Pelt yelled to his crew. "Ready!" he yelled, raising his arm. "Aim!" he commanded with a tight fist. But before he could utter the word *fire*, the neighboring galleon exploded into a magnificent fireball.

As a rain of splinters fell back to the water, Pelt could hear a hissing sound coming from the water. Looking over the ship's edge he then saw it. A torpedo was headed directly at another galleon! And as that ship disintegrated into a another cloud of fire, he knew that he had walked right into a trap that had been waiting all along. The drone-submarine blockade had them completely surrounded.

Sixty One
The Face of Death

In the shadows of the windmill, Ash had never felt so alone. So far away from everything he knew. He was careful not to allow the wings to touch anything as he huddled on the floor in the darkness. As much of a rush as it was, this mutation scared the hell out of him. He caught a skewed glimpse of himself in the moonlit sheen of a large moving gear.

The wings spiked high over his head, like that of a falcon. They were thin, leaf-like, and covered in what appeared to be white teardrop scales. Gray veins branched throughout the wings like a spiderweb, less visible now as his adrenaline cooled. As be breathed heavily, the milky-white wings contracted, accordion-like, glistening like a newborn covered in afterbirth. He should have been frozen in shock by the sight. But he wasn't. In a way he felt as though he had always known. They felt familiar, like he had seen them many times before. *Perhaps in his dreams? Perhaps when he was a very young child, before Logan had cut them off?* He closed his eyes. But when he opened them nothing had changed. These were his wings. They were as much a part of his anatomy as his arms. And the way they reacted to him; it was like they had always been there.

His skin was now glowing even brighter and his chest burned like fire. The Guardian was awake. But this time it was different. It was more. Not only was he adapting to this new power. This power was *becoming* him. Pulling the Enigma from his pocket, the new coordinates began to glow again in the palm of his hand. Suddenly he heard a sound.

A smell entered the darkness of the windmill. The rancid odor came like the first rumbles of thunder preceding a terrible storm. Ash pulled himself out of the moonlight and hid. As numbing as his newfound power was, he couldn't shake the trepidation Bontey's presence crippled him with. It was like the personification of how his own father made him feel, whenever around. Energy retreated along with his wings, which collapsed like an unused umbrella, retracting back into his scars.

"You finally know what your scars are," Bontey's unmistakable growl sifted into the air as his yellow eyes moved through the darkness. His words made Ash tremble. This beast knew too much about him. "Give me the medallion, boy."

Bontey's yellow eyes locked onto Ash's. Bolting away, Ash tumbled over another giant gear, moving faster now, as the stormy winds worked the windmill's blades. Bontey leaped through the shadows, his big boots landing on either side of Ash's fallen body.

"Your mother wasn't as lucky as you have been," Bontey said as the sound of his giant saber sliced the darkness. Thankfully, Ash already had his switch-sword in his hand. Quickly he ejected the blade. Their metal crossed with sparks and the duel was on.

Bontey roared maniacally as Ash made it to his feet and backed away. Navigating the maze of gears within the windmill was easier for Bontey, given his nocturnal vision. But Ash was not the same boy he had confronted in the swamps of Murk. Ash was a Guardian—a Guardian whose Mystery had since fully awakened. With his wings reemerged, Ash flew up into the upper beams; Bontey leaped and climbed like a black panther, his grip never failing.

Gale-force winds screamed through the walls as lightening lit up the night. Rain was streaming in through cracks, making the beams difficult to grip, even for Bontey. Ash seized this opportunity and kicked Bontey square in the face, trying to knock him down into the matrix of turning gears. But Bontey was fast. He instantly disengaged the saber into his prosthetic arm, replacing it with a large, sharp hook, which he pierced the wooden beam with. As he dangled there rather helplessly, Ash leaped into the air, flying straight up. He crashed through the withered shingles and landed on the mill's roof.

The storm swirled around him, rain whipping his face. The sky looked evil. He noticed the pirate galleons approaching the coast. But he didn't understand their presence, especially since they were clearly being vanquished by the Count's underwater blockade. In any other state Ash would have frozen in delirium. But emotions were now running high as he saw the lighthouse down the coast in the distance. Somewhere in its darkness Scar was captive. Hatred burned him when he thought of how wicked LePrey's scheme had been. Anger enraged him as he thought of the annihilation of Garbbit Harbor. He had the power now to put an end to all of this. *Only he,* as the White Dragon had claimed. Nothing was going to stop him. Then, just as another galleon became reduced to a cloud of fire below, the roof shook.

Bontey bludgeoned Ash with his heavy saber. But Ash was just quick enough to intercept the blow with his sword. Though the power of the dragon flowed through him like rushing waters, Ash was running out of room to move. Bontey was trying to back him off the edge. So once again, Ash used his new gift and flew away. But just as his feet left the wooden shingles, Bontey's saber caught his wing, slicing through part of the webbing.

Ash landed crudely on the roof of the next windmill over. Buckling under the pain, he looked to see the horror. Blood streamed from the laceration across his wing. The pain was nauseating every time he moved it. He would now have to limit its use. And with every drop of blood he lost, he felt the power of his Mystery draining just as rapidly. Looking up, he began to accept that this might very well be the end of the road.

Using the wind to his advantage, Bontey leaped onto one of the windmill's blades, allowing it to thrust him through the air. His body flew the great distance to the next windmill. Landing right next to Ash, he instantly resumed his bloody assault.

Trying to ignore the pain, Ash fought back with everything he had. The violent storm was now driving the mill's fan at a blurring speed, making it very difficult for Ash to maintain his balance. To his own amazement, Ash was still able to stave off Bontey's aggressive attack. The question of how long Ash could hold out had yet to be answered though. Suddenly the entire windmill shook as the sky flung a blinding bolt of lightening at one of the mill's blades.

The intense blast knocked the entire nacelle off its axis, rendering the mill useless. All four blades were now barely connected to the mill's hub, hanging at an angle over the cliff's edge. And in the shadows beneath one of the blades, Ash held on for his life.

Partially blinded by the lightening blast, his fingers fumbled around, digging helplessly into the wood of the broken fan blade. He couldn't even recall how he had ended up on the underside of it. Still disoriented from the blast, he scrambled to think of a way out. But he didn't trust his damaged wing enough to simply let go. Before he could even formulate a thought, the blade began to vibrate. It was more than the wind. Then something pierced his shoulder, causing him to lose grip with one hand.

In the darkness it was nearly impossible to tell what had pierced him. But when it happened again, and again, he quickly figured it out. *Bontey's saber!* The persistent pirate was standing above, thrusting his saber through the wood. Ash swung his body around wildly, trying to dodge the saber's thrusts, while trying not to fall. But his fingers were slipping. He focused his thoughts within and his eyes onto the next blade over. And then he just had to let go.

Ash's body arched through the air and onto the other smoldering blade. This one was jutted out, directly over the open water far down below. Regaining his balance as well as his focus, Ash stood tall. Bontey followed instantly.

Backing Ash down the length of the blade, Bontey almost appeared to be growing more powerful. As he foamed at the mouth, that mysterious black dust was now beginning to permeate from his oily fur. *What was this?* Ash wondered. *Dark energy.*

"Give me the medallion!" Bontey snarled, knowing he would have to kill Ash for it.

He began slashing at Ash almost randomly. Hatred curled out of his nostrils in the form of steam. He wanted Ash dead. And as he moved down the blade, Ash was beginning to succumb to fear in a way that overrode his powers. Exhaustion swept over him like a powerful drug. He couldn't allow this to happen. So as Bontey's black figure marched forward through the rain, Ash stopped, took a deep breath, and stood tall, glaring into the face of terror. Closing his eyes, he grasped the Enigma through his shirt, if for nothing else to reassure himself that it was still close. Then he focused on the energy of light deep within.

When Ash opened his eyes, he could hardly believe it. He was glowing so brightly it was almost difficult to look. Though he couldn't see it, his deep brown eyes were like white crystals, glowing in the night. His sword had burst into flame again and he was so light on his feet they were barely touching the blade. A surge of pure nirvana roared through him and he found himself screaming at the top of his lungs.

"I'm not afraid!" a deeper, thicker version of his voice exclaimed. And attached to the words was a swirling stream of fire! Smoke coiled out from his lips. With a shrilling, hissing scream Bontey fought the consuming flames as they quickly spread across his fur. Only the torrential rain saved him from becoming completely engulfed. Bontey's hateful glare was as evil as ever as his eyes narrowed in on Ash's. But Ash only returned it, and then he leaped forward.

Embers sprayed the night as the two collided in mid-air, their swords crossing with sparks. For a moment Ash wondered if they might have overshot the edge of the blade. But they quickly landed on its bowing mass. Ash had never felt so strong. Still, Bontey was displaying a force of beastly strength that kept Ash propelling backward, backward. The fowl smell of burnt hair permeated the cold air every time Ash struck Bontey with his fiery sword—slashing, slashing. Like the scream of a lion, Bontey howled, denouncing his pain. His yellowed eyes seemed to glow, possessed by the demons he had summoned. Suddenly there was a clamorous crunch. The blade split in two and both fell.

Ash barely caught himself on what was left of the blade, dangling over the edge of the cliff once again. But this time there was a gravity pulling him down with great force. Looking down to the violent black waters far below, Ash saw where a new excruciating, driving pain was coming from; Bontey had embedded his hook deep into his leg.

The only thing keeping Bontey from falling into the deadly waters far below was Ash's grip on the blade. He wasn't tired. He wasn't afraid. And he had nothing standing in his way, other than Ash's withering resistance. The amazing surge of energy Ash had summoned only moments ago, was now nothing more than a faint, smoldering numbness. But reality was beginning to outweigh even the most apparent advantages Ash had going for him. He couldn't see beyond the dark creature grasped to his leg, persistent on pulling him down to his death.

Blood drenched Ash's leg as Bontey's hook painfully drove deeper into his flesh, scraping the bone. But he would just as soon take Ash down with him than to give up. The Enigma would be *his* or nobody's. Their eyes made contact, and for the first time Ash saw panic taint Bontey's glare. He was about to lose it all. Yet rage prevailed as evil smoke seemed to curl from the beast's flared nostrils and he squinted with hatred. It was like staring into the face of death itself. Suddenly Ash had an incredible epiphany: Since Bontey's arm was merely a mechanical apparatus. Though Ash may have been helpless in forcing Bontey's surrender, he *could* prevail over a lifeless prosthetic limb.

Ash closed his eyes and began to channel his energy—what little he could. But then he heard the sound of small failing mechanical instruments inside the prosthetic arm. He could see the transformation in Bontey's expression as wild panic consumed the beast's eyes. Then, suddenly, a final clicking sound and the squeal of pressure-release gave way and the prosthetic arm detached itself from Bontey's body.

General Sayto Bontey instantly dropped—his heavy burnt mass falling away, quickly consumed by darkness. Only a ghostly plume of the mysterious black smoke remained, slowly dissipating to nothing.

Ash pulled himself up and took a deep breath. The magnitude of what had just taken place hadn't sunk in yet. But when he looked down and saw the prosthetic limb still dug deep into his leg, reality hit him hard, causing him to break down in tears. Clenching his teeth to muffle the pain, he ripped the bloody metal hook away. *It was never supposed to go like this.* He gave himself a moment to catch his breath and tried to figure out a plan. Looking up, he noticed the green glow of Machine beckoning from the lantern room of the lighthouse down the coast.

Sixty Two
Scarlett

Though he was amazed he could do it at all, flying was treacherously painful. The infected wound on Ash's wing almost made him pass out. Climbing through a broken lantern room window, Ash entered carefully. Machine floated before him like the embodiment of death. He struggled not to make eye contact with it. But its electrical vibrancy seemed to be reacting to Ash as he walked by.

Walking seemed like a journey in itself as the puncture from Bontey's hook gushed blood with every step. His wings fully retracted, Ash's entire body writhed in agony. The Guardian within had now subsided into a much-needed state of hibernation, allowing Ash's wounds to reveal their true pain. But this was no time to think of the pain. He had to press on. He had come for a reason.

Making his way carefully through the darkness, he heard a familiar voice. "I'm flattered that you've decided to return," LePrey's voice echoed like a ghost. For a moment, a ghost is exactly what Ash thought it was. After all, he had watched him die. But then LePrey's unmistakable silhouette moved in front of the moonlit windows. "Just as Machine had predicted, you've come back for the girl. But your transmutation is not yet quite complete." Ash pretended he didn't hear that comment.

"Where is she?" Ash asked with heavy breathing. He knew full well that what he was now doing went against everything he had been told. But he couldn't stop. After all he had just done, he saw no reason why he couldn't now save the one he loved. It was jeopardizing nothing.

"Closer than you think," LePrey answered as he slashed his wrists together, igniting his power-suit. The glow of his power-suit painted Scar blood-red as she knelt on the floor beside LePrey. His sword was pressed against her throat.

"Release the Enigma to me or she dies," LePrey threatened without compromise. "Don't make me say it again," he said pressing hard enough to cause a thin film of black blood to ooze out from behind the blade. He then drew the blade away and began pacing the lantern room, wearing an expression of deep, deep distress.

"I have spent my entire life developing this miracle of science," LePrey said with trembling passion in his voice as he gazed up at Machine. It seemed as though at any time he might break down in tears. "I am in the midst of evolving this world into a perfect, unified global mind—a world that has become far too divided by its own imperfections of mortality. I won't allow it to be destroyed or even threatened by the wild paranormals of the Chrysalis. Give me the Enigma and she goes free," he professed, reiterating his earlier promise.

Scar appeared to be slightly awake, but void of any form of strength to resists her captor. In spite of LePrey's sick obsession with her, it was clear that he wouldn't hesitate to sacrifice her for his own gain if need be.

Heavy with guilt, Ash painfully weighed his options. But he couldn't help feel that he was now at a place where there really weren't any to choose from. *Don't leave her side or she will die*, the gypsy witch's words echoed through Ash's mind. How prophetic those words were now. But the White Dragon's warning tore his will in the opposite direction. *Keep the Enigma close to you.*

After all he had gone through to hold on to the Enigma, as well as Scar, they were now both in jeopardy of being taken from him. The thrill of defeating Bontey had already drifted into the realm of the forgotten, washed away by the crisis before him. Once again he had allowed himself to walk right into the perfect trap.

"I sense your motives, boy," LePrey said as he pressed his sword even harder to Scar's throat. "Don't be rash," he warned. "I won't think twice to snuff the life out of her. She is just a number. One of many."

It was like LePrey was inside of Ash's mind, reading it. Indeed, Ash's motive was to wield his newfound powers and use them to defend Scar.

"Forget those mythic, heroic notions of the Vyne," LePrey continued. "Trust me. Allow me to bury the threat of your curse forever and I'll give you Scar—the one thing you can't live without," LePrey concluded with a frightful stare.

Ash reluctantly nodded his head in agreement. He wasn't even sure he could trust his own powers at this point anyway. His body shook all over with distress. He didn't have another fight in him.

Scar's eyes seemed to be growing even heavier as she observed Ash's desperate actions. It almost appeared as though she was subtly shaking her head *no*. But regardless, Ash was in no position to counteroffer. Just as he had been doing all along, LePrey had calculated this perfectly.

Ash felt numb. *Was he now merely a puppet of Machine? Had his exposure to synth poisoned him beyond the point of no return?* Ash feared his own lack of resistance. He felt he had no choice. All he could hope for now was for LePrey to live up to his end of the bargain.

Removing the Enigma from his pocket Ash slowly handed it over to LePrey, willing it out of his control. The moment it left his hand he could feel something else leaving his body. It was as if a force of energy had just been released. Guilt burned.

LePrey carefully received the Enigma, cautious of another supernatural assault, which had already burnt one of his hands. But the moment it touched his hand his power-suit surged with a sparking blast, glowing brighter than ever before. He stepped away from Scar with bright eyes and a wide grin. Even the storm outside seemed to pick up its pace as thunder and lightening rolled across the darkened sky.

Ash knelt on the floor and embraced Scar as LePrey began to laugh and mock them. Ash knew that he had just been duped. Tears streamed down his face as he squeezed Scar into himself. She felt so cold. LePrey hadn't killed her. But there was something about her that felt so lifeless.

Scar stared back up at Ash as he stroked her crimson hair with his fingers. A faint smile crossed her face. She was so beautiful. Ash's mind drifted back to their very first moments together—the evenings aboard his father's docked fishing trawler not so long ago. Everything seemed so innocent then, even though he had no idea who she really was at the time, even though his own life seemed to be at a pathetic standstill. The moment Scar entered, life finally had meaning. She was the first person to make Ash feel as though he was veritably someone with a life worth living. She made him feel needed. And now, here, in this cold, dark tower she needed him more than ever—but not for the reasons he wished.

Scar's mouth struggled to form a soundless word as her eyes began to gloss over in what appeared to be tears.

"What is it?" Ash whispered. "I'm going to get you out of here," he promised, looking around quickly.

Scar slowly shook her head. But then a fragile whisper emerged and it was clear. "Go," she said softly.

Ash didn't know what to make of such a request. It didn't make sense. Perhaps she was delirious. He tried to lead her to the stairs, but she wouldn't cooperate. "C'mon," Ash shot back at her in an almost irritated tone. He wouldn't have it. Leaving her was not an option. He didn't come this far and betray his destiny to leave her for dead. But then, like a revelation blossoming before his very eyes, he finally understood just what was happening.

Perhaps it was the remnants of synth in his system allowing Ash to communicate telekinetically with Scar. He wasn't sure. But it seemed as though he could see her thoughts.

Looking up, Ash saw LePrey standing before Machine in tranquilized anticipation. He appeared lucid. Green lightening leaped off Machine's black iron surface, encircling LePrey as though trying to pull him closer. He touched Machine with his hand, and an explosion of electricity lit up the room, smashing beakers and test tubes with its thunderous vibrations. Then Ash saw something he didn't expect to see.

With one hand still touching Machine, LePrey opened his other hand, which held the Enigma. The new set of coordinates were glowing! Somehow Machine had broken the code and extracted the encrypted coordinates. The map to the second cipher was now in the hands of darkness.

"I see the future," LePrey said to no one as he closed his eyes. Countless voices screamed in his head, louder than ever before. "Our armies have defeated terror. The world is in perfect unity. And I shall live forever!"

With Lord Yen and Sayto Bontey out of the picture, there was no stopping LePrey. Ash could save Scar now. But soon LePrey and his armies of evil would thrust the entire world into a state of dark tribulation. Little did Ash know, Scar had a plan.

Those blurry thoughts that once overcrowded her subconscious were now vividly clear. Her life as a simple farm girl in the northern plains was the real her—a life full of life itself. The little red-haired girl. The girl whose full name was Scarlett. And the person she was now was nothing more than pure enslavement. Her body was merely a physical host to this synthetic life-force forged by LePrey.

Scar finally realized why Isla Ruba had seemed so familiar. After all, it was where her life had been bartered for a sack of cash; slave lords had sold her into the hands of Count LePrey. That was the beginning of the end—before Machine sucked the life from her and turned her into an addict of synthetic collectivity—before she became Ninety-Seven.

Since removing the drone-implants from her hands, Scar had experienced feelings and emotions like never before. It was like being reborn. But as reality continued to slowly creep in, she was becoming less and less able to go on. Though her journey with Ash had been short-lived, it was worth everything, even her own fatality. Machine's grip was too powerful to escape. Destroying it was the only way.

Like a dream, inevitably giving way to reality, Scar slipped from Ash's arms, his fingers struggling to remain snagged on her sweater—*his* sweater. The one she had borrowed back when the future was yet unknown and full of hope. Her body slowly drifted away. And with outstretched arms, the scars on her palms were like testaments to the sacrifice she was about to make. Then, from the pockets of her black trousers, she pulled out two atomic grenades she had stolen from the drone-guards who had escorted her back up to the lantern room. *Indeed, she still had a bit of craft left in her.* She discreetly displayed them for Ash and then pulled the pins.

Time seemed to stand still. Aside from losing the one that he loved, he didn't understand what might happen if the Enigma was destroyed. Certainly its destruction was better than leaving it in the hands of LePrey. *But what about the rest of the world? How would the Chrysalis ever be found?* Unfortunately, there was no time to ponder this.

"Go," she whispered again. It was the first time Ash had actually witnessed Scar crying—her borrowed clothes hanging tiredly off of her thin frame.

As Ash approached the catwalk through the broken window, LePrey looked over at him with a perplexing expression. Standing there Ash could feel the winds of Cape Sparrow wrapping around him, trying to pull him away. This was it. One more step and Scar would be gone. Forever.

The last thing he saw was the panic in LePrey's eyes, as he figured out that it was actually *he* who had been duped. Without looking back, Ash closed his tear-filled eyes and dove.

Like a parachute, his wings erected, slowing his fall. As he glided through the rain, a painful explosion ripped the air, briefly lighting the entire coast. He could feel the heat of the blast on his back. His wounds stung. Everything hurt. And then he tumbled to the ground.

Kneeling in the grass, Ash wept in a way he had never before in his life. His throat ached and his eyes stung. His heart was broken. LePrey and his machine were gone, and with them the entire drone-armada. Ash had even faced and killed the dark creature from his nightmares—a feat that had seemed unimaginable. But none of this seemed to matter now. Scar was gone.

Sixty Three
Loss

Ash made his way down the coast, unable to watch the smoldering remains of the lighthouse any longer. Only one galleon remained in the water as fiery remnants were strewn across the rolling waves. He still didn't know whom the galleon belonged to. Suddenly a hand came to rest on his shoulder.

"I'm so sorry, kid," Lazlo said, his sad eyes studying the hemorrhaging scars on Ash's back, visible through his torn shirt. But he wasn't about to mention a word of it. As relieved as Ash was to see him, he was taken aback by the state he was in. Lazlo's leg appeared to be broken. And he was half doubled over, holding his ribs.

"I'm so sorry she's gone," he elaborated. He rested his weight on Ash's shoulder like a crutch. His face and arms were cut and bruised badly. Not aware of Lazlo's tussle with LePrey, it was obvious that he had gone through something quite violent.

"Where are the others?" Ash asked, unsure of what had actually transpired since he last saw his friends in the mist.

Lazlo's expression was unsettling. There was no telling what this meant. Suddenly they heard a voice yelling up from the rocky shores below.

"Is anyone up there?" Pelt yelled up, the wear of the fatal battle weakening his voice.

Looking over the edge of the cliff, through Lazlo's small telescope, Ash saw Captain Pelt standing on the bow of a long dory being rowed by two other men. Seated in the middle of the boat were four familiar figures: Driver, Boota, Wick, and Petra, who was standing on Boota's shoulder. He could almost see the relief in Wick's eyes. They were soon reunited aboard the galleon.

As they sailed away from Bald Rock, they unknowingly passed right over the *Venom*. However, the pirate submarine only dove deeper into the sea's darkness. After witnessing Bontey's burnt body come crashing into the waters, the crew of the *Venom* simply disappeared.

After turning down a hot meal (Ash had no appetite), he was informed of the terrible fate the Pirate Rogue had suffered at the hands of the drone-blockade. Captain Pelt's galleon was only spared because the hurricane winds stirring up the seabed had rendered the drone-subs blind. But now it mattered not. They, like the rest of the drone-armada network were nothing more than worthless lumps of metal, stopped dead in their tracks the moment Machine was destroyed.

That night, wrapped in a large blanket, Ash stood alone, in the ship's crow's nest, watching the fading distant storm. As the thunder drew to a faint whimper, he found himself living and reliving within the same short-term scenario: the moments between where Scar said *Go*, and when he felt the explosion behind him. He felt as if he was literally trapped in that torturous moment in time and he could not move forward.

Garbbit Harbor was gone forever, and with it, a childhood Ash couldn't revisit, even if he wanted to. He felt homeless and alone—just another face in the crowd. Scar, the only tangible reason Ash had to believe in himself was now gone too. But standing here in the midst of the greatest city in the world, Ash began to wonder if fate hadn't purposely brought him to this place in time.

His loss consumed him. He wondered if he even possessed the spirit of the Guardian any longer, now that he had allowed the Enigma to be destroyed. Though he still burned with anger, he recalled a fitting line Wick had told him as a boy. *We all have a purpose in this life. Some more challenging than others. But sometimes accepting it is the hardest part.*

Sixty Four
The Barter

A frail old doctor stood before King Basileus, slowly waving a small light-stick across Basileus's face. Though Basileus could detect a faint light source passing before his eyes, he couldn't quite make out what it was. The initial diagnosis didn't look good and things weren't changing. It was looking as though his eyesight may never improve beyond this nearly blind state. No matter what, life would never be the same for him.

Basileus remained alone in his chamber as the doctor let himself out. While the Royal Palace buzzed with preparations for the victory ceremony planned for the following day, Basileus could hardly get himself to eat. He wouldn't admit it, but he viewed this victory with much skepticism. Kingland had claimed many erroneous victories over the centuries, only to produce an even greater confrontation. But he had no substantial evidence to back his pessimism. His downward state was stemming from an entirely different source.

Her voice still echoed in his mind, as if she was sitting right next to him. He could feel his other senses intensifying without the solid presence of their visual counterpart. Even the smell of Arona seemed to be swirling about the room like she was actually present. He wondered where she was. He wondered if he would ever see her again.

Arona was far cleverer than she let on. The mastery behind her handiwork in saving Basileus's life was proof of that. So she knew exactly how dangerous it would be if she were to return to Crown City. Even with the Count out of the picture, there would certainly be loyalists obsessed with avenging his legacy. They would do anything to see Arona dead. Not to mention, there was no convincing way to make their secret affair public without instant allegations cropping up about ill-intentions to oust the Count.

No matter how he debated it in his own mind, the conclusion was the same: He had to let Arona go.

Swallowing his hatred against pirates was one of the hardest things Basileus had ever done. But the loyalty and bravery they displayed in the battle of Cape Sparrow could not be denied. They had fought to restore freedom to the very kingdoms that had turned on them. So easily could they have diverted their aggression *against* Kingland. Instead, Count LePrey and his machine were gone. And for the first time in a long time there was hope.

Basileus's ability to sense those he could not see took Lazlo by surprise as he hobbled into the room on a crutch.

"Who is there?" he asked the darkness.

"An old friend," Lazlo said, hoping this was still the case. "You said to come by next time I was around."

Basileus broke a smile. "Indeed I did. Sir Blackwood. My favorite pirate."

"That would be privateer, my Lord," Lazlo corrected. In spite of Basileus's humor, he still wasn't quite convinced that he wasn't about to be arrested for enlisting the Pirate Rogue to battle the drone-armada, an armada contracted by the King himself. After all, Basileus had specifically sent for him.

"I hear you were quite heroic in the battle of Cape Sparrow," Basileus said, attempting to make some sort of eye contact with Lazlo.

"There were many heroes, my Lord," Lazlo said. "Unfortunately most of them have found their resting place at the bottom of the cape."

"So you have remorse for your actions?"

Lazlo thought long and hard before answering. He knew Basileus too well to simply accept his words at face value. "I do not," he said proudly.

And as Lazlo rubbed his wrists, remembering how uncomfortable handcuffs were, Basileus stood to his feet, faced Lazlo and saluted him. "Good." Lazlo nearly passed out with relief. "You did a brave thing. Something I could never have done. I may be the King, but you are the people's hero."

"The real hero is a boy named Asher Meadows," Lazlo admitted.

"Yes, I've heard a great deal about this boy," Basileus said with reservation in his tone. "I know what he is. And it must remain a secret, for his sake." There was something in his mannerisms that gave away a sense of urgency about this topic. "You may not know this, but when I first became King, I gave secret protection to the order of the Vyne. I knew little about their sect, but enough to know that they were protectors of true virtue, something this world seems void of. After their demise I always wondered if their ancient prophecy might come true."

"Prophecy?" Lazlo asked, taken by the King's knowledge of the Vyne.

"The one," Basileus said. "This boy is the *one*, isn't he?"

Lazlo nodded and said, "He is here—here in Crown City."

"I know," Basileus said. "I will do everything I can to extend protection to him. But too much of a presence will only draw attention to him."

Basileus had enough of an understanding of the legend of the Chrysalis to know that its core prophecy claimed that *the one* would ultimately bring peace to the world. Even with the Pirate Rogue crippled, the militant-driven dessert tribes remained a major threat to global stability. However, the Imcot prophecy was to play out, Basileus would spare no expense in protecting this boy. The Zahartan dessert tribes remain determined to extinguish world freedoms in the name of a war that seemed less about their possession of the black crystal substance, and more to do with cultural and even religious differences. And if the prophecies were true, this boy is was only thing standing between this freedom and the forces trying to defeat it.

Lazlo became fidgety, struggling to find his words. He had come to discuss a different topic. "Look," he said awkwardly, "I actually came here to ask a favor."

"A favor?" Basileus asked, reeling back in disbelief. Lazlo knew that he was the last person who should be asking for favors at this time. After all, Basileus had more or less just pardoned him for his interaction with the Pirate Rogue.

"Y-yes," Lazlo stuttered. "In these delicate times, you'll need the support of the people more than ever before. That is why I am asking that you put to rest the relentless debate over Kingland's controversial detention camps and release the detainees instantly. They are more of a threat to you behind bars than they are walking free." His thoughts fell upon his old river gypsy friends. He couldn't stand the thought of what they might be going through at that moment, locked away in one of these camps.

Lazlo's request came as an obvious shock to Basileus. For a moment he couldn't even speak. But then his expression seemed to capture the essence of the struggle he was having within. He hated to admit it, but he knew that Lazlo was right. There wasn't a detainee that had actually been convicted of a crime. They were just easy targets. And in the time shortly after his wife's death, the people of Kingland were hungry to see someone pay for these crimes—but no one hungrier than the King.

"It's not that easy," Basileus replied, gazing into blackness. "I don't know if you know this already or not, but the latest virus, engineered by the Pirate Rogue, has gone missing. It's anyone's guess as to whose hands it might be in now. And almost more disturbing, General Bontey's body was never found off the coast of Bald Rock."

"Are you saying he's alive?" Lazlo interrupted in disbelief.

"I'm saying that without physically producing a criminal in chains, the people aren't going to feel as confident about me simply releasing more convicts in the name of passiveness."

"Well I'm sorry that I can't hand over the Pirate Rogue for you on a platter," Lazlo shot back with obvious anger driving his words. "But they're not available right now as most of them sacrificed their lives against the drone-armada to save your precious kingdom."

The room fell uncomfortably silent. Lazlo knew he had crossed a line. Even if Basileus was an old friend. But Basileus had no further argument. Lazlo had called his bluff. The only real motive behind his resistance in shutting down the detention camps was his own paranoia.

"Consider it done," Basileus replied with his head hung. "But you'll owe me one." As relieved as Lazlo was, he didn't know if he had offended his old friend. Perhaps his pardon had just been taken back. "I need someone to lead the secret operation of protection for the boy."

Lazlo didn't like the suspense. "And?" he asked.

"And I want it to be you," Basileus offered.

"In barter for releasing the detainees?" Lazlo said, knowing full well it was the case.

"Let's just say you'd be making the right choice by accepting the offer," Basileus said with a smile.

"Then I accept," Lazlo said with a bow that only he saw. "But I must say I'm a bit shocked that you'd stoop as low as to do business with a pirate." He laughed under his breath.

"You mean privateer," Basileus corrected. Their laughter escaped the room, echoing down the corridor. For Lazlo, it was good to see his old friend again. It was good to be alive.

As Lazlo left the chamber, King Basileus sat alone. He wanted a new beginning just as badly as anyone. But monumental change in a kingdom so grand would not be easy. The glory of Kingland's superpower status was as ironic as it was sad. Basileus knew better than anyone that in order to move forward, he would have to undo many of the very things that made Kingland the global superpower it was. What he underestimated, was how hard it would be to give up such power.

The majority of people simply wanted to believe that their kingdom was one of true virtue, a mighty force of *good* in the world. They hailed their king for cheating death and praised Kingland for once again restoring global peace. (Conveniently for them, the true, full story behind the drone-armada invasion had yet to be revealed.) Still, skeptics demanded an explanation for the devastation, refusing to buy the propaganda that blamed it entirely on the ill intensions of the deceased Count of Cape Sparrow.

Basileus would now have to prove that Kingland was an ally of the world rather than an enforcer of its own policy. But again, that was easier said than done when all that he had ever loved had been stripped away by the hands of cowards. Until now, the only thing keeping guilt from driving him completely mad was the simple act of turning a blind eye to the perils of war. But unless he could extinguish his own vengeance, he was ultimately doomed to such madness. Regardless. Until then, he was placing a lot of faith in an old friend and a boy he didn't even know.

Sixty Five
Rite of the Guardian

Just arriving in Crown City was an event in itself—the dazzling architecture, spires that seemed to touch the stars, and the simple fact that this vast city was floating above the clouds in the peaceful bliss of the sky. Since being a boy, Ash had dreamed of visiting this legendary city, which many called *the greatest city in the world*. But now being here, the magnitude of everything going on seemed to dwarf even the city's glory.

Ash had been briefed by aides to King Basileus that he was to be immediately placed under the protection of the throne. To Ash's bewilderment, the King was very intent on keeping the secret of the Chrysalis as well as Asher perfectly safe. As inveigling as it sounded, the thought of him being considered such an important asset to the throne scared him. It was difficult to comprehend. But saying goodbye would be even harder.

A sea of people spilled across the vastness of Crown City's Royal Courtyard. Even the countless garden-plates, floating above, were nearly overflowing with spectators awaiting what would certainly be one of the most defining moments in Kingland's history.

For many, they remembered a similar time when victory prevailed and the people of Kingland came together in a way they had never experienced before—the close of the Great War. But with the reemergence of their King, whom many had thought dead, this was indeed an occasion to unite as a kingdom.

The look on Lazlo's face was the usual smirk as Ash, with a large pack slung over his back, dressed in a gray coat and black slacks and boots (compliments of the King himself), stood before his friends at the foot of the zeppelin's boarding ramp. A twinkle in Lazlo's eye told Ash that *goodbye* wouldn't be any easier for him.

"I'll meet up with you soon, okay?" Lazlo promised with a tight one-armed embrace, as he leaned heavily on his crutch with the other.

Even Petra, who was perched on Lazlo's shoulder, was extremely melancholy as she hung her little head to hide her sad eyes. Driver and Boota gave a clumsy bow, accidentally knocking heads on their way down, bringing some much needed humor to the moment. Then Wick stepped forward. With regret in his eyes, he stood there shaking, the golden setting sun painting his tiny physique a soft gold.

When the old wharfling's eyes finally met Ash's it was obvious that whatever differences they had allowed to come between them, were valid no longer. After all, if Wick had actually been ill-intentioned in his taking of the Enigma, his little webbed hands would have never even been permitted to touch it.

Wick hugged Ash's leg with everything he had; fighting tears he never knew he had—tears that soaked Ash's trousers. To Ash, it seemed so long ago that they had had their falling out. It just didn't matter any longer. Theirs was a friendship that might bend but could never be broken, not completely.

"Why did my wings not reemerge until now?" Ash asked, just as intently as he had when he was a small boy. As he spoke, he readjusted his backpack multiple times. His wounds still burned.

Wick looked up and smiled. He missed the innocent boy who used to ask him anything. And he loved having the answers. "Because you never believed you had wings till now. It was not some fortuitous happening." His words made Ash emotional. "I'm proud of you, Asher," Wick continued, fighting back his tears.

"I'm afraid," Ash dared to admit to his old friend. "I feel weak. The Enigma also possessed the coordinates to the second cipher—something the White Dragon called the Koda." Wick's expression grew serious at the sound of that word. "But now with the Enigma gone, where do I even start? How will I find my way?"

"The same way you learned to fly without wings," Wick replied with a soft smile. "First you dreamed it, then you made it a reality. Follow your heart. You are a true Guardian now. *You have the power.*" Though Ash didn't know how to react to Wick's vote of confidence, the fact that he had just recited the exact line the White Dragon had spoken gave him unshakable chills. Perhaps he had underestimated his old friend. "Don't give up. Everything that has happened has only been to prepare you."

"For what?" Ash asked with reservation in his voice.

"For what's to come," Wick answered as he hung his head to hide his eyes. With that, the two embraced one last time and Ash finally boarded.

As the zeppelin drifted into the air, Ash peered through the cabin's window to the floating city below. He was being escorted to an undisclosed location, where he would eventually rendezvous with Lazlo and a small crew. From there, the horizon was as mysterious as the sea itself.

Basileus emerged onto a large balcony before the multitude, under a canopy of majestic billowing clouds. He was very animated as he spoke, raising his fists to the sky. Gauging by the crowd's reaction, his words were just the chorus they needed to hear.

Ash looked at the palm of his own hand. The lines across his skin seemed to be symbols of his destiny. Everything inside of him now, every memory, every pain and regret were all integral parts of the journey. Just like the White Dragon had said. Ash now understood that overcoming fear was not the mere riddance of it, but the understanding of it. No matter what form it took on, fear did not possess the ability to overcome him. And loss, as tragic as it was, was a necessary circumstance on such a path as this.

Scar came into his life to believe in him and give him the courage to realize and embrace his own Mystery. What Ash didn't learn until it was too late, was that she was never meant to be a possession of his. All of that energy spent on trying to save her was nothing more than futile efforts. Losing her was the only way for Ash to understand the true power of love. It had nothing to do with what he possessed and everything to do with what he was willing to let go. Her warning of how she would only hurt him did not burn like it did when the words first fell from her lips. Yes, her actions hurt him, but the irony was, no one wanted Ash to pursue his destiny more than Scar.

His strange power was not a *curse* as his father had claimed. It was his rite of becoming. His Mystery. And for the first time, Ash felt a sense of true being, knowing that he alone was the world's last and only hope for changing its fatal course—even if he didn't fully understand how this would play out in the end. But hiding behind the innocence of ignorance was no longer an option.

Life in Garbbit Harbor would have been such a safe and easy way to live, in spite of its misery. But Ash knew full well that the unchallenging lifestyle he had carved out for himself in that little fishing village would have eventually destroyed him as a person. This moment in time was his own personal *Decision Point*. It was one thing to find his life's purpose. It was another thing entirely to embrace it. And as scary as it was, he felt a strange sense of calm about the future. Though the road ahead would be filled with challenges and changes that might often yield unrest, in the end Ash realized that he had a far greater destiny to fulfill in hunting down the Chrysalis.

He gazed out over the clouds as the zeppelin rose through them. Ares's golden crown and the peaks of the snow-covered summits were now the only visible remnants of the world below. Something about the serenity of the moment made his thoughts fall upon his past, his parents. And in that very moment he became overwhelmed by emotion. In order to truly move on, there was one more thing he knew he had to do.

He had honestly never considered forgiving them for his unlived childhood. He always assumed that he would carry this heavy baggage with him the rest of his life. He knew no other way. But in leaving behind everything else he knew, he now saw no reason to carry it further. In spite of his father's abusive nature, in spite of his mother's abandonment, he had to let it go—even void of a formal apology. There was no way to make it right, not any more. But resentment was too heavy a burden to bear. He knew that eventually it would destroy him. So without another thought on the matter, he chose to forget.

Hesitant tears burned his eyes as he considered how much time and energy had been wasted on his own angst. He wondered how he had even made it this far. All he knew was that for the first time in a long time he felt good. This new sensation reminded him of what he felt the moment his wings re-birthed. *Freedom.* Peeling back his oily black bangs, he saw something that in any other instance he would have passed off as a trick of the eyes.

At the peak of the tallest summit stood a towering silhouette. The White Dragon. Her still body was erect, meditating, her long, thin tail slowly caressing the snow. She didn't appear as the frightening beast Ash had seen in the shadows of the cave. She was beautiful, the golden sun washing over her white feathers. Ash somehow knew that he was the only one able to see her. And she could see him. He felt her in his thoughts, beckoning. *In spite of your fears, I deem you estimable of this quest. You must find the Chrysalis. It is the only way to save the world. Follow me.*

Suddenly she lowered her head and made eye contact with him from where she stood. Her fiery eyes were hypnotic. But Ash didn't fear them anymore. He knew them. She spread her massive wings and dropped from the mountaintop, her movement like water as she drifted through the clouds and out over the sprawling ocean beyond. And as if leading the way, her figure receded into the dwindling glow of the setting sun.

Acknowledgements:

Writing this book has been unlike any other creative experience in my life. As wonderful and magical as it is to see the figments of my imagination come to fruition, it has been nothing shy of intense—especially for those at my side (e.g., my family).

I would like to thank Trinady, my beautiful wife, for her years of support, patience, and encouragement throughout the entirety of this journey. Without her, *The Vyne* would have never happened. Without her, I would have never discovered my Mystery.

photo by Sean Meszaros

About the Author

Daniel Walls is an award-winning art director/designer. As a boy growing up on the Canadian border of northern Minnesota, he spent most of his free time writing and illustrating fantasy stories, sharing them with his devoted audience, an English Springer Spaniel. *The Vyne* is his first full-length novel, and he promises it will not be his last.

Daniel lives with his wife, two children, three-legged dog, and sometimes-present cat in Minneapolis. Currently he is penning the second thrilling installment of *The Vyne* saga. For more information, visit vynesaga.com.